Lucas Davenport, "one of the best hard-case cops on the crime scene today" (*The Houston Post*), is back—on a relentless city-to-city search for a bizarre ritualistic killer . . .

SHADOW PREY

"Harrowing."
—*West Coast Review of Books*

"Sandford grabs you by the throat and never lets go!"
—Robert B. Parker

"Sandford knows all there is to know about detonating the gut-level shocks of a good thriller."
—*The New York Times Book Review*

"When it comes to portraying twisted minds, Sandford has no peers."
—The Associated Press

continued . . .

TITLES BY JOHN SANDFORD

THE KIDD NOVELS

SHADOW PREY

JOHN SANDFORD

BERKLEY BOOKS, NEW YORK

SHADOW PREY

A Berkley Book / published by arrangement with
the author

PRINTING HISTORY
G. P. Putnam's Sons edition / June 1990
Berkley edition / March 1991

ISBN: 0-425-12606-4

BERKLEY®
Berkley Books are published by The Berkley Publishing Group,
a division of Penguin Group (USA) Inc.,
375 Hudson Street, New York, New York 10014.
BERKLEY and the "B" design
are trademarks belonging to Penguin Group (USA) Inc.

PRINTED IN THE UNITED STATES OF AMERICA

45 44 43 42 41 40 39 38 37 36 35 34

SHADOW PREY

In the Beginning . . .

They were in a service alley, tucked between two dumpsters. Carl Reed, a beer can in his hand, kept watch. Larry Clay peeled the drunk Indian girl, tossing her clothes on the floor of the backseat, wedging himself between her legs.

The Indian started to howl. "Christ, she sounds like a fuckin' coon-dog," said Reed, a Kentucky boy.

"She's tight," Clay grunted. Reed laughed and said, "Hurry up," and lobbed his empty beer can toward one of the dumpsters. It clattered off the side and fell into the alley.

Clay was in full gallop when the girl's howl pitched up, reaching toward a scream. He put one big hand over her face and said, "Shut up, bitch," but he liked it. A minute later he finished and crawled off.

Reed slipped off his gunbelt and dumped it on top of the car behind the light bar. Clay was in the alley, staring down at himself. "Look at the fuckin' blood," he said.

"God damn," Reed said, "you got yourself a virgin." He ducked into the backseat and said, "Here comes Daddy. . . ."

The squad car's only radios were police-band, so Clay and Reed carried a transistor job that Reed had bought in a PX in Vietnam. Clay took it out, turned it on and hunted for something decent. An all-news station was babbling about Robert Kennedy's challenging Lyndon Johnson. Clay kept

1

turning and finally found a country station playing "Ode to Billy Joe."

"You about done?" he asked, as the Bobbie Gentry song trickled out into the alley.

"Just . . . fuckin' . . . hold on . . ." Reed said.

The Indian girl wasn't saying anything.

When Reed finished, Clay was back in uniform. They took a few seconds to get some clothes on the girl.

"Take her, or leave her?" Reed asked.

The girl was sitting in the alley, dazed, surrounded by discarded advertising leaflets that had blown out of the dumpster.

"Fuck it," Clay said. *"Leave her."*

They were nothing but drunk Indian chicks. That's what everybody said. It wasn't like you were wearing it out. It's not like they had less than they started with. Hell, they liked it.

And that's why, when a call went out, squad cars responded from all over Phoenix. Drunk Indian chick. Needs a ride home. Anybody?

Say "drunk Indian," meaning a male, and you'd think every squad in town had driven off a cliff. Not a peep. But a drunk Indian chick? There was a traffic jam. A lot of them were fat, a lot of them were old. But some of them weren't.

Lawrence Duberville Clay was the last son of a rich man. The other Clay boys went into the family business: chemicals, plastics, aluminum. Larry came out of college and joined the Phoenix police force. His family, except for the old man, who made all the money, was shocked. The old man said, "Let him go. Let's see what he does."

Larry Clay started by growing his hair out, down on his shoulders, and dragging around town in a '56 Ford. In two months, he had friends all over the hippie community. Fifty long-haired flower children went down on drugs, before the word got out about the fresh-faced narc.

After that it was patrol, working the bars, the nightclubs, the after-hours joints; picking up the drunk Indian chicks. You could have a good time as a cop. Larry Clay did.

Until he got hurt.

He was beaten so badly that the first cops on the scene thought he was dead. They got him to a trauma center and the docs bailed him out. Who did it? Dope dealers, he said. Hippies. Revenge. Larry Clay was a hero, and they made him a sergeant.

When he got out of the hospital, Clay stayed on the force long enough to prove that he wasn't chicken, and then he quit. Working summers, he finished law school in two years. He spent two more years in the prosecutor's office, then went into private practice. In 1972, he ran for the state senate and won.

His career really took off when a gambler got in trouble with the IRS. In exchange for a little sympathy, the gambler gave the tax men a list of senior cops he'd paid off over the years. The stink wouldn't go away. The city fathers, getting nervous, looked around and found a boy with a head on his shoulders. A boy from a good family. A former cop, a lawyer, a politician.

Clean up the force, they told Lawrence Duberville Clay. But don't try too hard. . . .

He did precisely what they wanted. They were properly grateful.

In 1976, Lawrence Duberville Clay became the youngest chief in the department's history. He quit five years later to take an appointment as an assistant U.S. attorney general in Washington.

A step backward, his brothers said. Just watch him, said the old man. And the old man was there to help: the right people, the right clubs. Money, when it was needed.

When the scandal hit the FBI—kickbacks in an insider-trading investigation—the administration knew where to go. The boy from Phoenix had a rep. He'd cleaned up the Phoenix force, and he'd clean up the FBI. But he wouldn't try too hard.

At forty-two, Lawrence Duberville Clay was named the youngest FBI director since J. Edgar Hoover. He became the administration's point man for the war on crime. He took the FBI to the people, and to the press. During a dope raid in Chicago, an AP photographer shot a portrait of a weary Lawrence Duberville Clay, his sleeves rolled above his elbows, a hollow look on his face. A huge Desert Eagle semiautomatic pistol rode in a shoulder rig under his arm. The picture made him a celebrity.

Not many people remembered his early days in Phoenix, the nights spent hunting drunk Indian chicks.

During those Phoenix nights, Larry Clay developed a taste for the young ones. Very young ones. And some of them maybe weren't so drunk. And some of them weren't so interested in backseat tag team. But who was going to believe an Indian chick, in Phoenix, in the mid-sixties? Civil rights were for blacks in the South, not for Indians or Chicanos in the Southwest. Date-rape wasn't even a concept, and feminism had barely come over the horizon.

But the girl in the alley . . . she was twelve and she was a little drunk, but not so drunk that she couldn't say no, or remember who put her in the car. She told her mother. Her mother stewed about it for a couple of days, then told two men she'd met at the res.

The two men caught Larry Clay outside his apartment and beat the shit out of him with a genuine Louisville Slugger. Broke one of his legs and both arms and a whole bunch of ribs. Broke his nose and some teeth.

It wasn't dope dealers who beat Larry Clay. It was a couple of Indians, on a comeback from a rape.

Lawrence Duberville Clay never knew who they were, but he never forgot what they did to him. He had a lot of shots at Indians over the years, as a prosecutor, a state senator, a police chief, an assistant U.S. attorney general.

He took them all.

And he didn't forget them when he became director of the FBI, the iron fist on every Indian reservation in the nation.

But there were Indians with long memories too.

Like the men who took him in Phoenix.

The Crows.

CHAPTER
1

Ray Cuervo sat in his office and counted his money. He counted his money every Friday afternoon between five and six o'clock. He made no secret of it.

Cuervo owned six apartment buildings scattered around Indian Country south of the Minneapolis Loop. The cheapest apartment rented for thirty-nine dollars a week. The most expensive was seventy-five. When he collected his rent, Cuervo took neither checks nor excuses. If you didn't have the cash by two o'clock Friday, you slept on the sidewalk. Bidness, as Ray Cuervo told any number of broken-ass indigents, was bidness.

Dangerous business, sometimes. Cuervo carried a chrome-plated Charter Arms .38 Special tucked in his pants while he collected his money. The gun was old. The barrel was pitted and the butt was unfashionably small. But it worked and the shells were always fresh. You could see the shiny brass winking out at the edge of the cylinder. Not a flash gun, his renters said. It was a shooter. When Cuervo counted the week's take, he kept the pistol on the desktop near his right hand.

Cuervo's office was a cubicle at the top of three flights of stairs. The furnishings were sparse and cheap: a black dial telephone, a metal desk, a wooden file cabinet and an oak swivel chair on casters. A four-year-old *Sports Illustrated* swimsuit calendar hung on the left-hand wall. Cuervo never changed it past April, the month where you could see the broad's brown nipples through the wet T-shirt. Opposite the calendar was a corkboard. A dozen business cards were tacked to the corkboard along with two fading bumper stickers. One said SHIT HAPPENS and the other said HOW'S MY DRIVING? DIAL 1-800-EAT-SHIT. Cuervo's wife, a Kentucky sharecropper girl with a mouth like barbed wire, called the office a shithole. Ray Cuervo paid no attention. He *was* a slumlord, after all.

Cuervo counted the cash out in neat piles, ones, fives and tens. The odd twenty he put in his pocket. Coins he counted, noted and dumped into a Maxwell House coffee can. Cuervo was a fat man with small black eyes. When he lifted his heavy chin, three rolls of suet popped out on the back of his red neck. When he leaned forward, three more rolls popped out on his side, under his armpits. And when he farted, which was often, he unconsciously eased one obese cheek off the chair to reduce the compression. He didn't think the movement either impolite or impolitic. If a woman was in the room, he said "Oops." If the company was all male, he said nothing. Farting was something men did.

A few minutes after five o'clock on October 5, an unseasonably warm day, the door slammed at the bottom of the stairs and a man started up. Cuervo put his fingertips on the Charter Arms .38 and half stood so he could see the visitor. The man on the stairs turned his face up and Cuervo relaxed.

Leo Clark. An old customer. Like most of the Indians who rented Cuervo's apartments, Leo was always back and forth from the reservations. He was a hard man, Leo was, with a face like a cinder block, but Cuervo never had trouble with him.

Leo paused at the second landing, catching his breath, then came up the last flight. He was a Sioux, in his forties, a loner, dark from the summer sun. Long black braids trailed down his back and a piece of Navaho silver flashed from his belt. He came from the West somewhere: Rosebud, Standing Rock, someplace like that.

"Leo, how are you?" Cuervo said without looking up. He had money in both hands, counting. "Need a place?"

"Put your hands in your lap, Ray," Leo said. Cuervo looked up. Leo was pointing a pistol at him.

"Aw, man, don't do this," Cuervo groaned, straightening up. He didn't look at his pistol, but he was thinking about it. "If you need a few bucks, I'll loan it to you."

"Sure you will," Leo said. "Two for one." Cuervo did a little loansharking on the side. Bidness was bidness.

"Come on, Leo." Cuervo casually dropped the stack of bills on the desktop, freeing his gun hand. "You wanna spend your old age in the joint?"

"If you move again, I'll shoot holes in your head. I mean it, Ray," Leo said. Cuervo checked the other man's face. It was as cold and dark as a Mayan statue's. Cuervo stopped moving.

Leo edged around the desk. No more than three feet separated them, but the hole at the end of Leo's pistol pointed unwaveringly at Ray Cuervo's nose.

"Just sit still. Take it easy," Leo said. When he was behind the chair, he said, "I'm going to put a pair of handcuffs on you, Ray. I want you to put your hands behind the chair."

Cuervo followed instructions, turning his head to see what Leo was doing.

"Look straight ahead," Leo said, tapping him behind the ear with the gun barrel. Cuervo looked straight ahead. Leo stepped back, pushed the pistol into the waistband of his slacks and took an obsidian knife from his front pants pocket. The knife was seven inches of beautifully crafted black volcanic glass, taken from a cliff at Yellowstone National Park. Its edge was fluted and it was as sharp as a surgeon's scalpel.

"Hey, Ray?" Leo said, stepping up closer to the slumlord. Cuervo farted, in either fear or exasperation, and the fetid smell filled the room. He didn't bother to say "Oops."

"Yeah?" Cuervo looked straight ahead. Calculating. His legs were in the kneehole under the desk: it'd be hard to move in a hurry. Let it ride, he thought, just a couple more minutes. When Leo was putting on the cuffs, maybe the right move . . . The gun glittered on the desk a foot and a half from his eyes.

"I lied about the handcuffs, Ray," Leo said. He grabbed Cuervo by the hair above his forehead and jerked his head back. With a single powerful slash, Leo cut Ray Cuervo's throat from ear to ear.

Cuervo half stood and twisted free and groped helplessly at his neck with one hand while the other crawled frantically across his desk toward the Charter Arms .38. He knew even as he tried that he wouldn't make it. Blood spurted from his severed carotid artery as though from a garden hose, spraying the leaves of green dollars on the desk, the *Sports Illustrated* broad with the tits, the brown linoleum floor.

Ray Cuervo twisted and turned and fell, batting the Maxwell House coffee can off the desk. Coins pitched and clattered and rolled around the office and a few bounced down the stairs. Cuervo lay faceup on the floor, his vision narrowing to a dim and closing hole that finally settled around Leo Clark, whose face remained impassively centered in the growing darkness. And then Ray Cuervo was dead.

Leo turned away as Cuervo's bladder and sphincter control went. There was $2,035 on the desktop. Leo paid it no attention. He wiped the obsidian knife on his pants, put it back in his pocket and pulled his shirt out to cover the gun. Then he walked down the stairs and six blocks back to his apartment. He was splattered with Cuervo's blood, but nobody seemed to notice. The cops got only a very slender description. An Indian male with braids. There were five thousand Indian males with braids in Minneapolis.

A large number of them were delighted to hear the news about Ray Cuervo.

Fuckin' Indians.

John Lee Benton hated them. They were worse than the niggers. You tell a nigger to show up, and if he didn't, he had an excuse. A reason. Even if it was bullshit.

Indians were different. You tell a guy to come in at two o'clock and he doesn't show. Then he comes in at two the next day and thinks that's good enough. He doesn't *pretend* to think so. He *really* thinks so.

The shrinks at the joint called it a cultural anomaly. John Lee Benton called it a pain in the ass. The shrinks said the only answer was education. John Lee Benton had developed another approach, all on his own.

Benton had seven Indians on his case load. If they didn't report on schedule, he'd spend the time normally used for an interview to write the papers that would start them back to Stillwater. In two years, he'd sent back nine men. Now he had a reputation. The fuckin' Indians walked wide around him. If you're going out on parole, they told each other, you didn't want to be on John Lee Benton's case load. That was a sure ride back inside.

Benton enjoyed the rep.

John Lee Benton was a small man with a strong nose and mousy hair combed forward over watery blue eyes. He wore a straw-colored mustache, cut square. When he looked at himself in the bathroom mirror in the morning, he thought he looked like somebody, but he couldn't think who. Somebody famous. He'd think of it sooner or later.

John Lee Benton hated blacks, Indians, Mexicans, Jews and Asians, more or less in that order. His hate for blacks and Jews was a family heritage, passed down from his daddy as Benton grew up in a sprawling blue-collar slum in St. Louis. He'd developed his animus for Indians, Mexicans and Asians on his own.

Every Monday afternoon Benton sat in a stifling office in the back of the Indian Center off Franklin Avenue and talked to his assholes. He was supposed to call them clients, but fuck that. They were criminals and assholes, every single one.

"Mr. Benton?"

Benton looked up. Betty Sails stood in the doorway. A tentative, gray-faced Indian woman with a beehive hairdo, she was the office's shared receptionist.

"Is he here?" John Lee spoke sharply, impatiently. He was a man who sweated hate.

"No, he's not," Betty Sails said. "But there's another man to see you. Another Indian man."

Benton frowned. "I didn't have any more appointments today."

"He said it was about Mr. Cloud."

Glory be, an actual excuse. "All right. Give me a couple of minutes, then send him in," Benton said. Betty Sails went away and Benton looked through Cloud's file again. He didn't need to review it but liked the idea of keeping the Indian waiting. Two minutes later, Tony Bluebird appeared at the door. Benton had never seen him before.

"Mr. Benton?" Bluebird was a stocky man with close-set eyes and short-cropped hair. He wore a gingham shirt over a rawhide thong. A black obsidian knife dangled from the thong and Bluebird could feel it ticking against the skin below his breast bone.

"Yes?" Benton let his anger leak into his tone.

Bluebird showed him a gun. "Put your hands on your lap, Mr. Benton."

Three people saw Bluebird. Betty Sails saw him both coming and going. A kid coming out of the gym dropped a basketball, and Bluebird stopped it with a foot, picked it up and tossed it back, just as Betty Sails started screaming. On the street, Dick Yellow Hand, who was seventeen years old and desperately seeking a taste of crack, saw him walk out the door and called, "Hey, Bluebird."

Bluebird stopped. Yellow Hand sidled over, scratching his thin beard. "You look bad, man," Bluebird said.

Yellow Hand nodded. He was wearing a dirty T-shirt with a fading picture of Mick Jagger on the front. His jeans, three sizes too large, were cinched at the waist with a length of clothesline. His elbow joints and arms looked like cornstalks. He was missing two front teeth. "I feel bad, man. I could use a few bucks, you know?"

"Sorry, man, I got no money," Bluebird said. He stuck his hands in his pockets and pulled them out empty.

"That's okay, then," Yellow Hand said, disappointed.

"I seen your mama last week," Bluebird said. "Out at the res."

"How's she?"

"She's fine. She was fishing. Walleyes."

Sails' hysterical screams became audible as somebody opened an outside door to the Indian Center.

"That's real good about Mama," said Yellow Hand.

"Well, I guess I gotta go," Bluebird said, easing away.

"Okay, man," said Yellow Hand. "See you."

Bluebird walked, taking his time, his mind in another place. What was her name? It had been years ago. Anna? She was a pretty woman, with deep breasts and warm hazel eyes. She'd liked him, he thought, though they were both married, and nothing ever happened; nothing but a chemistry felt across backyard hedges, deep down in Minneapolis' Indian Country.

Anna's husband, a Chippewa from Nett Lake, had been put in the Hennepin County Jail. Drunk, late at night, he'd seen a Coke machine glowing red-and-white through the window of a gas station. He'd heaved a chunk of concrete through the window, crawled in after it and used the concrete to crack the machine. About a thousand quarters had run out onto the floor, somebody told Bluebird. Anna's husband had still been picking them up, laboriously, one at a time, when the cops arrived. He'd been on parole and the break-in was a violation. He'd gotten six months on top of the remaining time from the previous conviction.

Anna and her husband had never had money. He drank up most of it and she probably helped. Food was short. Nobody had clothes. But they did have a son. He was twelve, a stocky, withdrawn child who spent his evenings watching television. One Saturday afternoon, a few weeks after his daddy was taken to jail, the boy walked down to the Lake Street bridge and jumped into the Mississippi. A lot of people saw him go and the cops had him out of the river in fifteen minutes. Dead.

Bluebird had heard, and he went down to the river. Anna was there, her arms wrapped around the body of her son, and she looked up at him with those deep pain-filled eyes, and . . . what?

It was all part of being Indian, Bluebird thought. The dying. It was something they did better than the whites. Or more frequently, anyway.

When Bluebird walked out of the room after slashing Benton's throat, he'd looked down at the man's face and thought he seemed familiar. Like a famous person. Now, on the sidewalk, as he left Yellow Hand behind, as he thought about Anna, Benton's face floated up in his mind's eye.

Hitler, he thought. John Lee Benton looked exactly like a young Adolf Hitler.

A young *dead* Adolf Hitler.

CHAPTER

Lucas Davenport lounged on a brocaded couch in the back of a used-book store, eating a roast beef sandwich. In his lap was a battered paperback copy of T. Harry Williams' biography of Huey Long.

T. Harry had gotten it right, Lucas reflected. The man in the white suit flashing among the Longites as they stood outside the governor's office. The shot. The Kingfish hit, the screaming, the running. The cops going berserk.

"Roden and Coleman fired at almost the same time, with Coleman's bullet probably reaching the man first," T. Harry wrote. "Several other guards had unholstered their guns and were blazing away. The man crumpled and fell facedownward near the wall of the corridor from which he had come. He lay there with his face resting on one arm and did not move and was obviously dead. But this did not satisfy some of the guards. Crazed with rage or grief, they stood over the body and emptied their guns into it. It was later discovered to have thirty bullet holes in the back and twenty-nine in the front (many of these were caused by the same bullet making an entry and exit) and two in the head. The face was partially shot away, and the white suit was cut to ribbons and drenched with blood."

Murder was never as neat as it was on television. No mat-

13

ter how brutal it was on the screen, in real life it was worse. In real life, there was always an empty husk lying there, the spirit departed, the flesh slack, the eyes like ball bearings. And it had to be dealt with. Somebody had to pick up the body, somebody had to mop up the blood. Somebody had to catch the killer.

Lucas rubbed his eyebrow where the scar crossed it. The scar was the product of a fishing accident. A wire leader had snapped back from a snag and buried itself in his face. The scar was not a disfigurement: the women he knew said it made him look friendlier. The scar was fine; it was his smile that was scary.

He rubbed his eyebrow and went back to the book. He did not look like a natural reader, sitting on the couch, squinting in the dim light. He had the air of the street about him. His hands, which were covered with a dark fuzz for three inches below his wrists, seemed too large and blocky as he handled the paperback. His nose had been broken, more than once, and a strong neck was rooted in heavy shoulders. His hair was black, just touched with gray.

He turned the page of the book with one hand and reached under his jacket and adjusted his holster with the other.

" 'Kingfish, what's the matter?'

" 'Jimmie, my boy, I've been shot,' Huey moaned. . . ."

Lucas' handset beeped. He picked it up and thumbed the volume control. A woman's voice said, "Lieutenant Davenport?"

"Go ahead."

"Lucas, Jim Wentz needs you down at the Indian Center on that guy that got cut. He's got a witness he wants you to look at."

"All right," Lucas said. "Ten minutes."

It was a beautiful day, one of the best of a good autumn. A murder would damage it. Murders were usually the result of aggressive stupidity mixed with alcohol and anger. Not always. But almost always. Lucas, given the choice, stayed away from them.

Outside the bookstore, he stood on the sidewalk for a moment, letting his eyes adjust to the sun and finishing the last bite of the sandwich. When he was done, he threw the sandwich bag into a trash barrel and crossed the street to his car. A panhandler was working the sidewalk, saw Lucas and said, "Watched yer car for ya?" and held out his hand. The panhandler was a regular, a schizophrenic pushed out of the state hospital. He couldn't function without his meds but wouldn't take the mind-numbing drugs on his own. Lucas passed him a dollar and dropped into the Porsche.

Downtown Minneapolis is a workbox of modernist architecture, blocks of glass and chrome and white marble. The aging red wart of City Hall hunkers in the middle of it. Lucas shook his head as he rolled past it, took a left and a right and crossed the interstate. The glitter fell behind, giving way to a ramshackle district of old clapboard houses cut into apartments, junker cars and failing businesses. Indian Country. There were a half-dozen squad cars outside the Indian Center and Lucas dumped the 911 at the curb.

"Three witnesses," the Homicide detective told him. Wentz had a flat, pallid Scandinavian face. His lower front teeth had been broken off in a fight, and he wore crowns; their silvery bases glittered when he talked. He counted the three witnesses on his fingers, as if he didn't trust Lucas' arithmetic.

"There's the receptionist," he said. "She saw him twice and says she can identify him. There's a neighborhood kid. He was playing basketball and says this guy had blood all over his pants. I believe it. The office looks like a fuckin' swimming pool."

"Can the kid identify him?" Lucas asked.

"He says he can. He says he looked the guy right in the face. He's seen him around the neighborhood."

"Who's number three?"

"Another kid. A junkie. He saw the killer outside the place, talked to him. We think they know each other, but he's not talking."

"Where is he?" Lucas asked.

"Out in a squad."

"How'd you find him?"

Wentz shrugged. "No problem. The receptionist—the one who found the body—called nine-one-one, then she went over to the window for some fresh air. She was feeling queasy. Anyway, she saw this kid and the killer talking on the sidewalk. When we got here, the kid was up the block. Standing there. Fucked up, maybe. We just put him in the car."

Lucas nodded, walked down the hallway and stepped inside the counseling office. Benton lay faceup on the tile floor in a pool of purplish blood. His hands extended straight out from his sides as though he had been crucified. His legs were spread wide, his blood-flecked wingtips pointing away from each other at forty-five-degree angles. His shirt and sport coat were saturated with blood. There were footprints and kneeholes in the puddle of blood, where the paramedics had tracked through, but no medical debris. Usually the packaging from the syringes, sponges, tape and compresses was all over the place. With Benton, they hadn't bothered.

Lucas sniffed at the coppery smell of the blood as the detective came in behind him.

"Looks like the same guy who did Ray Cuervo," Lucas said.

"Maybe," Wentz said.

"You better get him or the papers'll start peeing on you," Lucas said mildly.

"Could be worse than that," the Homicide cop said. "We got a rough description of the guy who did Cuervo. He had braids. Everybody says this guy had short hair."

"Could have cut it," Lucas suggested. "Got scared . . ."

"I hope, but it don't feel right."

"If it's two guys, that'd be big trouble. . . ." Lucas was getting interested.

"I know, fuck, I know." Wentz took off his glasses and rubbed a heavy hand up and down the side of his face. "Christ, I'm tired. My daughter piled up the car last Saturday. Right downtown by the IDS building. Her fault, she ran a light. I'm trying to deal with the insurance and the body shop and this shit happens. Two hours later and I'd be off. . . ."

"She okay?"

"Yeah, yeah." He settled his glasses back on his nose. "That's the first thing I asked. I say, 'You okay?' She says, 'Yeah.' I say, 'I'm coming down and I'm gonna kill you.' "

"As long as she was okay," Lucas said. The toe of his right loafer was in the blood puddle and he stepped back a few inches. He was looking at Benton's face upside down. It occurred to him that Benton resembled someone famous, but with the face upside down, he couldn't tell who.

". . . the apple of my eye," Wentz was saying. "If anything happened to her . . . You got a kid now, right?"

"Yeah. A daughter."

"Poor fuck. Wait a few years. She'll wreck that Porsche of yours and the insurance company will own your ass." Wentz shook his head. Goddamned daughters. It was nearly impossible to live with them and clearly impossible to live without them. "Look, you might know this kid we got in the car. He said we weren't to mess with him 'cause Davenport was his friend. We think he's one of your snitches."

"I'll go see," Lucas said.

"Any help . . ." The Homicide cop shrugged.

"Sure."

Outside, Lucas asked a patrolman about the junkie and was directed to the last car in line. Another patrolman sat behind the wheel and a small dark figure sat behind him, the two separated by a steel screen. Lucas bent over the open front window on the passenger side, nodded to the patrolman and looked into the backseat. The kid was bouncing nervously, one thin hand tangled in his dark hair. Yellow Hand.

"Hey, Dick," Lucas said. "How's things at K Mart?"

"Oh, man, Davenport, get me outta here." Yellow Hand's eyes were wide and frightened. He kept bouncing, faster now. "I didn't do nothing, man. Not a fuckin' thing."

"The people at K Mart would like to talk to you about that. They say you were runnin' for the door with a disc player. . . ."

"Shit, man, it wasn't me. . . ."

"Right. But I'll tell you what: You give me a name, and I'll put you on the street again," Lucas said.

"I don't know who it was, man," Yellow Hand squealed.

"Bullshit," grunted the uniform officer in the driver's seat. He shifted a toothpick and looked at Lucas. He had a wide Irish face and a peaches-and-cream complexion. "You know what he said to me, Lieutenant? He said, 'You ain't getting it out of me, dickhead.' That's what he said. He knows who it was."

"That right?" Lucas asked, turning back to Yellow Hand.

"Fuck, man, I didn't know him," Yellow Hand whined. "He was just this fuckin' guy. . . ."

"Indian guy?"

"Yeah, Indian guy, but I didn't know him. . . ."

"Bullshit," said the uniform.

Lucas turned his head and looked at the uniform. "You hold him here, okay? If anybody wants to transport him, you tell them I said to hold him here."

"Okay. Sure. Whatever." The uniform didn't care. He was sitting in the sunshine and had a pocket full of peppermint toothpicks.

"I'll be back in twenty minutes," Lucas said.

Elwood Stone set up a hundred feet from the halfway house. It was a good spot; the inmates could get their cocaine on the way home. Some of them, the inmates, were running on tight schedules: they were clocked out of their jobs and allowed a set amount of time to get home. They didn't have the leisure to run all over the place, looking for toot.

Lucas spotted Stone at the same time Stone spotted Lucas' Porsche. The dealer started running south down the street, but it was all two- and three-story apartments and townhouses with no spaces between them to run into. Lucas cruised alongside until Stone gave up, breathing hard, and sat on the stoop of one of the apartments. As he sat down, it occurred to Stone that he should have tossed the tube of crack into the weeds. Now it was too late.

"Stone, how are you?" Lucas said amiably, as he walked around the nose of the 911. "Sounds like you're a little out of shape."

"Fuck you, Davenport. I want a lawyer." Stone knew him well.

Lucas sat on the stoop beside the dealer and leaned back, tilted his head up to the sun, taking in the rays. "You ran the four-forty in high school, didn't you?"

"Fuck you, Davenport."

"I remember that track meet against Sibley, they had that white boy, what's his name? Turner? Now that boy could motor. Christ, you don't see that many white boys . . ."

"Fuck you, I want a lawyer."

"So Turner's old man is rich, right?" Lucas said conversationally. "And he gives the kid a Corvette. Turner takes it up north and piles it into a bridge abutment, you know? They had to stick him together with strapping tape to have a funeral."

"Fuck you, I got a right to an attorney." Stone was beginning to sweat. Davenport was a stone killer.

Lucas shook his head with a stage sigh. "I don't know, Elwood. Can I call you Elwood?"

"Fuck you. . . ."

"Sometimes life ain't fair. You know where I'm coming from? Like the Turner kid. And take your case, Elwood. They've got all bureaucrats on the sentencing commission. You know what they did? They cranked up the guidelines on possession with intent. Guess what the guidelines are for a three-time loser going down on possession with intent?"

"I ain't no fucking lawyer. . . ."

"Six years, my friend. Minimum. Cute guy like you, your asshole will look like the I-94 tunnel when you come out. Shit, if this had been two months ago, you'd of got off with two years."

"Fuck you, man, I want an attorney."

Lucas leaned close to him and bared his teeth. "And I need a few rocks. Now. You lay a few rocks on me, now, and I walk away."

Stone looked at him in wild surmise. "You? Need rock?"

"Yeah. I need to squeeze a guy."

The light in Stone's eyes went out. Blackmail. That made sense. Davenport actually smoking the stuff, that didn't make sense. "I walk?"

"You walk."

Stone thought about it for a few seconds, then nodded,

stood up and fished in his shirt pocket. He pulled out a glass tube stoppered with black plastic. There were five chunks of crack stacked inside.

"How much you need?" he asked.

"All of it," Lucas said. He took the tube away from Stone. "And stay the fuck away from that halfway house. If I catch you here again, I'll bust your ass."

The medical examiner's assistants were hauling Benton's body out of the Indian Center when Lucas got back. A TV cameraman walked backward in front of the gurney as it rolled down the sidewalk carrying the sheet-shrouded body, then did a neat two-step-and-swivel to pan across the faces of a small crowd of onlookers. Lucas walked around the crowd and down the line of squad cars. Yellow Hand was waiting impatiently. Lucas got the patrolman to open the back door and climbed in beside the kid.

"Why don't you hike over to that 7-Eleven and get yourself a doughnut," Lucas suggested to the cop.

"Nah. Too many calories," the cop said. He settled back in the front seat.

"Look, take a fuckin' hike, will you?" Lucas asked in exasperation.

"Oh. Sure. Yeah. I'll go get a doughnut," the uniform said, finally picking up the hint. There were rumors about Davenport. . . .

Lucas watched the cop walk away and then turned to Yellow Hand.

"Who was this guy?"

"Aw, Davenport, I don't know this guy. . . ." Yellow Hand's Adam's apple bobbed earnestly.

Lucas took the glass tube out of his pocket, turned it in his fingers so the kid could see the dirty-white chunks of crack. Yellow Hand's tongue flicked across his lips as Lucas slowly worked the plastic stopper out of the tube and tipped the five rocks into his palm.

"This is good shit," Lucas said casually. "I took it off Elwood Stone up at the halfway house. You know Elwood? His mama cooks it up. They get it from the Cubans over on the West Side of St. Paul. Really good shit."

"Man. Oh, man. Don't do this."

Lucas held one of the small rocks between a thumb and index finger. "Who was it?"

"Man, I can't . . ." Yellow Hand was in agony, twisting his thin hands. Lucas crushed the rock, pushed the door open with his elbow, and let it trickle to the ground like sand running through an hourglass.

"Please, don't do that." Yellow Hand was appalled.

"Four more," Lucas said. "All I need is a name and you can take off."

"Oh, man . . ."

Lucas picked up another rock and held it close to Yellow Hand's face and just started to squeeze when Yellow Hand blurted, "Wait."

"Who?"

Yellow Hand looked out the window. It was warm now, but you could feel the chill in the night air. Winter was coming. A bad time to be an Indian on the streets.

"Bluebird," he muttered. They came from the same reservation and he'd sold the man for four pieces of crack.

"Who?"

"Tony Bluebird. He's got a house off Franklin."

"What house?"

"Shit, I don't know the number. . . ." he whined. His eyes shifted. A traitor's eyes.

Lucas held the rock to Yellow Hand's face again. "Going, going . . ."

"You know that house where the old guy painted the porch pillars with polka dots?" Yellow Hand spoke in haste now, eager to get it over.

"Yeah."

"It's two up from that. Up towards the TV store."

"Has this guy ever been in trouble? Bluebird?"

"Oh, yeah. He did a year in Stillwater. Burglary."

"What else?"

Yellow Hand shrugged. "He's from Fort Thompson. He goes there in the summer and works here in the winter. I don't know him real good, he was just back on the res, you know? Got a woman, I think. I don't know, man. He mostly knows my family. He's older than I am."

"Has he got a gun?"

"I don't know. It's not like he's a friend. I never heard of him getting in fights or nothing."

"All right," Lucas said. "Where are you staying?"

"In the Point. The top floor, with some other guys."

"Wasn't that one of Ray Cuervo's places? Before he got cut?"

"Yeah." Yellow Hand was staring at the crack on Lucas' palm.

"Okay." Lucas tipped the four remaining rocks back into the test tube and handed it to Yellow Hand. "Stick this in your sock and get your ass back to the Point. If I come looking, you better be there."

"I will," Yellow Hand said eagerly.

Lucas nodded. The back door of the squad had no handles and he had carefully avoided closing it. Now he pushed it open and stepped out, and Yellow Hand slid across and got out beside him. "This better be right. This Bluebird," Lucas said, jabbing a finger into Yellow Hand's thin chest.

Yellow Hand nodded. "It was him. I talked to him."

"Okay. Beat it."

Yellow Hand hurried away. Lucas watched him for a moment, then walked across the street to the Indian Center. He found Wentz in the director's office.

"So how's our witness?" the cop asked.

"On his way home."

"Say what?"

"He'll be around," Lucas said. "He says the guy we want is named Tony Bluebird. Lives down on Franklin. I know the house, and he's got a sheet. We should be able to get a photo."

"God damn," Wentz said. He reached for a telephone. "Let me get that downtown."

Lucas had nothing more to do. Homicide was for Homicide cops. Lucas was Intelligence. He ran networks of street people, waitresses, bartenders, barbers, gamblers, hookers, pimps, bookies, dealers in cars and cocaine, mail carriers, a couple of burglars. The crooks were small-timers, but they had eyes and memories. Lucas was always ready with a dollar or a threat, whatever was needed to make a snitch feel wanted.

He had nothing to do with it, but after Yellow Hand produced the name, Lucas hung around to watch the cop machine work. Sometimes it was purely a pleasure. Like now: when the Homicide cop called downtown, several things happened at once.

A check with the identification division confirmed Yellow Hand's basic information and got a photograph of Tony Bluebird started out to the Indian Center.

At the same time, the Minneapolis Emergency Response Unit began staging in a liquor store parking lot a mile from Bluebird's suspected residence.

While the ERU got together, a further check with utility companies suggested that Bluebird lived in the house where Yellow Hand had put him. Forty minutes after Yellow Hand spoke Bluebird's name, a tall black man in an army fatigue jacket and blue jeans ambled down the street past Bluebird's to the house next door, went up on the porch, knocked, flashed his badge and asked himself inside. The residents didn't know any Bluebird, but people came and went, didn't they?

Another detective, a white guy who looked as if he'd been whipped through hell with a soot bag, stopped at the house before Bluebird's and went through the same routine.

"Yeah, Tony Bluebird, that's the guy's name, all right," said the elderly man who met him at the door. "What's he done?"

"We're not sure he did anything," said the detective. "Have you seen this guy lately? I mean, today?"

"Hell, yes. Not a half an hour ago, he came up the walk and went inside." The old man nervously gummed his lower lip. "Still in there, I guess."

The white detective called in and confirmed Bluebird's presence. Then he and the black detective did a careful scan of Bluebird's house from the windows of the adjoining homes and called their information back to the ERU leader. Normally, when they had a man pinned, they'd try to make contact, usually by phone. But Bluebird, they thought, might be some kind of maniac. Maybe a danger to hostages or himself. They decided to take him. The ERUs, riding in nondescript vans, moved up to a second stage three blocks from Bluebird's.

While all that was going on, Betty Sails picked Bluebird out of a photo spread. The basketball player confirmed the identification.

"That's a good snitch you got there, Lucas," Wentz said approvingly. "You coming along?"

"Might as well."

The ERU found a blind spot around the back door of Bluebird's house. The door had no window, and the only other window near it had the shade pulled. They could move up to the door, take it out and be inside before Bluebird had even a hint of their presence.

And it would have worked if Bluebird's landlord hadn't been so greedy. The landlord had illegally subdivided the house into a duplex. The division had been practical, rather than aesthetic: the doorway connecting the front of the house to the back had been covered with a sheet of three-quarter-inch plywood.

When the tac commander said "Go," one of the ERUs tossed a flash-bang grenade through Bluebird's side window. The terrific explosion and brilliant flash would freeze anyone inside for several seconds, long enough for the ERU team to get on top of him. When the flash-bang went off, another ERU blew the back door open with an AVON round fired from his shotgun, and the team leader went through the door, followed by three of his men.

A young Mexican woman was lying half asleep on the sofa, a baby on her stomach. An older kid, a toddler, was sitting in a dilapidated playpen. The Mexican woman had been nursing the baby and her shirt was open, her breasts exposed. She struggled to sit up, reacting to the flash-bang and the AVONs, her mouth and eyes wide with fear.

The team leader blocked a hallway, and the biggest man on the squad hit the plywood barrier, kicked it twice and gave up.

"We're blocked out, we're blocked out," he shouted.

"Is there any way to the front?" the team leader yelled

at the Mexican woman. The woman, still dazed, didn't understand, and the team leader took his men out and rotated them down the side of the house.

They were ten seconds into the attack, still hoping to do it clean, when a woman screamed from the front of the house. Then there were a couple of shots, a window shattered, and the leader figured Bluebird had a hostage. He called the team off.

Sex was strange, the team leader thought.

He stood with his back against the crumbling white siding of the house, the shotgun still in his hand, sweat pouring down his face. The attack had been chaotic, the response—the shooting—had been the kind of thing he feared, a close-up firefight with a nut, where you might have a pistol right up your nose. With all that, the image of the Mexican woman's thin breast stayed in his mind's eye and in his throat, and he could barely concentrate on the life-and-death confrontation he was supposed to be directing. . . .

When Lucas arrived, two marked squads were posted in front of Bluebird's house, across the street, and ERUs waited on the porches of the houses on either side of Bluebird's. A blocking team was out back. Drum music leaked from the house.

"Are we talking to him?" Lucas asked the tac commander.

"We called him on the phone, but we lost the phone," the tac commander said. "Phone company says it's out of order. We think he pulled the line."

"How many people are in there?"

The tac commander shrugged. "The neighbors say he's got a wife and a couple of kids, preschool kids. Don't know about anybody else."

A television truck rolled up to the end of the street, where a patrolman stopped it. A *StarTribune* reporter appeared at the other end of the block, a photographer humping along behind. One of the TV crew stopped arguing with the patrolman long enough to point at Lucas and yell. When Lucas turned, she waved, and Lucas ambled down the block. Neighbors were being herded along the sidewalk.

There'd been a birthday party going on at one house and a half-dozen kids floated helium balloons over the gathering crowd. It looked like a carnival, Lucas thought.

"What's happening, Davenport?" the TV reporter yelled past the patrolman. The reporter was a Swede of the athletic variety, with high cheekbones, narrow hips and blood-red lipstick. A cameraman stood next to her, his camera focused on the Bluebird house.

"That killing down at the Indian Center today? We think we got the guy trapped inside."

"He got hostages?" the reporter asked. She didn't have a notebook.

"We don't know."

"Can we get any closer? Any way? We need a better angle. . . ."

Lucas glanced around the blocked-off area.

"How about if we try to get you in that alley over there, between those houses? You'll be further away, but you'll have a direct shot at the front. . . ."

"Something's going down," the cameraman said. He was looking at the Bluebird house through his camera's telephoto setting.

"Ah, shit," said the reporter. She tried to ease past the patrolman to stand next to Lucas, but the patrolman blocked her with a hip.

"Catch you later," Lucas said over his shoulder as he turned and started back.

"C'mon, Davenport . . ."

Lucas shook his head and kept going. The ERU team leader on the porch of the left-hand house was yelling at Bluebird's. He got a response, stepped back a bit and took out a handset.

"What?" asked Lucas, when he got back to the command unit.

"He said he's sending his people out," said a cop on a radio.

"I'm backing everybody off," said the tac commander. As Lucas leaned on the roof to watch, the tac commander sent a patrolman scrambling along the row of cars, to warn the ERUs and the uniformed officers that people were com-

ing out of the house. A moment later, a white towel waved
at the door and a woman stepped out, holding a baby. She
was dragging another kid, maybe three years old, by one
arm.

"Come on, come on, you're okay," the detective called
out. She looked back once, then walked quickly, head down,
on the sidewalk through the line of cars.

Lucas and the tac commander moved over to intercept
her.

"Who are you?" the tac commander asked.

"Lila Bluebird."

"Is that your husband in there?"

"Yes."

"Has he got anybody with him?"

"He's all alone," the woman said. Tears streamed down
her face. She was wearing a man's cowboy shirt and shorts
made of stretchy black material spotted with lint fuzzies.
The baby clung to her shirt, as though he knew what was
going on; the other kid hung on her hand. "He said to tell
you he'll be out in a minute."

"He drunk? Crack? Crank? Anything like that?"

"No. No alcohol or drugs in our house. But he's not
right."

"What's that? You mean he's crazy? What . . ."

The question was never finished. The door of the Bluebird
house burst open and Tony Bluebird hurdled onto the lawn,
running hard. He was bare-chested, the long obsidian blade
dangling from his neck on a rawhide thong. Two eagle
feathers were pinned to his headdress and he had pistols in
both hands. Ten feet off the porch, he brought them up and
opened fire on the nearest squad, closing on the cops behind
it. The cops shot him to pieces. The gunfire stood him up
and knocked him down.

After a second of stunned silence, Lila Bluebird began to
wail and the older kid, confused, clutched at her leg and
began screaming. The radio man called for paramedics.
Three cops moved up to Bluebird, their pistols still pointed
at his body, and nudged his weapons out of reach.

The tac commander looked at Lucas, his mouth working
for a moment before the words came out. "Jesus Christ,"
he blurted. "What the fuck was that all about?"

CHAPTER
3

Wild grapes covered the willow trees, dangling forty and fifty feet down to the waterline. In the weak light from the Mendota Bridge, the island looked like a three-masted schooner with black sails, cruising through the mouth of the Minnesota River into the Mississippi.

Two men walked onto a sand spit at the tip of the island. They'd had a fire earlier in the evening, roasting wieners on sharp sticks and heating cans of SpaghettiOs. The fire had guttered down to coals, but the smell of the burning pine still hung in the cool air. A hundred feet back from the water's edge, a sweat lodge squatted under the willows.

"We ought to go up north. It'd be nice now, out on the lakes," said the taller one.

"It's been too warm. Too many mosquitoes."

The tall man laughed. "Bullshit, mosquitoes. We're Indians, dickhead."

"Them fuckin' Chippewa would take our hair," the short one objected, the humor floating through his voice.

"Not us. Kill their men, screw their women. Drink their beer."

"I ain't drinkin' no Grain Belt," said the short one. There was a moment's comfortable silence between them. The

29

short one took a breath, let it out in an audible sigh and said, "Too much to do. Can't fuck around up north."

The short man's face had sobered. The tall man couldn't see it, but sensed it. "I wish I could go pray over Bluebird," the tall man said. After a moment, he added, "I hoped he would go longer."

"He wasn't smart."

"He was spiritual."

"Yep."

The men were Mdewakanton Sioux, cousins, born the same day on the banks of the Minnesota River. One had been named Aaron Sunders and the other Samuel Close, but only the bureaucrats called them that. To everyone else they touched, they were the Crows, named for their mothers' father, Dick Crow.

Later in life, a medicine man gave them Dakota first names. The names were impossible to translate. Some Dakota argued for Light Crow and Dark Crow. Others said Sun Crow and Moon Crow. Still others claimed the only reasonable translation was Spiritual Crow and Practical Crow. But the cousins called themselves Aaron and Sam. If some Dakota and white-wannabees thought the names were not impressive enough, that was their lookout.

The tall Crow was Aaron, the spiritual man. The short Crow was Sam, the practical one. In the back of their pickup, Aaron carried an army footlocker full of herbs and barks. In the cab, Sam carried two .45s, a Louisville Slugger and a money belt. They considered themselves one person in two bodies, each body containing a single aspect. It had been that way since 1932, when the daughters of Dick Crow and their two small sons had huddled together in a canvas lean-to for four months, near starving, near freezing, fighting to stay alive. From December through March, the cousins had lived in a cardboard box full of ripped-up woolen army blankets. The four months had welded their two personalities into one. They had been inseparable for nearly sixty years, except for a time that Aaron had spent in federal prison.

"I wish we would hear from Billy," said Sam Crow.

"We know he's there," Aaron Crow said quietly.

"But what's he doing? Three days now, and nothing."

"You worry that he's gone back to drinking. You shouldn't, 'cause he hasn't."

"How do you know?"

"I know."

Sam nodded. When his cousin said he knew, he knew. "I'm worried about what'll happen when he goes for the hit. The New York cops are good on a thing like this."

"Trust Billy," said Aaron. Aaron was thin, but not frail: wiry, hard, like beef jerky. He had a hundred hard planes in his face, surrounding a high-ridged nose. His eyes were like black marbles. "He's a smart one. He'll do right."

"I hope so. If he's caught right away, the television coverage will come and go too fast." Sam had a broad face, with smile lines around a wide, soft chin. His hair was salt-and-pepper, his eyes deep and thoughtful. He had a belly, which bore down on a wide belt with a turquoise buckle.

"Not if Leo moves. He should be in Oklahoma City tomorrow, if his car holds out," said Aaron. "If the two . . . attacks . . . come right on top of each other, the TV'll go nuts. And the letters are ready."

Sam paced down to the water's edge, watched it for a moment, then turned and spoke back up the sand spit.

"I still think the first two were a mistake. We wasted Bluebird, doing that second one. Those killings won't have the impact we need. . . ."

"We needed some low-risk attacks to start. . . ."

"Wasn't low-risk for Bluebird . . ."

"We knew he might have a problem . . . but we had to set a tone. We had to make it a war. We can't just have a couple of assassinations. We have to make the media think . . . War. We have to pump this motherfucker up. It has to be big, if we want to get . . ."

"The Great Satan," Sam snorted. "It'll be for nothing if we can't get him out here."

"It wouldn't be for nothing—the ones we've already taken are bad enough. But he'll come," Aaron said confidently. "We know he comes out here. We know why. We know where. And we can get at him."

"No," said Sam. "We know he *used* to come here. But

maybe no more. He's got the media watching. He wants to be president. . . . He's careful. . . ."

"But once he's here, he won't stay away. Not with the monkey he's got on his back."

"Maybe," said Sam. He thrust his hands into his pockets. "I still think the first two were bullshit killings."

"You're wrong," Aaron said flatly.

Sam stared out at the water. "I don't want to waste anybody, that's all." He bent, picked up a flat rock and tried to skip it across the river. Instead of skipping, it cut into the surface like a knife and was gone. "Shit," he said.

"You never were any good at that," Aaron said. "You need more of a sidearm."

"How many times have you told me that?" Sam asked, hunting up another rock.

"About a million."

Sam flipped the second rock out at the water. It hit and sank. He shook his head, thrust his hands back into his jean pockets, stood quietly for a moment, then turned to his cousin. "Have you talked to Shadow Love?" he asked.

"No."

"Are you still planning to send him to Bear Butte?"

"Yeah. I want him out of here," Aaron said.

"Shadow Love is a weapon," Sam Crow said.

"He's our kid."

"Every man comes to earth with a purpose. I'm quoting the famous Aaron Crow himself. Shadow Love is a weapon."

"I won't use him," said Aaron, walking down to the water's edge to stand by his cousin.

"Because he's our kid," Sam said. "Don't let that fuck you up."

"It's not that. The fact is, Shadow scares the shit out of me. That's the real problem." Aaron kicked off his battered sneakers and took a half-step so his toes were in the water. It felt cool and healing. "I fear for what we did to that boy, when we left him with Rosie. We had work to do, but . . . She wasn't quite right, you know. She was a lovely woman, but she had some wrong things in her mind. You say we made a weapon. I think we made a crazy man."

"Remember, once, a Crazy Horse . . . ?"

"Not the same. Crazy Horse loved a kind of life. A warrior life. A warrior life. Shadow's not a warrior. He's a killer. You've seen him; he hungers for pain and the power to create it."

The two men fell silent for a moment, listening to the water ripple past the sandbar. Then Aaron said, in a lighter tone, "How long before we fuck up, do you think?"

Sam threw back his head and laughed. "Three weeks. Maybe a month."

"We'll be dead, then," Aaron said. He made it sound funny.

"Maybe not. We could make it up to Canada. Sioux Valley. Hide out."

"Mmmm."

"What? You think we don't have a chance? We're just a couple of dead flatheads?" asked Sam.

"People who do this kind of thing . . . don't get away. They just don't." Aaron shrugged. "And there's always the question, *Should we try?*"

Sam ran a hand through his hair. "Jesus," he muttered.

"Exactly," Aaron said, with a quick, barking laugh. "If we go down . . . it'd make the point. Everybody knows Sitting Bull, because he died. Everybody knows Crazy Horse, because he died. Who knows about Inkpaduta? He was maybe the greatest of them all, but he went to Canada and got old and died. Not many remember him now. We're going to . . . *war* . . . to wake up the people. If we just sneak off, I don't think that'll be the same."

Sam shook his head but said nothing. He found another flat rock and sidearmed it at the water. It sank instantly. "Asshole," he called after the rock.

Aaron looked down at the sandbar at his cousin, sighed and said, "I'm going back to town with you. I hear too many voices tonight. I can't handle it."

"You shouldn't come here so often. Even I can feel them, groaning under the sand." He made a brushing motion that took in the sandbar, the river and the hillside. The land around the island had once been a concentration camp. Hundreds of Sioux died in it, most of them women and children.

"Come on," Aaron said. "Let's load the truck and get our ass out of here."

Billy Hood lay on the Jersey motel bed and stared at the ceiling. He'd made a preliminary reconnaissance, across the river into Manhattan, and concluded that he could do it. He could kill the man. The stone knife weighed on his chest.

To cut a man's throat . . . Hood's own throat tightened. Last year, hunting out of Mille Lacs in central Minnesota, he'd taken a deer. He'd spotted it walking through a grove of birches, a tan wraith floating through the white-on-white of trees and snow. It had been a doe, but a big one. The .30-.30 had knocked it down and it hadn't gotten up again. It hadn't died, either. It had lain there on its side in the shallow snow, its feet making feeble running motions, its visible eye blinking up at him and his brother-in-law Roger.

"Better cut her throat, brother," Roger had said. Roger was smiling. Turned on? Feeling the power? "Put her out of her misery."

Hood had taken his hunting knife from its sheath, a knife he'd honed to a razor sharpness. He'd grabbed the doe by an ear and lifted its head and cut its throat with a quick, heavy slash. Blood had spurted out on the snow and the doe had kicked a few times, its eye still blinking up at him. Then the death film crossed it and the doe went.

"It's the only place you ever see red blood, you know?" Roger had said. "In the snow. You see blood out in the woods in the fall, or in the summer, it always looks black. Boy, in this snow, it sure does look red, don't it?"

Andretti's blood would look black on the beige carpet of his office. That's how far Hood had gotten on his recon run. Andretti was famous for his long hours. The hall all around his office was closing down, but his "team" stayed on the job. Andretti called it a team. A photograph on an employee bulletin board outside his office showed Andretti and his staff gathered around a cake, wearing basketball jerseys. Andretti, of course, wore number 1.

"Mother," Hood said, closing his eyes to dream and maybe to pray. The stone pressed on his chest. Andretti's

blood would be black on the carpet. He would do it tomorrow, just after the hall closed.

The night was dark and filled with visions, even in the
suffocating motel room. Hood woke at one o'clock, and
three, four and five. At six, he got up, weary but unable to
sleep. He shaved, cleaned up, put on his best suit, feeling
the stone weight around his neck, the small pistol in his
pocket.

He walked to the train station, caught a ride across
the river, walked to Central Park. Checked the zoo and the
Metropolitan Museum. Cruised the van Goghs and the
Degas, lingered with the Renoirs and Monets. He liked
the outdoor lushness of the Impressionists. His own country, out along the Missouri in South Dakota, was all brown
and tan for most of the year. But there were times, in the
spring, when you'd find small mudflats overflowing with
wildflowers, where side creeks ran down to the river. He
could peer at the Monets and smell the hot prairie spice of
the black-eyed Susans. . . .

It took forever for the time to come. When it did, he rode
downtown on the subway, pinching out his emotions, one
by one. Thinking back to his hours on Bear Butte, the arid,
stoic beauty of the countryside. The distant scream of the
Black Hills, raped by the whites who promoted each natural
mystery with a chrome-yellow billboard.

By the time he reached the hall, he felt as close to stone
as he ever had. A few minutes before five, he walked into
the hall and took the stairs to the fifth floor.

Andretti's welfare department took up twelve floors of
the hall, but his personal office consisted of a suite of four
rooms. Hood had calculated that six to eight people regu-
larly worked in those rooms: Andretti and his secretary; a
receptionist; three aides, one male and two female; and a
couple of clerks on an irregular basis. The clerks and receptionist fled at five o'clock on the dot. He shouldn't have
more than five people to deal with.

On the fifth floor, Hood checked the hallway, then
walked quickly down to the public rest room. He entered
one of the stalls, sat down and opened his shirt. The obsidian
knife hung from his neck on a deerhide thong, taken from

the doe killed the year before. He pulled the thong over his neck and slipped the knife into his left jacket pocket. The gun was in his right.

Hood looked at his watch. Three minutes after five. He decided to wait a few more minutes and sat on the toilet, watching the second hand go 'round. The watch had cost twelve dollars, new. A Timex; his wife had bought it when it looked as if he might get a job with a state road crew. But the job had fallen through and all he had left was the Timex.

When the Timex said 5:07, Hood stood up, his soul now as hard as the knife. The hallway was empty. He walked quickly down to Andretti's office, looking to his right as he passed the main hall. A woman was waiting for the elevator. She glanced at him, then away. Hood continued to Andretti's office, paused with his hand on the knob, then pushed it open. The receptionist had gone, but he heard laughter from the other side of the panel behind her desk.

Putting his hand in his jacket pocket, on the gun, he stepped around the panel. Two of the aides, a man and a woman, were leaning on desks, talking. Through an open door, he could see Andretti, working in shirtsleeves behind a green goosenecked lamp. There was at least one more person in his office with him.

When he came around the panel, the woman didn't notice him for a moment, but the man saw him and frowned slightly. Then the woman turned her head and said, "I'm sorry, we're closed."

Hood took his hand from his pocket, with the gun in it, and said, "Don't say a word or make a sound. Just walk into Mr. Andretti's office."

"Oh, no," said the woman. The man clenched his fists and slipped off the desk.

Hood pointed the gun at his head and said, "I don't want to kill you, but I will. Now walk." He had now moved out of Andretti's line of sight. "Move," he said.

They moved reluctantly, toward Andretti's office. "If you do anything, if you touch a door, if you say anything, I will shoot you," Hood said quietly as they approached Andretti's office.

The man stepped inside, followed by the woman. Hood said, "Off to the side." The man said, "Boss, we've got a problem." Andretti looked up and said, "Oh, shit."

A woman was slumped in a chair in front of Andretti's desk, her face caught in a smile which seeped away when she saw Hood; Hood thought the word *seeped,* because of the slowness with which it left. As though she didn't want to disturb him. As though she wanted to think it was a joke.

"Where's the secretary?" Hood asked Andretti.

"She went home early," Andretti said. "Listen, my friend . . ."

"Be quiet. We've got some business to do, but I have to arrange these people first. I don't want them rushing me while we talk."

"If you've got a problem . . ."

"I've got a problem, all right," Hood interrupted. "It's how to keep from shooting one of these people if they don't do what I say. I want you to all lay down, facedown, on the rug against that wall."

"How do we know you won't shoot us?"

"Because I promise not to. I don't want to hurt you. But I promise I *will* shoot you if you don't get down on the floor."

"Do it," Andretti ordered.

The three backed away toward the wall, then sat down. "Roll over, facedown," Hood said. They flattened themselves out, one of the women craning her neck to see him. "Look at the rug, lady, okay?"

When they were staring at the rug, Hood moved slowly around Andretti's desk. Andretti was a big man, and young; early thirties. No more than thirty-five.

"Let me explain what I'm about to do, Mr. Andretti," Hood said as he moved. He and Bluebird and the others had thought this out, and decided that lying would be best. "I'm going to put some cuffs on you and then I'm going to make some phone calls downtown on behalf of my people. I'm going to put the cuffs on because I don't want you causing trouble. If everybody cooperates, nobody gets hurt. Do you understand?"

"I understand what you're saying, but I don't understand what you want."

"We'll talk that out," Hood said reassuringly. He was behind Andretti, and he reached out and touched him on the temple with the barrel of the pistol. "Put your hands behind your back, clasp them."

When Andretti had done that, Hood said, "Now, look straight back. No, arch your back and tilt your head back. I want to show you this before I do it."

"What?" Andretti asked, dropping his head straight back.

"This," Hood said. He'd changed the gun for the knife, caught Andretti's hair in his left hand and slashed him with the stone, cutting deeper, much deeper, much fiercer, than he had with the doe.

"Ahh," he grunted as the blood spurted from Andretti's neck. Andretti's hands pounded on his desk and he began coughing, choking, looking for Hood. One of the women half sat, saw Andretti and screamed. Hood fired a single shot at her white face and she dropped down. He didn't know whether he had hit her or not, but the man now rolled and the other woman began scrambling across the rug. Hood hollered "Stop" and fired a shot into the man's back. The man arched and Hood was out the door, down the hallway and in the stairwell, running, the screams fading as doors closed.

Gun in pocket, knife in pocket, first landing down. He looked at his hands. Clean. Looked at his pants. Clean. Blood on his shirt, a spot on his jacket. He pulled the jacket shut, third landing down. Ground floor. Into the lobby. Guard at the desk, looking up. Past the guard, into the street. Down a block. Into the subway. The token. Wait. Wait. Wait for running feet, shouts, cops, but nothing but the damp smell of the subway and the clatter of an approaching train.

It took him an hour to get back to Jersey. A half-hour after that, he was in his car, heading west into the setting sun.

In Oklahoma City, Leo Clark stood outside the federal courthouse and looked up. Scouting. The stone blade hung heavy around his neck.

CHAPTER
4

Jennifer came out of the bathroom, still naked. She was tall, slender, small-breasted and blonde; she had dark eyebrows under her champagne bangs and blue eyes that sometimes, when she was angry, went the color of river ice. Lucas hooked her with his arm as she passed the bed, and pulled her stomach into his face.

"That was nice," he said. "We should do it more often."

"I'm here," she said.

Lucas nuzzled her stomach and she pushed his head away.

"You're messing with my flab."

"It's all gone."

"No, it's not." Jennifer flipped on the room light, pushed the door shut and pirouetted in the full-length mirror mounted on the back. "I've got tummy-stretch and butt-hang. I can handle the butt. The tummy is tough."

"You goddamn yuppie women have the weirdest enthusiasms," Lucas said lazily, lying back on the bed, watching her. "You look perfect."

She skipped past him, eluding his arm, and took a cotton nightgown off the dresser. "I can't decide whether you're just naturally full of shit or unnaturally horny," she said as she slipped it over her head.

Lucas shrugged, grinned and leaned back on the oversize pillow. "Whichever it is, it works. I get laid a lot."

"I should kick you out of here, Davenport," Jennifer said. "I . . . Is that the baby?"

He listened and heard the baby's low crying from the next room. "Yup."

"Time to eat," Jennifer said.

They had never married, but Lucas and Jennifer Carey had an infant daughter. Lucas pressed for a wedding. Jennifer said maybe—sometime. Not now. She lived with the baby in a suburban townhouse south of Minneapolis, fifteen minutes from Lucas' house in St. Paul.

Lucas rolled off the bed and followed Jennifer into the baby's room. The moment the door opened, Sarah stopped crying and began to gurgle.

"She's wet," Jennifer said when she picked her up. She handed Sarah to Lucas. "You change her. I'll go heat up the glop."

Lucas carried Sarah to the changing table, pulled the tape-tabs loose from the diaper and tossed the diaper in a disposal can. He whistled while he worked, and the baby peered at him in fascination, once or twice pursing her lips as though she were about to start whistling herself. Lucas cleaned her bottom with wet-wipes, tossed the wipes after the diaper, powdered her and put a new diaper on her. By the time he finished, Sarah was bubbling with delight.

"Jesus Christ, you are positively dangerous around *any-thing* female," Jennifer said from the doorway.

Lucas laughed, picked up Sarah and bounced her on the palm of one hand. The baby chortled and grabbed his nose with surprising power.

"Whoa, whoa, wet go ub Daddy's nose. . . ." Jennifer said he sounded like Elmer Fudd when he spoke in baby talk. Sarah whacked him in the eye with her other hand.

"Jesus, I'm getting mugged," Lucas said. "What do you think you're doing, kid, whopping on your old man . . . ?"

The phone rang. Lucas glanced at his wrist, but he'd taken his watch off. It was late, though, after midnight. Jennifer stepped down the hall to the phone. A second later, she was back.

"It's for you."

"Nobody knew I was here," Lucas said, puzzled.

"It's the shift commander, what's-his-name . . . Meany. Daniel told him to try here."

"I wonder what's going on?" Lucas padded down the hall to the phone, picked it up and said, "Davenport."

"This is Harry Meany," said an old man's voice. "The chief said to track you down and get your ass in here. He'll see you in his office in half an hour."

"What happened?"

"I don't know. Lester and Anderson are already here and Sloan's on his way."

"You've got nothing going?" Lucas asked.

"Not a thing," Meany said. "A 7-Eleven got knocked off over on University, but that's nothing new. Nobody hurt."

"Hmph." Lucas scratched his chin, considering. "All right, I'll be down."

Lucas hung up and stood with his hand on the phone, staring blankly at the picture hung above it, a hand-colored print of an English cottage. Jennifer said, "What?"

"I don't know. There's a meeting. Daniel, Lester, Anderson, Sloan. Me."

"Huh." She posed with her hands on her hips. "What are you working?"

"Not much," Lucas said. "We're still getting rumors about guns going out of here, but nothing we can pin down. There's been a lot of crack action. That's about it."

Jennifer nodded. She had been TV3's top street reporter for ten years. After Sarah had arrived, she'd taken a partial leave of absence and begun working as a producer. But the years on the street were still with her: she had both an eye and a taste for breaking news.

"You know what it sounds like?" she asked, a calculating look on her face. "It sounds like the team Daniel set up last year. The Maddog group."

"But there's nothing going on," Lucas said. He shook his head again and walked to the bathroom.

"You'll let me know?" she called after him.

"If I can."

•   •   •

Lucas suspected that early city fathers had built the Minneapolis City Hall as an elaborate practical joke on their progeny. A liverish pile of granite, it managed to be both hot in the summer and cold in winter. In the spring and fall, in the basement, where his office was, the walls sweated a substance that looked like tree sap. Another detective, a lapsed Catholic like Lucas, had suggested that they wait for a good bout of sweating, carefully crack his office wall in a likeness of Jesus and claim a holy stigmata.

"We could make a buck," he said enthusiastically.

"I'm not real big in the Church anymore," Lucas said dryly, "But I'd just as soon not be excommunicated."

"Chickenshit."

Lucas circled the building, dumped the Porsche in a cops-only space. The chief's corner office was lit. As he walked around the nose of the car and stepped onto the curb, a Chevy station wagon pulled up behind the Porsche and the driver tapped the horn. A moment later, Harrison Sloan climbed out of the wagon.

"What's happening?" Lucas asked.

Sloan shrugged. He was a thin man with soft brown puppy eyes and a thin mustache. He might have played an RAF fighter pilot in a World War II movie, a pilot named Dicky. He was wearing a sweatsuit and tennis shoes. "I don't know. I was asleep. Meany called and told me to get my ass down here."

"Same with me," Lucas said. "Big mystery."

As they pushed through the outer doors, Sloan asked, "How's the hand?"

Lucas looked down at the back of his hand and flexed it. The Maddog had broken several of the bones between his wrist and knuckles. When he squeezed hard, it still hurt. The doctors said it might always hurt. "Pretty good. The strength is back. I've been squeezing a rubber ball."

"Ten years ago, if you'd been hurt like that, you'd have been a cripple," Sloan said.

"Ten years ago I might have been quick enough to shoot the sonofabitch before he got to me," Lucas said.

City Hall was quiet, smelling of janitor's wax and disinfectant. The soles of their shoes made a rubbery flap-flap-

flap as they walked down the dim hallways, and their voices rattled off the marble as they speculated about Daniel's call. Sloan thought the hurried meeting involved a political problem.

"That's why the rush in the middle of the night. They're trying to sort it out before the newspapers get it," he said.

"So why Lester and Anderson? Why bring Robbery–Homicide into it?"

"Huh." Sloan nibbled at his mustache. "I don't know."

"It's something else," said Lucas. "Somebody's dead."

The outer door of the chief's office was open. Lucas and Sloan stepped inside and found Quentin Daniel in the dark outer office, poking at his secretary's desk. Daniel was a broad man with the open, affable face of a neighborhood butcher. Only his eyes, small, quick, probing, betrayed the brain behind the friendly face.

"Stealing paper clips?" Sloan asked.

"You can never find any goddamn matches when you need them, and nobody smokes anymore," Daniel grumbled. He was an early-to-bed, early-to-rise type, but he looked alert and almost happy. "Come on in."

Frank Lester, the deputy chief for investigations, and slat-thin Harmon Anderson, a computer savant and Lester's assistant, were perched on side chairs opposite Daniel's desk. Lucas and Sloan took empty chairs and Daniel settled behind the desk.

"I've been on the phone all evening. Frank and Harmon have been here for most of it," Daniel told Lucas and Sloan. "There's been a killing in New York City. A commissioner of welfare. A little after five o'clock this evening, their time. He was a prize Italian named John Andretti. Either of you guys hear of him?"

Lucas and Sloan both shook their heads. "Nope," said Sloan. "Should we?"

"He's been in the *Times* quite a bit," said Daniel, with a shrug. "He was a businessman who was getting into politics. Had some different ideas about welfare . . . Anyway, he's got big family money. Construction, banking, all that. Went to Choate. Went to Harvard. Went to Yale Law. He had these great teeth and this great-looking old lady with great-looking tits and four great-looking kids and nobody in the family pushes dope or drinks too much or fucks anybody else's husband or wife, and they all go to church on Sunday. His old man had him set to run for Congress this fall and then maybe the Senate in four years. You know, the New York media were starting to call him the Italian John Kennedy. . . ."

"So what happened?" Lucas asked.

"He got himself killed. In his office. There were three witnesses. This guy comes in, he's got a pistol. He backs everybody off, then steps around behind Andretti. Before anybody can say 'Boo,' this guy—he's an Indian, by the way—he grabs Andretti, pulls his head back and slits his throat with a weird-looking stone knife."

"Oh, fuck," said Lucas. Sloan was sitting in his chair with his mouth open. Anderson watched them in amusement, while Lester looked worried.

"That's exactly right," said Daniel. He leaned forward, took a cigar from a brand-new humidor, held it under his nose, sniffed, then put the cigar back in the humidor. " 'Oh, fuck.' The Indian also shot one of Andretti's aides, but he'll be okay."

Anderson picked up the story. "The Andretti family went berserk and started calling in debts. The governor, the mayor, everybody is getting in on the act." Anderson was wearing plaid pants, a striped shirt and shiny yellow-brown vinyl shoes. "The New York cops are running around like chickens with their heads cut off."

"Andretti was one of the best-connected guys in New York City," Daniel added. "He's got twenty brothers and sisters and cousins and his old man and his old lady. They got an ocean of money and two oceans of political clout. They want blood."

"And they think whoever killed Andretti was working with this Bluebird guy?" asked Lucas.

"Look at the killings," Daniel said, spreading his arms. "It's obvious. And there's more to it. Andretti's office building had a videotape monitor on a continuous loop. The witnesses picked out the killer. It's a horseshit picture and they've only got him for about ten seconds, walking through the lobby, but they released it to the television stations an hour ago. A few minutes after they put it on TV, a motel owner from Jersey called up and said the guy might have been at his motel. The Jersey cops checked and they think he's right. They've got no license-plate number—it wasn't that kind of motel—but the owner remembers the guy had Minnesota plates. He remembers that when the guy was checking out, he said he was heading back home. The motel owner said there was no question about him being an Indian. And then there was the other thing."

"What's that?" Sloan asked.

"The New York cops held back the part about the stone knife," Daniel said. "They told the media that Andretti had been stabbed, but nothing about the knife. So this motel owner asked the Jersey cops, 'Did he stab him with that big fucking stone knife?' The cops say, 'What?' And this motel owner, he says his Indian wore a stone knife around his neck, on a leather thong. He saw him at the Coke machine, wearing an undershirt with the knife hanging down."

"So we know for sure," Sloan said.

"Yeah. And he seems to be coming this way." Daniel leaned back in his chair, put his hands on his stomach and twiddled his thumbs.

Lucas pulled his lip, thinking about it. After a moment of silence, he looked up at the chief. "This guy have braids?"

"The killer? Didn't say anything about braids . . ." He hunted around his desktop for a moment, picked up a piece of computer printout, read it and said, "Nope. Hair down over the tops of his ears and just over his shirt collar. Longish, but not long enough for braids."

"Shit."

"Why?"

"Because the guy who did Cuervo had braids."

The others glanced at each other and Daniel said, "He could have cut it."

"I said the same thing about Bluebird, when we took him down," Lucas said.

"Oh, boy," Lester rasped, rubbing the back of his neck. He was the department's front man on cases that drew media attention. "That'd make three. If there are two, the media's gonna go nuts. If there's three . . . I've been burned before, I don't need this shit."

Sloan grinned at him. "It's gonna be bad, Frank," he said, teasing. "This guy sounds like big headlines. When the networks and the big papers get a whiff of conspiracy, they'll be on you like white on rice. Especially with the part about the stone knives. They'll love the stone knives."

"The local papers already figured it out. Five minutes after the news came across on the Indian angle, we were getting calls on Bluebird. *StarTribune, Pioneer Press,* all the stations. AP's got it on the wire," said Anderson.

"Like flies on a dead cat," Sloan said to Lester.

"So we're setting up a team, just like we did with the Maddog. I'll announce it at a press conference tomorrow morning," said Daniel. "Frank will run the out-front investigation and handle the press on a daily basis. Harmon will get the database going again. Just like with the Maddog. Every goddamn scrap of information, okay? Notebooks for everybody."

"I'll set it up tonight," Anderson said. "I'll get somebody to duplicate copies of the Bluebird mug shot."

"Good. Get me a bunch for the press conference." Daniel turned to Sloan. "I want you to backtrack everybody connected with Bluebird. He's our hold on this thing. If we get an ID on the New York killer, I want you to track down everybody who knew him. You'll be pretty much independent, but you report to Anderson every day, every move. Everything you get goes into the database."

"Sure," Sloan nodded.

"Lucas, you're on your own, just like with the Maddog," Daniel said. "Our contacts with the Indian community are fuckin' terrible. You're the only guy who has any."

"Not many," said Lucas.

"They're all we got," said Daniel.

"What about bringing in Larry Hart? We've used him before. . . ."

"Good." Daniel snapped his fingers and pointed at Lester. "Call Welfare tomorrow and ask them if we can detach Hart as a resource guy. We'll pick up his salary."

"What is he?" asked Sloan. "Chippewa?"

"Sioux," said Lucas.

"He's strange, is what he is," said Anderson. "He's got some genealogical stuff stored away in the city computers. The systems guys would shit if they knew about it."

Lucas shrugged. "He's an okay guy."

"So let's get him," said Daniel. He stood up and paced slowly away from his desk, his hands in his pants pockets. "What else?"

Bluebird's funeral would be monitored. Intelligence would attempt to identify everyone who attended and run histories on them. Sloan would build a list of friends and relatives who might have known about Bluebird's activities. They would be interviewed by selected Narcotics and Intelligence detectives. Anderson would press the Jersey cops for any available details on the killer's appearance and his car and run them against known Indian felons from Minnesota, Wisconsin, Nebraska and the Dakotas.

"It'll be a fuckin' circus, starting bright and early tomorrow morning," said Daniel. "And I'll tell you what: When this New York guy gets here, I want us on top of this thing. I want us to look good, not like a bunch of rube assholes."

Anderson cleared his throat. "I don't think it's a guy, chief. I think it's a woman," he said.

Sloan and Lucas glanced at each other. "What are you talking about?" asked Sloan.

"We told you, didn't we? No? The goddamn Andretti family is putting the screws on the New York cops. They want to send somebody out here to *observe* our investigation," said Daniel. He turned to Anderson. "You say it's a woman?"

"Yeah. That's what I understood. Unless they got male cops named Lillian. She's a lieutenant."

"Huh," said Daniel. He stroked his chin, as though grooming a goatee. "Whoever it is, I can guarantee she's heavy-duty."

"Where'll we put her?" asked Lester.

"Let her work with Sloan," Daniel said. "That'll give her

some time on the street. Give her the feeling she's doing something."

He looked around the room. "Anything else? No? Let's do it."

CHAPTER
5

The barbershop had one chair, a turn-of-the-century model with a cracked black leather seat. A mirror was mounted on the wall behind the chair. Below the mirror, on a shelf, stood a line of bottles with luminescent yellow lotions and ruby-red toilet waters. Sunlight played through them like a visual pipe organ.

When Lucas walked in, William Dooley was pushing a flat broom around the floor, herding snips of black hair into a pile on the flaking brown linoleum.

"Officer Davenport," Dooley said gravely. Dooley was old and very thin. His temples looked papery, like eggshells.

"Mr. Dooley." Lucas nodded, matching the old man's gravity. He climbed into the chair. Dooley moved behind him, tucked a slippery nylon bib into his collar and stood back.

"Just a little around the ears?" he asked. Lucas didn't need a haircut.

"Around the ears and the back of the neck, Mr. Dooley," Lucas said. The slanting October sunlight dappled the linoleum below his feet. A sugar wasp bounced against the dusty window.

"Bad business about that Bluebird," Lucas said after a bit.

Dooley's snipping scissors had been going chip-chip-chip. They paused just above Lucas' ear, then resumed. "Bad business," he agreed.

He snipped for another few seconds before Lucas asked, "Did you know him?"

"Nope," Dooley said promptly. After another few snips, he added, "Knew his daddy, though. Back in the war. We was in the Pacific together. Not the same unit, but I seen him from time to time."

"Did Bluebird have any people besides his wife and kids?"

"Huh." Dooley stopped to think. He was halfbreed Sioux, with an Indian father and a Swedish mother. "He might have an aunt or an uncle or two out at Rosebud. That's where they'd be, if there are any left. His ma died in the early fifties and his old man went four or five years back, must have been."

Dooley stared sightlessly through the sunny window. "No, by God," he said in a creaking voice after a minute. "His old man died in the summer of 'seventy-eight, right between those two bad winters. Twelve years ago. Time passes, don't it?"

"It does," Lucas said.

"You want to know something about being an Indian, Officer Davenport?" Dooley asked. He'd stopped cutting Lucas' hair.

"Everything helps."

"Well, when Bluebird died—the old man—I went off to his funeral, out to the res. He was a Catholic, you know? They buried him in a Catholic cemetery. So I went up to the cemetery with the crowd from the funeral and they put him in the ground, and everybody was standing around. Now most of the graves were all together, but I noticed that there was another bunch off in a corner by themselves. I asked a fellow there, I said, 'What's them graves over there?' You know what they were?"

"No," said Lucas.

"They were the Catholic suicides. The Catholics don't allow no suicides to be buried in the regular part of the cemetery, but there got to be so many suicides that they just kind of cut off a special corner for them. . . . You ever hear of anything like that?"

"No, I never did. And I'm a Catholic," Lucas said.

"You think about that. Enough Catholic suicides on one dinky little res to have their own corner of the cemetery."

Dooley stood looking through the window for another few seconds, then caught himself and went back to work. "Not many Bluebirds left," he said. "Mostly married off, went away east or west. New York and Los Angeles. Lost their names. Good people, though."

"Crazy thing he did."

"Why?" The question was so unexpected that Lucas half turned his head and caught the sharp point of the scissors in the scalp.

"Whoa, did that hurt?" Dooley asked, concern in his voice.

"Nah. What'd you . . . ?"

"Almost stuck a hole in you," Dooley interrupted. He rubbed at Lucas' scalp with a thumb. "Don't see no blood."

"What do you mean, 'Why?' " Lucas persisted. "He cut a guy's throat. Maybe two guys."

There was a long moment of silence, then, "They needed them cut," Dooley said. "There weren't no worse men for the Indian community. I read the Bible, just like anybody. What Bluebird did was wrong. But he's paid, hasn't he? An eye for an eye. They're dead and he's dead. And I'll tell you this, the Indian people got two big weights off their backs."

"Okay," said Lucas. "I can buy it. Ray Cuervo was an asshole. Excuse the language."

"I heard the word before," Dooley said. "I wouldn't say you was wrong. And not about this Benton fella, either. He was bad as Cuervo."

"So I'm told," Lucas said.

Dooley finished the trim above Lucas' ear, pushed his head forward until his chin rested on his chest, and did the back of his neck.

"There's been another killing, in New York," Lucas said. "Same way as Cuervo and Benton. Throat cut with a stone knife."

"Saw it on TV," Dooley acknowledged. He pointed at the

black-and-white television mounted in the corner of the shop. "*Today* show. Thought it sounded pretty much the same."

"Too much," Lucas said. "I've been wondering . . ."

"If I might of heard anything? Just talk. You know Bluebird was a sun-dancer?"

"No, I didn't know," Lucas said.

"Check his body, if you still got it. You'll find scars all over his chest where he pulled the pegs through." Lucas winced. As part of the Sioux ceremony, dancers pushed pegs through the skin of their chests. Cords were attached to the pegs, and the dancers dangled from poles until the pegs ripped out. "There's another thing. Bluebird was a sun-dancer for sure, but there's folks around saying that a couple years ago, he got involved in this ghost-dance business."

"Ghost dance? I didn't think that was being done," Lucas said.

"Some guys came down from Canada, tried to start it up. They had a drum, went around to all the reservations, collecting money, dancing. Scared the heck out of a lot of people, but I haven't heard anything about them lately. Most Indian people think it was a con game."

"But Bluebird was dancing?"

"That's what I heard. . . ." Dooley's voice trailed off and Lucas turned and found the old man staring out the window again. There was a park across the street, with grass worn brown by kids' feet and the fall frosts. An Indian kid was working on an upturned bike in the middle of the park and an old lady tottered down the sidewalk toward a concrete drinking fountain. "I don't think it means much," Dooley said. He turned back to Lucas. "Except that Bluebird was a man looking for religion."

"Religion?"

"He was looking to be saved. Maybe he found it," Dooley said. He sighed and moved close behind Lucas and finished the trim with a few final snips. He put the scissors down, brushed cut hair off Lucas' neck, unpinned the bib and shook it out. "Sit tight for a minute," he said.

Lucas sat and Dooley found his electric trimmers and

shaved the back of Lucas' neck, then slapped on a stinging palmful of aromatic yellow oil.

"All done," he said.

Lucas slid out of the chair, asked, "How much?" Dooley said, "The regular." Lucas handed him three dollars.

"I haven't heard anything," Dooley said soberly. He looked Lucas in the eyes. "If I had, I'd tell you—but I don't know if I'd tell you what it was. Bluebird was the Indian people, getting back some of their own."

Lucas shook his head, sensing the defiance in the old man. "It's hard to believe you said that, Mr. Dooley. It makes me sad," he said.

Indian Country was full of Dooleys.

Lucas quartered through it, touching the few Indians he knew: a seamstress at an awnings shop, a seafood broker, a heating contractor, clerks at two gas stations and a convenience store, an out-of-business antique dealer, a key-maker, a cleaning lady, a car salesman. An hour before Bluebird's funeral was scheduled to begin, he left his car in an alley and walked across the street to Dakota Hardware.

A bell over the door jingled, and Lucas stopped for a moment, waiting for his eyes to adjust to the gloom. Earl May came out of the back room wearing a leather apron and flashed a smile. Lucas walked back and watched the smile fade.

"I was about to say, 'Good to see you,' but I guess you're here to ask questions about Bluebird and that killing in New York," May said. He turned his head and yelled into the back, "Hey, Betty, it's Lucas Davenport."

Betty May stuck her head through the curtain between the back room and the store. "Lucas, it's been a while," she said. She had a round face, touched by old acne scars, and a husky voice that might have sung the blues.

"There's not much around about Bluebird," said Earl. He looked at his wife. "He's asking about the killings."

"That's what everybody tells me," Lucas said. Earl was standing with his arms crossed. It was a defensive position, a push-off stance, one that Lucas had not seen before with the Mays. Behind her husband, Betty unconsciously took the same position.

"You'll have trouble dealing with the community on this one," she said. "Benton was bad, Cuervo was worse. Cuervo was so bad that when his wife got down to his office, after the police called her, she was smiling."

"But what about this guy in New York, Andretti?" Lucas asked. "What the hell did he do?"

"Andretti. The liberal with good accountants," Earl snorted. "He called himself a realist. He said there were people that you have to write off. He said that it made no difference whether you threw money at the underclass or just let it get along. He said the underclass was a perpetual drag on the people who work."

"Yeah?" said Lucas.

"A lot of people want to hear that," Earl continued. "And he might even be right about some people—winos and junkies. But there's one big question he doesn't answer. What about the kids? That's the question. You're seeing a genocide. The victims aren't the welfare queens. The victims are the kids."

"You can't think this is right, these people being killed," Lucas argued.

Earl shook his head. "People die all the time. Now some folks are dying who were hurting the Indian people. That's too bad for them and it's a crime, but I can't get too upset about it."

"How about you, Betty?" Lucas asked. He turned to the woman, disturbed. "Do you feel the same way?"

"Yeah, I do, Lucas," she said.

Lucas peered at them for a moment, studying Earl's face, then Betty's. They were the best people he knew. What they thought, a lot of people would think. Lucas shook his head, rapped the counter with his knuckles and said, "Shit."

Bluebird's funeral was . . . Lucas had to search for the right word. He finally settled on *peculiar*. Too many of the gathered Indians were shaking hands, with quick grins that just as quickly turned somber.

And there were too many Indians for one guy who wasn't

that well known. After the coffin had been lowered into the ground, and the last prayers said, they gathered in groups and clusters, twos and threes, talking. An air of suppressed celebration, Lucas thought. Somebody had lashed out. Bluebird had paid, but there were others still at it, taking down the assholes. Lucas watched the crowd, searching for faces he knew, people he might tap later.

Riverwood Cemetery was a working-class graveyard in a working-class neighborhood. Bluebird was buried on a south-facing slope under an ash tree. His grave would look up at the sun, even in winter. Lucas stood on a small rise, next to one of the city's increasingly rare elms, thirty yards from the gravesite. Directly opposite him, across the street from the cemetery and a hundred feet from the grave, were more watchers. The catsup-colored Chevy van fit into the neighborhood like a perfect puzzle piece. In the back, two cops made movies through the dark windows.

Identifying everyone would be impossible, Lucas thought. The funeral had been too big and too many people were simply spectators. He noticed a white woman drifting along the edges of the crowd. She was taller than most women and a little heavy, he thought. She glanced his way, and from a distance, she was a sulky, dark-haired madonna, with an oval face and long heavy eyebrows.

He was still following her progress through the fringe of the crowd when Sloan ambled up and said, "Hello, there." Lucas turned to say hello. When he turned back to the funeral crowd a moment later, the dark-haired woman was gone.

"You talk to Bluebird's old lady?" Lucas asked.

"I tried," Sloan said. "I couldn't get her alone. She had all these people around, saying, 'Don't talk to the cops, honey. Your man is a hero.' They're shutting her down."

"Maybe later, huh?"

"Maybe, but I don't think we'll get much," Sloan said. "Where're you parked?"

"Around the corner."

"So am I." They picked their way between graves, down the shallow slope toward the street. Some of the graves were well tended, others were weedy. One limestone gravemarker

was so old that the name had eroded away, leaving only the
fading word FATHER. "I was talking to one of the people
at her house. The guy said Bluebird hadn't been around that
much. In fact, he and his old lady were probably on the edge
of breaking up," Sloan said.

"Not too promising," Lucas agreed.

"So what're you doing?"

"Running around picking up bullshit," Lucas said. He
looked one last time for the dark-haired woman but didn't
see her. "I'm headed over to the Point. Yellow Hand's up
there. Maybe he's heard something more."

"It's worth a try," Sloan said, discouraged.

"He's my last shot. Nobody wants to talk."

"That's what I get," Sloan said. "They're rootin' for the
other side."

The Point was a row of red-brick townhouses that had been
converted to single-floor apartments. Lucas stepped inside
the door, pushed it shut and sniffed. Boiled cabbage, a few
days old. Canned corn. Oatmeal. Fish. He reached back to
his hip, slipped the Heckler and Koch P7 out of its holster
and put it in his sport coat pocket.

Yellow Hand's room was five floors up, in what had once
been a common-storage attic. Lucas stopped on the landing
at the fourth floor, caught his breath and finished the climb
with his hand on the P7. The door at the top of the stairs
was closed. He tried the knob without knocking, turned it
and pushed the door open.

A man was sitting on a mattress reading a copy of *People*
magazine. An Indian, wearing a blue work shirt with the
sleeves rolled above his elbows, and jeans and white socks.
An army field jacket lay next to the mattress, along with
a pair of cowboy boots, a green ginger-ale can, another copy
of *People* and a battered volume of *Reader's Digest Con-
densed Books.* Lucas stepped inside.

"Who are you?" the man asked. His forearms were tattooed—a rose inside a heart on the arm nearer to Lucas,
an eagle's wing on the other. Another mattress lay across
the room with two people on it, asleep, a man and a woman.
The man wore jockey shorts, the woman a rose-colored

rayon slip. Her dress lay neatly folded by the mattress and next to that were two chipped cups with a coil heater inside one of them. The floor was littered with scraps of paper, old magazines, empty food packages and cans. The room stank of marijuana and soup.

"Cop," said Lucas. He stepped fully into the room and looked off to his left. A third mattress. Yellow Hand, asleep. "Looking for Yellow Hand."

"He's passed out," said the tattooed man.

"Drinking?"

"Yeah." The man rolled off the mattress and picked up his jacket. Lucas pointed a finger at him.

"Stick around for a minute, okay?"

"Sure, no problem. You got a cigarette?"

"No."

The woman on the second mattress stirred, rolled onto her back and propped herself up on her elbows. She was white, and older than Lucas thought when he first saw her. Forties, he thought. "What's going on?" she asked.

"Cop to see Yellow Hand," said the tattooed man.

"Oh, shit." She squinted at Lucas and he saw she was missing her front teeth. "You got a cigarette?"

"No."

"God damn, nobody ever got no smokes around here," she whined. She looked at the man beside her, poked him. "Get up, Bob. The cops are here." Bob moaned, twitched and snored.

"Leave him," said Lucas. He moved over to Yellow Hand and pushed him with his toe.

"Don't fuck w' me," Yellow Hand said sleepily, batting at the foot.

"Need to talk to you."

"Don't fuck w' me," Yellow Hand said again.

Lucas prodded him a little harder. "Get up, Yellow Hand. This is Davenport."

Yellow Hand's eyes flickered and Lucas thought he looked too old for a teenager. He looked as old as the woman, who was now sitting slouched on the mattress, smacking her lips. The tattooed man stood bouncing on his toes for a second, then reached for a cowboy boot.

"Leave the boots," Lucas said, pointing at him again. "Wake up, Yellow Hand."

Yellow Hand rolled to a sitting position. "What is it?"

"I want to talk." Lucas turned to the tattooed man. "Why'n't you come over here and sit on the mattress?"

"I ain't done a fuckin' thing," the man snarled, suddenly defiant. He was rake thin and had one shoulder turned toward Lucas in an unconscious boxing stance.

"I'm not here to fuck with anybody," Lucas said. "I'm not asking for ID, I'm not calling in for warrants. I just want to talk."

"I don't talk to the fuckin' cops," the tattooed man said. He looked around for support. The woman was staring at the floor, shaking her head; then she spat between her feet. Lucas put his hand in his pocket. The attic space was crowded. Ordinarily, he wouldn't worry about a couple of derelicts and a drifter, but the tattooed man exuded an air of toughness. If there were a fight, he wouldn't have much room to maneuver.

"We can do it the easy way or we can do it the hard way," he said softly. "Now get your ass over here or I'll kick it up between the ears."

"What you gonna do, cop, you gonna fuckin' shoot me? I ain't got no knife, I ain't got no gun, I'm in my own fuckin' apartment, I ain't seen no warrant, you gonna shoot me?"

The man stepped closer and Lucas took his hand back out of his pocket.

"No, but I might beat the snot out of you," Lucas said. Both the older man and the woman were looking away. If the tattooed man jumped, he would have no support from them. Yellow Hand wasn't likely to help the stranger, so it would be one on one. He braced himself.

"Take it easy, Shadow, you don't want to fight no cop," Yellow Hand said from the mattress. "You know what'd happen then."

Lucas looked from Yellow Hand to the tattooed man and guessed that the tattooed man was on parole.

"You know Benton?" he snapped. "He your PO?"

"No, man. I never met him," the tattooed man said, suddenly closing his eyes and half turning away. The tension ebbed.

"All I want to do is talk," Lucas said mildly.

"You want to talk with a gun in your pocket," said the tattooed man, turning back to him. "Like all whites."

He looked straight at Lucas, and Lucas saw that his eyes were light gray, so light they looked as though cataracts were floating across his irises. The man's body trembled once, again, and then settled into a low vibration, like a guitar string.

"Take it easy," Yellow Hand said again, rubbing his face. "Come on over and sit down. Davenport won't fuck with you."

There was another moment of stress; then, as suddenly as he'd become angry, the tattooed man relaxed and smiled. His teeth were a startling white against his dark face. "Sure. Jeez, I'm sorry, but you come on sudden," he said. He bobbed his head in apology.

Lucas backed up a few steps, wary of the sudden change, uneasy about the eyes. Witch eyes. The tattooed man moved over to Yellow Hand's mattress and sat down on a corner. Lucas watched him for a second, then stepped closer to Yellow Hand, until he was looming over him. He spoke at the top of the teenager's head.

"What do you hear, Yellow Hand? I need everything about Ray Cuervo getting his throat cut. Anything about this guy Benton. Anybody who was friends with Bluebird."

"I don't know about that shit," Yellow Hand said. "I knew Bluebird from out on the res."

"At Fort Thompson?"

"Yeah, man. His sister and my mom used to walk down below the dam and go fishing."

"What do you hear about him lately?" Lucas reached down and grabbed Yellow Hand's hair, just above his ear, and pulled his head back. "Gimme something, Yellow Hand. Talk to me."

"I don't know shit, man, I'm telling the truth," Yellow Hand said sullenly, jerking his hair free. Lucas squatted so he could look Yellow Hand straight in the face. The tattooed man watched Lucas' face over Yellow Hand's shoulder.

"Look. When Benton got killed, you got picked up as a witness," Lucas said, putting a friendly note in his voice. "That's on the record. There are some cops putting together a list. Your name is on it. That means some hardasses from Robbery–Homicide will be checking you out. They aren't going to be friendly, like me. They aren't gonna be no fuckin' pussycats. They aren't going to take care of you, Yellow Hand. If you give me something, I can deal them off. But I got to have something. If I don't get something, they'll figure I didn't squeeze hard enough."

"I could go back to the res," Yellow Hand said.

Lucas shook his head. "What are you going to smoke on the res? Sagebrush? What are you gonna do, sneak down to the tribal store and shoplift boomboxes? Gimme a break, Yellow Hand. You got all these nice K Marts you can work in the Cities. You got the candy man coming around every night. Shit, you got guys peddling crack at Fort Thompson?"

A tear trickled down Yellow Hand's face and he sniffed. Lucas looked at him. "What have you got, man?" Lucas asked again.

"I heard one thing," Yellow Hand admitted. He glanced at the tattooed man, then quickly looked away. "That's all. It probably don't mean shit."

"Let me hear it. I'll decide."

"You know that hassle last summer? Like two, three months ago, between the bikers and the Indian people out in the Black Hills?"

"Yeah, I saw something about it in the papers."

"What it was, was these bikers come in from all over. They have this big rally up in Sturgis and they have like a truce. There's Angels and Outlaws and Banditos and Satan's Slaves and every fuckin' thing. A whole bunch of them stay in this campground out at a place called Bear Butte. They call it the Bare Butt campground, which already makes some Indian people angry."

"What's this got to do with Bluebird?"

"Let me finish, man," Yellow Hand said angrily.

"Okay."

"Some of these bikers, they get drunk at night and they like to run up the side of the butte on their bikes. The butte's a holy place and there were some medicine people up there, with some guys looking for visions. They came down and they had guns. That's what started the trouble."

"And Bluebird was there?" asked Lucas.

"That's what I heard. He was with this group, searching for visions. And they came down with guns. Yesterday, when this guy in New York gets killed, I was in Dork's Pool Hall down on Lyndale?"

"Yeah?"

"Some guy had a picture cut out of the *StarTribune* from the biker thing. He was showing it around. There was a bunch of cops and a bunch of bikers and the Indian medicine people. One of the guys with a rifle was Bluebird."

"Okay, that's something," Lucas said, patting Yellow Hand on the knee.

"Jesus," said the tattooed man, looking at Yellow Hand.

"What about you?" Lucas asked him. "Where were you during this shit?"

"I got back from Los Angeles yesterday. I still got the bus ticket over by my bed. And I ain't heard nothing, except bullshit."

"What bullshit?"

"You know, that Bluebird went crazy and decided to kill a few of the white people sitting on his back. And how that's a good thing. Everybody says it's a good thing."

"What do you know about Bluebird?"

The tattooed man shrugged. "Never met him. I know the family name, but I'm from Standing Rock. I never went over to Fort Thompson except once, for a powwow. The place is out of the way of everything."

Lucas looked at him and nodded. "What were you doing in Los Angeles?"

"Just went there to look around, you know. Look at movie stars." He shrugged.

"All right," Lucas said after a moment. He looked down at Yellow Hand. There wouldn't be much more. "You two just sit here for a minute, okay?"

Lucas stepped over to the tattooed man's bed. On the floor on the far side, out of sight from the door, was a willow stick with a small red rag tied around the tip in a bundle, what looked like a crumpled bus ticket, and a money clip. Inside the clip were a South Dakota driver's license and a photograph pressed between two pieces of plastic. Lucas bent over and scooped it up.

"What you doin' with my stuff, man?" the tattooed man said. He was on his feet again, vibrating.

"Nothing. Just looking," Lucas said. "Is this what I think it is?"

"It's a prayer stick, from an old ceremony down on the river. I carry it for luck."

"Okay." Lucas had seen one once before. He carefully laid it on the mattress. The bus ticket was out of Los Angeles, dated three days earlier. It might have been an arranged alibi, but didn't feel that way. The SoDak license carried a fuzzy photo of the tattooed man in a white T-shirt. The white eyes glistened like ball bearings, like the eyes of Jesse James in nineteenth-century photographs. Lucas checked the name. "Shadow Love?" he said. "That's a beautiful name."

"Thank you," said the tattooed man. His smile clicked on like a flashlight beam.

Lucas looked at the fading color snapshot. A middle-aged woman in a shapeless dress stood by a rope clothesline. The line was strung between a tree and the corner of a white clapboard house. There was a board fence in the background, and in the distance, a factory chimney. A city, maybe Minneapolis. The woman was laughing, holding up a pair of jeans that had frozen board-stiff. The trees in the background were bare, but the woman was standing on green grass. Early spring or late fall, Lucas thought.

"This your mom?" he asked.

"Yeah. So what?"

"So nothing," Lucas said. "A guy who carries a picture of his mom, he can't be all bad."

●   ●   ●

After the Point, Lucas gave up and headed back toward City Hall, stopping once at a public telephone outside the *StarTribune*.

"Library," she said. She was small and wistful, falling into her forties. Nobody at the paper paid her any attention.

"You alone?" he asked.

"Yes." He could feel her catch her breath.

"Could you call something up for me?"

"Go ahead," she said.

"Last week of July, first week of August. There was a confrontation between bikers and Indians out in South Dakota."

"Do you have a key word?" she asked.

"Try 'Bear Butte.' " Lucas spelled it for her. There was a moment's silence.

"Three hits," she said.

"Did you use any art?" There was another moment of silence.

"Yes," she said. "August first. Three columns, page three."

"Yours or AP?"

"Ours." She named the photographer.

"What are the chances of getting a print?"

"I'd have to lift it from the files," she said, in a hushed voice.

"Could you?"

Another few seconds passed. "Where are you?"

"Right down at the corner, in my car."

"It'll be a minute."

Sloan was leaving City Hall when Lucas arrived.

"Winter coming," he said as they stopped on the sidewalk.

"Still warm," said Lucas.

"Yeah, but it's already getting dark," Sloan said, looking up the street. Cars were creeping out toward the interstate, their lights on.

"Did you get anything today? After I left you?"

"Naw." Then the other man brightened. "I did get a look at that woman cop from New York."

Lucas grinned. "She's worth looking at?"

"Oh, yeah. She's got a lip, you know? She's got this little
overbite and she's got this kind of soft look about her like,
I don't know, like she'd *moan* or something. . . ."

"Jesus, Sloan . . ."

"Wait'll you take a look at her," Sloan said.

"Is she still here?"

"Yeah. Inside. She went out with Shearson this morning," Sloan laughed. "The lover boy. The good suits."

"He made a move on her?" Lucas asked.

"I'd bet on it," Sloan said. "When he came back, he spent
two hours studying his files awful hard. She was sitting
around looking cool."

"Hmph." But Lucas grinned. "How'd she get with Shearson? I thought she was going out with you."

"Naw. Shearson gave Lester a blow job and got her as-
signed to him. Squire her around."

"He's so suave," Lucas said. He said "swave."

"Good title. You ought to write a song," Sloan said, and
went on his way.

Lucas saw her in the hallway outside the Robbery–
Homicide office. The madonna from the cemetery. She was
walking toward him on high heels and he noticed her legs
first, then her dark eyes, like pools. He thought about the
tattooed man, the shiny pale eyes like flint, eyes you
bounced off. With the woman, you fell in. She was wearing
a tweed jacket and skirt with a ruffled-front blouse and black
tie. She had a paper coffee cup in her hand and Lucas held
the door for her.

"Thanks." She smiled and went through, headed for Anderson's cubbyhole. Her voice was low and buttery.

"Um," said Lucas, tagging behind. Her hair was done up
in a slightly lopsided bun and a few loose strands fell across
her neck.

"I'm leaving," she told Anderson, leaning into his cubbyhole. "If anything comes overnight, you've got the number."

Anderson was sitting behind an IBM terminal, chewing
on the end of a chopstick. The remains of a Chinese dinner

were congealing in a white foam carton on his desk and the office stank of overcooked water chestnuts and rum-soaked cigars. "Okay. We'll see if we can find something better for you tomorrow."

"Thanks, Harmon."

She turned and almost bumped into Lucas. He caught a faint scent that was neither water chestnut nor cigar, something expensive from Paris. Anderson said to her, "Do you know Lucas? Davenport?"

"Nice to meet you," she said, stepping back and offering her hand. Lucas took it and shook once, smiling politely. She was larger than he'd thought at first. Deep-breasted, a little pudgy. "You're the guy who blew up the Maddog."

"He's the one," Anderson said from behind her. "You get anything, Lucas?"

"Maybe," Lucas said, still looking at the woman. "Harmon didn't mention your name."

"Lily Rothenburg," she said. "Lieutenant, NYPD."

"Homicide?"

"No. I work out of the . . . out of a precinct in Greenwich Village."

Anderson's head was swiveling between them like a spectator at a tennis match.

"How come you're on this one?" Lucas asked. Inside his head, he was doing an inventory. He was wearing a $400 Brooks Brothers tweed sport coat with a pale rose stripe, a dark-blue shirt, tan slacks and loafers. He should look pretty good, he thought.

"Long story," she said. She nodded at the manila envelope in his hand. "What did you get? If you don't mind my asking?"

"A photograph of Bluebird taken on the first of August," he said. He took the photo out of the envelope and handed it to her. "He's the guy with the rifle over his shoulder."

"Who are these people?" A small frown line appeared on her forehead, connecting her bushy dark eyebrows.

"A group of Sioux vision-seekers and a couple of medicine men. I don't know who's who, but they had guns and Bluebird was with them a month ago."

She looked at him over the top of the photograph and

their eyes clicked together like two pennies in a pocket. "This could be something," she said. "Where did you get it?"

"Friend," Lucas said.

She broke her eyes away and turned the photo over. The remnants of routing slips were pasted on the back. "A newspaper," she said. "Can we get the other shots on the roll?"

"Think it'd be worth the trouble?"

"Yes," she said. She put her index finger on the head of one of the figures in the photo. "See this guy?"

Lucas looked at the photo again. The tip of her finger was touching the head of a stocky Indian man, but only the outer rim of his face and one eye were visible. The rest was eclipsed behind the head of another figure in the foreground.

"What about him?" He took the photograph and looked more closely at it.

"That could be our man," she said. "The guy who lit up Andretti. It looks a lot like him, but I need a better shot to be sure."

"Whoa." Anderson eased out of his chair to take a look. The lumpy mound of Bear Butte was in the background, gray and brooding, a lonely northern outpost of the Black Hills. In the foreground, a group of Indians, wearing calico shirts and jeans, were gathered behind one of the elderly medicine men. Most of the men were looking to the left of the camera, toward a group of sheriff's deputies. Bluebird was there with his gun, one of the few who were looking more or less at the camera.

"So how do we get back to your friend and see what else is on the negatives?" Lily asked.

"I'll talk to the chief tonight," Lucas said. "We'll have to meet with some of the people at the paper tomorrow morning. First thing."

"Tomorrow?" she snapped, incredulous. "Christ, the guy's on his way here right now. We've got to get going tonight."

"That would be . . . difficult," Lucas said hesitantly.

"What's difficult? We get the negs, print them and find somebody who knows my guy's name."

"Look, I know the papers here. They'll need three meetings and eight consultations before they'll make the pictures," Lucas said. "That won't get done tonight. There's no way that we'll see the negatives."

"If we put on enough heat . . ."

"We're talking bureaucracy here, okay? We can't move it faster than it's willing to move. And if we go tonight, there's a good chance I'll burn my friend. The first thing they'll do is look at their files, and they'll find their record photo's gone. I don't want to do that. I want to get it back in the file."

"Jesus Christ, you fuckin' . . ." She snapped her mouth shut.

"Shitkickers?"

"I wasn't going to say that," she lied.

"Bullshit. I'll tell you what. I'll get as much done tonight as can get done. All the newspaper people will get called, it'll all be explained, they can have all their meetings, and we'll be over there at eight tomorrow morning, looking at prints."

Her eyes searched his face for a moment. "I don't know," she said finally.

"Look," said Lucas, trying to win her over. "Your killer is driving a junker. If he pushed it as hard as he could, he wouldn't get here until tomorrow night anyway. Not unless he's got a relief driver and they really hammered it out the whole way."

"He was alone in the motel. . . ."

"So we don't lose anything," Lucas said. "And I save my friend's ass, which is a pretty high priority."

"Okay," Lily said. She nodded, her eyes on his face, then stepped past him toward the door. "I'll see you tomorrow, Harmon."

"Yeah." Anderson looked after her as she went through the door. When she was gone, he turned to Lucas, a small smile playing on his face.

"You got the look," he said.

"What's that?"

"Like a bunch of people look after they talk to her. Like you been hit on the forehead with a ball-peen hammer," Anderson said.

• • •

Daniel was eating dinner.

"What happened?" he asked when Lucas identified himself.

"We came up with a photo from the *StarTribune*," Lucas said. He explained the rest of it.

"And Lillian thinks he might be the killer?" Daniel asked.

"Yeah."

"Damn, that's good. We can get some mileage out of this. I'll talk to the people at the *Trib*," Daniel said. "What do you think about the approach?"

"Tell them we need the rest of the negatives on that roll and any other rolls they have. Argue that the photos were taken at a public news event, that there is no secret film involved—nothing involving sources, nothing confidential. Tell them if they help catch Andretti's killer, we'll give them the story. And they'll already have the exclusive pictures that solved the assassination."

"You don't think they'll pull the confidentiality shit?" Daniel asked.

"I don't see why they should," Lucas said. "The pictures weren't confidential. And we're talking about serial assassination of major political figures, not some kind of horseshit inciting-to-riot thing."

"Okay. I'll call now."

"We need them as early as we can get them."

"Nine o'clock. We'll get them by nine," Daniel said.

Lucas hung up and dialed the *StarTribune* library. He gave his friend a summary of what had happened and arranged to meet her near the paper's offices.

"It's kind of exciting," she whispered as she leaned over his car. He handed her the manila envelope. "It's like being a mole, in John le Carré."

He left her in a glow and headed home.

Lucas lived in St. Paul. From his front-room window, he could see a line of trees along the Mississippi River gorge and the lights of Minneapolis on the other side. He lived alone, in a house he once thought might be too big. Over ten years, he'd spread out. The double garage took an aging Ford four-wheel-drive that he used for backcountry trips and boat-towing. The basement filled up with weights and workout pads, a heavy bag and a speed bag, shooting gear and a gun safe, tools and a workbench.

Upstairs, the den was equipped with a deep leather chair for dreaming and watching basketball on television. One bedroom was for sleeping, another for guests. He'd converted a third bedroom into a workroom, with an oak drawing table and a bookcase full of references.

Lucas invented games. War games, fantasy games, role-playing games. Games paid for the house and the Porsche and a cabin on a lake in northern Wisconsin. For three months, he had been immersed in a game he called Drorg. "Drorg" was an invented word, inspired by *cyborg,* which itself was a contraction of the words *cybernetics organism.* Cyborgs were humans with artificial parts. A drorg, in Lucas' game, was a drug organism, a human altered and enhanced by designer drugs. To see in the dark, to navigate by sonar with enhanced hearing, to have the strength of a gorilla, the reflexes of a cat. The brain of a genius.

Not all at once, of course. That's where the game came in. And the drugs had penalties. Some lingered: Call for superstrength and it hung on when you needed superintelligence. Call for superintelligence and the drug pushed you to madness and suicide if you couldn't acquire the antidote. Take the pan-effects drug and it flat killed you, period; but not before you achieved superabilities and eventually intolerable pleasure.

It all took work. There was the basic plot to write—Drorg was essentially a quest, like most role-playing games. There were also scoring systems to build, opponents to create, boards to design. The publisher was excited about it and was pressing. He wanted to do a computer version of it.

So five or six nights a week, for three months, Lucas had been in the workroom, sitting in a pool of light, plotting his patterns. He listened to classic rock, drank an occasional beer, but mostly laid out a story of information bureaucracies, corporate warfare, 'luded-out underclasses and drorg warriors. Where the story came from, he didn't know; but every night the words were there.

When he got home, Lucas put the car in the garage, went inside and popped a frozen chicken dinner into the microwave. In the five minutes before it was ready, he checked the house, got the paper off the front porch and washed his hands. He'd eaten all the french fries and three of the four chicken nibbles—he wasn't exactly sure what part they were, but they did have bones—when Lily Rothenburg's face popped into his mind.

She came out of nowhere: he hadn't been thinking about her, but suddenly she was there, like a photograph dropped on a table. A big woman, he thought. A little too heavy, and not his style; he liked the athletes, the small muscular gymnasts, the long sleek runners.

Not his style at all.

Lily.

CHAPTER

Leo Clark was a drunk by the time he was fifteen. At forty, he had been twenty-two years on the street, begging nickels and dimes from the rich burghers of Minneapolis and St. Paul. A lifetime lost.

Then one bitterly cold night in St. Paul, he and another drunk, a white man, were turned out of the mission after an argument with a clerk. They stopped at a liquor store and bought two bottles of rye whiskey. After some argument, they walked down to the railroad tracks. An old tunnel had been boarded up, but the boards were loose. They pried them back and crawled inside.

Late that night, Leo went out, found sticks of creosote-covered scrap lumber along the tracks, dragged it back to the tunnel and started a fire. The two men finished the whiskey in the stinking smoke. Their cheeks, hands and stomachs felt like fire, but their legs and feet were blocks of ice.

The white man had an idea. Up along the bluffs on the Mississippi, he said, were storm sewers that led into the tunnel system under the city. If they could crawl back there, they could lie up on steam pipes. The tunnels would be as warm as the mission and it wouldn't cost them a dime. They could get a Coleman lantern, a few books. . . .

When Leo Clark woke the next morning, the white man

was dead. He was lying facedown on the cold ground and had taken a few convulsive bites of the earth as he died: his mouth was half full of oily dirt. Leo Clark could see one of his eyes. It was open, and as flat and silvery and empty as the dime that the steam tunnels wouldn't cost him.

"He died in a fuckin' cave, man; they let him die in a fuckin' hole in the ground," Leo told the cops. The cops didn't give a shit. Nobody else did either: the body went unclaimed, and was eventually dumped in a pauper's grave. Dental X rays were filed with the medical examiner in the improbable case that somebody, someday, showed up looking for the dead man.

After the white man died in the cave, Leo Clark stopped drinking. It didn't happen all at once, but a year later he was sober. He drifted west, back to the res. Became a spiritual man, but with a twist of hate for people who would let men die in holes in the ground. He was forty-six years old, with a face and hands like oak, when he met the Crows.

Leo Clark hid in a corner of a dimly lit parking ramp, between the bumper of a Nissan Maxima and the outer wall of the ramp. He was thirty feet from the locked steel door that led into the apartment building.

A few minutes earlier, he had looped a piece of twelve-pound-test monofilament fishing line around the doorknob. He led the line to the bottom of the door, fastened it with a piece of Magic mending tape and trailed it on to the Maxima. In the low light, the line was invisible. He was waiting for somebody to walk through the door—going in, he hoped, but out would be okay, as long as it wasn't to the Maxima. That would be embarrassing.

Leo Clark lay bathed in the odors of exhaust and oil and thought about his mission. When he had killed Ray Cuervo, the overwhelming emotion had been fear—fear of failure, fear of the cops. He'd known Ray personally, had suffered from his greed, and anger and hate had been there too. But this judge? The judge had been bribed by an oil company in a lawsuit involving the illegal disposal of toxic wastes at the Lost Trees reservation. Leo Clark *knew* that, but he

didn't *feel* it. All he felt was the space in his chest. A . . .
sadness? Was that what it was?

He had thought his years on the street had burned all of
that away: that he'd lost all but the most elemental survival
emotions. Fear. Hate. Anger. He wasn't sure whether this
discovery, this renewal of feeling, this *sadness,* was a gift or
a curse. He would have to think about that: Leo Clark was
a careful man.

As for the judge, it would make no difference. He had
been weighed and he would die.

Leo Clark had been waiting for twenty minutes when a
car pulled into an empty space halfway down the garage.
A woman. He could hear her high heels rapping on the concrete. She had her keys in her hand. She opened the door
into the building, stepped inside. The door began to swing
shut and Leo pulled in the line, popping off the Magic mending tape, putting tension on the line, easing the door shut . . .
but not quite enough to latch. He kept up the tension, waiting, waiting, giving the woman time for the elevator, hoping
that nobody else came out. . . .

After three minutes, he slid from beneath the car. Keeping the line tight, he walked to the door and eased it open.
Nobody in the elevator lobby. He stepped inside, walked
past the elevator to the fire stairs, and went up.

The judge was on the sixth floor, one of three apartments.
Leo listened at the fire door, heard nothing. Opened the
door, looked through, stepped into the empty hallway. Six
C. He found the door, rapped softly, though he was sure
it was empty. No answer. After another quick look around,
he took a bar from his jacket, slipped it into the crack between the door and the jamb and slowly put his weight to
it. The door held, held; then there was a low ripping sound
and it popped open. Leo stepped inside, into the dark room.
Found a chair, sat down and let the sadness flow through
him.

Judge Merrill Ball and his girlfriend, whose name was
Cindy, returned a few minutes after one in the morning. The
judge had his key in the lock before he noticed the damage
to the door.

"Jesus, it looks like . . ." he started, but the door flew

open, freezing him. Leo Clark was there, his long black braids down on his chest, his eyes wide and straining, his mouth half open, his hand driving up. And in his hand, the razor-edged stone knife . . .

An hour later, in a truck stop off I-35 north of Oklahoma City, Leo Clark sat at the wheel of his car and wept.

Shadow Love walked into the wind, his shoulders hunched, his running shoes crunching through the fallen maple leaves. The black spot floated out ahead of him.

The black spot.

When Shadow Love was a child, his mother had taken him to a neighbor's home. The house smelled of cooking gas and boiled greens, and he could remember the neighbor's fat white legs as she sat on a kitchen table, sobbing. Her husband had a black spot on his lungs. The size of a dime. Nothing to be done, the woman said. Make him comfortable, the doctors said. Shadow Love remembered his mother, gripping the other woman around the shoulders. . . .

And now he had a name for the thing on his mind. The black spot.

Sometimes the invisible people would talk to his mother, plucking at her arms and face and her dress and even her shoes, to get her attention, to tell her what Shadow Love had done. He couldn't remember doing all those things, but the invisible people said he had. They were never wrong, Rosie Love said. They saw everything, knew everything. His mother would beat him with a broom handle for doing those things. She would chase him and pound him on the back, the shoulders, the legs. Afterward, when the invisible people had gone, she would fall on him weeping, begging forgiveness, trying to rub off the bruises as if they were shoe polish. . . .

The black spot had come with the invisible people. When Shadow Love got angry, the black spot popped up in front of his eyes, a hole in the world. He never told his mother about the black spot: she would tell the invisible people and they would demand a punishment. And he never showed his anger, for the same reason. Defiance was the worst of all sins, and the invisible people would howl for his blood.

At some point, the invisible people stopped coming. His mother killed them with alcohol, Shadow Love thought. Her bouts of drunkenness were bad enough, but nowhere near as bad as the invisible people. Although the invisible people were gone, the black spot stayed. . . .

And now it floated in front of his eyes. The fuckin' cop. Davenport. He treated them like dirt. He came in and pointed his finger. Made them sit. Like a trained dog. *Sit,* he said. *Speak,* he said. *Arf.*

The black spot grew and Shadow Love felt dizzy with the humiliation of it. Like a *dog.* His pace picked up, until he was almost running; then he slowed again, threw his head back and groaned, aloud. *Fuckin' dog.* He balled a fist and hit himself on the cheekbone, hard. The pain cut through his anger. The black spot shrank.

Like a fuckin' dog, you crawled like a fuckin' dog. . . .

Shadow Love was not dumb. His fathers were running their war and would need him. He couldn't be taken by the cops, not for something as stupid as a fistfight. But it ate at him, the way Davenport had treated him. Made him be *nice . . .*

Shadow Love bought a pistol from a teenaged burglar. It wasn't much of a gun, but he didn't need much of a gun. He gave the kid twenty bucks, slipped the pistol into his waistband and headed back to the Point. He would need a new place to stay, he thought. He couldn't move in with his fathers: they were already jammed into a tiny efficiency. Besides, they didn't want him in their war.

A place to stay. The last time he was in town, he'd have gone to Ray Cuervo. . . .

Yellow Hand's day had been miserable. Davenport had started it, kicking him out of a stupor. A stupor he'd valued. The longer he was asleep, the longer he could put off his problem. Yellow Hand needed his crack. He rolled his upper lip and bit it, thinking about the rush. . . .

After Davenport had gone, Shadow Love had put on his boots and jacket and left without a word. The old white woman had fallen back on her mattress and soon was snoring away with her man, who had never woken up. Yellow

Hand had made it out on the street a half-hour later. He'd cruised the local K Mart, but left with the feeling he was being watched. It was the same way at a Target store. Nothing obvious, just white guys in rayon neckties . . .

He wished Gineele and Howdy were still in town. If Gineele and Howdy hadn't gone to Florida, they'd all be rich.

Gineele was very black. When she was working, she wore her hair in corn rows and sported fluorescent pink lipstick. She had a nasty scar on her right cheek, the end product of an ill-considered fight with a man who had a beer can opener in his hand. The scar scared the shit out of everybody.

If Gineele was bad, Howdy was a nightmare. Howdy was white, so white he looked as if he'd been painted. A quick glance at his eyes suggested that this boy was snorting something awful. Ether, maybe. Or jet fuel. Toxic waste. In any case, his eyes were always cranked wide, his mouth was always open, his tongue flicking out like a snake's. To complement his insane face, Howdy wore steel rings around his neck, black leather cuffs with spikes, and knee-high leather boots. He was twenty years old—you could see the youth in his carriage—but his hair was dead-white and fine as spun silk. When Howdy and Gineele went into a K Mart, the white guys in the rayon neckties went crazy. While the two decoys caromed around the store, Yellow Hand took boomboxes out the front door by the cartload.

Jesus. Yellow Hand really needed them. . . .

An hour after he hit the street, he scored a clock-radio and three calculators at a Walgreen's drugstore. He cashed them for a chunk, smoked it, floated away to never-never land. But it was a soiled trip, because even as he went out he was anticipating the cold reality of the crash.

Early in the evening, he tried to steal a toolbox from a filling station. He almost made it. As he was turning the corner, a guy by the gas pumps spotted him and yelled. The box was too heavy to run with, so he dumped it and hauled ass through two blocks of backyards. The gas jockey called the cops and Yellow Hand spent an hour hiding under a boat trailer as a squad car cruised the neighborhood. By the time he started back to the Point, it was fully dark. He had to think. He had to plan. He had only two more days at the Point; then he'd need money for the rent. The nights were getting cold.

Shadow Love was smoking a cigarette when Yellow Hand came in.

"Loan me a couple bucks?" Yellow Hand begged.

"I don't have no money to spend on crack," Shadow Love said. He reached for the hardpack of Marlboros. "I can give you a smoke."

"Aw, man, I wouldn't buy no crack," Yellow Hand whined. "I need to eat. I ain't had nothin' to eat all day." He took the cigarette and Shadow Love held a paper match for him.

"Tell you what," Shadow Love said after a moment, fixing Yellow Hand with his pale eyes. "We can walk up to that taco joint by the river road. I'll buy you a half-dozen tacos."

"That's a long way, man," Yellow Hand complained.

"Fuck ya, then," Shadow Love said. "I'm going. Thanks for lettin' me stay." He'd paid Yellow Hand three dollars to use the mattress.

"All right, all right," Yellow Hand said. "I'm coming. I'm so fuckin' hungry. . . ."

Walking slow, they took twenty minutes to get from the Point to the Mississippi. The river was a hundred feet below them and Shadow Love sidestepped down the slope.

"Where are you going, man?" Yellow Hand asked, puzzled.

"Down to the water. Come on. It's not much further this way." Shadow Love thought about Yellow Hand and Davenport. Yellow Hand had told the cop about the newspaper clipping: that was something. The black spot popped up.

"We gotta climb back up, man," Yellow Hand complained.

"Come on," Shadow Love snapped. The black spot floated out in front of him. His heart was pounding, and the rising power flowed through his blood like gold. He wasn't arguing anymore. Yellow Hand looked back toward the lights of the street, undecided, and finally followed, still bitching under his breath.

They crossed a river access road and continued down to the water, where the riverbank was supported by a concrete wall. Shadow Love stepped onto the wall, drew in a breath of the river air and exhaled. Smelled real. He turned to Yellow Hand, who had climbed onto the wall behind him.

"Lights look great from down here, don't they?" Shadow Love asked. "Look at the reflections in the water."

"I guess," Yellow Hand said, puzzled.

"Look over there, under the bridge," Shadow Love said.

Yellow Hand turned to look. Shadow Love stepped closer, taking the pistol from his waistband. He put it behind Yellow Hand's ear, waited a delicious second, then another and a third, thrilling to the darkness of the act; when he couldn't stand it anymore, the glorious tension, he pulled the trigger.

There was a sharp *pop* and Yellow Hand went down like a puppet whose strings had been cut. Shadow Love had intended that the body fall into the river. Instead it landed on the concrete wall. It took a minute to get it off the edge, into the water.

Yellow Hand's shirt ballooned up around his body, supporting it, a white lump in the current. Then there was a bubble, and another, and Yellow Hand was gone.

A traitor to the people. The man who'd put the hunter cop onto the Bluebird picture.

While Leo Clark sat at a truck stop and wept, Shadow Love sat in the taco stand eating ravenously, hunched over his food like a wolf. His body sang with the kill.

CHAPTER
7

Lucas worked on Drorg until four in the morning, and Daniel called at eight. When the phone rang, Lucas rolled onto his side, thrashing at the nightstand like a drowning swimmer. He hit the phone and the receiver bounced on the floor, and he took another moment to find it.

"Davenport? What the hell . . . ?"

"Dropped the phone," Lucas said sleepily. "What happened?"

"They did another one. A federal judge in Oklahoma City."

"Shit." Lucas yawned and sat up. "The way you're talking, the killer got away."

"Yeah. He had braids, like . . ."

". . . the guy who did Cuervo. So there had to be at least three of them, counting Bluebird."

"Yeah. Anderson's getting everything he can out of the Oklahoma cops. And those pictures—we're getting them at nine. We'll meet in Wink's office."

"No problems?"

"Aw, we gotta go through the usual bullshit, but we'll get them," Daniel said.

"Somebody ought to call Lily," Lucas said.

"My secretary'll take care of it. There's one more thing. . . ."

"What?"

"The feds are in it."

Lucas groaned. "Aw, no, please . . ."

"Yeah. With both feet. Made the announcement an hour ago. I talked to the Minneapolis agent-in-charge and he says Lawrence Duberville Clay himself is taking a personal interest."

"Sonofabitch. Can we keep them off the street? Those guys could screw up a wet dream."

"I'll suggest that they focus on intelligence, but it won't work," Daniel said. "Clay thinks he can ride the crime business into the attorney general's job, and maybe the presidency. The papers are calling these killings 'domestic terrorism.' That'll get him out here for sure, just like when he went out to Chicago on that dope deal, and L.A. for the Green Army bust. When he gets here, he'll want some action."

"Fuck him. Let him find his own action."

"Try to be nice, all right? And in the meantime, let's get these pictures from the *Trib* and start hammering the street. If we nail these cocksuckers, Lawrence Duberville won't have any reason to come out."

They met with *StarTribune* executives in the office of Louis Wink, the paper's bald-as-a-cueball editor. Harold Probst, the publisher, and Kelly Lawrence, the city editor, sat in. Lily arrived on Daniel's arm; his elbow, Lucas noticed, was pressing Lily's breast. Daniel wore a gray suit that was virtually a mirror image of Wink's, and a self-satisfied smile. The meeting lasted ten minutes.

"The reason I object is that it brings up the question of whether we're an arm of the police. It damages our credibility," said the round-faced Lawrence.

"With who?" Lily asked heatedly. She was dressed in a rough silk blouse and another tweed skirt. She either had the world's best complexion or did the world's best makeup, Lucas thought.

"With people on the street," said the city editor. Lawrence was wearing a rumpled cotton dress that was just the wrong color of blue for her eyes. Lily looked so much better that Lucas wished she'd waited outside.

"Oh, bullshit," Lily snapped. "You have this great big goddamned building full of yuppies in penny loafers and you're worried about damaging your reputation with street people? Jesus H. Christ on a crutch."

"Take it easy," Lucas said soothingly. "She's right. It's a sensitive question."

"We wouldn't even ask, if the crimes weren't so horrendous. They killed a federal judge last night; butchered him. They killed one of the brightest up-and-coming politicians in the country and two people here," Daniel said in a syrupy voice. He turned to Lily. "The fact is, the press is in a very delicate situation."

He turned back to Wink and Probst, where the power was. "All we want to do is look at the face of the man that Lily thinks might be the New York killer. And we want to look at the people around him, so we can question them. You might very well have run all of those pictures in the paper, for anyone to see. You promised confidentiality to nobody. In fact, they were soliciting attention by their very presence at this confrontation."

"Well, that's right," said Probst. A flash of irritation crossed Wink's face. Probst had come up on the advertising side.

"And you'll get a tremendous story out of it," Lucas put in. "You'll stick it right up the *Pioneer Press*'s ass."

Lawrence, the city editor, brightened, but Lily continued to stew. "And if you don't we'll go to court and drag it out of you anyway," she snarled.

"Hey . . ." Wink sat up.

Daniel broke in before he could go any further. He pointed a finger at Lily's face and said, "No, we won't, Lieutenant. If they decide against us in this room, we'll look for other pictures, but we won't go to court. And if you keep this up, I'll ship your ass back to New York faster than you can say 'Avenue of the Americas.' "

Lily opened her mouth and just as suddenly snapped it shut. "Okay," she said. She glanced at Wink. "Sorry."

Daniel smiled his most charming smile at Wink and said, *"Please?"*

"I think . . . we should get some prints in here," Wink said. He nodded at Lawrence. "Get them."

They all sat silently until the city editor came back with three manila envelopes and handed them to Wink. Wink opened one, took out a set of eight-by-ten prints, looked at them, then passed them to Daniel. Daniel dealt them out across the table to Lily, who stood up, spread them out and began studying them.

"It's him," she said after a moment. She tapped one of the faces. "That's my man."

They got two sets of photos and stopped on the street corner before Daniel walked back to City Hall.

"Larry Hart is coming over this afternoon. He had to get his case load closed out," Daniel said to Lucas. "I'll get him a set of photographs. He may know somebody."

"All right. And I'll show my set around."

Daniel nodded and looked at Lily. "You should watch your temper. You almost lost it for us."

"Newsies piss me off," she said. "You were getting pushed around."

"I wasn't getting pushed. Everybody knew what would happen. We had to go through the ritual," Daniel said mildly.

"Okay. It's your turf. I apologize," she said.

"You should apologize. Being a hell of guy, I accept," Daniel said, and started off across the street.

Lily looked after him. "He's a piece of work," she said after a moment.

"He's okay. He can be an asshole, but he isn't stupid," Lucas said.

"So who's this Larry Hart?" Lily asked.

"He's a Welfare guy, a Sioux. Good guy, knows the streets, probably knows a thousand Indians. He's fairly large in Indian politics. He's written some articles, goes out to all the powwows and so on."

"We need him. I spent six hours on the street yesterday and didn't learn a thing. The guy I was with—"

"Shearson?"

"Yeah. He wouldn't know an Indian from a fire hydrant. Christ, it was almost embarrassing," she said, shaking her head.

"You're not going back out with him?"

"No." She looked at him without a sign of a smile. "Besides his woefully inadequate IQ, we had a little problem yesterday."

"Well . . ."

"I thought I might ride along with you. You're showing the pictures around, right?"

"Yeah." Lucas scratched his head. He didn't like working with a partner: he sometimes made deals that were best kept private. But Lily was from New York and shouldn't be a problem that way. "All right, I guess. I'm parked down this way."

"Everybody says you've got the best contacts in the Indian community," Lily said as they walked along. Lucas kept looking at her and tripped on an uneven sidewalk slab. She grinned, still looking straight ahead.

"I know about eight guys. Maybe ten. And not well," Lucas said when he recovered.

"You came up with the picture from the paper," she pointed out.

"I had a guy I could squeeze." Lucas stepped off the curb and walked around the nose of his Porsche. Lily walked behind him.

"Uh, around there," he said, pointing back to the passenger-side door.

She looked down at the 911, surprised. "Is this your car?"

"Yeah."

"I thought we were crossing the street," Lily said as she stepped back to the curb.

Lucas got in and popped open her door; she climbed inside and fastened the seat belt. "Not many New York cops would have the guts to drive around in a Porsche. Everybody would figure he was in the bag," she said.

"I've got some money of my own," Lucas said.

"Even so, you wouldn't have to buy a Porsche with it," Lily said primly. "You could buy a perfectly good car for

ten or fifteen thousand and give the other twenty or thirty
thousand to charity. You could give it to the Little Sisters
of the Poor."

"I thought about that," Lucas said. He gunned the Porsche through an illegal U-turn and punched it up to forty
in the twenty-five-mile-per-hour business zone. "And I decided, fuck 'em."

Lily threw back her head and laughed. Lucas grinned at
her and thought that maybe she was carrying a few too
many pounds, but maybe that wasn't all bad.

They took the photographs to the Indian Center, showed
them around. Two of the men in the photos were known
by face but not by name. Nobody knew where they lived.
Lucas called Anderson, told him about the tentative IDs,
and Anderson promised to get more photos on the street.

After leaving the Indian Center, they stopped at an
Indian-dominated public housing project, where Lucas
knew two old men who worked as caretakers. They got no
new IDs. The hostility was palpable.

"They don't like cops," Lily said as they left.

"Nobody around here likes cops," Lucas said, looking
back at the decrepit buildings. "When they see us, we're
mostly getting their cars towed away in the winter. They
don't like us, but at least they're not against us. But this is
something else. This time, they're against us."

"Maybe they got reasons," Lily said. She was looking out
the window at a group of Indian children sitting on the
porch of a decaying clapboard house. "Those kids ought to
be in school. What you've got here, Davenport, is a clean
slum. The people are fucked up, but the street gets cleaned
twice a week."

They spent the rest of the morning running the photos
down Lucas' Indian acquaintances. Lily trailed behind, not
saying much, studying the faces of the Indians, listening to
them, the Indians looking curiously back.

"They think you might be an Indian, or part Indian, but
they're not sure until they hear your voice," Lucas said between stops. "You look a little Indian."

"I don't sound Indian."

"You sound Lawn Guyland."

"There's an Indian reservation on Long Island," she said.

"No shit? Jesus, I'd like to hear those people talk. . . ."

Late in the morning, Lucas drove to Yellow Hand's apartment at the Point, describing him to Lily as they went. Outside, on the stoop, he reached back and freed the P7 in its holster.

"Is this trouble?" she asked.

"I doubt it," he said. "But you know."

"Okay." When they were inside the door, she slipped her hand into a mufflike opening in her shoulder bag, took out a short Colt Officer's Model .45 and jacked a shell into the chamber.

"A forty-five?" Lucas said as she put it back in the purse.

"I'm not strong enough to wrestle with assholes," she said bluntly. "If I shoot somebody, I want him to go down. Not that the P7 isn't a nice little gun. But it's a bit light for serious work."

"Not if you can shoot," Lucas said through his teeth as he headed up the stairs.

"I can shoot the eyes out of a moving pigeon," she said. "And not hit the feathers."

The door on the top floor was open. Nobody home. Lucas eased inside, looked around, then tramped across a litter of paper, orange peels and empty personal-size catsup packs from McDonald's. "This is where he was," Lucas said, kicking Yellow Hand's mattress.

"Place feels vacant," Lily said. She touched one of the empty catsup packs with the toe of her shoe. Street people stole them from fast-food joints and used the catsup to make tomato soup. "They're really hurting for money."

"Crackheads," Lucas said.

Lily nodded. She took the Colt out of the purse, pulled the magazine, stuck it between the little and ring fingers of her gun hand, cupped the ejection port with her free hand and jacked the slide. The chambered round ejected into her palm. She snapped it back into the magazine and pushed the magazine back into the butt of the pistol. She'd done it smoothly, without thinking, Lucas thought. She'd spent some time with the gun.

"The trouble with single-action weapons," Lucas said, "is that shit happens and you're caught with an empty chamber."

"Not if you've got half a brain," she said. She was looking around at the litter. "I've learned to anticipate."

Lucas stopped and picked up an object that had been almost hidden by Yellow Hand's mattress where it had pressed against the wall.

Lily asked, "What?" and he tossed it to her. She turned it over in her hands. "Crack pipe. You said he was a crack-head."

"Yeah. But I wonder why he left it here? I wouldn't think the boy would be without it. All of his other shit is gone."

"I don't know. Nothing wrong with it. Yet," Lily said. She dropped the glass pipe on the floor and stepped on it, crushing it.

On the street again, Lucas suggested a check at Cuervo's rental office. If there was anyone running the place, he told Lily, there might be some word of where Yellow Hand had gone. She nodded. "I'm following you," she said.

"I hope the dipshit hasn't gone back to the res," Lucas said as they climbed back in the car. "Yellow Hand would be hell to find out there, if he didn't want to be found."

Lucas had been in Cuervo's office a dozen times over the years. Nothing had changed in the shabby stairway that went up to it. The building had permanent bad breath, compounded of stale urine, wet plaster and catshit. As Lucas reached the top of the stairs, Cuervo's office door opened on a chain and a woman looked out through the crack.

"Who're you?" Lucas asked.

"Harriet Cuervo," the woman snapped. All Lucas could see were her eyes, which were the color of acid-washed jeans, and a pale crescent of face. "Who in the hell are you to be asking?"

"Police," Lucas said. Lucas fished his badge case out of his jacket pocket and flashed the badge at her. Lily waited behind him, down a step. "We didn't know you'd taken over Ray's operation."

"Know now," the woman grunted. The chain rattled off and she let the door swing open. Her husband's murder had left a faint stain on the wooden floor and Harriet Cuervo was standing in the middle of it. She was wearing a print dress that fell straight from her neck to her knees. "I told the other cops everything I knew," she said bluntly.

"We're looking for a different kind of information," Lucas said. The woman went back around Cuervo's old desk. Lucas stepped inside the office and glanced around. Something had changed, something was wrong, but he couldn't put his finger on it. "We're asking about one of his tenants."

"So what do you want to know?" she asked. She was five feet, nine inches tall and weighed perhaps a hundred pounds, all of it rawboned knobs. There were short vertical lines above and below her lips, as though they'd once been stitched shut.

"You've got a renter named Yellow Hand, down at the Point?"

"Sure. Yellow Hand." She opened a ledger and ran a finger down an open column. "Paid up 'til tomorrow."

"You didn't see him yesterday or today?"

"Shit, I don't do no surveys. I just rent the fuckin' apartments," she said. "If he don't have the money tomorrow, out he goes. Today, I don't care what he does."

"So you haven't seen him?"

"Nope." She peered around Lucas at Lily. "She a cop too?"

"Yeah."

Cuervo looked Lily up and down. "Dresses pretty good for a cop," she sniffed.

"If Yellow Hand doesn't pay, do you go down and evict him yourself?" Lily asked curiously.

"I got an associate," Cuervo said.

"Who's that?" Lucas asked.

"Bald Peterson."

"Yeah? I thought he'd left town."

"He's come back. You know him?"

"Yeah. We go back."

"Say . . ." Harriet Cuervo's eyes narrowed and she made a gun of her index finger and thumb and pointed it at Lucas' heart. "You ain't the cop that pounded him, are you? Years ago? Like fuckin' crippled him?"

"We've had some disagreements," Lucas said. "Tell him hello for me." He took a step toward the door. "How about a guy named Shadow Love? You seen him around?"

"Shadow Love? Never even heard of him."

"He was living up at the Point. . . ."

She shrugged. "Didn't rent from me," she said. "Must've been one of those other flatheads let him in. You know how it goes."

"Yeah," Lucas said as he turned away again. "Sorry about Ray."

"It's nice somebody is, 'cause I ain't," Cuervo said flatly. Her face showed some animation for the first time. "I was trying to think what I remembered best about Ray. One thing, you know? And you know what come to mind? He had a bunch of porno videotapes. He had one called *Airtight Brunette*. You know what an airtight brunette is? That's one who is filled up everyplace, if you know what I mean. Three guys. Anyway, his favorite part was when this guy 'jaculates on the brunette's chest. He was running that back and forth, back and forth. Everytime he stopped the VCR and rewound the tape, the regular TV show come on. You know what that was?"

"Uh, no, I wouldn't," Lucas said. He glanced quickly at Lily, who was staring at Cuervo, fascinated.

"*Sesame Street.* Big Bird was finding out how doctors take your blood pressure. So this guy 'jaculates on the brunette's chest and we get Big Bird. And he 'jaculates again and we get Big Bird. It was like that for fifteen minutes. 'Jaculate, Big Bird, 'jaculate, Big Bird."

She stopped to take a breath. "That," she said, "is how I remember Ray."

"Okay. Well, jeez, we gotta get going," Lucas said desperately. He pushed Lily out the door toward the stairs. They were ten steps down when Harriet Cuervo came to the landing.

"I wanted to have kids," she shouted down at them.

Lily grinned at him as they walked back to the car. "Nice girl," she said. "We wouldn't do much better in New York."

"Fuckin' gerbil," Lucas grumbled.

"Did you see the calendar on the wall? Big Boys' Buns?"

Lucas snapped his fingers. "I knew there was something different about the place," he said. "Ray used to have this old *Sports Illustrated* swimsuit calendar. A wet–T-shirt shot. These great . . . ah . . ."

"Tits?"

"Right. Anyway, it was always the same picture. He found one he liked and stopped right there."

"So what we got is a change in management, but no change in style," Lily said.

"You got it."

In the car, Lucas checked the time. They had been on the street for three hours. "We ought to think about lunch."

"Is there a deli in town?" Lily asked.

Lucas grinned at her. "Can't stand to be away?"

"It's not that," she said. "I've been eating hotel food for too long. Everything tastes like oatmeal."

"All right, a deli," Lucas agreed. "There's one a couple blocks from my place, over in St. Paul. Got a restaurant in the back."

They headed east on Lake, across the Mississippi, then south down along the river through a forest of maples, elms and oaks, past a couple of colleges.

"All religious colleges. Highest density of virgins in the Twin Cities, right here," Lucas said.

"Your neighborhood too. What a shame; what a workload," she said.

"What's that mean?" Lucas asked.

"When I told people I was planning to go out with you, they all gave me the look. Like, Uh-oh, into the hands of Lothario."

"Bullshit," said Lucas.

• • •

The deli was in a yellow cinder-block building with a parking lot in back. When they got out of the car, an old woman was watching them through a restaurant window while she gnawed on the end of a whole pickle. Lily's face lit up when she saw it.

"That pickle . . . There's a marginal chance that this place could be all right," she said. Inside, she scanned the sandwich menu, then ordered a corned beef and cheese combo with coleslaw, a side order of french fries, a seven-layer salad and a raspberry-flavored Perrier.

"A thousand calories," she said five minutes later, looking ruefully at the brown plastic tray the counterman had just delivered. The counterman snorted as he turned away. "What, you think more than a thousand?" she called after him.

"Honey, the sandwich is six, seven hundred and that's only half of it," the counterman said.

"I don't want to hear it," Lily said, turning back to the food.

Lucas got a sausage on rye, a bag of potato chips and a Diet Coke and led the way to the back.

"I'm an eater," Lily said as they slid into the booth. "I'll weigh two hundred pounds when they bury me."

"You look all right," Lucas said.

Her eyes came up. "I'd look great with ten less pounds."

"I'll stand by my original statement."

Lily got busy with her food, keeping her eyes away from his. "So," she said a moment later. "I understand you've got a new kid but aren't married."

"Yup."

"Doesn't that embarrass you a little?" She licked a fleck of slaw off her upper lip.

"Nope. I wanted to get married, but the woman wouldn't do it. We're still together, more or less. We don't live together."

"When did you last ask her to marry you?" Lily asked.

"Well, I used to ask her once a week. Then I just made a general open offer."

"Do you love her?"

"Sure," Lucas said, nodding.

"Does she love you?"

"She says so."

"So why doesn't she marry you?" Lily asked.

"She says I'd be a great father but a fuckin' terrible husband."

"Hmph." Lily took a big bite of her sandwich and chewed thoughtfully, watching him. "Well," she said after she swallowed, "it sounds like you might fool around a little."

"Not since she got pregnant," Lucas said. "Before that . . ."

"A little?"

"Yeah." He grinned. "Now and then."

"How about you?" Lucas asked. "You're wearing a ring."

"Yup." She snapped off a french fry. "My husband's a sociology professor at NYU. He did position papers for Andretti. That's one of the reasons I'm out here. I knew the family."

"Good guy?"

"Yeah, for a politician, I guess."

"I meant your husband."

"David? David's great," Lily said positively. "He is the gentlest man I've ever known. I met him when I was going to school. He was a graduate assistant, I took a class. It was about the time everything was going to hell up at Columbia, people were in the streets, McCarthy was running for president. . . . Good times. Interesting times."

"So, what, you got married right after college?"

"Before graduation. Then I got my degree, applied to the department under a special program to bring in women, and here I am."

"Huh. How about that." Lucas watched her for a few seconds, finished a last chip and slid out of the booth. "I'll be right back."

They've got problems, Lily and David, he thought as he walked to the counter. He ordered another bag of chips and another Diet Coke. *She likes him okay, but there's no heat.* When he looked back, she was watching people in the street, a shaft of sunlight cutting across the table and her hands. She's beautiful, he thought.

When he got back to the table, she was licking her finger-tips. "Done," she said. "Where to next?"

"Gotta go see a nun."

"Say what?"

A seven-foot-tall alabaster statue of the Virgin Mary hung over the driveway. Lily looked doubtfully up at it.

"I've never been to a nunnery," she muttered.

"It's not a nunnery," Lucas said. "It's a college."

"You said nuns lived here."

"There's a residence on the other side of the campus," Lucas said.

"How come her eyes are rolled back like that?" Lily asked, still looking up at the Virgin.

"The ecstasy of perfect grace," Lucas suggested.

"What's she doing to that snake?" The tail of a snake was visible beneath the Virgin's sandals. The snake's body curled up one of her robed legs, its head poised to strike at knee level.

"Crushing it. That's the devil."

"Huh. Looks like one of the investigators on my squad. The snake, I mean."

Lucas had been to grade school with Elle Kruger. They'd tracked each other over the years, Lucas on the Minneapolis police force, Elle Kruger as a psychologist and a Sister of Mercy. Her office was on the third floor of Albertus Magnus Hall. Lucas led Lily down a long, cool hallway that echoed with their footsteps. At Elle's office, he knocked once, opened the door and stuck his head inside.

"About time," Elle Kruger snapped. She was a tradition-alist, and wore the black habit with a band of beads hanging down beside her hand.

"Traffic," said Lucas in way of apology. He stepped in-side, Lily close behind. "Elle, this is Lieutenant Lily Ro-thenburg of the New York Police Department, out here investigating the death of John Andretti. Lily, this is my friend Sister Mary Joseph. She's the chief shrink around here."

"Pleased to meet you, Lily," Elle said, and reached out a bony hand.

Lily took it and smiled. "Lucas tells me you've helped on some of his cases."

"Where I can. But we mostly play games," Elle said.

Lily looked at Lucas, and Lucas explained, "We have a gaming group that meets once a week."

"That's interesting," Lily said, looking from one of them to the other. "Like Dungeons and Dragons?"

"No, no role playing," Elle said. "Historical reconstruction. Get Lucas to tell you about his Gettysburg. We played it three times last year and it always comes out wildly different. Last time, Bobby Lee almost got himself into Philadelphia."

"I've still got to do something about that damn Stuart," Lucas said to the nun. "When he gets loose too early, he fouls up all the calculations. I'm thinking of . . ."

"No game talk," Elle said. "Let's get some ice cream."

"Ice cream?" Lily said. She put her fingers over her mouth to cover a tiny burp. "Sounds good."

As they walked down the hall, Lily turned to Elle and asked, "What did you mean when you said, 'his Gettysburg'? Did Lucas make the game or something?"

Elle raised an eyebrow. "Our boy is a famous games inventor. Didn't you know that?"

"No, I didn't," Lily said, looking at Lucas.

"He surely is," Elle said. "That's how he got rich."

"Are you rich?" Lily asked Lucas.

"No," Lucas said. He shook his head.

"He is, take my word for it," Elle said to Lily with a phony confidentiality. "He bought me a gold chain last year that has scandalized my entire wing of the residence."

"For a good German Catholic girl, I think the influence of the Irish is beginning to seep in," Lucas said.

"The Irish?"

"The blarney." Lucas turned to Lily and said in a stage whisper, "I'd never use a word like 'bullshit' around a nun."

They sat in a booth in the ice cream shop, Lucas and Lily side by side, Elle across the table. Elle ate a hot-fudge sundae while Lily worked on a banana split. Lucas blew into a cup of coffee and thought about Lily's warm thigh next to his.

"So you're working on Andretti," Elle prompted them.

"There's some kind of conspiracy," Lily said.

"The Indian man who killed the people in Minneapolis, and the Indian man who killed Andretti?"

"Yeah," said Lucas. "Except we think that two different guys killed the people in Minneapolis. And now the judge in Oklahoma City . . ."

"I haven't heard . . ."

"Last night . . . I was wondering . . . what kind of group would we be dealing with? If there is a group."

"Religious," Elle said promptly.

"Religious?"

"There are few things in the world that can hold together a murder conspiracy. Hate by itself is not enough, because it's too unfocused and not intellectual enough. There has to be some positive energy, as it were. That usually comes from religion. It's difficult to be intellectual and murderous at the same time, without some complicated rationale."

"How about these groups that develop in prison?" asked Lily. "You know, a group of guys gets together and they start holding up armored cars . . ."

". . . raising money for a cause. Which usually has some kind of quasi-religious doctrine behind it. Save the white race from mongrelization by blacks, Arabs, Jews, whatever. You see the same thing in the leftist radical groups and even the groups or pairs of psychotic killers you get from time to time. There's a religious aspect, there's a group feeling of oppression. Usually there's a messiah figure who tells the others that it's all right to kill. That it's necessary."

"One of my people in the Indian community said that Bluebird—"

"That was the man killed in Minneapolis?" Elle interrupted.

"Yeah. He said Bluebird was a man looking for religion."

"I'd say he found it," Elle said. She had been saving the maraschino cherry for last, and finally she ate it, savoring the sweetness.

"You know how they make maraschino cherries?" Lucas asked, covering his eyes with his hand as it disappeared.

"I don't want to hear," Elle said. She pointed her long spoon at Lucas' nose. "If there's a group doing these killings, there probably aren't more than a dozen people in it and that would be an extreme. More likely it's five or six. At the most."

"Six? Jesus," Lily blurted. "Excuse me, my language. But six?"

"What are the chances that it's three?" Lucas asked. "Bluebird and this guy in New York and the guy in Oklahoma?"

Elle tipped her head back and peered at the ceiling, calculating. "No. I don't think so, but then, who knows? But I have the sense . . . these men in New York and Oklahoma, they traveled some way to do the killings, if they came from here. If they know Bluebird. I have a sense that they were sent out . . . that they are on missions. Bluebird was apparently ready to die. That would be more typical of people who saw themselves as part of a process, rather than as a last chance to strike back."

"So there'll be more?"

"Yes. But there is a limit on size. There really is no such thing as a grand criminal conspiracy. Or at least no such thing as a secret one. I suppose Adolf Hitler and his henchmen were a grand criminal conspiracy, but they needed the collaboration of a nation to pull it off."

"So there'd probably be at least two or three more, and maybe six or eight," Lucas said. "Probably held together by some sort of religious mania."

"That's right," Elle said. "If you want to stop it, look for the preacher."

In the car going back to Lucas' office, Lily looked him over.

"I have the feeling I'm being looked over," Lucas said.

"You have interesting friends," Lily said.

He shrugged. "I'm a cop."

"You invent games and play them with nuns?"

"Hey, I'm a wild kind of guy." He looked at her over the top of his sunglasses, winked and turned back to the traffic.

"Oooh, Mr. Cool," she said. "It makes my thighs hot."

Lucas thought, Mine too. He glanced quickly at her and she turned away, a blush creeping up her neck. She knew what he was thinking, and she had been aware of him in the booth. . . .

At home, Larry Hart wore cowboy boots, blue jeans and work shirts with string ties. The string ties always had a chunk of turquoise buried in a silver slide. He could have worn that outfit to work, with a jacket to complete it, but he never did. He wore brown suits, with neckties in shades of brown and gold, and brown wingtip shoes. In the dead of summer, with the temperatures climbing into the nineties, Hart would sweat through the tiny tinderbox apartments of his welfare clientele, always in a brown suit.

Lucas had once asked him why. Hart shrugged and said, "I like it." What he meant was, *I have to*.

Hart jammed himself into the cookie-cutter frame of a municipal executive. It never worked, as hard as he tried. There was no way a brown suit could disguise his heritage. He was broad-shouldered and powerfully built, with black eyes and gray-shot hair. He was Sioux. Hart had the biggest case load in Welfare. Some of his clients refused to talk to anyone else.

"Lucas, what's happenin', babe?" Hart asked. Lucas lounged in his office chair with his feet on the rim of a wastebasket, while Lily rolled back and forth, a few inches one way and then a few inches the other, in an office chair on casters. Hart stepped inside the tiny office and dropped his bulk on a corner of Lucas' desk.

"Larry Hart, Lily Rothenburg, NYPD," Lucas said, gesturing between them.

"Nice to meet you," Lily said, taking Hart in. "You've been out?"

"Yup. Down on Franklin . . ."

Hart had been working through Indian Country with the photos. He knew two of the men himself.

"Bear is down at Rosebud and so is Elk Walking," Hart said. "They're pretty tough, but they ain't crazy. I can't see them getting involved in anything like this."

"You didn't know anybody else in the pictures?" Lily asked.

"Not names, but I know some of the faces. There are a couple of guys I see down at the Indian Center. You were asking Anderson about one of them. I played basketball against him last year."

"Could we get the team rosters?"

"They're mostly pickup games," Hart said. "But if I ask around enough, I could probably find out who he is. There are a couple more faces I've seen at powwows, at Upper Sioux and Flandreau, Sisseton, Rosebud, all over the landscape."

"All Sioux?" asked Lucas.

"I think all but one. Give me the pictures again, let's see. . . ." Hart thumbed through the stack of photographs until he found the one he wanted. He poked a finger at a man's face. "This guy's Chippewa. I don't know his name, it's Jack something, maybe like Jack Bordeaux. I think he's from White Earth, but I'm not sure."

"So how do we find out about Lily's man?" Lucas asked.

"There're a couple of guys out in SoDak who'd probably know him. Deputies. I gave Daniel the names, he called them and they're driving down to Rapid City tonight. I'm catching a plane out at six o'clock. I should be in Rapid City by seven-thirty. I'll take the pictures along."

"You think they'll know all these guys?" Lily asked.

"Most of them. They try to keep track of who has guns," Hart said.

"Why don't we just wire the pictures out . . . ?"

"The technical guys said we'd lose too much resolution. We decided it'd just be best all around if I went. I could spend some time talking to them."

"That sounds right," Lily said.

"What about this computer tree you're building?" Lucas asked. "I understand you got all kinds of family stuff in there from Minnesota Sioux. Anything on Bluebird or Yellow Hand?"

"I looked up Bluebird. He's just about the last of the family. A lot of Bluebirds went East and married into the Mohawks and that bunch. There are still quite a few Yellow

Hands out at Crow Creek and Niobrara. Those used to be Minnesota Indians before they got run out. But I know this Yellow Hand you talked to. He doesn't have much to do with the other Yellow Hands. This one is a loser."

"Nothing else?"

" 'Fraid not." Hart checked his watch. "I've got a plane to catch."

"When will you know? About the pictures?" asked Lily.

"About five minutes after I get off the plane. Do you want me to call tonight?"

"Could you? I'll come back here and wait for the call," Lucas said.

"So will I," Lily added.

" 'Bout seven-thirty, we should know," Hart said.

"So now what?" Lily asked. They were standing on the sidewalk. Hart was on his way to the airport, riding in a squad.

Lucas glanced at his watch. "I've got to see my kid, get something to eat," he said. "Why don't we meet back here at seven o'clock? We can wait for Larry to call and figure out what we're going to do tomorrow."

"Depending on what he finds out," Lily said.

"Yeah," Lucas said, flipping his key ring around his finger. "Need a ride down to your hotel?"

"No, thanks." She smiled, starting away. "It's a nice walk."

Sarah was crawling around on the living room rug when Lucas arrived. He got down on his hands and knees, his tie dragging on the carpet, and played backup with her. First he backed up and she crawled toward him, gurgling; then, with her eyes wide, she backed away and he prowled forward.

"That'd be a lot more charming if you didn't have that big bump on your ass," Jennifer said from the kitchen. Lucas reached back, pulled out the P7 and put it on a lamp table.

"Jesus, not there," Jennifer said with asperity. "She could pull herself up and grab it."

"She can't pull herself up yet," Lucas objected.

"She will soon. It's a bad habit."

"Okay." Lucas stood up, slipped the pistol back in its holster and scooped up his daughter, who had been quivering in anticipation of the flight. He bounced her in his hands as he wandered toward the kitchen and propped himself in the doorway. "Have we got some kind of problem?"

Jennifer was making a salad. She turned her head. "No. Not unless you have."

"I just got here and I'm fine," Lucas said. "You sound a little tight."

"Not at all. I just don't want guns lying around the house."

"Sure," he said. "Come on, Sarah, time for bed. Besides, your mom's being a grouch."

Lucas waited for it during dinner, watching Jennifer's face. Something was going on.

"Any lines on the guy from New York?" Jennifer asked finally. Rumors about the meeting at the *StarTribune* were circulating through all the media. Daniel had already fended off a half-dozen inquiries, but leaks were inevitable. Jennifer, called by her former partner at TV3, had spent the afternoon talking to old sources by phone. By the time Lucas had arrived, she had most of the story.

"Maybe. I've got a call coming in at seven-thirty."

"You're going back?"

"Yeah. Around seven."

"If Kennedy called you from the station, could you give him something for the ten-o'clock broadcast?"

"He'd have to talk to Daniel," Lucas said.

"Is he going to be there tonight?"

"No, I don't think so."

"How about this New York cop lady?"

Lucas thought, Ah, and said, "She'll be there."

"I hear she's terrific-looking," Jennifer said. She looked up from her dinner plate, straight into Lucas' eyes.

"She's pretty good," Lucas said. "A little `chubby, maybe . . . Is this going to be a problem? Who I work with?"

"No, no." Jennifer looked down at her plate again. "There's something else too," she said.

"Okay," Lucas said, putting his fork down. "Let's have it."

"A guy at the station asked me out."

"Who?"

"Mark Seeton."

"What'd you say?"

"I said . . . I'd get back to him."

"So you want to go?"

Jennifer stood up, picked up her plate and carried it to the sink. "Yes, I think so," she said. "No big heavy deal. Mark's a nice guy. He wants somebody to go to the symphony with."

Lucas shrugged. "So go."

She looked sideways at him. "You wouldn't mind?"

"I'd mind. I just wouldn't try to stop you."

"Jesus, that's worse than trying to stop me," she said, one fist planted against her hip. "You're trying to mind-fuck me, Davenport."

"Look, if you want to go, go," Lucas said. "You know I'm not going to take you to the symphony. Not on any regular basis."

"It's just that you have your friends and the things you do, the games, the fishing, the police work . . . me and Sarah. You see somebody almost every day, one way or another. I hardly see anybody at all, outside of work. And you know what I'm like about music. . . ."

"So go," Lucas said shortly. Then he grinned. "I can take Mark Seeton, I'm not worried," he said. He pointed a finger at her. "But I don't want to hear any shit about this New York cop. She *is* good-looking, but she's also happily married to a big-shot professor at NYU. Shearson made some kind of move on her yesterday and he's now carrying his nuts around in his lunch box."

"You're protesting too much," Jennifer said.

"No, I'm not. But you're looking for an excuse. . . ."

"Let's not fight, okay?"

"Are we still in bed?" Lucas asked.

"You might get lucky," Jennifer said. "A little romance wouldn't hurt, though."

•   •   •

Lily had a short white line on her upper lip when she got back to Lucas' office. They were alone in the tiny office, the door open on the darkened hallway.

"Did you have a glass of milk?"

She cocked her head. "You're also psychic, right? In addition to the game-making and the money."

He grinned and reached out and wiped his thumb across her lip. "No. Just a little rim of milk, here. Like my daughter."

"What's her name? Your daughter?"

"Sarah."

"We've got a Marc and a Sam," Lily said. "Marc's fifteen now, God, I can't believe it. He's started high school and he plays football. Sam's thirteen."

"You've got a kid who's fifteen?" Lucas asked. "How old are you, anyway?"

"Thirty-nine."

"I thought maybe thirty-four."

"Oh, la, such a gentleman," Lily laughed. "How about you?"

"Forty-one."

"Poor guy. Your daughter will be hanging out with all the metal-heads at the high school and you'll be too old and feeble to do anything about it."

"I'm looking forward to my feebletude," Lucas said. "Sit around in a good leather chair, read poetry. Go up to the cabin, sit on the dock, watch the sun go down . . ."

"With your fly down and your dick hanging out because you're senile and can't remember how to dress yourself . . ."

"Jesus, I can barely stand the flattery," Lucas said, laughing despite himself.

"You were getting a little carried away with the retirement bullshit," Lily said wryly.

Hart called at quarter to eight from the Rapid City airport. "They knew him right away," he said. "His name's Bill Hood. He's a Sioux from Rosebud, but he married a Chippewa woman a few years ago. He lives in Minnesota. Somewhere up around Red Lake, they think."

"What?" Lily said. There was no extension in the office and she was watching Lucas' face.

Lucas nodded at her and said into the phone, "How about the other people. You got any more names?"

"Yeah, they know quite a few of them. During the trouble with the bikers, they did a bunch of IDs. I'll give them to Anderson, get him to crank them through the computer."

"What?" Lily asked again, when Lucas got off the phone.

"Your man's name is Bill Hood. He supposedly lives somewhere up by Red Lake. . . ."

"Where's Red Lake?" she asked.

"It's a reservation up north."

"Let's get going. We'll have to stop at my—"

"Whoa. We've got things to do. We'll start with our identification people tonight, see if we can figure out exactly where he lives. The Indians are always back and forth from here to the res. For all we know, he may be down here, with Bluebird. If he's not, we'll arrange some contacts up north, then go. If we head up there tonight, we'd spend most of our time thrashing around."

Lily stood and put her hands on her hips and leaned toward him. "Why do guys always have to wait another day? Jesus, in New York . . ."

"You're not in New York. In New York, you want to go somewhere, you take a taxi. You know how far Red Lake is from here?"

"No. I don't know."

"About the same distance as it is from New York to Washington, D.C. It ain't just a taxi ride. I'll get some calls going tonight, and tomorrow . . ."

"We go."

CHAPTER

"You heard?" She called.

Lily strode down the hall toward him, a sheaf of papers clutched in one hand. Before, she'd always worn soft pink-ish lipstick, and just a touch. This morning, her lipstick was hard and heart-red, the color of street violence and rough sex. She had changed her hair as well; black bangs curled down over her brow, and she looked out from under them, like the wicked queen in *Snow White.*

"What?" Lucas was carrying a paper cup of microwaved coffee and had a *Trib* pinched under his arm.

"We found Hood. Right here in town. Anderson got on the computers early this morning," she said. The papers were computer printouts with notes scrawled in the margins in blue ink. She looked down at the top one. "Hood used to live at a place called Bemidji. It's not on a reservation, but it's close."

"Yeah. It's right next to Red Lake," Lucas said. He opened the metal door of his office and led the way in.

"But we got a problem," Lily said as she settled into the second chair in the office. Lucas put the coffee on his desk, pulled off his sport coat, hung it on a hook and sat down. "What happened is . . ."

Lucas rubbed his face and she frowned. "What's wrong?"

"My face hurts," Lucas said.

"Your face hurts?"

"It's sensitive to morning light. I think my grandfather was a vampire."

She looked at him for a moment and shook her head. "Jesus . . ."

"So what's the problem?" Lucas prompted, smothering a yawn.

She got back on track. "Hood's not driving his own car. He's the listed owner of a 1988 Ford Tempo four-wheel-drive. Red. That car's still at his former home up in Bemidji, along with his wife and kid. The Bemidji cops have some kind of source in his neighborhood—some cop's sister-in-law—and the red car's been there all along. We're not sure what Hood was driving out of that Jersey motel, but it was big and old. Like a 'seventy-nine Buick or Oldsmobile. It had bad rust."

"So we've got no way to spot him on the highway."

"Unfortunately. But . . ." She thumbed through the print-outs. "Anderson did a computer run on him and talked to the state people. He's got a Minnesota driver's license but no second-car registration. So Anderson went through everything else in the computers and *bingo*. Found him listed as a defendant in a small-claims-court filing. He bought a TV on time and couldn't make the payments."

"And his address was on the filing."

"Nope. Anderson had to call Sears. They looked up the address on their accounts computer. It's an apartment on Lyndale Street."

"Lyndale Avenue," Lucas said. He sat forward now, intent.

"Whatever. The thing is, the apartment's rented to a guy named Tomas Peck. Sloan and a couple of Narcotics guys are over in the neighborhood now, trying to figure it out."

"Maybe he moved."

"Yeah, but Peck has been listed as the occupant for two years. So maybe Hood's living with him."

"Huh." Lucas thought it over as she sat leaning forward,

waiting for a comment. "Are you sure you've got the right Bill Hood? There have got to be a lot of them. . . ."

"Yeah, we're sure. The Sears account had a change of address."

"Then I'd bet he's still living at that apartment," Lucas said. "We're on a roll, and when you get on a roll . . ."

". . . it all works," Lily said.

Lily had not gone down to look for Hood, she said, because Daniel wanted to keep the police presence in the neighborhood to a minimum. "The FBI's all over the streets. They must have half a dozen agents going through the community," she said.

"Isn't he going to tell them about identifying Hood?"

"Yeah. He's already talked to a guy." She glanced at her watch. "There's a meeting in half an hour. We're supposed to be there. Sloan should be back and Larry Hart's coming in sometime this morning," Lily said. She was quivering with energy. "God damn, I was afraid I'd be here for a month. I could be out of here tomorrow, if we get him."

"Did Daniel say who the FBI guy is?" Lucas asked.

"Uh, yeah. A guy named . . ." She looked at her notes. "Kieffer."

"Uh-oh."

"Not good?" She looked up at him and he shook his head, frowning.

"He doesn't like me and I don't like him. Gary Kieffer is a most righteous man. Most righteous."

"Well, get your phony smile in place, then, because we're meeting with him in twenty-seven minutes." She looked at her watch again, then at his nearly empty coffee cup. "Where can we get more coffee and a decent Danish?"

They walked through the tunnel from City Hall to the Hennepin County Government Center, took a couple of escalators to the Skyway level, walked along the Skyway to the Pillsbury building. Standing on the escalator a step above him, she could look straight into his eyes; she asked if he had had a long night.

"No, not particularly." He glanced at her. "Why?"

"You look a little beat."

"I don't get up early. I usually don't get going until about noon." He yawned again to prove it.

"What about your girlfriend? Is she a night person too?"

"Yeah. She spent half her life reporting for the ten-o'clock news, which meant she got off work about eleven. That's how we met. We'd bump into each other at late-night restaurants."

Going across the Skyway, Lily looked through the windows at the glossy downtown skyscrapers, monuments to the colored-glass industry. "I've never been in this part of the country," she said. "I made a couple of cross-country trips when I was doing the hippie thing, back in college, but we always went south of here. Through Iowa or Missouri, on the way out to California."

"It's out of the way, Minnesota is," Lucas conceded. "Lake Michigan hangs down there and cuts us off, with Wisconsin and the Dakotas. You've got to want to come here. And I suppose you don't often get out of the Center of the Universe."

"I do, once in a while," she said mildly, refusing to rise to the bait. "But it's usually on vacation, down to the Bahamas or the Keys or out to Bermuda. We went to Hawaii once. We just don't get into the middle part of the country."

"It's the last refuge of American civilization, you know—out here, between the mountains," Lucas said, looking out the windows. "Most of the population is literate, most people still trust their governments, and most of the governments are reasonably good. The citizens control the streets. We've got poverty, but it's manageable. We've got dope, but we've still got a handle on it. It's okay."

"You mean like Detroit?"

"There are a couple of spots out of control . . ."

"And South Chicago and Gary and East St. Louis . . ."

". . . but basically, it ain't bad. You get the feeling that nobody even knows what goes on in New York or Los Angeles and that nobody really cares. The politicians have to lie and steal just to get elected."

"I think my brain would shrivel up and die if I was living

here. It's so fuckin' peaceful I don't know what I'd do," Lily said. She looked down at a street-cleaning machine. "The night I came in, I got here late, after midnight. I caught a cab at the airport and went downtown, and I started seeing these women walking around alone or waiting for buses by themselves. Everywhere. Jesus. That's such . . . an odd sight."

"Hmph," Lucas said.

They left the Skyway and got on an escalator to the main floor of the Pillsbury building. "You have a little hickey on your neck," she said lightly. "I thought maybe that's why you looked so tired."

They sat in the dining area of a bakery, Lily eating a Danish with a glass of milk, Lucas staring out the window over a cup of coffee.

"Wish I was out there with Sloan," she said finally.

"Why? He can handle it." Lucas sipped at the scalding coffee.

"I just wish I was. I've handled a lot of pretty serious situations."

"So have we. We ain't New York, but we ain't exactly Dogpatch, either," Lucas said.

"Yeah, I know. . . ."

"Sloan's good at talking to people. He'll dig it out."

"All right, all right," she said, suddenly irritable. "But this means a lot to me."

"It means a lot to us too. We're up to our assholes in media; Jesus, the street outside the office this morning looked like the press parking lot at a political convention."

"Not the same," she insisted. "Andretti was a major figure. . . ."

"We're handling it," Lucas said sharply.

"*You're* not handling much. You didn't even get here until ten o'clock, for Christ's sake. I'd been standing around for two hours."

"I didn't ask you to wait for me; and I told you, I work nights."

"I just don't have the right feeling from this. You guys—"

"And if I read the newspapers right, you guys in New York have screwed more than your share of cases to the wall," Lucas interrupted, talking over her. "If you guys aren't deliberately blowing up some black kid, you're taking money from some fuckin' crack dealer. We're not only pretty good, we're clean. . . ."

"I never took a fuckin' nickel from anybody," Lily said, her voice harsh. She was leaning over the table, her jaw tight.

"I didn't say you did, I said . . ."

"Hey, fuck you, Davenport, I just want to nail this sonofabitch, and the next thing I hear is that New York cops are taking payoff money. . . ." She threw a paper napkin on the table, picked up the Danish and the carton of milk, and stood and stalked away.

"Hey, Lily," Lucas said. "God damn it."

Gary Kieffer didn't like Lucas and made no effort to hide it. He was waiting in Daniel's office when Lily arrived, with Lucas just behind her. He and Lucas nodded at each other.

"Where's Daniel?" Lily asked.

"Off somewhere," Kieffer said coldly. He was wearing a navy-blue business suit, a tie knotted in a full Windsor, and well-polished black wingtips.

"I'll go check," Lucas grumped. He backed out of the office, looking at Lily. She dropped her purse beside the chair next to Kieffer's and sat down.

"You'd be the New York lady officer," Kieffer said, looking her over.

"Yes. Lily Rothenburg. Lieutenant."

"Gary Kieffer." They shook hands, he with an exaggerated gentleness. Kieffer wore thick glasses and his large red nose was pitted with old acne scars. He crossed his hands over his stomach.

"What's the problem with you and Davenport?" Lily asked. "There's a certain chill. . . ."

Kieffer's blue eyes were distorted by the heavy glasses and looked almost liquid, like ice cubes in a glass of gin and tonic. He was in his early fifties, his face lined by weather and stress. He was silent for a moment, then asked, "Are you friends?"

"No. We're not friends. I just met him a couple of days ago," she said.

"I don't like to talk out of turn," Kieffer said.

"Look, I've got to work with him," Lily prompted.

"He's a cowboy," Kieffer continued. His voice dropped a notch and he looked around the office, as though checking for recording devices. "That's my estimation. He's gunned down six people. Killed them. I don't believe there's another officer in Minnesota, including SWAT guys, who has killed more than two. No FBI man has. Maybe nobody in the country has. And you know why? Because in most places, if a guy kills two people, he goes on a desk. They won't let him out anymore. They worry about what they've got on their hands. But not with Davenport. He does what he pleases. Sometimes that's killing people."

"Well, I understand that in his area . . ."

"Yeah, yeah, that's what everybody says. That's what the news people say. He's got the media people in his pocket, the reporters. They say he does dope, he does vice, he does intelligence work on violent criminals. I say he's a gunman, and I don't hold with that. Except for Davenport, we don't have the death penalty in Minnesota. He's a gunman, plain and simple."

Lily thought it over. A gunman. She could see it in him. She'd have to be careful. But gunmen had their uses. . . . Kieffer was staring straight ahead, at the photos on Daniel's wall, caught in his own thoughts of Davenport.

Lucas came back a moment later, Daniel trailing behind him with a cup of coffee. Sloan and another cop, the second one unshaven and dressed like a parking-lot attendant, were a step behind Daniel. Everybody called the second cop Del, but nobody introduced him to Lily. She assumed he was undercover Narcotics or Intelligence.

"So what do we got?" Daniel asked as he settled behind his desk. He looked into his humidor, then snapped it shut.

"We've got a map. Let me explain the situation," Sloan said. He moved up to Daniel's desk and unrolled a copy of a plat map from the City Planner's Office.

•   •   •

Billy Hood had apparently left Bemidji a year before, drifted
down to the Twin Cities and moved into an apartment with
two friends. The apartment was on the first-floor corner of
the building, just to the right of the entrance. A careful, se-
cretive questioning of the elderly couple who worked as
building superintendents suggested that Hood's roommates
were in residence. Hood had been gone for more than a
week, perhaps ten days, but his clothes were still in the
apartment.

"What are the chances of getting a search warrant?"
Lucas asked.

"If Lily will swear that she has probable cause to think
Hood's the man who killed Andretti, there'd be no problem," Daniel said.

"The problem is, we've got those two guys who live with
him," said Sloan. "We've got nothing against them, so we
can't kick the door and bust them. But if we go talk nice
to them, what happens if they're part of the whole deal?
Maybe Hood's calling them every night to find out what's
happening. They could have a voice code to warn him
off. . . ."

"So what are you suggesting?" Daniel asked.

The cop named Del pointed at the map. "See this building
across the street? We can get a ground-floor apartment and
set up there. There's only two ways out of Hood's building—the other way's on the side—and we can see both of
them from the apartment across the street. We think the
ideal thing would be to set up a surveillance. Then, depending on how he arrives, grab him just before he goes in, or
when he comes back out."

"What do you mean, 'how he arrives'?" Daniel asked,
looking up from the map.

"There're not many cars on the street. He could pull up
right to the front door, hop out and go inside. If he's nuts,
we want to be in a position where we can tackle him. You
know, a couple guys walk down the street, talking, and
when they get to him, wham! Take him down, put on the
cuffs."

"We could put somebody inside . . ." Daniel suggested,
but Del was already shaking his head.

"We've got those goddamned roommates to worry about. Or, as far as we know, somebody else in the building. If he's warned off somehow, we'd never know it. We could be there watching the building and he's laying on a beach in San Juan."

They talked for another five minutes before Daniel nodded.

"All right," he conceded, standing up. "It looks like you've got it figured. When do you think he'll get back?"

"No sooner than tonight, even if he drove like crazy," Sloan said. "He'd have to do six, seven hundred miles a day to get here tonight. New York says he's driving an old car."

"That's what we got from his motel," Lily said.

Lucas looked at Daniel. "If there was some way to make sure the other two guys were out of there, it might not be a bad idea to go in and take a look," he said. "We could check for weapons and anything that might tell us where he is right now."

"Are we talking about an illegal entry?" Kieffer blurted suddenly. They were the first words he had spoken since the meeting began, and everybody turned to look at him.

"No. We're not, Gary," Daniel said promptly. "Everything will be on the up-and-up. But instead of kicking in the door, Lieutenant Davenport, I take it, is proposing to go in without disturbing the place."

"That is very close, very close to an illegal search. You know that searches are supposed to be announced. . . ."

"Hey, take it easy, everything will be okayed by a judge, all right?" Daniel said, staring Kieffer down. "And if it wasn't, it's still better'n getting one of my people shot."

Kieffer grunted in disgust. "I've got nothing to do with this. In my judgment, it's a bad move. And I think we ought to grab him the minute we see him. Put some guys in cars, take him. Or if he gets in that apartment, kick the door. We could put an entry team in there, take the door off, and we're inside before they can move. . . ."

"But what if he's willing to die? Like Bluebird?" Lucas asked. "You can get the drop on somebody, but if he's willing to die, and if he goes for a gun, what're you gonna do?

You're gonna shoot him. I don't give a shit if you kill him, but I'd like to talk to him first."

Kieffer shook his head. "It's a bad plan," he said. "He'll slip away. I'm telling you that on the record."

"Lemme know when the record's released," Lucas said.

Lily grinned without thinking, but killed the smile when Lucas looked at her. She was still mad.

Daniel turned to Del. "These two guys, the roommates. What do we know about them?"

"One of them works at a bakery. One of them's unemployed. He spends most of his time at a health club, lifting. He supposedly does some modeling for art classes, big scandal in the building. You know, nude stuff. Anyway, that's what we get from the super."

"Can you locate them, put a guy on each one of them?"

"I think so."

"Do it. Lily, we're going to need you for the warrant." Daniel looked at Lucas. "And you better figure out how you'll get in. We'll want you to do the search."

Kieffer got up and walked to the door. "I don't know anything about this," he said, and left.

Lucas stopped Del in the hallway.

"How are we going to do this?" he asked.

"I could get a key. . . ."

"That'd be quicker'n a power pick. The fuckin' pick sounds like you dropped a tray full of silverware."

"I'll talk to the super. . . ."

"You got a little weight on them?" Lucas asked.

"A little," Del said. "They push some toot out the back door, supplement the old man's Social Security."

"Okay. As long as they're fixed. Are you going down there now?"

"Yeah."

"I've got to stop in my office, pick up a tape recorder and a Polaroid. I'll be right behind you."

The building across from Hood's had an alleyway access. Lucas dumped the Porsche a block away and walked in. Del was waiting with the key.

"The baker's halfway through his shift. He gets off at four. The other guy's at the club. He's doing bench presses and he told Dave that he always sits in the whirlpool after a heavy workout, so he'll be a while." Del handed Lucas a Yale key. "The warrant's on the way. Daniel said to stick it into one of Hood's coat sleeves before you leave. Like in a parka or something. Someplace he won't look right away."

Lily arrived five minutes later, with Sloan.

"We've got a warrant," she told Lucas. She made no move to hand it to him. "I'm coming along."

"Fuck that."

"I'm coming," she insisted. "He's my man and two of us can go through the place faster than one."

"Not a bad idea," said Del. "No offense, man, but you kinda smell like a cop. If somebody sees you in the hallway, before you get in . . . Lily'd be a little camouflage."

Lucas looked from Lily to Del and back. "All right," he said. "Let's go."

"Hope there's nobody crashing in here. You know, a guest," Lily said as they crossed the street. Hood's building was made of old red sandstone; the wooden windows showed dry rot.

"Don't worry, I'll cover you," Lucas said. He tried to make it light, a joke, but it came out macho.

She stared back at him. "You can be a pain in the ass, you know?"

"That was supposed to be a joke."

"Yeah. Well." Her eyes broke away.

Lucas shook his head. He wasn't doing anything right. He followed her up the stoop into the building. First door on the right. He knocked once. No answer. And again. No answer. He put the key in the lock, cracked the door. Lily looked down the hall, checking the other doorways for watchers.

"Hello?" Lucas made it loud, but not too loud. Then he whistled. "Here, boy. Here, pup."

After a few seconds of silence, Lily said, "Nobody home."

"Probably a fuckin' Rottweiler under the bed with its

tongue cut out to make it mean," Lucas said. He pushed open the door and they stepped inside.

"That's a heck of a door," Lucas said as he eased it shut.

"What?"

"It's an old building. They still have the original doors—solid oak or walnut or something," Lucas said, rapping on the door with his knuckles. "By the time apartments get this old, one landlord or another has usually stripped out all the original doors and sold them. They're probably worth as much as the apartment building."

They were in the living room. Two rickety occasional chairs, a recliner with a stained fabric cover, the brown metal cube of an aging color television. Two red vinyl bean-bag chairs lay on the floor in front of the TV, leaking tiny white Styrofoam beads on the wooden floor. The apartment smelled of some kind of stew or soup—lentils, maybe. White beans.

Lucas led the way through a quick check of the apartment, glancing into two bedrooms, a tiny kitchen with its peeling linoleum and thirties gas stove with a fold-down top.

"How do we know which is Hood's room?" Lily asked.

"You look at the stuff on the chests," Lucas said. "There's always some shit."

"You sound like you do this quite a bit," she said.

"I mostly talk to a lot of burglars," Lucas said, suppressing a grin. He headed toward a bedroom.

"What do you want me to do?" Lily asked.

"Look in the kitchen, around the telephone," Lucas said. He took the miniature tape recorder out of his pocket. "Push the red button to record. Dictate any phone numbers you find written around. Any times or place names. Any-place Hood might have been."

The first bedroom had one bed and a ramshackle chest. The bed was unmade, the bedclothes twisted in a pile. Lucas stooped and looked under it. There were several boxes, but a patina of dust suggested that they hadn't been moved recently. He stood and went over to the six-drawer chest. Notes, gas-station charge slips, cash-register receipts, ball-point pens, paper clips and pennies were scattered across the top. He checked the charge slips: Tomas Peck. Wrong guy. Lucas quickly looked through the drawers and the closet for weapons. Nothing.

The second bedroom had two beds and no chests. All the clothing was stacked inside boxes, some plastic and made for storage, some cardboard and made for moving. Personal papers were scattered across a windowsill next to one of the beds. He picked up a letter, glanced at the address: Billy Hood. The return address was in Bemidji and the handwriting was feminine. His wife, probably. Lucas looked through the letter, but it was mostly a litany of complaints followed by a request for money for the wife and a daughter.

He quickly went through the boxes stacked beside the bed. One was half full of underwear and socks, a second was stacked with several pairs of worn jeans and a couple of belts. A third held winter-weight shirts and sweaters, with a couple sets of thermal underwear.

The bedroom had one closet. The door was standing open and Lucas patted down the shirts and jackets hanging inside. Nothing. He dropped to his knees and pushed the clothing out of the way and checked the bottom. A lever-action Sears .30-.30. He cranked the lever down. Unloaded. A box of shells sat on the floor beside the butt. He got up, looked around, found a torn pair of underpants.

"What're you doing?" Lily was in the doorway.

"Found a gun. I'm going to jam it. What'd you get in the kitchen?" He ripped a square of material out of the underpants.

"There were some phone numbers on papers around the phone. I got them."

"Look in all the drawers."

"I did. Paged through the calendar, looked through a kind of general catchall basket and drawer full of junk. Went through the phone book. There was a number written in the back with a red pen and there was a red pen right next to the book, so it might be recent. . . ." She glanced at a piece of paper in her hand. "It has a six-one-four area code. That's the Twin Cities, right? Maybe . . ."

"No, we're six-one-two," Lucas said. "I don't know where six-one-four is. Sure it was six-one-four?"

"Yeah . . ." She disappeared and Lucas made a tight little

ball of the underpants material and pushed it down the muzzle with a ballpoint. The material was tightly packed, and after two or three inches, he couldn't force it down any farther. Satisfied, he put the rifle back in the closet and closed the door.

"That six-one-four code is southwestern Ohio," Lily said from the doorway. She was looking at a phone book.

"He could be coming back that way," Lucas said.

"I'll get somebody to run down the number," Lily said. She closed the phone book. "What else?"

"Check the front-room closets. I gotta finish here."

There was a box under Hood's bed. Lucas pulled it out. A photo album, apparently some years old, covered with dust. He glanced through it, then pushed it back under the bed. A moment later, Lily called, "Shotgun." Lucas stepped into the living room just as she cracked open an old single-shot twelve-gauge.

"Shit," Lucas said. "No point in trying to jam that. He'll be looking right through the barrel when he puts a shell in."

"Don't see any shells," Lily said. "Should we take it?"

"Better not. If his roommates are involved, we don't want anything missing. . . ."

Lucas went back to the bedroom and looked through the other man's boxes. There was nothing of interest, no letters or notes that might tie the others more intimately to Hood. He went back into the living room. "Lily?"

"I'm in the bathroom," she called. "Find anything else?"

"No. How about you?" He poked his head into the bathroom and found her carefully going through the medicine cabinet.

"Nothing serious." She took a prescription-drug bottle out of the cabinet and looked at it, her forehead wrinkling. "There's a prescription here for Hood. Strong stuff, but I don't see how you could abuse it."

"What is it?"

"An antihistamine. The label says it's for bee stings. My father used it. He was allergic to bees and fire ants. If he got stung, his whole body would swell up. It used to scare the shit out of him; he'd think he was smothering. And he might have too, if he didn't have his medicine around. The swelling can pinch off your windpipe. . . ."

Lucas shrugged. "No use to us."

Lily put the plastic bottle of pills back in the cabinet, closed it and followed him into the living room. "Anything else?"

"I guess not," Lucas said. "We fucked up a gun; I hope there aren't any shells for the shotgun."

"Didn't see any. Are you going to do any pictures?"

"Yeah. Just a few views." Lucas took a half-dozen Polaroid photos of the rooms and paced off the main room's dimensions, which he dictated into the tape recorder.

"You know, we really could spend more time going through the place," Lily suggested.

"Better not. What you get quick is probably all you're going to get," Lucas said. "Never push when you're inside somebody else's house. All kinds of shit can happen. Friends stop by unexpectedly. Relatives. Get in and get out."

"You sound more and more experienced. . . ."

Lucas shrugged. "You got the warrant?"

"Oh, yeah." Lily took it out of her purse and stuck it in the sleeve of a winter coat in the living room closet. "We'll tell the court we put it one place he'd find it for sure. Of course, he's got to put on the coat."

"Which he probably wouldn't do until winter . . ."

"Which is not that far away," Lily said.

"So all right," Lucas said. "Did we change anything?"

"Nothing I can see," Lily said.

"Let me take a last look in the bedroom." He stepped into the bedroom, looked around and finally opened the closet door an inch. "I'm slipping," he said. "The damn door was open when I came in and I closed it."

Lily was looking at him curiously. Lucas said, "What?"

"I'm really kind of impressed," she conceded. "You're pretty good at this."

"That's the nicest thing you ever said to me."

She grinned and shrugged. "So I'm a little competitive."

"I'm sorry about ragging you this morning," Lucas said, the words tumbling out. "I'm not a responsible human being before noon. I don't daylight; I really don't."

"I shouldn't have picked on you," she said. "I just want to get this job done."

"Are we making up?"

She turned away toward the door, her back to him.

"It's all right with me," she said. "Let's get out of here." She opened the door and peered down the hallway.

"Clear," she said.

Lucas was just behind her. "If we're going to make up, we ought to do it right," he said.

She turned and looked at him. "What?"

He leaned forward and kissed her on the mouth, and the kiss came back for just the barest fraction of a second, a returned pressure with a hint of heat. Then she pulled away and stepped out into the hall, flustered.

"Enough of that shit," she said.

It was a five-minute walk down the block, around the corner, up the alley and into the surveillance apartment. Lily kept her head turned, apparently interested in watching the apartment buildings go by. Once or twice, Lucas felt her glance at him, and then quickly away. He could still feel the pressure of her lips on his.

"How'd we do?" Del asked when they got back to the apartment. Sloan stood up and wandered over. A third detective had arrived and was sitting on an aluminum lawn chair, reading a book and watching the street. A man in a gray suit sat on a folding canvas camp stool next to the window. He was reading a hardcover book and smoking a pipe.

"Found a couple of guns, fucked one of them up," Lucas said. Under his breath he asked, "Feeb?"

Del nodded, and they glanced at the FBI man in the gray suit. "Observing," Del muttered. In a louder voice he said, "Get anything else?"

"A phone number," Lily said. "I'll call Anderson and see how quick he can run down that Ohio phone."

Anderson called Kieffer and Kieffer called Washington. Washington made three calls. Ten minutes after Lily talked to Anderson, Kieffer got a call from the agent-in-charge in Columbus, Ohio. The number was for a motel off Interstate

70 near Columbus. An hour later, an FBI agent showed a motel desk clerk a wire photograph of Hood. The clerk nodded, remembering the face, and said Hood had stayed at the motel the night before. The clerk found the registration, signed as Bill Harris. There was a license-plate number, but a check showed that the number had never been issued in Minnesota.

"He's careful," Anderson said. They were gathered in Daniel's office.

"But he's moving right along," said Kieffer.

"He ought to be here. Or close," Lily said, looking from Lucas to Anderson to Daniel to Kieffer.

Kieffer nodded. "Very late tonight or sometime tomorrow, if he keeps pushing it. He's got Chicago in the way. He either has to go through it, or go way around it. . . . He'd have to push like a sonofabitch to make it here tonight. It's more likely that he'd make it to Madison tonight and get into the Cities tomorrow."

"How far is Madison?" Lily asked.

"Five hours."

"He is pushing it," she said. "So it could be tonight. . . ."

"We'll keep a watch," Daniel said. He looked around. "Anything else?"

"I can't think of anything," Lucas said. "Lily?"

"I guess we wait," Lily said.

CHAPTER
9

Lily went back to the surveillance post with Del, the under-
cover cop, while Lucas filled out the return on the search
warrant. As he was finishing, Larry Hart walked in, carrying an overnight bag.

"Anything more?" Lucas asked.

"Nothing but a bunch of rumors," Hart said, dumping
the bag against the wall. "There was something weird going
on, just about the time of the bikers. There was a sun dance
up at Standing Rock, but that was on the up-and-up. But
there was maybe a ceremony of some kind at Bear Butte.
A midnight deal. That's the rumor."

"Any names?"

"No. But the guys out there are asking around."

"We need names. In this business, names are the game."

Hart checked in with Anderson, then went home to clean
up. Lucas filed the return on the search warrant, walked
across the street to a newsstand and bought half a dozen
magazines, then headed down to Indian Country.

Del was asleep on an inflatable mattress, his mouth half
open. He looked exactly like a bum, Lucas decided. Two
Narcotics cops were perched on matching aluminum lawn
chairs, watching the street. A cooler sat next to the cop on
the left and a boombox was playing "Brown Sugar." The

FBI man was gone, although his stool was still there: the seat read L. L. BEAN. Lily was sitting on a stack of newspapers, leaning back against a wall.

"You guys are such a bunch of cutups," Lucas said as he walked in.

"Fuck you, Davenport," the two surveillance cops said in unison.

"I second that," Lily said.

"Anytime, anyplace," Lucas said. The cops laughed, and Lily said, "You talking to me or them?"

"Them," said Lucas. "Duane's got such a nice ass."

"Takes a load off my mind," said Lily.

"*Puts* a load on mine," said Duane, the fat surveillance cop.

"Nothing happening?" asked Lucas.

"Lot of fuckin' dope," Duane said. "I was kinda surprised. We don't hear too much about it from this area."

"We don't know too many Indians," Lucas said. He looked around the bare apartment. "Where's the feeb?"

"He went out. Said he was coming back. He seems kinda touchy about his chair, if that's what you were thinking," said the thin cop.

"Yeah?"

"Stacks of newspaper down the hall," Lily said.

One of the magazines had a debate on ten-millimeter automatic pistols. A gun writer suggested that it was the perfect defensive cartridge, producing twice the muzzle energy of typical nine-millimeter and .45 ACP rounds and almost half again as much as the .357 Magnum. The writer's opponent, a Los Angeles cop, worried that the ten-millimeter was a little *too* hot, tending to punch holes not only through the target but also through the crowd at the bus stop two blocks away. Lucas couldn't follow the details of the argument. His mind kept straying to the shape of Lily's neck, the edge of her cheek from the side and slightly behind, the curve of her wrist. Her lip. He remembered Sloan saying something about her overbite, and he smiled just a bit and nibbled at his own lip.

"What're you smiling about?" Lily asked.

"Nothing," Lucas said. "Magazine."

She heaved herself to her feet, stretched, yawned and wandered over. "Hot-hot-hot," she said. "It's a ten-MM?"

Lucas closed the magazine. "Dumb fucks," he said.

Anderson called on the portable a few minutes after one o'clock: The killer in Oklahoma City had vanished. Kieffer had talked to FBI agents in South Dakota about the rumors Hart had heard of a midnight ceremony, Anderson added, but nobody had much.

"There's some question about whether there ever was such a thing," he said.

"What do you mean?"

"Kieffer talked to the lead investigator out there and this guy thinks the rumors came out of the confrontation with the bikers. One night the Indians surrounded Bear Butte, wouldn't let the bikers down the road around it. The bikers supposedly saw fires and so on, and heard drum music—and that eventually got turned into this secret-ceremony business."

"So it could be another dead end," Lily said.

"That's what Kieffer says."

"I could be watching *The Young and the Restless*," Lily said twenty minutes later.

"Go for a walk?" Lucas suggested.

"All right. Take a portable."

They went out the alley, two blocks to a 7-Eleven, bought Diet Cokes and started back.

"So fuckin' boring," Lily complained.

"You don't have to sit there. He probably won't be in until this evening," Lucas said.

"I feel like I oughta be there," Lily said. "He's my man."

On the way back, Lucas took a small gun-cleaning kit out of the Porsche. Inside the apartment, he spread newspapers on the floor, sat cross-legged, broke down his P7 and began cleaning it. Lily went back to her stack of newspapers for a few minutes, then moved over across from him.

"Mind if I use it?" she asked after watching for a moment.

"Go ahead."

"Thanks." She took her .45 out of her purse, popped the magazine, checked the chamber to make sure it was empty and began stripping it. "I break a fingernail about once a week on this damn barrel bushing," she said. She stuck her tongue out in concentration, rotated the bushing over the recoil spring plug and eased the spring out.

"Pass the nitro," she said.

Lucas handed her the cleaning solvent.

"This stuff smells better than gasoline," she said. "It could turn me into a sniffer."

"Gives me headaches," Lucas said. "It smells good but I can't handle it." He noticed that her .45 was spotless before she began cleaning it. His P7 didn't need the work either, but it was something to do.

"Ever shot a P7?" he asked idly.

"The other one. The eight-shot. The big one, like yours, has a lot of firepower, but I can't get my hand around the butt. I don't like the way it carries either. Too fat."

"That's not exactly a Tinker Toy you've got there," he said, nodding at her Colt.

"No, but the shape of the butt is different. It's skinnier. That's what I need. It's easier to handle."

"I really don't like that single-action for street work," Lucas said conversationally. "It's fine if you're target-shooting, but if you're only worried about hitting a torso . . . I like the double-action."

"You could try one of the forty-five Smiths."

"They're supposed to be good guns," Lucas agreed. "I probably would have, if the P7 hadn't come out first. . . . How come you never went to a Smith?"

"Well, this thing just feels right to me. When I was shooting in competition I used a 1911 from Springfield Armory in thirty-eight Super. I want the forty-five for the street, but all that competition . . . the gun feels friendly."

"You shot competition?" Lucas asked. The cops at the window, who had been listening in an abstract way, suddenly perked up at an undertone in Lucas' voice.

"I was New York women's champ in practical shooting for a couple of years," Lily said. "I had to quit competition because it was taking too much time. But I still shoot a little."

"You must be pretty good," Lucas offered. The cops by the window glanced at each other. A bet.

"Better than anybody you're likely to know," she said offhandedly.

Lucas snorted and she squinted at him.

"What? You think you can shoot with me?"

"With you?" Lucas said. His lip might have curled.

Lily sat up, interested now. "You ever compete?"

He shrugged. "Some."

"You ever win?"

"Some. Used a 1911, in fact."

"Practical or bull's-eye?"

"A little of both," he said.

"And you think you can shoot with me?"

"I can shoot with most people," Lucas said.

She looked at him, studied his face, and a small smile started at the corners of her lips. "You want to put your money where your mouth is?"

It was Lucas' turn to stare, weighing the challenge. "Yeah," he said finally. "Anytime, anyplace."

Lily noticed the cops by the window watching them.

"He's sandbagging me, right?" she said. "He's the North American big-bore champ or some fuckin' thing."

"I don't know, I never seen him shoot," one of the cops said.

Lily stared at him with narrowed eyes, gauging the likelihood that he was lying, then turned back to Lucas. "All right," she said. "Where do we shoot?"

They shot at a police pistol range in the basement of a precinct house, using Outers twenty-five-foot slow-fire pistol targets. There were seven concentric rings on each target face. The three outer rings were marked but not colored, while the inner four rings—the 7, 8, 9 and 10—were black. The center ring, the 10 ring, was a bit smaller than a dime.

"Nice range," Lily said when Lucas turned on the lights. A Hennepin County deputy had been leaving just when they arrived. When he heard what they were doing, he insisted on judging the match.

Lily put her handset on the ledge of a shooting booth, took the .45 from her purse, held it in both hands and looked downrange over the sights. "Let's get the targets up."

"This P7 ain't exactly a target pistol," Lucas said. He squinted downrange. "I never did like the light in here either."

"Cold feet?" Lily asked.

"Making conversation," he said. "I just wish I had my Gold Cup. It'd make me feel better. It'd also punch a bigger hole in the paper. The same size as yours. If you're as good as you say, that could make the difference."

"You could always chicken out if the extra seven-hundredths of an inch makes you nervous," Lily said. She pushed a magazine into the Colt and jacked a shell into the chamber. "And I don't have my match guns either."

"Fuck it. We'll flip to shoot," Lucas said. He dug in his pocket for a quarter.

"How much?" Lily asked.

"It's got to be enough to feel it," Lucas said. "We ought to give it a little bite of reality. You say."

"Best two out of three rounds . . . One hundred dollars."

"That's not enough," Lucas said, aiming the P7 downrange again. "I was thinking a thousand."

"That's ridiculous," Lily said, tossing her head. The deputy was now watching them with real interest. The story would be all over the sheriff's department and the city cops, and probably St. Paul, before the night was done. "You're trying to psych me, Davenport. A hundred is all I can afford. I'm not a rich game-inventor."

"Hey, Dick," Lucas said to the deputy. "Lily's not gonna let me put the targets up, you want to . . ."

"Sure . . ."

The deputy began running the target sheets out to twenty-five feet. Lucas stepped closer to Lily, his voice low. "I'll tell you what. If you win, you take down a hundred. If I win, I get another kiss. Time and place of my choosing."

She put her hands on her hips. "That's the most goddamned juvenile thing I ever heard. You're too fuckin' old for that, Davenport. You've got lines in your face. Your hair is turning gray."

Lucas reddened but grinned through the embarrassment. Dick was walking back toward them. "It might be juvenile, but that's what I want," he said. "Unless you're chicken."

"You really do a number on a person's head, don't you?"

"Puk-puk-puk," he said, doing an imitation of a chicken's cackle.

"Fuck you, Davenport," she said.

"So maybe we just have a pleasant afternoon shooting guns. We don't have to compete. I mean, if you've got cold feet."

"Fuck you."

"Anytime, anyplace."

"What an asshole," she muttered under her breath.

"What does that mean?" Lucas asked.

"It means you're on," she said.

Lucas tossed the quarter and won. They shot a round of five shots for familiarization. Neither showed the other the practice target.

"You ready?" Lucas asked.

"Ready."

Lucas fired first, five shots. He used both hands, his right shooting hand cupped in his left, the left side of his body slightly forward of the right. He kept both eyes open. Lily could tell he was hitting the black, but she couldn't tell how close he was to the center 10 ring. When Lucas finished, she stepped to the line and took a position identical to the one Lucas had used. She fired her first shot, said, "Shit," and fired four more.

"Problem?" Lucas said when she took down the gun after the last shot.

"First shot was a flier, I think," she said. The deputy rolled the targets back to the shooting line. Two of Lucas' five shots had clipped the 10 ring. The third and fourth counted 9, a fifth was in the 8 ring. Forty-six.

Three shots from Lily's .45 had obliterated the center of

the target, a fourth was in the nine, but the flier was out in the four. Forty-three.

"Without the flier, I'd of won," Lily said. She sounded angry with herself.

"If pigs had wings they could fly," said Lucas.

"That's the worst round I've shot in a year."

"It's the less than ideal conditions, shooting targets with a gun you don't use on the range," Lucas said. "It gets you range shooters every time."

"I'm not a range shooter," she said, now angry at Lucas. "Let's get the new targets up, huh?"

"Jesus, what'd you guys bet? Must be something, huh?" asked the deputy, looking from one of them to the other.

"Yeah," said Lily. "A hundred bucks and Davenport's honor. He loses either way."

"Huh?"

"Never mind."

Lucas grinned as he finished reloading. "Bitch, bitch, bitch," he said, just barely audibly.

"Keep it up, buster," she said through her teeth.

"Sorry. Wasn't trying to psych you," he said, trying to psych her. "You shoot first this time."

She fired five shots and all five felt good. She smiled at him this time and said, "I just shot a fifty or close to it. Stick that in your nose, asshole."

"Temper, temper . . ."

Lucas fired his five. After the last shot he looked at her and said, "If that doesn't beat you, I'll kiss your ass in Saks' front window."

"Side bet?" she asked before the deputy reeled in the targets. "I got fifty bucks that says I win this round. And don't give me any shit about anything else."

"All right," he said. "Fifty."

Dick pulled in the targets and whistled. "I'll have to count these careful," he said.

All ten shots were deep in the black. Dick spread the targets on a workbench and started counting, Lily and Lucas looking over his shoulder.

"Wait a minute," Lucas started, when the deputy wrote down an eight.

"Not a fuckin' word," Lily said, pointing her finger at Lucas' nose.

The deputy added up the totals, turned to Lucas and said, "You owe the lady fifty bucks. I count it forty-seven to forty-six."

"Bullshit. Let me see those. . . ."

Lucas counted them forty-eight to forty-seven. He took two twenties and a ten out of his wallet and handed them to her.

"This pisses me off," he said, his voice tight.

"I hope being pissed off doesn't make your hand shake," she said sweetly.

"It won't," he promised.

Lucas shot first on the third round. All five shots felt good, and he turned to her and nodded. "If you beat me this time, you deserve it. This time, I got the fifty."

"We'll see," she said.

She fired her five and they followed Dick down to the targets. He shook his head. "Jesus. You guys . . ."

He took five minutes to count, then glanced at Lily. "I think he's got you, Lily, Lieutenant. Either one point or two . . ."

"Let me see that. . . ."

Lily went over the targets, counting, her lips moving as she totaled them up. "I don't believe it," she grunted. "I shoot two of the worst rounds of my fuckin' career and you take me out by a point."

Lucas was grinning. "I'll collect tonight," he said.

She peered at him for a second, then said, "Double or nothing. One round, five shots."

Lucas thought about it. "I'm happy where I'm at."

"Yeah, maybe, but the question is, Are you greedy enough to go for more? And do you have the balls for it?" Lily said.

"I'm happy," he repeated.

"Think how happy you'll be if you win."

Lucas looked at her for a moment, then said, "One shot. Just one. Double or nothing."

"You're on," she said. "You shoot first."

Dick sent down a new target sheet. When he was out of

the way, Lucas lined up in a one-handed bull's-eye–shooter's stance, brought the P7 up once, lowered it, scratched his forehead, brought the gun up again, let out half a breath and fired.

"That's a good one," he said to her.

"I thought you shot practical."

"Most of the time," he said. Then he added, innocently, "But I was really better at bull's-eye."

She took her two-handed stance and squeezed off the shot. "A hair to the left."

"I win, then."

"We ought to look." They looked. Lucas' shot wiped out the 10 ring. Lily's shot counted nine. "God damn it," she said.

Outside the precinct station, it was already getting dark. They turned a corner into the parking lot and were alone for a moment.

"Well," she said.

He took in her big dark eyes and the heavy breasts beneath her tweed jacket, looked down at her and shook his head. "Later."

"God damn it, Davenport . . ." But Lucas was already popping open the door to the car. They were back at the surveillance post in fifteen minutes, Lily stewing.

"Anything?" Lucas asked, as they stepped into the surveillance room. The FBI man's camp stool had disappeared.

"Quiet as death," said one of the cops. Del was still asleep. "Who won?"

"He did," Lily said grimly. "Two points out of a hundred and fifty."

"All right," said the heavier of the two cops. He held out his hand and the other cop gave him a dollar.

"A whole fuckin' dollar?" Lucas said. "I'm impressed."

The street was absolutely empty. At times it seemed as though an hour passed between cars. Sloan stopped by, watched an hour and finally said, ' Why don't you get a portable and come down to King's Place. My wife is gonna meet me there. It's about two minutes away."

"What is it?" Lily asked.

"Tex-Mex cowboy-lumberjack bar down on Hennepin. They don't allow fights, they've got a band and terrific tacos, three for a dollar," Sloan said.

"Food," said Lily.

Lily expected Lucas to collect at the car, in the dark, but he walked around her again.

"Jesus, you're an asshole sometimes," she said.

"You're so impatient," he said. "Why can't you relax?"

"I want to pay off and be done."

"We got plenty of time," he said. "We got all night."

"In a pig's eye we got all night," she said.

The bar had thirty-pound muskies and deer heads on the wall, a stuffed black bear in the entrance and a wooden cactus in the middle of a room full of picnic tables. A three-piece Mexican rock band banged away in a corner, and pitchers of Schmidt beer went for two dollars.

Sloan got things rolling by ordering a round of pitchers, which only Lily thought was excessive. The band came on with a south-of-the-border version of "Little Deuce Coupe."

"Let's dance," Lucas said, pulling Lily away from her tacos and pitcher. "Come on, they're playing rock 'n' roll." Lucas danced with Lily and then with the wife of a local cowboy while the cowboy danced with Lily. Then Lily danced with Sloan, and Lucas with a tall single woman whose beehive hairdo had just begun to topple, while Sloan's wife danced with the cowboy. Then they did it again. Lily was giggling when she finally got back to the table. Lucas waved at the waitress and pointed at Lily's pitcher.

" 'Nother round, all the way," Lucas called.

"You're trying to get me drunk, Davenport," Lily said. Her voice was clear, but her eyes were moving too much. "It'll probably work."

Sloan laughed immoderately and started on the second round.

At midnight, they checked the surveillance room. Nothing. Both of Hood's roommates were home. The lights were out. At one o'clock, they checked again. Nothing.

"So what do you want to do?" Lucas asked when King's closed.

"I dunno. I guess you better take me back to the hotel. I doubt he'd be driving this late."

Lucas pulled the Porsche into the hotel parking lot and hopped out.

"Time to collect?" Lily asked.

"Yeah."

A half-dozen people were walking through the lot, and more were going in and out.

"This is not an invitation, so I don't want you to read anything into it. . . ."

"Yeah?"

"You can come up for just long enough to collect."

They rode up in the elevator without speaking and walked down the hall to her room, Lucas feeling increasingly awkward. Inside, when she closed the door, it was dark. Lucas fumbled for the light switch but she caught his hand and said, "Don't. Just collect and then you can leave."

"All of a sudden, I feel like a fuckin' idiot," Lucas said, abashed.

"Let's get it over with," she said, a little drunkenly.

He found her in the dark, pulled her in and kissed her. She hung in his arms for just a fraction of a moment, then returned the kiss, powerfully, pushing him against the door, her face and pelvis pressed to his, her hands clenching his rib cage. They clung together for a long moment; then she broke her lips away and squeezed him tighter and groaned, "Oh, Jesus."

Lucas held her for a moment and then whispered in her ear, "Double or nothing," and found her lips again and they walked in a tight little circle and Lucas felt the bed hit the back of his knees and he dropped on it, pulling her with him. He expected her to resist, but she did not. She rolled to one side and held him, kissing him again on the lips, then on the edge of the jaw, and Lucas rolled over half on top of her and pulled at her shirt, getting it out of her trousers, slipping his hand inside, fighting the brassiere, finally reaching around her, unsnapping the bra and then catching one of her breasts in his hand. . . .

"Oh, God," she said, arching against him. "God, Davenport . . ."

He found her belt, pulled it open, slipped his hand inside her trousers, under the edge of her underpants, down, to the hot liquid center. . . .

"Ah, Jesus," she said, and she rolled away from him, pushing his hand away, off the side of the bed onto the floor.

"What?" It was pitch black in the room, and Lucas was groggy from the sudden struggle. "Lily . . ."

"God, Lucas, we can't. . . . I'm sorry, I don't mean to tease. Jesus, I'm sorry."

"Lily . . ."

"Lucas, you're going to make me cry, go away. . . ."

"Jesus, don't do that." Lucas stood up, pushed his shirt back in his pants, discovered he was missing a shoe. He groped in the dark for a second, found the light. Lily was sitting on the floor on the far side of the bed, clutching her shirt around her.

"I'm sorry," she said. Her eyes were black with remorse. "I just can't."

"That's okay," Lucas said, trying to catch his breath. He half laughed. "My fuckin' shoe is missing. . . ."

Lily, her face drawn, looked around the edge of the bed and said, "Under the curtain. Behind you."

"Okay. Got it."

"I'm sorry."

"Look, Lily, whatever is right, okay? I mean, I'm going back home to blow my brains out, to relieve the pressure, but don't worry about it."

She smiled a tentative smile. "You're a nice guy. See you tomorrow."

"Sure. If I survive."

When he was gone, Lily stripped off her clothes and stood in the shower, letting the water pour down her breasts and then her back. After a few minutes, she began reducing the temperature until finally she stood in what felt like a torrent of ice water.

Sober, she went to bed. And just before she went to sleep,

she remembered that last shot. Had she flinched? Or had she deliberately thrown the shot?

Lily Rothenburg, faithful wife, went to sleep with lust in her heart.

CHAPTER
10

The knock came a few minutes after ten o'clock. Sam Crow was washing a coffee cup in the kitchen sink. He stopped at the knock and looked up. Aaron Crow was sitting in front of a battered Royal typewriter, pecking at a press release on the Oklahoma killing. Shadow Love was in the bathroom. When the knock came, Aaron went to the door and spoke through it.

"Who is that?"

"Billy."

Billy. Aaron fumbled at the lock, pulled the door open. Billy Hood stood in the hallway, bowlegged in his cowboy boots, a battered, water-stained Stetson perched on his head. His square face was drawn and pale. He took a step forward and Aaron wrapped his arms around him and picked him up off his feet.

"God damn, Billy," he said. He could feel the stone knife dangling beneath Billy's shirt.

"I feel bad, man," Billy said when Aaron released him. "Man, I've been fucked up all the way back. I can't stop thinking about it."

"Because you're a spiritual man."

"I don't feel so fuckin' spiritual. I cut that dude," Billy

said as he walked farther into the room. Aaron glanced once into the hallway and pushed the door shut.

"A white man," said Aaron.

"A man," Shadow Love said from the bathroom. He stood squarely in the doorway, arms slightly away from his sides, like a gunslinger. His cheeks were hollow. His white eyes hooked up at the corners, like a starving wolf's. "Don't make it sound small."

"I don't mean that it's small," said Aaron. "I mean that it's different. Billy killed the enemy in a war."

"A man is a man," Shadow Love insisted. "It's all the same."

"And an Indian man is an Indian man, and that's different, to be one of the people," Sam retorted. "One reason Aaron won't use you is that you don't understand the difference between war and murder."

The two Crows were squared off against their son. Hood broke it.

"Everybody's looking for me," he said. Billy looked scared, like a rabbit that's been chased until there's no more room to run. "Me and Leo. Christ, I heard about Leo and the judge. He took him off, man. Have you heard from him?"

"No. We're getting worried. They haven't got him, but we haven't heard a thing."

"Unless they've got him but they aren't saying, so they can squeeze him," said Shadow Love.

"I don't think so. This is too big to hide something like that," Sam Crow said.

Billy took off his hat, tossed it on a chair and wiped his hair back with his hand. "We've been on the radio every hour. In all the newspapers all the way from New York. Every town I come to."

"They don't know your names," Sam said.

"They connected us with Tony Bluebird. They'll be looking for us here in the Cities."

"That won't help them if they don't know who you are, Billy," said Aaron, trying to reassure him. "There are twenty thousand Indians in the Cities. How will they know which one? And we knew they'd connect you to Bluebird; that was the whole point."

"They'll find out who you are," Shadow Love said. His voice was gravelly, cold. He looked at the Crows. "It's time for you guys to go to the safe house, get out of this place. If you want to live."

"Too early," said Sam. "When we feel some pressure, we go to the safe house. Not before. If we go in too early and there's nothing happening, we'll get careless. We'll fuck around and somebody will see us."

"And they still don't have any names, nothing that will identify Billy or Leo," Aaron said again.

Shadow Love stepped out into the room and put a hand on Billy Hood's shoulder, ignoring his fathers. "I'll tell you now: They'll find your name. And they'll find Leo's. Eventually, they'll get the rest of us. They've got some movies from a camera in the building where you killed Andretti, so they've got your face. The cops'll take the pictures and go around and squeeze and squeeze, and somebody will tell them. And there was a witness who saw Leo. They'll have her looking at mug shots right now."

"You're a big authority?" Aaron asked sarcastically. "You know all the rules?"

"I know enough," Shadow Love said. His eyes were white and opaque, like marble chips from a tombstone. "I've been on the street since I was seven. I know how the cops work. They pick-pick-pick, talk-talk-talk. They'll find out."

"You don't know that. . . ."

"Don't be an old woman, Father," Shadow Love snapped. "It's dangerous." He held the older man's eyes for a moment, then turned back to Billy. "Somebody will tell. Somebody will tell on us all, sooner or later. I met one of the cops doing the investigation. He's a hunter, you can smell it on him. He'll be after us, and he's not some South Dakota sheriff's cousin, some retreaded shitkicker calling himself a cop. He's a hard man. And even if he doesn't get us, somebody will. Sooner or later. Everyone in this room is a dead man walking."

Billy Hood looked into Shadow Love's face for a moment, then nodded and seemed to grow taller. "You're right," he said, his voice suddenly calm. "I should do another while I can. Before they get me."

Sam clapped him on the back. "Good. We have a target."

"Where's John? Is he out?"

"Yeah. Out in Brookings."

"Ah, Jesus, he's going after Linstad?"

"Yup."

"That's a big one," Billy said. He ran his hand through his hair. "I gotta get home, get some sleep. Maybe I'll go up north and see Ginnie and the girl, you know? Tomorrow or the day after."

"Come on down to the river with us," Sam suggested. "We're doing a sweat. You'll feel a hundred percent better afterwards. We got some bags too, and a couple of tents. You can sleep out on the island."

"All right," Billy nodded. "My ass is whipped, man. . . ."

"And we've got to talk about a man in Milwaukee," said Sam. "The guy who's figuring the strategy for attacking the land rights up north. Smart guy . . ."

"I don't know if I can do the knife again, man. This Andretti guy, the blood was coming out of his neck like a hose." Billy sounded shaky again and Sam stopped him with a wave of his hand.

"The knife is good because it means something to the people and something to the media," he said, "But it's not the main thing. In Milwaukee, use a pistol. Use a rifle. The important thing is to kill the guy."

Aaron nodded. "Wear the knife around your neck. If you're taken, that'll be good enough."

"I won't be taken," Billy said. His voice was trembling and low, but he held it together. "If I can't get away, I'll go like Bluebird."

They talked for another fifteen minutes while Aaron gathered up the dried sage and red willow he used in the sweats. Sam couldn't sleep without a pillow, so he got one off the bed. They were walking out the door when the phone rang.

Aaron picked it up, said hello, listened a second, smiled and said, "Leo, God damn. We were worried. . . ."

Leo Clark was calling from Wichita. Oklahoma City was

a war zone, he said. The police and the FBI were crawling through the Indian community. He'd gotten out of town immediately after the killing, hidden at a friend's house the next day, gotten a haircut and then driven to Wichita.

"What's happening there?" Leo asked.

"Not much. But there are FBI agents all over the place. So it's just a matter of time. . . ."

"I wish we'd hear . . ."

"The media's talking about *war,* so we got that across."

"Gotta keep pumping . . ."

"Yeah. Tell me what the judge said just before you took him," Aaron said. He listened intently and finally said, "Okay. I'm going to put some of that in the press release, so they'll know it's for real . . . and I'll put in a quote from you, like we agreed."

They talked for another minute and then Aaron hung up. "He's on his way in," he said. "He cut his hair. No more braids."

"Too bad," said Sam. "That boy had a good hair on him."

"No more. He's got sidewalls and a flattop," Aaron Crow said, chuckling. "He says he looks like a fuckin' Marine."

The sweat lodge was on the island below Fort Snelling, at the junction of the Minnesota and Mississippi, on the ground that held Sioux bones from the death camp. Aaron Crow could feel them there, still crying, tearing his flesh like fishhooks. Sam Crow held him, fearing that his other half would die of a burst heart. Billy Hood prayed and sweated, prayed and sweated, until the fear and anguish of the Andretti kill ran out of him into the ground. Shadow Love glowered in the heat, watching the others. He felt the bones in the ground, but he never prayed a word.

Long after midnight, they sat on the edge of the river, watching the water roll by. Billy lit a cigarette with a Zippo lighter, took a drag.

"Killing a man is a lot harder than I thought. It's not *doing it* that's so hard. It's afterwards. Doing it, it's like cutting the head off a chicken with a hatchet. You just do it. Later, thinking about it, I got the sweats."

"You think too much," said Shadow Love. "I've killed

three. The feeling isn't bad; it's pretty good, really. You win. You send another one of them assholes straight to hell."

"You killed three?" Aaron said sharply. "I know two. One in South Dakota, one in Los Angeles: the drug man and the Nazi."

"There's another one now," Shadow Love said. "I put his body into the river below the Lake Street bridge." He gestured at the river. "He may be floating past right now, while we smoke."

The Crows looked at each other, and a tear ran down Aaron's face. Sam reached out and thumbed it away.

"Why?" Aaron asked his son.

"Because he was a traitor."

"You mean he was one of the people?" Aaron's voice rose in fear and anguish.

"A traitor," Shadow Love said. "He put the police on Bluebird."

Aaron was on his feet, his hands at the sides of his head, pressing together. "No, no no no no . . ."

"Yellow Hand he was, from Fort Thompson," Shadow Love said.

"I can hear the bones," Aaron groaned. "Yellow Hand's people were free warriors. They died for us and now we have killed one of theirs. They are screaming at us. . . ."

Shadow Love stood and spit into the river. "A man is a fuckin' man and that's all," he said. "Just a fuckin' piece of meat. I'm trying to keep you free and you won't even give me that."

Billy Hood never could get his head quite right in the borrowed sleeping bag. After a difficult night, he woke well before dawn with a crick in his neck. While the Crows and Shadow Love slept, he crawled out of the tent and lit the Coleman lantern, moved quietly into the woods, dug a cathole and used it. When he finished, he kicked dirt in the hole and started collecting wood.

A jungle of dead trees stood along the waterline. Hood gathered a dozen limbs as long and thick as his forearm and hauled them back to the campsite. Using twigs and finger-thick sticks, he built a foot-high tepee-shaped starter fire, fanned it, waited until it was going good, then stacked on the heavier wood and topped the structure with a steel grate. The Crows kept a blue enameled-steel coffeepot in their truck, with a jar of instant coffee inside. He got it, filled the pot with water from a jug, dumped in what looked like enough coffee and put it on the grate.

"God damn." Aaron Crow, moving. "Nothing smells as good as cookout coffee."

"Got a couple of quarts of it out here," Billy said.

Aaron crawled out of the tent, wearing a V-necked T-shirt and green boxer shorts. "Cups in the cooler, in the back of the truck," he said.

Billy nodded and went to get them. Aaron looked toward the east, but there was no sign of the sun. He sniffed and the air smelled like morning, redolent of dew and river mud and boiling coffee. When Billy returned, Sam and Shadow Love were stirring.

"John ought to be in Brookings by now," Billy said.

"Yeah." Aaron handled the coffeepot off the fire with a hot pad and poured two cups. "So what are you going to do?"

"Go home, get cleaned up, maybe catch a few more hours of sleep, then go on up to Bemidji and see Ginnie and the kid. I'll give you a call," Billy said.

"Did you think about Milwaukee?" Aaron asked.

"All night." Billy took a sip of the scalding coffee, looking at Aaron over the rim of the cup. "I think I can handle it. The sweat helped."

Aaron looked back at the sweat lodge. "Sweats always help. Sweats'd cure cancer, if they'd give them a chance."

Billy nodded, but after a moment he said, "Don't seem to help Shadow. No offense, Aaron, but that boy is one crazy motherfucker."

CHAPTER

11

The phone woke Lucas a few minutes before six.

"Davenport," he groaned.

"This is Del. Billy Hood just walked into his building."

Lucas sat up: "You made him for sure?"

"No question, man. It's him. He pulled up, hopped out and went inside before we could move. You better get your ass over here."

"Did you call Lily?" Lucas put a finger behind his bedroom curtain and looked out. Still dark.

"She's next on the list."

"I'll call her. You call Daniel. . . ."

"Already did. He said go with the plan, like we talked," Del said.

"How about the feebs?"

"The guy here called his AIC."

Lily answered on the third ring, her voice croaking like a rusty gate.

"You awake?" Lucas asked.

"What do you want, Davenport?"

"I thought I'd call and see if you were lying there naked."

"Jesus Christ, are you nuts? What time . . . ?"

"Billy Hood just rolled into his apartment."

"What?"

"I'll pick you up outside your hotel in ten minutes. Ten to fifteen. Brush your teeth, take a shower, run downstairs. . . ."

"Ten minutes," she said.

Lucas showered, brushed, pulled on jeans, a sweatshirt and a cotton jacket, and was outside five minutes after he talked to Lily. Rush hour was beginning: he punched the Porsche down Cretin Avenue, driving mostly on the wrong side of the street, jumping one red light and stretching a couple of greens. He put the car on I-94 and made it to Lily's hotel twelve minutes after he had hung up the phone. She was walking out of the lobby doors when he pulled in.

"No question about the ID?" she snapped.

"No." He looked at her. "You're a little pale."

"Too early. And I'm a little queasy. I thought about stopping in the coffee shop for a roll, but I thought I better not," she said. Her voice was all business. She wouldn't meet his eye.

"You had a few last night."

"A few too many. I appreciate . . . you know."

"You were hot," Lucas said bluntly, but with a smile.

She blushed, furious. "Christ, Davenport, give me a break?"

"No."

"I shouldn't be riding with you," she said, looking out the window.

"You wanted to roll, last night. You backed out. I can live with it. The big question is . . ."

"What?"

"Can you?"

She looked at him and her voice carried an edge of disdain. "Ah, the Great Lover speaks. . . ."

"Great Lover, bullshit," Lucas said. "You were hungry. That didn't develop since you met me."

"I happen to be . . ." she started.

". . . very happily married," they said in unison.

"I want you pretty bad," Lucas said after a moment. "I feel like I'm smothering."

"Jesus, I don't know about this," she said, looking away.

Lucas touched her on the forearm. "If you really . . . rule it out completely . . . we probably ought to hang out with different people. . . ."

She didn't say she ruled anything out. She did change the subject.

"So why didn't they take Hood when he pulled in? Was it like they thought . . ."

A half-dozen detectives and the FBI agent were waiting in the surveillance apartment when Lucas and Lily arrived. Del took them aside. He was wide-awake.

"Okay. Talked to Daniel, we all agreed. We wait until the baker leaves for his job. He leaves at seven-thirty, twenty minutes of eight, something like that."

Lucas glanced at his watch. Six-twenty.

"The other guy, the lifter, we can't tell when he leaves," Del continued. "The super says that some days he's out of there by nine, other days he sleeps 'til noon. We can't wait that long. We figure that if Hood comes in at six, he's probably pretty beat. Maybe driving all night. Anyway, there's a good chance he's asleep. So we call it this way: We go in and cut their phone, just in case somebody else in the building is with them. Then we put an entry team in the hall, four guys, and stick a microphone on the door. Listen awhile. See who's up. Then, when the baker opens the door to come out, we grab him and boom—we're in."

"Jesus, if Hood's awake and has the gun handy . . ."

"He'd hardly have time to get at it," Del said confidently. "You know that Jack Dionosopoulos guy, that big Greek with the ERU? Used to play ball at St. Thomas?"

"Yeah." Lucas nodded.

"He's going in first, bare hands. If Hood's there with a gun in his hand, we got no choice. Jack goes down and the second man takes Hood with the shotgun. If there's no gun showing, Jack takes him down. If he can't see him, he hits the bedroom. Just fucking jumps him, pins him. Hood's not that big a guy. . . ."

"Fuckin' Jack, he's taking a chance. . . ."

"He's all armored up. He thinks he's back at St. Thomas."

"I don't know," Lucas said. "It's your call, but it sounds like Jack might have played too long without a helmet."

"He did it before. Same deal. Gang guy, needed him to talk. He had a gun in his belt when Jack went in. He never had a chance to pull it. Jack was on him like holy on the pope."

"So we sit some more," Lily said, peering through the venetian blinds at the apartment across the street.

"Not here," Del said. "We sent your drawing of the apartment down to the ERU—they're staging in the garage of that Amoco station three blocks up. We need you to go down there and talk to them about the apartment."

"All right," said Lucas. "If anything happens, call."

"Del's pretty sharp for this time in the morning," Lily said on the way down to the ERU meeting.

"Uh." Lucas glanced at her.

"He's maybe got his nose in the evidence? He was sleeping so hard yesterday it kinda looked like a chemical crash."

Lucas shook his head. "No coke," he muttered.

"Something?"

Lucas shrugged. "There're some stories," his voice still low. "He maybe does a black beauty from time to time."

"Like once a fuckin' hour," she said under her breath.

The ERU felt like a ball team. They were psyched, already on their toes, talking with the distracted air of a team already focusing on the game. The apartment diagram had been laid out on plastic board with a black marker. The Polaroid photos Lucas had shot in the apartment were Scotch-taped to one side. He spent a few minutes spotting chairs, sofas, tables, rugs.

"What kind of rug is that? Is that loose?" Dionosopoulos asked. "I don't want to run in there and fall on my ass."

"That's what you did at St. Thomas," one of the other ERU men said.

"Fuck you and all pagan Lutherans," Dionosopoulos said casually. "What about the rug, Lucas?"

"It's small, that's all I can tell you. I don't know, I'd say be careful, you could slide. . . ."

"It's one of those old fake Persian carpets, you know, you can see the threads," said Lily. "I think it'd slide."

"Okay."

"Lucas?" One of the other team members moved up. "Del just called. He sounds weird, man, but he says to get your ass back to the surveillance post. Like instantly."

"What do you mean, 'weird'?" Lucas asked.

"He was whispering, man. On the radio . . ."

Del met them in the hallway outside the apartment. His eyes looked like white plastic poker chips.

"What?" asked Lucas.

"The feds are here. They've got an entry team on the way in."

"What?" Lucas brushed past him into the apartment. The Minneapolis agent-in-charge was standing by the window, next to the FBI surveillance man. Both were wearing radio headsets and looking across the street.

"What the fuck is going on?" Lucas asked.

"Who are you?" the AIC asked, his voice cold.

"Davenport, lieutenant, Minneapolis Police. We've got this scene wrapped. . . ."

"It's not your scene anymore, Lieutenant. If you doubt that, I suggest you call your chief—"

"We got guys on the street," a Minneapolis surveillance man suddenly blurted. "We got guys on the street."

"Motherfucker," Del said, "motherfucker . . ."

Lucas looked through the slats of the venetian blind. Lily was at his shoulder. There were six men on the street, two in long coats, four in body armor. Three of the men in armor and one man in a coat were climbing the stoop into the apartment building; the other man in a coat waited at the base of the steps, while the last man in armor posted himself at the corner of the building. One of the men on the steps showed a shotgun just before going inside. The man in the coat turned and looked at the surveillance post. Kieffer.

"Oh, no, no," Lily said, "He's got an AVON, they're gonna hit the door with AVONs."

"It'll never fall, man," Lucas said urgently to the AIC. "The door's a solid chunk of oak. Call them down, man, it'll never fall."

"What?" The AIC couldn't sort it out, and Lily said, "The door won't fall to AVONs."

Lucas turned and ran out of the apartment and down the hall to the front door of the building. He could hear Del chanting, *Motherfuckers, motherfuckers . . .*"

Lucas crashed through the front door, startling the FBI man on the street. The agent made a move toward his hip and Lucas swerved, screaming "No, no . . ."

There was a boom, then a second and a third, not sharp reports, but a hollow, echoing *boom-boom-boom,* as though someone in the distance were pounding a timpani. Lucas stopped, waiting, one second, two, three; then another *boom, boom . . .* And then a pistol, a sharper sound, nastier, with an edge, six, seven rounds, then a pause, then an odd cracking explosion . . .

"Minneapolis cops," Lucas shouted to the FBI man at the base of the stairs. Lily was with him now and they crossed the street. The FBI man had one hand out at them, but with the series of pistol shots he turned and looked at the building.

"Get out of the fuckin' street, dummy," Lucas screamed. "That's fuckin' Hood with the pistol. If he comes to the window, you're a dead sonofabitch."

Lucas and Lily crossed the sidewalk to the building until they were standing behind the stoop. The FBI man came over and stood with them, his pistol out now. There was shouting in the hallway.

"They got him," the agent said, looking at them. He sounded unsure.

"Bullshit," said Lily. "They never got inside. If you got a radio, you better call the paramedics, because it sounds like Hood sprayed the place. . . ."

The building door popped open and Kieffer, in a crouch, his gun drawn, stepped down onto the stoop.

"What's happening, what's happening?" shouted the armored agent on the corner.

"Back it off, back it off," Kieffer shouted. "He's got hostages."

"You dumb sonofabitch, Kieffer . . ." Lucas shouted.

"Get out of here, Davenport, this is a federal crime scene."

"Fuck you, asshole. . . ."

"I'll arrest your ass, Davenport."

"Come down here and you can arrest me for kicking a federal agent's ass, 'cause I will," Lucas shouted back. "You dumb cocksucker . . ."

The federal entry team and the Minneapolis teams stabilized the area and hustled the other tenants out of the apartment building and adjacent buildings. The city's hostage negotiator set up a mobile phone to call Hood.

When Lucas and Lily returned to the surveillance apartment, Daniel was talking with the AIC and Sloan was leaning against the apartment wall, listening.

". . . go on television and explain exactly what happened," Daniel was droning piously. "We've had substantial experience with this type of situation, we had the scene cleared and stable, we had an excellent action plan prepared by our best officers. Suddenly, with no coordination and without proper intelligence—intelligence that we had: we knew that door wouldn't fall to AVONs, which is one reason we didn't try them—suddenly, an FBI team takes jurisdiction and promptly launches what I can only describe as a rash action, which not only endangered the lives of many police officers and innocent people in adjoining apartments, but also jeopardizes the chances of capturing Bill Hood alive, and cracking this terrible conspiracy which has taken the lives of so many people. . . ."

"It should have worked," the AIC said bitterly.

Daniel discarded his pious-preacher voice and turned hard. "Bullshit. You know, I never would have believed you'd have tried this. I thought you were too smart. If you'd come in with your team, taken some time, talked it over, we could have done a joint operation and you would have gotten the credit. The way it happened . . . I ain't taking the rap."

"Could I get everybody out of here? Just for a minute," the AIC asked loudly. "Everybody?"

"Lucas, you stay," Daniel said.

When the other cops were gone, the AIC looked briefly at Lucas, then turned to Daniel.

"You need a witness?"

"Never hurts," Daniel said.

"So what do you want?"

"I don't know. I'll probably want your seal of approval and some active lobbying on a half-dozen federal law-enforcement-assistance grant applications . . ."

"No problem . . ."

". . . and a line into your files. When I call you on something, I want what you got and no bullshit."

"Jesus Christ, Daniel."

"You can write me a letter to that effect."

"Nothing on paper . . ."

"If there's nothing on paper, there's no deal."

The AIC was sweating. He could have had a coup. He was now in charge of a disaster. "All right," he said finally. "I gotta trust you."

"Hey, we've always been friends," Daniel offered, slapping the FBI man on the back.

"Fuck that," said the AIC, wrenching away. "That fuckin' Clay. He's calling me every fifteen minutes, screaming for action. He's coming here, you know. He'll have that fuckin' gun in his armpit, the asshole."

"I feel for you," Daniel said.

"I don't give a shit about that," the AIC said. "Just find something that'll get me off the hook."

"I think we can do that," Daniel said. He glanced at Lucas. "We'll say that Minneapolis made the call and we decided to use FBI experts to attempt an entry. When that couldn't be accomplished, we went to an alternate plan that used city officers to negotiate a surrender."

"The fuckin' TV'll never buy it," the agent said unhappily.

"If we both agree, what choice have they got?"

• • •

Del, Lily and Sloan were standing together in the hallway when Lucas and Daniel left the surveillance apartment.

"What'd we do?" Del asked.

"A deal," Daniel said.

"I hope you got a lot," Del said.

"We did all right, as long as we can pull Hood out of there," Daniel said.

"Maybe this wasn't a time to deal," Sloan suggested. "Maybe this was a time to tell it like it is."

Daniel shook his head. "You always deal," he said.

"Always," said Lucas.

Lily and Del nodded and Sloan shrugged.

Hood had fired seven shots with a big-bore pistol through the oak door after the molded-compound AVON rounds had failed to blow it open. When they saw that the door wasn't going to fall, the agents had cleared away from it and nobody was hurt. The firing stopped, there was the odd explosion, and then silence.

Twenty minutes after the attempted entry, with Daniel still meeting with the agent-in-charge, the police hostage negotiator called Hood. Hood answered, said he wasn't coming out, but that his friends in the apartment had nothing to do with any of it.

"You know me?" he asked.

"Yeah, we've had a line on you, Billy," the negotiator said. "But that wasn't us at the door, that was another *agency*."

"The FBI . . ."

"We're just trying to get everybody out, including you, without anybody getting hurt. . . ."

"These guys in here, they didn't have anything to do with it."

"Could you send them out?"

"Yeah, but I don't want any of those white guys to snipe them. You know? The fuckin' FBIs, man, they shoot us down like dirty dogs."

"You send them out, I guarantee no harm will come to them."

"I'll ask them," Hood said. "They're scared. They're sleeping, and all of a sudden somebody tries to blow up the fuckin' apartment, you know?"

"I guarantee . . ."

"I'll ask them. You call back in two minutes." He hung up.

"What's going on?" Lucas asked. He and Lily had cut around the building to come up on the negotiator's car.

"I think he's gonna let the other two guys out."

"Just like that?"

"Just like that. He's not thinking like they're hostages."

"They're not. They're his friends."

"What happened with Daniel?" the negotiator asked.

"The feebs are out," Lucas said.

"All right."

The negotiator called back after a little more than two minutes.

"They're coming out, but they gotta come out the window. The goddamn door is all fucked up, we can't get it open," Hood said.

"All right. That's fine. Break the window, whatever you have to do."

"Tell those white boys, so they don't get sniped."

"We'll pass the word right now. Give us a minute, then send them out. And you ought to think about it too, Billy; we really don't want to do you any harm."

"Save the bullshit and pass the word not to snipe these guys," Hood said, and hung up.

"The two guys are coming out," the negotiator told the radio man next to him. "Pass the word."

As they watched, with Lucas and Lily standing beside the car, a chair sailed through the front window and broken glass was knocked out of the window frame with a broom. Then a blanket was thrown over the window ledge. The first man stood in the window, jumped the five feet to the ground and hurried down the street toward the blocking police cars. A patrolman met him as he crossed the line of cars.

Lily looked at him and shook her head. "Don't know him. Wasn't in any of the photos."

The second man followed a half-minute later, sitting on the window ledge with his legs dangling, talking back into the apartment. After a few seconds, he shrugged, hopped down and walked to the police line. The negotiator got back on the phone.

"Billy? Billy? Talk to me, man. Talk to me. . . . Come on, Billy, you know that's not right. That was the FBI, we cleared those fuckers out of here. . . . I know, I know. . . . No, bullshit, I don't do that and the men here don't do that. You tell me one time . . . Billy? Billy?" He shook his head and dropped the receiver to his lap. "Fuck it, he hung up."

"What's he say?" Lily asked.

"He says us white boys are going to snipe him," the negotiator said. The negotiator, who was burly and black, smiled and picked up the phone and started dialing again. "He's probably right, fuckin' white boys with guns."

The line was busy.

"Where's that file Anderson made?" the negotiator asked his radio man. The radio man passed a notebook. "Call the phone company, tell them what's happening and ask them to check the number, see where the call's going."

"Check his family," Lucas suggested. "There oughta be a phone number."

The negotiator found the Bemidji number in Anderson's notebook, dialed it, found it busy. "That's it," he said. "We ought to have somebody get onto the sheriff's office up there, get them to go see his wife. We might want to talk to her. We can get her to call here, and then switch her in, so we can hear what they're saying."

A plainclothes cop hurried up. "One of the roommates says that Hood tried to fire a rifle and it blew up on him. He's hurt. He's got a cut on his face, he's bleeding. The roommate doesn't think it's too bad."

Lucas looked at Lily, and Lily grinned and nodded.

Five minutes later, the negotiator got through again.

"You can't get out, Billy. All that's gonna happen is that somebody's gonna get hurt. We'll get you a lawyer, free, we'll get you . . . Fuck."

"Try his wife?" Lucas suggested.

"How about those two guys who came out?" asked Lily. "Maybe they'd help. . . ."

Kieffer drifted up to the car. "I thought you were out of here," Lucas said, standing to confront him.

"We're observing," Kieffer said bitterly.

"Observe my ass." Lucas stood directly in front of Kieffer, their chests almost touching.

"Fuckin' touch me, Davenport," Kieffer said. "I'll have your ass in jail. . . ."

"I'll touch you," Lily said, pushing between them. Lucas reluctantly gave a step. "You gonna put me in jail for assault? I'm not so polite as these Minneapolis assholes, Kieffer, and I don't have to honor any of Daniel's deals. I can go talk to the TV on my own."

"Fuck it," Kieffer said, stepping back. "I'm observing."

The negotiator tried again, spoke longer this time. "You can trust us. . . . Wait a minute, let me talk to a guy. . . ."

He finally turned to Lucas, covered the mouthpiece on the phone and said, "You know any Indians?"

"A few."

"You want to try him? He's scared. Mention these people you know. . . ."

Lucas took the phone. "Billy Hood. This is Lucas Davenport from the Minneapolis cops. Listen, you know Dick Yellow Hand, a friend of Bluebird's? Or Chief Dooley, the barber? Do you know Earl and Betty May? They're friends of mine, man. They'd be worried about you. I'm worried about you. There's nothing you can do in there. You'll just get hurt. If you come out, you'll be okay. I swear."

There was another moment of silence. Then Hood said, "You know Earl and Betty?"

"Yeah, man. You could call them. They'd tell you I'm okay."

"You white?"

"Yeah, yeah, but I don't want to hurt anybody. Come on out, Billy. I swear to God nobody wants to shoot at you. Walk on out and we can all go home."

"Let me think, man. Let me think, okay?"

"Okay, Billy." The line went dead.

"What?" Lucas asked the negotiator, who had been listening on a headset.

"He may be calling these people. Earl and Betty, was that their names?"

"Yeah. Just about everybody knows them."

"We'll give him two minutes and try again."

Two minutes later, the line was busy. After three, they got through. The negotiator said a few words, then handed the phone to Lucas.

"Is this the guy who knows Earl and Betty?" Hood asked.

"Yeah. Davenport," Lucas said.

"I'll come out, but I want you to come up here and get me. If I just come outside, one of those white boys is gonna snipe me."

"No, they won't, Billy. . . . Listen . . ." Lucas hunched over the phone.

"Bullshit, man, don't bullshit me. Those guys been against me for a long time. Ever since I was born, man. They're just waiting. I got nothing against you, so you'd be safe. You want me out, you come up here."

Lucas looked at the negotiator. "What do you think?"

"He killed the guy in New York," the negotiator said. "He tried to kill the FBI team."

"He had a reason. Maybe he really wants the protection."

"He's scared," the negotiator agreed.

"What are you going to do?" Hood asked.

"Hold on a minute, we're talking," Lucas said. He looked at Lily. "There might not be any other way to take him alive."

"You'd be nuts to go in there," Lily objected. "We've got him. Sooner or later he's got to come out and nobody has to get hurt. Nobody out here . . ."

"We need to talk to him."

"I don't need to talk to him," she said. "I just need him any way we can get him. Dead or alive."

"You don't care if we get the rest of the group?" Lucas asked.

"Sure. Theoretically. But Hood's my man. After he's taken care of, the rest is up to you and the feebs."

Kieffer had been standing back from the car, looking down the street at the apartment. "It'd take some balls to go in there," he said.

His tone was ambiguous, as if he weren't sure that Lucas would do it.

"Hey, we aren't talking balls here," the negotiator said, anger in his voice.

"Yeah, what the fuck did that crack mean, Kieffer?" Lily asked, turning to Kieffer with her hands on her hips.

"Take it easy," Lucas said, waving them off. He didn't look at Kieffer but stared past the negotiator at the apartment window. With the glass broken out, it was a black square in the red stone. "I'll give it a try."

"God damn it, Davenport, you're crazy," Lily said. But then she said, "Talk to him through the window. Don't go inside, just talk over the ledge."

Lucas got back on the phone. "Billy? I'm ready, man."

"Well, come on."

"You're not bullshitting me?"

"I'm not, I just don't want one of them white boys to snipe me, man."

"They see him from across the street. They got a gun on him. He's halfway up into the room," the radio man said quietly, as he listened on his headset. "Del says that when you get up there, if he tries anything, you drop below the window; we'll hose him down."

"Okay." Lucas glanced at Lily, nodded and said into the phone, "I'm stepping out, Billy. I'm down the street, way to your right as you look out the window."

"Come on, man. This is getting old."

Lucas stepped out from behind the car, his hands held wide and open at shoulder height.

"Okay, man," he yelled at the window.

He walked slowly down the street, his hands wide, conscious of two dozen sets of eyes following him. The day was cool, but he could feel sweat starting on his back. A line of blue-and-white pigeons watched from a red-tiled roof down the street. On another roof, beside a chimney and out of Hood's line of sight, an ERU officer was lined up on the window with an M-16. A police radio poked unintelligible sentences into the morning air. Lucas was thirty feet out.

"Come on, man, you're okay," Hood called from the window. Lucas moved closer, his hands still away from his side. When he was five feet from the window, Hood called again. "Come straight on in. I'll be off to the left. I don't want to see no gun pointing at me, man. I'm really tight, you know?"

Lucas reached out, touched the outer wall of the building and eased up to the window. Looking in at a sharp angle, he could see nothing but a broken-down chair. He moved a little farther into the window opening. There was nobody in his line of sight. The red beanbag was squashed in the middle of the floor, with a dent in it, as though somebody had been thrown on top of it.

"I'm giving up, man," Hood said. His voice came from off to the right, but Lucas still couldn't see him. He took another step.

"I want you inside," Hood said.

"I can't do that, Billy," Lucas said.

"You're just setting me up, man. You're just making me a target. If I come to that window, I'm a dead man, aren't I?"

"I swear to God, Billy. . . ."

"You don't have to swear to God. Just get up in that window. I'll be there. I want you to go out right in front of me, man, so those white boys don't snipe me."

Lucas looked around once, muttered "Fuck it" under his breath, put his hands on the window ledge and boosted himself up. As he crawled onto the ledge, Hood was suddenly there, his back to the outer wall. He was looking at Lucas over the shotgun.

"Step in further," he said. The muzzle of the shotgun followed Lucas' head like a steel eye.

"Come on, man," Lucas said. There hadn't been any shells in the closet with the shotgun. Since Hood was using it, he either had found the shells or was bluffing with an empty weapon. Why would he bluff? He'd used a pistol of some kind, anyone would be willing to believe that the pistol was loaded. . . . "This can't do any good."

"Shut up," Hood said. He was wound tight as a spring, frightened. "Get in here."

Lucas hopped down from the window ledge.

"Did one of you wise-ass cops fuck up my rifle? You did, didn't you?"

"I don't know about a rifle," Lucas said. Hood's face was bleeding from a long cut over one eye. On the floor near his foot was a .45, the slide locked open. Out of ammo, Lucas decided.

"Pulled the trigger on that cocksucker rifle and almost blew my face off. There was a rag in it," Hood said.

"I don't know anything about that," Lucas said. He could feel the P7 pushing into his back.

"Bullshit," Hood snapped. "But I *know* you didn't know about these. . . ."

He kept the shotgun muzzle on Lucas' head but opened the hand under the shotgun's fore-end. He had two shells in his hand.

"Buckshot, for deer," Hood said. "I had them stuck in with the thirty-thirty shells. Somebody missed them, huh?"

"Bill . . ." Lucas started. Inside, he was cursing himself for not taking the .30-.30 shells, or at least checking the box. "You won't get out of here this way. . . ."

"Buckshot's no good when those fuckers out there got M-16s, but this buckshot is going to get me out of here, because I got you, white boy," he said. He gestured with the muzzle. "Lay down. On the floor."

"Billy, I trusted you, man. This is no good." Lucas felt the sweat start at his temples, felt the heat in his armpits.

"So I lied, motherfucker," Hood said. "Get the fuck down." He dipped the barrel of the shotgun an inch, to indicate *down*.

Lucas got down on his knees, thought about going for the P7, but the shotgun muzzle never wavered.

"Keep your hands away from your body. . . ."

From outside, the ERU team leader called on a loudspeaker. "You coming out? Everything okay?"

"Everything fine," Hood yelled back. "We're talking. Let us talk."

"Nothing you can do is going to help ..." Lucas started.

"On your fuckin' belly," Hood snapped.

Lucas let himself down on the floor. It smelled of city grime. Grit cut into his chin.

"I'll tell you what we're doing, so you don't fuck me up," Hood said. Sweat was pouring down his face, and Lucas could smell the fear on him. "I'm going to march you out of here with this gun. We're going to take a car and we're going down the Mississippi to the res. Someplace along the way I'll get out and get off in the woods. Once I'm in the woods, I'm gone, man."

"They'll come through with dogs. . . ."

"Let them. There'll be Indians all over the place, running them fuckin' dogs to death, man. They'll never get me out of them swamps down there." Lucas felt Hood easing up close to him; then the shotgun muzzle touched the back of his head. "Just to let you know I'm here. I want your face straight down, until I tell you different."

Lucas lay facedown, still thinking about the gun on his hip. Hood was doing something behind him, but he couldn't see what it was. There was a ripping sound and he tried tipping his face, but Hood said, "Hey," and Lucas tipped it back. "I gotta breathe," Lucas said.

"You can breathe, don't bullshit me. . . . Now you're going to feel the gun on your head. I 'spect you've got a gun and maybe you're one of them karate experts, but if you so much as jiggle, I'm going to blow your fucking brains out. . . . I got my finger on the trigger and the safety is off, you got it?"

"I got it," Lucas said.

He felt the cold touch of the muzzle on the skin behind his ear. "Now push your head back until you're looking off the floor. Look out into the kitchen, but don't move anything else but your head," Hood said. Lucas lifted his head, and a second later Hood took a quick turn of tape around his forehead, then another. Lucas gritted his teeth.

"The muzzle of the gun is taped to your head," Hood said when he had finished. His voice was a notch less tense. "If one of them white boys snipes me, you're dead. If anything happens, you're dead. A couple of pounds of pull on the trigger and you're gone, man. You know what I'm saying? Lights out." A third and fourth loop of tape overlapped the first two. The last loop partially covered Lucas' left eye. He could feel the buttons on his shirt pressing into his chest and suddenly found it hard to breathe.

"Jesus Christ, man, be careful," he said, struggling to keep a whine out of his voice.

"You just be cool, man. . . . Now get up."

Lucas got to his hands and knees and shakily stood up. The muzzle of the gun stayed with him, behind his right ear.

"Everything all right?" the ERU team leader called.

"Everything is great, motherfucker," Hood yelled back. "We're coming out in a minute." He turned back to Lucas. "My car's about fucked up. I want a cop car and I need some time. We're going out there and get it."

"Tell them what you're doing," Lucas said. The weight of the gun pulled his head to the side. The tape over his left eye was sticking to his eyelid, and he struggled with a sudden feeling of claustrophobia. "If they see me with my hands up and you behind me, maybe somebody who can't see what's going on will take a shot at you."

"You tell them," Hood said. "They'll believe you. Over to the window."

Lucas stepped over to the window. Hood held onto his shirt collar with his left hand. The shotgun was in his right and he used the end of the barrel to push Lucas to the windowsill.

"Everybody hold it," Lucas screamed as he stepped into the opening. He put his arms up over his head, his fingers spread. "Everybody fuckin' hold it. He's got a shotgun taped to my head. Everybody fuckin' hold it."

There was movement inside the apartment across the street, just a flicker at the window. Hood pulled him closer, the shotgun cutting into the flesh behind his ear.

"Billy . . ." said the loudspeaker.

"I want a car, man," Hood shouted. He prodded Lucas forward until he was sitting on the windowsill. Carefully,

carefully, he climbed up beside him. "You get down first," he said.

"Jesus," said Lucas. "Don't jar anything."

"Get down."

Lucas dropped the five feet, flexing his knees, his eyes closed as he landed. The world was still there. Hood landed next to him. Lucas took another breath. "I want a cop car and I want everybody out of my way," Hood screamed.

"Billy, this isn't going to help, man, everything was fine," the team leader called. The loudspeaker echoed in Lucas' ears. He looked at the street, the cars blocking it, the people half visible behind them, and he wondered if they would suddenly wink out and Lucas Davenport would be a shell on the cold ground, with a crowd looking down at him. . . .

"Just give me the car, man, bring a car down here." Hood was tensing up again, his voice screeching toward blind panic.

"Give him the fuckin' car," Lucas yelled. The scent of pines came through. There were no pines there; no vegetation at all, but the scent of pines was there, just as though he were at his Wisconsin cabin. A refrain started running through the back of Lucas' mind, *Not yet, please not yet,* but the cold circle of the shotgun muzzle pressed into the flesh behind his ear. . . .

"Okay, okay, okay, we're calling for a car, take it easy, Billy, we don't want anybody else hurt. . . ."

"Where's the car?" Hood screamed. "Where's the car?" He jerked on the shotgun and Lucas' head snapped back.

"Take it easy, take it easy, man," Lucas said, his heart in his throat. His neck hurt, his head hurt, and Hood pressed against him like an unwanted partner in a three-legged race. "If you fire this thing accidentally, you're a dead motherfucker just like me."

"Shut up," Hood snapped.

"You can have a car, Christ, take it easy," the ERU team leader called. He was directly across the street. "Take the car down to your right, down to your right. See the cop getting out? The keys are in that car."

Hood turned to look at it and Lucas looked with him.

The car was next to the negotiator's car. He could see Lily behind it.

"Okay, we're walking to the car," Hood yelled toward the ERU leader. They edged sideways, like crabs, slowly, the shotgun pressing. . . . Twenty feet out from the car.

"Billy? Billy? I'm the guy on the telephone. We've got a doctor here," the negotiator called. The negotiator took a step away from his car and Lucas noticed that he'd taken off his sidearm. "We got a doctor, a registered psychologist, we want you to talk with her. . . ."

Lily stepped out from behind the car and stood beside the negotiator, clutching her purse in both hands. She looked like a very scared public-health nurse.

"We brought her in to see if you were okay. She says she'll ride with the two of you, in case there's any trouble, she wants to talk. . . ."

"I don't want any talk, man, I just want the car." Hood prodded Lucas and Lucas sidestepped toward the car, his head twisted by the angle of the shotgun.

"I can help you," Lily called. She was fifteen feet away.

"I don't want you, man," Hood said. He was sweating, and the odor of the fear sweat filled the air around him. "Just get the fuck out of my way."

"Listen, you've got to listen to me, Billy. Please? I've worked with a lot of Indian people and this is not the Indian way." She took a step closer, and another, and with their movement toward the car, she was now less than ten feet away.

"Just get away from me, will you?" Hood said in exasperation. "I don't need no fuckin' shrink, okay?"

"Billy, please . . ." Lily said, a pleading note in her voice. Six feet. She let the purse drop to her side on its shoulder strap, one hand gesturing while the other plucked at her jacket. "Let me . . ." Her voice suddenly changed from persuasion to urgency. "Billy, you've got a problem. Okay? Let me tell you about this, okay? You've got a problem that you don't know about. I mean it. Billy, there's a wasp on your hair. Above your right ear. If it stings, don't pull the trigger, it's just a wasp. . . . We don't want a tragedy."

"A wasp, man . . . where is it?" Hood stopped, his voice

suddenly tight. Lucas' mind flashed to the box of antihistamine tablets in Hood's medicine cabinet.

"On your hair just above your right ear, right there, it's
crawling down toward your ear. . . ."

Hood had his left hand around Lucas' neck and Lucas
felt the stock of the gun come up as Hood tried to brush
the nonexistent wasp away with his gun hand. With his finger through the trigger guard, he couldn't quite reach his
ear; for just the barest part of a second, not thinking, he
pulled his trigger finger out of the guard, reaching toward
his head. As his finger came out of the guard, Lily went into
her belly with her right hand, the hand that had been nervously plucking at her jacket button, and came out with the
full-cocked .45. She thrust it at Hood's head almost as if
she were throwing a dart, and he saw it just soon enough
to flinch. Lucas closed his eyes and started to turn away;
the .45 went off and Lucas felt a hot stinging on his face,
as though he'd been hit by a handful of beach sand. Hood
kicked back onto the ground as Lucas fell to his knees and
screamed:

"Get it off get it off get it off get it off."

The negotiator knelt beside him and said, "You're okay,
you're okay." A hand grasped the shotgun barrel, held it,
and Lucas, his breath ragged, groaned, "Get it off, get it
off," and there was a flat cutting sound and the muzzle was
gone.

Again, everything was sharp, the blacktop beneath his
knees, the smell of tar and city garbage, the sound of the
radios, an ERU officer running, Lily saying "Jesus, Jesus,"
the team leader's knee next to his face, Billy Hood's gym
shoe twisted in the dirt. Then Lucas' breakfast came up, and
he knelt outside Billy Hood's apartment and vomited and
vomited; and when he couldn't vomit anymore, dry heaves
shook his shoulders and racked his stomach. Members of
the ERU team were gathering around the body, and from
somewhere he could hear a woman's wail over the shouting
and the chatter. The team leader's hand was on the back
of his neck, warm against his cold skin. He heard somebody
crack the shotgun and a green-cased shotgun shell flipped
out.

When the stomach spasms stopped, when he had controlled them, Lucas turned his head and saw Billy Hood's face. The front of it was caved in, as though somebody had hit him with a claw hammer.

"One shot in the ten ring," Lily said. She was standing above him, her face pale as winter, looking down at Hood. "Right on the bridge of his nose." And although her voice was brave, she sounded ineffably sad. Lucas got to his hands and knees, then to his feet, wobbling.

The team leader helped him strip the tape off his head, and turned to look at Lily. "You okay?" he asked.

"I'm okay," Lily said.

"How about you?" the negotiator asked Lucas.

"Fuck, no." Lucas took a couple wobbly steps and Lily slipped an arm around his waist. "It could take a couple of minutes. I was a dead man."

"Maybe he would have let you go," Lily said, looking back at Hood's body.

"Maybe, but I don't think so. Billy Hood was an angry man," Lucas said. "He was ready to die and he wasn't going alone."

He stopped and turned and, like Lily, looked back at the body. Hood's face wasn't peaceful in death. It was simply dead, and empty, like a beer can crushed on the side of a road. A red-hot anger washed through Lucas.

"God damn, we needed him. We needed the motherfucker to talk, the stupid shit. The stupid shit, why'd he do this?" He was shouting and the ERU team was looking at him.

Lily tightened her grip around his waist and gave him a gentle push toward the house across the street.

"Did I say 'Thank you'?" Lucas asked, looking down at Lily.

"Not yet."

"You could have blown my fuckin' brains out, Rothenburg. And I've got all kinds of shit buried in my face."

"I'm too good a shot to have hit you. And the shit in your face is better than shotgun pellets behind your ear," she said.

"So, thanks. You saved my ass."

"I accept your abject gratitude, and while it's not enough . . ."

"I'll give you all the gratitude you can handle. You know that," he said. The hair on the top of her head brushed against his cheek.

"Fuckin' men," she muttered.

CHAPTER
12

Lucas sat on a stack of newspapers.

"Are you all right?" Daniel asked, squatting beside him. Lily realized that he was trying to be gentle but didn't know how.

"In a bit," Lucas said.

Larry Hart came in, saw them and stopped. "The whole area is surrounded by media," he said. "Channel Eight had a camera on a roof down the street. They had the whole thing on the air, live. Everybody'll be looking for you and Lily."

"Fuck that," said Lucas, his elbows on his legs, his head hung down to his knees. "Has anybody talked to Jennifer?"

"I gave her a call right after Lily took Hood out," Daniel said. "She was watching. She sounded pretty calm. She even tried to screw some details out of me, for their newscast."

"Sounds like Jennifer," Lucas said. He thought about the shotgun behind his ear and gripped his knees. "If you can get somebody to take the Porsche back to my place, maybe I could sneak out in a squad. . . ."

"Sloan'll take it," Daniel said. Lucas nodded and dug the keys out of his pocket. "We've got more problems. I hate to bother you with them. . . ."

"Jesus, what?"

"The St. Paul water patrol took a body off the Ford dam this morning. It got hung up on an abutment. It's an Indian. He was carrying an ID that said 'Richard Yellow Hand.'"

"Aw, fuck," said Lucas.

"We'd like you to take a look. We're not sure yet . . . well, we're pretty sure, but he was your snitch. . . ."

"All right, all right, all right . . ."

"I'll go with you if you want," Lily offered.

"Uh, you better not," Daniel said, looking up at her. "We'll have some shooting reports to make out. You'll have to talk to our attorney, you not being a certified police officer in Minnesota. . . ."

"What . . . ?"

"No, no, there won't be any problems," Daniel said hastily. "But there's some bureaucratic rigmarole to go through. Jesus, I wish I had a cigar."

"So I look at this body . . ." said Lucas.

"There's something else," Daniel said, almost reluctantly. "They did another one."

"Another one?" asked Lily. "Where?"

"Brookings, South Dakota. It's just coming in now. The fuckin' state attorney general. They were having some kind of harvest-festival thing and they had these polka dancers. This guy, the attorney general, always went to the polka dances because he knew he'd make the local TV. A gunman was waiting for him."

"Our friend with the braids?" asked Hart.

"No. And they got this guy. They shot him, anyway. He's in a trauma room right now. Some cowboy saw the shooting, pulled a rifle out of his pickup and nailed him."

"Okay. Well, fuck. Better go see Yellow Hand, first thing. If it is Yellow Hand. I can't worry about this SoDak thing, not yet." Lucas stood up and wandered in a circle, stopped by the door. Lily, Daniel and Hart watched him, worried, and he tried to smile. "You guys look like Dorothy, the Lion and the Tin Man. Cheer up."

"So what, that makes you the Wizard of Oz?" asked Lily, still worried.

"I feel more like the Wicked Witch when the house fell on her," Lucas said. He lifted a hand. "See you."

• • •

Yellow Hand's body was at the Ramsey County Medical Examiner's Office, lying faceup on a stainless-steel tray. Lucas hated floaters. They no longer looked human. They looked . . . melted.

"Yellow Hand?" asked a deputy medical examiner.

Lucas looked the melted thing in face. Yellow Hand's eyes were open and bloated and had no pupils; they resembled milk-jug plastic. His features were twisted, some enlarged, some not. But the thing was still recognizable. He turned away. "Yeah. Yellow Hand. He's got people out in Fort Thompson, that's in South Dakota. His mother, I think."

"We'll call . . ."

"Do you have a cause of death yet?" Lucas asked.

"We took a quick look. He's got a hole at the base of his skull. Like one of those Chinese executions, one bullet. That's not official yet: the wound might not have killed him, he might have drowned or something. . . ."

"But he was shot?"

"Looks like it . . ."

Sloan arrived with the Porsche as Lucas was getting out of the squad car at his house.

"What a fuckin' car," Sloan said enthusiastically. "A hundred and fifty-five on the interstate, I couldn't believe it. . . ." He checked Lucas' face. "Just joking," he said. "Jesus, you okay? You look like shit."

"It's been a bad day. And not even noon yet," Lucas said, trying to put some humor in his voice. It came out flat.

"Was it . . . ?"

"Yeah. It was Yellow Hand."

Sloan gave him the keys and said that Lily would be up to her neck in paperwork. A couple of local stations, and one from New York, were already asking why she had been carrying a pistol in Minneapolis. Daniel was handling it, Sloan said.

"Well, I gotta go, if I want a ride back in the squad," Sloan said.

"Yeah. Thanks for bringing the car."

"Take it easy. . . ." Sloan seemed reluctant to leave him, but Lucas turned his back and walked to the house. As he unlocked the front door, he could hear the phone ringing. The answering machine kicked in before he could reach it. Jennifer Carey's voice said, "It's ten twenty-eight. We've been on the air about the Hood thing. Call me . . ."

Lucas picked up the phone. "Whoa. You still there?"

"Lucas? When did you get in?"

"Just this minute. Hang on a second, I've got to shut the front door."

When he got back to the phone, Jennifer pounced: "Damn you, Davenport, I've been going crazy. I talked to Daniel and he said he didn't know where you were, but that you were okay."

"I'm fine. Well, I'm not fine, I'm feeling a little fucked up. Where are you?"

"At the station. When I found out what was happening— thanks for not calling, by the way, we got our asses kicked by Eight, and since everybody knows that we go together, they're looking at me like I'm an alien toad. . . ."

"Yeah, yeah. Where's the baby?" Lucas asked.

"I called Ellen, the college girl. She has her. She can stay as late as I need. She can stay over if she has to."

"Can you come over later?"

"You're okay?" she asked.

"Yeah. But I could use some heavy-duty succor."

"Things are going crazy here. You heard about Elmer Linstad, out in South Dakota?"

"Yeah. The attorney general."

"Dead as a mackerel. The guy they shot, this Liss guy—"

"Whoa, whoa, you're ahead of me now. Who is he?"

"He's an Indian guy named John Liss. He's from right here in the Cities. He's in the operating room, but the word is, he's going to make it. They're talking about putting me on a plane later this afternoon. I'll be running the crew out there . . ."

"Okay." Lucas tried to keep the disappointment out of his voice.

". . . but I could sneak away around lunchtime."

"I'd like to see you," Lucas said. "I'm feeling kind of weird."

"If we sent a crew over there, could you talk . . . ?"

"No, I can't, Jen. Really. Tell them I'm not here. I'm going to turn off the phone. I've got to lie down."

"All right . . . Love you."

Lucas crawled into bed, but sleep wouldn't come. His brain was turning over, hot, he could feel the touch of muzzle behind his ear, the grotesquely bloated face of Yellow Hand floated up in front of his eyes. . . .

He was lying flat on his back, sweating. He turned his head and looked at the clock. He'd been in bed for more than an hour; he must have been asleep, he must have been somewhere, it felt like five minutes. . . .

Lucas sat up and winced as the headache hit him. He went out to the kitchen, got a bottle of lime-flavored mineral water from the refrigerator and walked unsteadily back to his workroom. The answering machine was blinking at him: eight messages. He punched the replay button. Six calls were from TV stations and the two papers. One was from Daniel, the last from Lily. He called her back.

"I'm up to my ass in paperwork," she said.

"I heard."

"And I've got a deposition tomorrow morning. . . ."

"Lunch, maybe?"

"I'll call you."

"I'll be on the street. I'll have a handset. . . ."

Daniel had called to see how he was. "We've got the feebs by the nuts," he said. "We've got one team working the people in Hood's apartment house and his roommates; Sloan and Anderson are digging for stuff on this guy in South Dakota. You heard he was from here?"

"Yeah. Jen told me."

"Okay. Listen, I've got to go. You take it easy. We got it covered."

When he got off the phone with Daniel, Lucas poured the mineral water into a tumbler and followed with three fingers of Tanqueray gin. The combination made a bad gin and tonic. He sat in the kitchen and drank it down. Fuckin'

Yellow Hand. Hood and the shotgun. He reached back and rubbed the spot where the shotgun had been, then walked unsteadily back to the bathroom and got in the shower. The liquor was working on him and the hot water beat on his face, but the images of Hood and Yellow Hand would not go away.

He was out of the shower, toweling off, when the doorbell rang. He wrapped the towel around his waist, padded through the kitchen and peeked out a window at his porch.

Jennifer.

"Hi," she said, taking him in. "You still okay?"

"Kind of drunk," he said.

A worry line appeared between her eyebrows, and she leaned forward and kissed him. "Gin," she said. "I never would have believed it."

"I'm fucked up," he said, trying on a grin.

"Follow me," she said, tugging at his towel. "We'll try to unfuck you."

The afternoon sun dropped below the eaves and lit up the curtain in Lucas' bedroom. Jennifer pushed him off and swung her legs over the side of the bed, and looked back and said, "That was . . . frantic."

"I'm not sure I'm still alive," Lucas said. "Christ, I could use a cigarette."

"Were you scared?"

"Almost paralyzed. I wanted to plead, but . . . it just . . . I don't know, it wouldn't have done any good. . . . I just wanted to get it off me. . . ."

"This policewoman from New York . . ."

"Lily . . ."

"Yeah. There was a press conference, a short one, with Daniel and her and Larry Hart. She looked tough," Jennifer said, watching his face. "She looked like your type."

"I could give a shit about that," Lucas grunted. "The best thing about her is that she used to shoot in combat competition. She had that forty-five in Billy Hood's face in maybe a tenth of a second. Boom. *Adiós,* motherfucker."

"She looked pretty nice," Jennifer said.

"Jesus, yeah. She looks pretty nice. She's a little chubby, but nice-looking."

"She looked a little chubby," Jennifer agreed. Jennifer worked out every morning at a hard-core muscle gym.

"She eats everything in sight," Lucas said. "Jesus, I wish I still smoked."

"So you're all right. . . ."

"Nothing like this has ever happened," he said, bewildered. "I've come close before, shit, with the Maddog I almost got my ass killed. But this got to me . . . I don't know."

She rubbed his still damp hair and he asked, "Did you go on the date? To the symphony?"

"Yeah."

"How was it?"

"It was okay," she said. "I'll go with him again if he asks, but I won't be sleeping with him."

"Ah. Decent of you to tell me."

"He's just too fuckin' nice," Jennifer said. "No edges. Everything I said, he agreed with."

"He's probably hung like a Tennessee stud horse."

Jennifer's forehead wrinkled. "Men worry about the goddamnedest things," she said.

"I wasn't worried."

"Sure. That's why you mentioned it," she said. "Anyway, even if I did plan to sleep with him, I'd put it off for a while. I keep looking at the baby, and I keep thinking I want to do it again. With the same daddy."

Lucas turned on his side and kissed her on the forehead. "I'd like to help, whenever you want to. Soon?"

"I think so. In a couple, three months. This time, I'll tell you when I go off the Pill."

He kissed her again and his hand crept over her breast, circling and pressing her nipple with the palm of his hand.

"I'd like a boy," she said.

"Whatever," said Lucas. "Another daughter would be fine with me."

"Maybe we could move it up. Next month, maybe."

"I'll be on the job," he said.

She laughed, shook her head and looked at her watch.

"Think you could stand some more succor? I've got barely enough time."

"Christ, I don't know, I'm getting old. . . ."

They made love again, more sedately, and later, when Jennifer was getting dressed, Lucas said, hoarsely, "I didn't want the world to go away. I would never have known, but I kept thinking . . . I don't even know if I was thinking it, but I was feeling it . . . I wanted more. More life. Jesus, I was afraid I'd just wink out, like a soap bubble. . . ."

After Jennifer left for the airport, Lucas tried again to nap. Failing, he turned on the television and caught the cable news from Sioux Falls. John Liss was out of surgery; he'd live, but he'd never walk again. The cowboy's shot had taken out a piece of spinal cord just above the hips. They ran the tape of the shooting again, then another time, in slow motion, and then cut to a picture of Lawrence Duberville Clay. It was a well-known shot, the director in shirt-sleeves on the Chicago waterfront, working a cocaine bust. He had a huge Desert Eagle automatic pistol packed under his arm in an elaborate shoulder holster.

"In a related development, FBI director Lawrence Duberville Clay has announced that he will go personally to Brookings to take charge of the investigation, and said he expects to set up a temporary national FBI headquarters in Minneapolis until the conspirators are captured," the anchorwoman said. "Clay said the move should be accomplished in the next two or three days. This is the third time that the FBI director has involved himself with a specific investigation. His action is seen as an administration effort to emphasize the importance given to its war on crime. . . ."

Lucas poked the remote control and Clay's face went away. Three o'clock. He stood, thought a moment, then went back in the kitchen for the rest of the Tanqueray.

CHAPTER

13

Shadow Love saw Billy Hood's death on a television set in the corner of a Lake Street grill. The camera was a full block from the scene, but up high, and it was all as clear as a running play on *Monday Night Football*.

Billy and the hunter cop. The woman with the purse. Billy moving. Why did he do that? Why did he take his finger off the trigger? The woman's hand coming up with the pistol. The shot, Billy going down like a rag doll, and Davenport kneeling on the pavement, vomiting . . .

Shadow Love watched it once, watched it again, watched it a third time as the station endlessly ran the tape loop. *"The following news broadcast contains scenes of violence and death and may not be appropriate for children. If there are any children in the viewing area . . ."*

And then a running press conference at the shooting scene. Larry Hart: *". . . have developed evidence that these people are not just killing whites, but have killed one of our own, a Dakota man from Fort Thompson, Yellow Hand . . ."*

Larry Hart on the TV. Sweating. Pleading. Twisting his hands like Judas Iscariot.

The black spot popped up, twitching, growing, blurring his vision. Shadow Love tried to blink it away, but the anger was stirring through his chest.

Judas. Sweating, pleading . . .

Hart's face vanished in an electronic instant, to be replaced by that of a woman newscaster. "We've just gotten word that there has been another assassination attempt in Brookings, South Dakota, apparently related to the killings done by the Indian extremist group responsible for the assassinations of the New York commissioner of welfare and a federal judge in Oklahoma. The target of the South Dakota attempt was Elmer Linstad, the state's attorney general. . . ."

The woman paused, looked at her desk, then up again. "CBS news is reporting that Elmer Linstad, attorney general of South Dakota, is dead in an assassination in Brookings, South Dakota. His assailant was shot by a bystander and has been taken to a Brookings hospital. . . ."

"Billy's dead and John's been shot." Shadow Love, carrying a long cardboard box, pushed into the apartment. He kicked the door shut and tossed the box on the couch. A printed label on the side of the box said CURTAIN RODS.

"What?" The Crows, startled, stared at him.

"You deaf?" Shadow Love asked. "I said Billy's dead. John's been shot. It's on the TV."

The Crows' apartment had come with a television, but they rarely turned it on during the day. Now they did, and the loops were running.

William Two Horses Hood, the anchorman said, had been positively identified as the slayer of John Andretti, the New York City welfare commissioner. He had been shot to death by a New York police officer after Hood had taken a Minneapolis officer hostage. The Minneapolis officer was not hurt. John Liss, a Sioux Indian from Minneapolis, was in guarded condition in a Brookings hospital. . . .

"That's the hunter cop," Shadow Love said, tapping the screen over the film sequence of Lucas. "He found him."

"Motherfucker," Sam whispered as they watched the tape. Aaron began to weep and Sam patted him on the shoulder. They watched the tape again, then the one of the killing of Linstad, and then a rerun of the on-street press conference, with Larry Hart.

Sam looked at his cousin. "Remember him? He's one of the Wapeton Harts, Carl and Mary's boy?"

"Yeah. Good people." said Aaron. He turned to Shadow Love. "He's working with this cop?"

"Yes. And everybody likes him, Larry Hart. I went to school with him. Everybody liked him in school. Everybody likes him now. The hunter and Hart and this bitch from New York, they'll find us. There are people who know the Crows, who've probably seen you on the streets. And they'll talk. . . ."

"You don't know that," said Aaron.

"Yes, I do. Just like I knew they'd find Billy. If they don't find us by accident, somebody will turn us in. And it could be one of you, or Leo, or John. Or maybe one of their wives."

"Nobody would do that . . ." Aaron objected.

"Sure they would, if this hunter pushes the right buttons," Shadow Love said.

"And of all of us, you'd be the only one who wouldn't break?"

"That's right," said Shadow Love. "Because you know what gets people? Love. That's what it is. Cops use it. They say, *Help your friend; betray him.* They catch Sam and they want Aaron. So they say on the news that Sam is dying, he wants his cousin to pray him into death. . . . Could you stay away?"

Aaron didn't answer.

"I'd never betray us, because I don't have anyone I love enough," Shadow Love said with a subdued sadness. "Sometimes . . . I wish I could. I never had a laugh, you know. Never got to play catch-me-fuck-me with some chick. The only one, ever, they could use against me was Mama. With her dead, there's no pressure they could put on me."

After a moment, Aaron said, "That's the most awful thing I ever fuckin' heard." Behind him, Sam nodded, and Shadow Love turned away.

"That's the way it is," he said.

Aaron, tears running down his face, said, "They're all going. There's only Leo now."

"And us," said Sam.

Aaron nodded. "If Clay doesn't come in after South Dakota, one of us may have to go to Milwaukee."

Sam glanced at Shadow Love, involuntarily, just a peek, but Aaron caught it. "No," he said.

"Why not?" Shadow Love asked, his words like an axedge. "I'm part of the group; I have a stone knife."

"This action is not for you. If you want to help, go out to Rosebud and talk to the old men. Learn something."

"You don't want me here," Shadow Love said.

"That's right," Aaron said.

"You assholes," Shadow shouted. "You fuckin' assholes."

"Wait, wait, wait . . ." Sam said, pointing at the television.

Clay and his gun: ". . . to Brookings and will establish a temporary national headquarters in Minneapolis. This is the third time . . ."

The mood changed in an instant:

"The sonofabitch is coming," Sam whooped. "The cocksucker's on his way."

They had a quiet lunch, the three of them sitting around a rickety table eating cold-cut sandwiches with mustard and Campbell's chicken noodle soup.

"So what now?" Shadow asked. "There are cops all over the place, and the FBI. In a few more days, we won't be able to go on the streets."

Aaron glanced at Sam. "I'll call Barbara. Tell her we may be coming. I don't want to go in too soon; we'd fuck up, go outside, somebody'd see us."

"If you're not going out to Bear Butte, you ought to come over to Barbara's," Sam told Shadow Love. "She talks like you were her kid."

Shadow Love nodded. "Yeah. I saw her before I went to L.A. I don't know . . . we'll be a danger to her."

"She knows that," Aaron said. "We've been on the run before. She says we'll be welcome, no matter what."

"She didn't know exactly what you were planning to do. . . ."

"She'll take us," said Sam.

"Not a bad piece of ass either," Aaron said with a grin.

Sam snorted and even blushed. He and Barbara had been lovers. Nothing had been said when he talked to her on the telephone a month before, but he knew it would start again. He looked forward to it. "Jealousy. It's an ugly sight," he said into his soup.

Shadow Love stepped to the couch, picked up the cardboard box and opened it. Inside was a flat black assault rifle. He took it out of the box. "M-15," he said. He pointed it out the window at a streetlight.

"Where'd you get it? What's it for?" asked Sam.

"I got it on the street. It's for the cop, maybe. Or Hart."

Aaron had stepped toward the stove, reaching for the teapot. He stopped in mid-stride and whirled toward his son. "No. Not Hart. You don't kill the people," he said furiously.

Shadow Love looked at him with a cold glint in his eye. "I do what I think best. You and Sam disagree all the time, but you still act."

"We always agree before we do anything," said Aaron.

"That's a luxury you won't have much longer. You can argue. You can sit and think. You can fuck up. I'll try to buy you some time."

"We don't want that," Aaron said furiously.

Shadow Love shook his head, aimed out the window again and squeezed the trigger. The *click* hung in the air between them.

CHAPTER
14

Hart worked through an Indian-dominated housing project while Sloan did background on John Liss. Lucas, fighting a blinding hangover, made the rounds of barbershops, bars, fast-food joints and rooming houses.

A little after noon, Lucas called the dispatcher to check on Lily and was told that she was still meeting with the county attorney. He stopped at an Arby's, ordered a roast beef sandwich and carried it outside. He was leaning on his car when his handset squawked and the shotgun touched him behind the ear again. He almost dropped the sandwich. He stood paralyzed, and the cold metal pressed against his head and Hood's apartment rose up in front of his eyes, the circle of squad cars, the radios squawking . . . A few seconds later, it all faded and Lucas staggered from the car and half fell onto a mushroom-shaped concrete stool. He sat sweating for a few moments, then got up and walked shakily to the car and started off again.

A half-hour later, the dispatcher gave him a number to call. Lily's hotel. Lucas called from a street booth across from a leather shop, staring at a Day-Glo–green sign advertising hand-tooled belts.

"Lunch?" Lucas asked, when Lily said hello.

"I can't," she said. There was a second's silence, and then she said, "I'm going home."

Lucas considered it, staring at the Day-Glo sign, then down at the telephone receiver in his hand. After a few seconds he said, "I thought you might stay over, see what happens."

"I thought about it, but then . . . I finished with the county attorney and called to see when I could get a flight out. I was thinking tonight, but they said they could get me on a flight at one-thirty. I've got a cab coming downstairs. . . ."

"I could come . . ."

"No, don't," she said quickly. "I'd really prefer that you didn't."

"Jesus, Lily . . ."

"I'm sorry . . ." she said. There was a moment's silence before she finished the sentence. "I hope you're okay. And I'll see you. Maybe. You know, someday."

"Okay," he said.

"So. Bye."

"Bye."

She hung up and Lucas stood leaning against the booth. "God damn it," he said aloud.

Two young girls were passing, carrying schoolbooks. They heard him, glanced his way and hurried on. Lucas walked slowly back to his car, confused, unsure whether he was feeling disappointment or relief. He spent another hour touring Lake Street bars, apartment buildings and stores, looking for a toehold, an edge, a whisper, anything. He came up dry; and although he was given more names, more people to check, his heart wasn't in it. He looked at his watch. Ten after two. She'd be off the ground, on her way to New York. Lily.

Daniel was in his office. He had turned the overhead fluorescent lights off and sat in a pool of yellow light cast by an old-fashioned goosenecked desk lamp. Larry Hart was sitting in the chair in front of his desk, Sloan, Lester and Anderson off to the side. Lucas took the last chair.

"Nothing?" asked Daniel.

"Not a thing," Hart said. Lucas shook his head as he sat down.

"We've been getting some stuff about Liss. He worked for a metal fabrication plant out in Golden Valley. They said he was all right, but weird, you know, about Indian stuff."

"Big help," Anderson said.

Sloan shrugged. "I got some names of his friends, I can feed them to you, maybe the computer'll have something."

"Family?" asked Lucas.

"Wife and kid. Wife works a couple of jobs. She's a check-out at Target and works at a Holiday store at night, part-time. And they got a kid. Harold Richard, aka Harry Dick, seventeen. He's trouble, a doper. He's been downtown a half-dozen times, minor theft, possession of pot, possession of crack. Small stuff."

"That's it?" asked Daniel.

"Sorry," Sloan apologized. "We're hitting it as hard as we can."

"What about Liss himself? Are they getting anything out of him?"

Anderson shook his head. "Nope. About fifteen minutes after Liss went down, Len Meadows flew in from Chicago in his private jet. The first thing he did was bar any cops from talking to his client."

"Fifteen minutes? Did Meadows know in advance?" Lucas asked.

"It wasn't really fifteen minutes—" Sloan started.

Hart interrupted. "The Fire Creek Reservation office is in Brookings. When they heard about the shooting, they got scared about what might happen. They called Meadows' office. He'd done some pro bono criminal work for them. So then Meadows had his people call around, working with the information they were getting off the TV. They found out who Liss' old lady was. Meadows called her—Louise, that's her name—and offered his services. She said yes, so he flew out to Brookings. When Liss woke up after the docs got finished with him, Meadows went in and talked to him. That was it. No more cops."

"Damn it," Lucas said, chewing his lip. "Meadows is pretty good."

"He's a grandstanding asshole," said Lester.

"Frank, *you're* an asshole, but nobody ever said you weren't pretty good," said Daniel.

"I did once," Sloan said. "He made me go out and investigate supermarket thefts."

Lester grinned. "And I'd do it again," he said.

"The problem with Meadows is, he won't deal," Lucas said. "He's an ideologue. He prefers the crucifix to the plea bargain."

They all chewed it over for a minute, then Daniel said, "Our Indian friends are putting out press releases now."

"Say what?" asked Hart.

"We got a press release. Or rather, the media got press releases. All of them—newspapers, TV stations, WCCO radio. We got copies. They're supposedly from the killers," Daniel said.

Lucas sat up. "When did this happen?"

"They started arriving in the morning mail." Daniel passed out photocopies of the press releases. "Channel Eight was out on the street for the noon news, asking Indians to read the press releases and then asking them if they agreed."

Lucas nodded absently as he read. The authors took responsibility for all four killings, the two in the Cities, and those in New York and Oklahoma City. Nothing about the Brookings killing, so they were mailed before that. The killings were done as the beginning of a new uprising against white tyranny. There were unconvincing quotes from the Oklahoma assassin, but there were also details from Oklahoma that Lucas hadn't seen.

"This Oklahoma stuff . . ." he said, looking up at Daniel.

The chief nodded. "They got it right."

"Huh." He finished the release, glanced at the second sheet Daniel had given him, a copy of the envelope the release had arrived in, and said "Huh" again.

"Interesting envelope," Sloan remarked.

"Yeah."

"What's that?" asked Hart. He had been looking at the press release and now turned to the envelope.

"Look at the cancellation," Lucas said. "Minneapolis."

Anderson looked up. "We thought they were working out of here."

"Now everybody will know," Daniel said. "That'll crank up the pressure."

"That TV stuff we put out about Yellow Hand last night, blaming this group, I think it backfired," Hart said. "A lot of people knew Yellow Hand. They know he was a crack-head. They figure he was killed by a dealer or another crack-head. Some kind of ripoff. They think the TV stuff is just more white-cop bullshit."

"Shit," Daniel said. He pulled at his lip, then looked at Lucas. "Any ideas? We gotta break something loose."

Lucas shrugged. "We could try money. There're a lot of poor people out there. A little cash might loosen things up."

"That's ugly," Hart objected.

"We're about to get lynched by the media," Daniel snapped. He looked at Lucas. "How much?"

"I don't know. We'd be on a blind trip, just fishing. But I don't know what else to do. I've got no net with the Indians. You show me a problem with the black community, I can call two hundred guys. With the Indians . . ."

"You won't make any friends by spreading money around," Hart insisted. "That's too . . . white. That's what the people will say. That it's just like the white men. They get in trouble, and they go out and buy an Indian."

"So it's not the best way. The question is, Will it work?" Daniel said. "We can worry about rebuilding community relations later. Especially since we don't have any in the first place."

Hart shrugged. "There's always some people who'll talk for money. Indians are no different than anybody else, that way."

Daniel nodded. "And we have a source of money," he said. "We don't even have to tap the snitch fund."

"What's that?" Lucas asked.

"The Andretti family. When the word got out that we'd nailed Billy Hood, I got a call from old man Andretti him-self, thanking us for our help. . . ." He frowned, remember-ing, and looked at Lucas. "Where's Lily? I haven't seen her."

"She headed back to New York," Lucas said. "She was done here."

"God damn it, why didn't she check out with me?" Daniel asked irritably. "Well, she'll just have to come back."

"What?"

"The Andrettis were happier'n hell about Hood, but apparently they're no longer satisfied with getting what the old man calls 'small fry.' He's convinced the NYPD that Lily should stay out here and observe until this whole crazy bunch is busted."

"So she's coming back?" Lucas asked, his breath suddenly coming harder.

"I expect she'll be back tomorrow, as hot as the Andrettis are," Daniel said. "But that's neither here nor there. Anderson has started putting together some interview files. . . ."

Daniel kept talking, but Lucas lost track of what he was saying. A slow fire of anticipation spread though his chest and stomach. Lillian Rothenburg, NYPD. Lucas bit his lip and stared into a dark corner of Daniel's office, as the chief rambled on.

Lily.

A moment later he realized Daniel had stopped talking and was staring at him.

"What?" asked Daniel.

"I got an idea," Lucas said. "But I don't want to talk about it."

An hour after dark, Lucas found Elwood Stone standing under a streetlight on Lyndale Avenue. This time, Stone didn't bother to run.

"What the fuck you want, Davenport?" Stone was wearing sunglasses and a brown leather bomber jacket. He looked like an advertisement for rent-a-thug. "I ain't holding."

Lucas handed him a deck of photographs. "You know this kid?"

Stone looked them over. "Maybe I seen him around," he said.

"They call him Harry Dick?"

"Yeah. Maybe I seen him around," Stone repeated. "What you want?"

"I don't want anything, Elwood," Lucas said. "I just want you to give the boy some credit on a couple of eight-balls."

"Shit, man . . ." Stone turned away and looked up the street, doing a comic double-take in disbelief. "Man, I don't give no credit, man. To a crackhead? You fuckin' crazy?"

"Well, it's like this, Elwood. Either you give Harry a little credit—and it's got to be tomorrow—or I'll talk to Narcotics and we'll run your little round ass right off the street. We'll have somebody in your back pocket every day."

"Shit . . ."

"Or, I can have a talk with Narcotics and tell them you're temporarily on my snitch list. I'll give you some status for say . . . two months? How about that?"

"Why me?"

" 'Cause I know you."

Stone considered. If he went on the snitch list, he'd have virtual immunity from prosecution. It was an opportunity not to be missed, as long as nobody else found out.

"Okay," Stone said after a moment. "But keep it between you and me. You don't tell Narcotics, but if I get hassled, you jump in."

Lucas nodded. "You got it."

"So where do I find this motherfucker, Harry Dick? It's not like I know where he lives."

"We'll spot him for you. You give me your beeper number and I'll call you. Tomorrow. Probably early afternoon."

Stone looked at him for another long minute, then nodded. "Right."

CHAPTER
15

Lucas put a thousand dollars on the street between ten o'clock and noon, then headed out to the airport in a city car. Sloan called him on the way.

"He's there," Sloan said. "I talked to the next-door lady. She said he's usually out of there in the early afternoon. Sleeps late, usually leaves between one and two. His mother's gone out to South Dakota to see the old man."

"All right. Keep an eye on the place," Lucas said. "You got our friend's number?"

"Yeah."

"Lily's plane's on time, so I ought to hook up with you before one. If our boy goes for a walk before then, take him. No fuckin' around."

"Gotcha. Uh, our little Indian helper . . ."

"I'll pick him up. Don't worry about Larry."

"He could be a problem, the way he's talking," Sloan warned.

"I'll take care of it," Lucas said.

Hart bitterly fought the idea of putting money on the street, and threatened to quit. Daniel went to the director of Welfare and Hart got a call.

191

When Lucas talked to him that morning, Hart seemed
more sad than angry, but the anger was there too.

"This could fuck me forever, man," Hart said. "With the
Indian people."

"They're killing guys, Larry," Lucas said. "We gotta stop
it."

"This is not right," Hart said.

And when Lucas outlined the proposal to pick up Harold
Richard Liss, Hart laughed in disbelief.

"Don't fuck with me, Lucas," he said. "You're setting
that boy up. You're going to plant the stuff on him."

"No, no, this is a legitimate tip," Lucas lied.

"Bullshit, man . . ."

They'd left it like that, Hart heading down to Indian Country with a pocket full of cash and a growing anger. He could
be handled, Lucas thought. He loved his job too much to
risk it. He could be cooled out. . . .

Lily's plane was early. He found her in the luggage pickup area, watching the carousel with the suppressed embarrassment of somebody who suspects she has been stood up.

"Jesus, I missed you at the gate," Lucas said, hurrying
over. She was wearing a beige silk blouse with a tweed skirt
and jacket and dark leather high heels. She was beautiful
and he had trouble saying the words.

"God damn it, Davenport," she said.

"What?"

"Nothing. That was just a general 'God damn it.' About
everything." She rose on her tiptoes and pecked him on the
cheek. "I didn't want to come back."

"Mmm."

"There's a bag," she said. She stopped a suitcase and
Lucas lifted it off the carousel. "And there's the other, coming through now."

Lily's second bag came around, and Lucas grabbed the
two of them and led the way to the parking ramp. On the
way, he looked down at her and said, "How've you been?"

"About the same as I was yesterday," she said with mild
sarcasm, squinting as the outdoor light hit her face. "I was
out of here. Finished. Job done. I got to our apartment,

opened the door, and the phone was ringing. David was in the shower, so I picked it up. It was a deputy commissioner. He said, 'What the fuck are you doing here?' "

"Nice guy," Lucas said.

"If there were honorary degrees for assholes, he'd be a doctor of everything," Lily said.

"How's David?" Lucas asked, as though he knew her husband.

"Not so good the first time, 'cause he was a little overexcited. After that, he was great," she said. She looked up at him and suddenly blushed.

"Women are no good at that kind of talk," Lucas remarked. "But it wasn't a bad try."

They stopped at the gray Ford and Lily lifted an eyebrow.

"We got something going," Lucas said. "In fact, we're in kind of a hurry. I'll tell you about it as we go along."

Hart was worse. He'd tried to talk money with some of his acquaintances, and everything, he said, had changed. He'd be a pariah. The Indian man who bought people. And he worried about Harold Richard Liss.

"Man, I don't like this, I don't like this." He sat in the backseat, twisting his hands. Tears ran down his face. He wiped them away with the sleeve of his tweed jacket.

"He's a fuckin' criminal, Larry," said Lucas, annoyed. "Jesus Christ, quit whining."

"I'm not whining, man, I'm . . ."

Lucas let the Ford idle along. A hundred yards ahead, Harold Richard Liss ambled down Lake Street looking in the store windows. "He was making money selling chloroform to little kids. And glue," Lucas said, interrupting.

"This still isn't right, man. He's a fuckin' teenager." Hart shivered.

"It's only for a couple of days," Lucas said.

"It still isn't right."

"Larry . . ." Lucas started in exasperation. Lily touched his shoulder to stop him and turned and looked over the seat.

"There's a big difference between Welfare work and police work," she said to Hart, keeping her face and voice soft and sympathetic. "In a lot of ways, we're on different sides. I think you'd be more comfortable if we just dropped you off."

"We might need his help," Lucas objected, glancing sideways at Lily.

"I won't be much help, man," Hart said. There was a new note in his voice, the sound of a trapped man who sensed an opening. "I mean, I spotted him for you. I don't know shit about surveillance. It's not like you need to interrogate him."

Lucas thought about it, sighed and picked up the radio. "Hey, Sloan, this is Davenport. You still got him?"

Sloan came back: "Yeah, no sweat. What's happening?"

"I'm dropping Larry. Don't worry when you see us stop."

"Sure. I'll hang with Harry."

Lucas pulled over to the side and Hart scrambled to get out. "Thanks, man," he said, leaning over the driver's side window. "I mean, I'm sorry. . . ."

"That's okay, Larry. We'll see you back downtown," Lucas said.

"Sure, man. And thanks, Lily."

They pulled away from the curb and Lucas turned to Lily. "I hope we don't need him to talk to the guy."

"We won't. Like he said, you're not planning to interrogate him."

"Hmph."

Lucas watched Hart in his rearview mirror. Hart was peering after them as they continued down the street after Harry. Then Hart turned and walked away, around a corner. Up ahead, Harry stopped on the street corner to talk to a fat white man in a black parka. The parka was a full season too big, the kind you wore in January when the temperature went down to minus thirty. Harry and the white man exchanged a few words, the white man shook his head and Harry started pleading. The white man shook his head again and stepped away. Harry said something else and then turned, despondent, and started down the street again.

"Dealer," said Lily.

"Yeah. Donny Ellis. He wears that parka 'til June, puts

it back on in September. He pisses in it, never washes. You don't want to get downwind of him."

"This is going to be stupid, Lucas. . . . Nobody ever sold anybody that much crack on credit. Especially not . . ."

"Hey, we don't have to convince anybody. It's just . . . Okay, there's Stone. . . ." Lucas picked up the radio and said, "Stone just came around the corner."

"I got him," Sloan said.

Lucas looked at Lily. "You know what? We should have gotten rid of Larry sooner than we did. He's the kind of guy who might go to the Human Rights Commission."

"Maybe, but I don't think so. That's why he was sweating," she said. She was watching as Elwood Stone walked toward Harry Dick, who was still shambling along the sidewalk. "It's not like we're going to do anything with the Liss kid. Hold him a couple of days and then kick him out of the system. My sense of Larry Hart is that his career means everything to him. He's a success. He makes some money. People like him. They depend on him. If he went outside with this, he'd be on the city's shit list. End of career. Back to the res. I don't think he'd risk that. Not if we kick the kid back out on the street after a couple of days."

"Okay."

"But it *will* make him feel like a small piece of shit," Lily added. "We whipsawed him between his job and his people and he's smart enough to see that. He'll never trust you again."

"I know," Lucas said uncomfortably. "God damn, I hate to burn people."

"Professionally, or personally?"

"What?" Lucas asked, puzzled by the question.

"I mean, you hate to burn a guy because it loses a contact, or because it loses a friend?"

He thought about it and after a minute said, "I don't know." Up the street, Harry spotted Elwood Stone and quickened his step. Stone was one of the tightest dealers on the street, but it never hurt to ask. All he needed was a taste. Just a taste to tide him over.

"They're talking," Sloan said on the radio. "That goddamn Stone is shuckin' like he's on Broadway."

"I told him not to overdo it," Lucas muttered to Lily. Lucas had pulled into a parking place and couldn't see well from the driver's side. He crowded against Lily, who had her face pressed against the passenger-side window, and let his hand drop on her thigh.

"Watch it."

"What?"

"The hand, Davenport . . ."

"God damn it, Lily."

"It's going down," she said.

"It's going down," Sloan said. "He's got it."

"Let's take him," Lucas said.

Sloan came in from the west, Lucas from the east. Sloan pulled into the curb ahead of Harry, Lucas did a U-turn into a fire-hydrant zone behind him. Harry was still grinning, still had his hand in his jacket pocket, when Sloan hopped out of his car. He was inside fifteen feet before Harry figured out something was happening. He turned to run and almost bumped into Lucas, who was closing in from behind. Lily stayed in the street, blocking a dash to the side. Lucas grabbed Harry by the coat collar and said, "Whoa." A second later, Sloan had him by the arm.

"Hey, man," Harry started, but he knew he had been bagged.

"Come on, on the wall," Lucas said, "on the wall." They pushed him onto the wall. Sloan frisked him and found the baggies in his pocket.

"Holy shit," Sloan said. "We got us a dealer."

He opened his palm to Lucas, showed him the two eight-balls.

"I'm no fuckin' dealer, man. . . ."

"A quarter-ounce of dog-white cocaine," Lucas said to Harry. "That's a dealer load, kid. That's presumptive prison term."

"I'm a juvenile, man, look at my ID." Harry was old enough to be worried.

"You don't get no juvenile break on a presumptive-dealer rap," Lucas said. "Not unless you're ten years old. You look older than that."

"Oh, man," Harry moaned. "I just got it, a guy give it to me. . . ."

"Right," Sloan said skeptically. "He gave it to you all right. He gave it to you right in the ass." He cranked down one arm while Lucas hung onto the other, and Sloan put on his handcuffs. "You got the right to remain silent . . ."

Daniel wanted to push as hard as they could. If they waited, he thought, Len Meadows would get Liss' family organized and protected.

"You can fly out to Sioux Falls and rent a car . . ." Daniel started.

"Fuck fly," Lucas said. "I'm driving. We'll be there in four hours. We wouldn't get there any faster if we waited for an airplane and then drove up from Sioux Falls."

"Are you going?" Daniel raised an eyebrow and looked at Lily.

"Yeah. We'll be dealing with this Louise Liss. Maybe a woman would do it better."

"Okay. But take it easy with the Liss woman, will you? This whole thing is a little shaky. Larry Hart is shitting bricks. He's scared," Daniel said. "Worse than that, he's pissed off."

"Can you talk to him?"

"I already did and I'll go back with him again. I'll tell him if we squeeze anything out of Liss, we can probably send him back to work at Welfare. . . ."

They took overnight bags to Brookings. If they didn't get the information the first night, there wouldn't be much point in staying a second.

"Your friend . . . Jennifer. She's in Brookings, right?"

"Yeah. They sent out a crew. She's producing." They were crossing the Minnesota River at Shakopee. A flock of Canada geese were standing on the riverbank, watching the water go by. Lucas said, "Geese."

"Mmm. Will you stay with her?"

"What?"

"Jennifer. Will you stay with her?"

Lucas downshifted as they came into town and rolled up

to a stoplight. He glanced at her, then turned right on the red light. "No. I'd rather that she not know I was there. She has a way of reading my mind. If she sees me, she'll know something is up."

"Do you know where she's staying?"

"Sure. It's out by the interstate that comes up from Sioux Falls. The Brookings cops told me that Louise Liss is staying in a place downtown. I thought we'd check in there."

They were going through the town of Sleepy Eye on Highway 14 when they passed a man on bicycle, dressed in cycling clothes: a green-striped polo shirt, black cycling shorts, white helmet. It was cool, but his bare legs were exposed and pumped like machine pistons. Lucas estimated that he was breaking the speed limit through the downtown.

"He looks like David," Lily said. "My husband."

"David's a cyclist?"

"Yeah. He was pretty serious about it, once." She turned her head to watch the cyclist as they went by. "He'd go out every Saturday with a group of people and they'd ride centuries. Sometimes two. A century's a hundred miles."

"Jesus. He must be in great shape."

"Yeah." She was watching the storefronts in the tiny town. "Bicycles bore the shit out of me, to tell you the truth. They always break down, then you've got to fix them. Or they're not broken, then you've got to fiddle with them to get them tuned up exactly right. The tires go flat all the time."

"That's why I bought a Porsche," Lucas said.

"A Porsche's probably cheaper too," Lily said. "Those goddamned racing bikes cost a fortune. And you can't have just one."

A few minutes later, back in the countryside, they passed a herd of black-and-white dairy cows.

"Neat cows," she said. "What kind are they?"

"Beats the hell out me," Lucas said.

"What?" she said in amusement. "You're from Minnesota. You ought to know about cows."

"That's the cheeseheads over in Wisconsin who know

about cows. I'm a city kid," he said. "If I had to guess, I'd say they're Holsteins."

"Why's that?"

" 'Cause that's the only cow name I know. Wait a minute. There's also Guernseys and Jerseys. But I don't think they're the spotted ones."

"Brown Swiss," Lily said.

"What?"

"That's a kind of cow."

"I thought that was a kind of cheese," Lucas said.

"I don't think so. . . . There's another bunch." She watched a herd of cows ambling down the pasture toward the barn, walking in ones and twos, like tourists coming back to a bus, shadows trailing behind them. "David knows the names of everything. You drive up toward the mountains and you say, 'What's that tree?' And he says, 'That's a white oak,' or, 'That's a Douglas fir.' I used to think he was bullshitting me, so I started checking. He was always right."

"I don't think I could stand it," Lucas said.

"He's really smart," she said. "He might be the smartest man I ever knew well."

"Sounds like fuckin' Mahatma Gandhi."

"What?"

"You once told me he was the gentlest man you ever knew. Now you say he's the smartest."

"He's really quite the guy."

"Yeah, I doubt Gandhi rode a racing bike, so he's one up . . ."

"I don't think I want to talk about this anymore."

"All right."

But a few minutes later she said, "Sometimes, I don't know . . ."

"What?"

"He's so centered. David is. Peaceful. Sometimes . . ."

"It bores the shit out of you," Lucas suggested.

"No, no . . . I just feel like I'm so taken care of, I can't hardly stand the weight of it. He's such a good guy. And I hang out at the refrigerator and eat too much and I walk around with a gun and I've shot people. . . . He was freaked out when I went back home. I mean, he wanted to know all about it. He had this friend come over, a shrink, Shirley Anstein, to make sure I was all right. He was wild when he heard I was coming back. He said I was damaging myself."

"You think he's screwing this Anstein broad?"

"Shirley?" She laughed. "I don't think so. She's about sixty-eight. She's like an adoptive mother."

"He's faithful, then."

"Oh, yeah. He's so faithful it's almost like it's part of the weight on me. I can't even get away from that."

"Walnut Grove," Lily said, looking at a highway sign as they rolled through the edge of another small town. The sun was dipping toward the horizon. It'd be dark before they got to Brookings. "When I was a kid, I used to read the Laura Ingalls Wilder books. I loved them. Then they put the TV show on, you know, *Little House on the Prairie.* I was grown-up and the show was pretty bad, but I watched anyway, because of Laura. . . . The show was set in a place called Walnut Grove."

"This is it," Lucas said.

"What?" Lily looked at the sign again. "Same place?"

"Sure."

"Jesus . . ." She looked out the windows as they went through and saw a small prairie town, a little shabby, very quiet, with side streets that Huckleberry Finn would have been comfortable on. When they were out of the town, she still looked back, and said, "Walnut Grove . . . Damn. You know, given the change in time, it looks right."

They found Louise Liss through the Brookings Police Department and went to her motel. She was in the coffee shop, sitting by herself, staring into a glass of Coke. She was overweight, worn, with tired eyes now rimmed with red. She'd been crying, Lucas thought.

"This'll be bad," Lily muttered.

"Let's get her down to her room," Lucas said.

"I'll talk," Lily said.

They closed in the last few steps to the table and Lily took her ID case from her purse. "Mrs. Liss?"

Louise Liss looked up. Her eyes were flat, dazed. "Who are you?"

"We're police, Mrs. Liss. I'm Lily Rothenburg and this is Lucas Davenport from Minneapolis. . . ."

"I'm not supposed to talk to police," Louise said defensively. "Mr. Meadows said I wasn't supposed . . ."

"Mrs. Liss, we don't want to talk about your husband. We want to talk about your son, Harold." Lily sounded like somebody's mother, Lucas thought, then remembered that she was.

"Harold?" Louise reached out and gripped the Coke, her knuckles turning white. "What happened to Harold? Harold's okay, I talked to him before I left. . . ."

"I think we should talk in your room. . . ." Lily took several steps away from the table and Louise slipped out of the booth, following.

"Your purse," Lucas said.

She reached back to get her purse, saying, "What happened, what happened?" And she started to cry. The cashier was watching them. Lucas handed him three dollars, flashed his badge and said, "Police."

Outside the coffee shop, they turned toward the room. Louise grabbed Lily's coat and said, "Please . . ."

"He was arrested on cocaine charges, Mrs. Liss."

"Cocaine . . ." She suddenly pulled herself together and looked at Lucas; her voice rose to a screech. "You did this, didn't you? You framed my boy to get at John."

"No, no," Lucas said as he tried to keep her walking toward her room. "He'll tell you himself. The Narcotics people saw him touch a dealer. They stopped him and found two eight-balls in his pockets. . . ."

"Eight-balls?"

"Eighth-ounce packets. That's a lot of cocaine, Mrs. Liss." They got to her room and she opened the door with the key. Lily followed her inside and Lucas stepped in and closed the door. Louise sat on the bed. "It's what they call a presumptive amount. With that big an amount of cocaine, the law presumes he's dealing and it's a felony."

"He's just seventeen," Louise said. She seemed barely able to hold up her head.

Lucas put a sad expression on his face. "With that much cocaine, the county attorney will put him on trial as an adult. If he's convicted, it'd be a minimum of three years in prison."

The blood drained out of Louise's face. "What do you want?" she whispered.

"We're not Narcotics people," Lily said. She sat on the bed beside Louise and touched her on the shoulder. "We're investigating these murders with the Indians, like the one with your husband. So anyway, one of the Narcotics guys, his name is Sloan, came in this afternoon and said, 'Guess what? You know that guy they got out in South Dakota? The guy who killed the attorney general? We just busted his kid.' And then he said, 'I guess the whole family is rotten.' "

"We're not rotten," Louise protested. "I work hard. . . ."

"Well, we've got some room to maneuver with Harold, your son," Lily said in a quiet voice. "The court could treat him as a juvenile. But we have to give something to the Narcotics people. Some reason. We said, 'Well, his father is refusing to talk, and that thing is a lot more important than another dope charge.' We said, 'If we can get him to tell us just a few things, could we promise that we'd treat Harold as a juvenile?' The Narcotics officers thought it over, and we talked to the chief, and they said, 'Yes.' That's why we're here, frankly. To see if we can make a deal."

"You want John to sell out his friends," Louise said bitterly. "Sell out the people."

"We don't want any more murders," Lucas said. "That's all we want to do. We want to stop them."

Louise Liss had been pressing her hands to her cheeks as she listened to the pitch; now she dropped them into her lap. It was a gesture of either despair or surrender. Lily leaned closer to her. "Hasn't your family paid enough? Your husband is going to prison. He'll never walk again. You don't see the people who are behind this thing, you don't see those people in prison. They're still out walking around. *Walking* around, Louise."

"I don't know anything myself . . ." she said tentatively.

"Could you talk to John?" Lily asked gently.

"It would really be good if he could just give us a few names. We don't need a lot of details, just a few names. Nobody would have to know, even," Lucas said.

There was a moment of silence, and then Louise said, "Nobody would have to know?"

"Nobody," Lily said flatly. "And it would save your family a lot of grief. I hate to bring this up, but I noticed that Harold was a very good-looking youth. I mean, if they put him in the prison up in St. Cloud, with some men who have not had sexual relationships in a long time . . . Well."

"Oh, no, not Harold."

"It's not like they really have a choice," Lucas said. "Some of those guys up there are bigger than football players. . . ."

When Louise had gone, Lily asked, "How bad do you feel?"

Lucas cocked his head and rolled his eyes up, as though thinking about it, and said, "Actually, not that bad."

"I don't feel that bad myself. And I think we should. It makes me a little sad that we don't feel worse," Lily said. "We're missing some parts, Davenport."

Lucas shrugged. "They got worn off. And . . ."

"What?"

"It's a game, you know," he said, testing her. "You can't back off in a game and win. You either go balls to the wall, or somebody takes you out and you're no good anymore."

Louise Liss was back from the hospital an hour later.

"I had trouble getting in," she apologized.

"Did you talk to John?"

"Yes . . . you'll help Harold?"

"If you help us, Mrs. Liss, I'll do everything I can to see that Harold is released," Lucas promised.

"It's some people named Crow," she said in a low voice. "They may be brothers or cousins. They're big Dakota medicine men."

"Dakota?" asked Lily.

"That's Minnesota Sioux," Lucas said. "Where are they at?"

"I wrote it down," Louise said, fumbling a piece of paper out of her purse. It was the corner of an envelope, with a street address. "He thinks this is right. . . ."

"Are there any more killings planned?" Lily pressed.

"All he would give me are the names and that address," Louise said. "I think it might kill him, just doing that."

"Okay, that's fine," Lily said. "We'll see about Harold tonight. We'll call on the telephone."

"Please," Louise Liss said, snatching at Lily's coat sleeve, "help him. Please?"

"The Crows? He said the Crows?" Larry Hart was astonished.

"You know them?" asked Daniel. Lucas was in a phone booth. Daniel, Anderson, Sloan and Hart were in Daniel's office, using a speaker phone.

"I know about them." There was a long pause, as Hart thought it over. "God damn. I might even have seen them once. They're famous. Two old men, they travel around the country and up in Canada, organizing the Indian nations. They've been on the road all their lives. Aaron is powerful medicine. Sam is supposed to be brilliant. . . . Jesus, you know, it all fits. They'd be right."

"What was that on their names? Aaron?" Anderson asked.

"Aaron and Sam. They supposedly come through the Cities a lot. It's like their home base. They have a son here, you see him from time to time. I went to school with him, years ago. Shit, you might even see the Crows from time to time, but I wouldn't know them. . . ."

"What about the son?" asked Sloan.

"The son is a freak. He has visions. He doesn't know which one of the Crows is his father. They were both sleeping with his mother that winter. . . . That's how he got his name, Shadow Love, love-in-the-shadows . . . it's like an Indian joke, based on his mother's last name. He's supposed to have some of the power of Aaron. . . ."

"Wait a minute, wait a minute," Lucas said. "Shadow Love?"

"Yeah. Skinny guy . . ."

"With tattoos. God damn." Lucas slapped his forehead. He took the phone away from his mouth and spoke to Lily. "We got them. These are the right motherfuckers." He went back to the phone. "Shadow Love's the guy I saw with Yellow Hand, before Yellow Hand was killed. Sonofabitch. Shadow Love. And two guys named Crow?"

"Yeah." Hart sounded distant, almost pensive.

"All right, listen," Lucas said. He hesitated a moment, trying to remember each step of his brief encounter with Shadow Love. "All right: Shadow Love's got a South Dakota driver's license and it's in his own name. I looked at it and that's how I remember the name, because it was so strange. And I don't know why, I can't remember, but something he said made me think he'd done time in prison. Harmon, can you run that down? Check with the NCIC or whatever?"

"I got it," said Anderson.

"We'll get some guys on the way to that address, check it out," Daniel said. "We ought to know something in an hour."

"Call us," Lucas said. He gave them his room number. "We'll get something to eat, then I'll be in my room."

"Soon as we know," Daniel promised. "This is fuckin' great, you two. This is what we needed. We got those motherfuckers."

CHAPTER

16

Anderson got the location of the Crows' apartment and a
bonus—a phone number—from the 911 center, and ran
them down to Daniel's office.

"I'll start pulling guys," Anderson said. "I can get Del
and a couple of his Narcotics people down there in ten minutes. They can check the place out while we get the entry
team together. We'll stage at the Mobil station on Thirty-
sixth."

"Don't tell anyone but Del what we're doing. Not until
the last minute, when we have the place nailed down," Daniel said. "I don't want the feebs moving in."

"All the local feebs are out in Brookings," Sloan said with
an edge of sarcasm. "That fuckin' Clay came in like the
President of the Universe. Eight hundred guys running
around with microphones in their ears . . ."

"Okay, but still keep it under your hat," Daniel said.

Anderson hurried away to his office. "You guys stick
around," Daniel said to Hart and Sloan. "If this works out,
you'll want to be in on the kill."

Sloan nodded and glanced at Larry. "Want to walk down
to the machines and get a bite? Could be our last chance
for a while . . ."

"I'll catch you down there," Larry said. "I gotta take a leak."

The Crows had mailed the press release on the Linstad killing earlier in the day, and Sam was rereading it as he tried to get comfortable on the battered couch. "I hope John sticks to it, the Indian Nation stuff," he said. "Hope he doesn't fall apart."

"He's got Meadows covering him," Aaron said. "Meadows is pretty good. . . ."

"Fuckin' wannabee," Sam grunted.

"John's got his reasons to hold out. He ever tell you his hot-dog story?"

Aaron was sitting at the kitchen table and Sam had to crank his head around to see him. " 'Hot dog'?"

John Liss had been twelve, a weedy kid in an army shirt and jeans. His father had been gone for weeks, his mother for two days with a man he didn't know. Her car was still out front, with maybe two gallons of gas. Neither John nor his nine-year-old sister had eaten since noon the day before—a can of Campbell's cream of mushroom soup.

"I'm so hungry," Donna cried. "I'm so hungry."

John made up his mind. "Get in the car," he said.

"You can't drive."

"Sure I can. Get in the car. We'll find something to eat."

"Where? We don't got no money," she said skeptically. But she was pulling on her jacket. She wore flip-flops for shoes.

"In town."

Friday night. The lights at the football field on the edge of town were the brightest things for miles.

"Must be about done," John Liss said. He could barely see over the steering wheel on the old Ford Fairlane. They bumped off the road and across a dirt parking lot. The temperature was in the forties. As long as the car was running, the heater would work, but he worried about running out of gas. If they were careful, they could make it back home.

"Watch the hot-dog stand," John told his sister. The year before, he had gone to a game and afterward had watched the woman who ran the concession stand peel a half-dozen wieners off the spits of an automatic broiler and toss them into a garbage can. A partial bag of buns had gone with them. The stand was in the same place, and a garbage can still stood next to it. Even the woman was the same.

The game ended twenty minutes later. The hometown fans spilled out of the stands, pushing and shoving in celebration of the victory. A tall blond kid stopped at the hot-dog stand, bought a dog and a Coke, and started walking away with friends. After a few steps, he spotted a girl in the crowd and yelled, "Hey, Carol."

"What do *you* want, Jimmy?" she asked teasingly. They were both wearing red wool letter jackets with white leather sleeves and yellow letters. John and his sister watched as they sidled toward each other, grinning, friends backing up each of them.

"This remind you of anything?" Jimmy asked, sliding the wiener out of his bun.

Her friends feigned shock while his slapped themselves on their foreheads, but Carol was ready: "Well," she said, "I suppose it might look a teensy bit like your dick, only the weenie's a lot bigger."

"Oh, *right*," he said, and flipped the wiener at her. She ducked and laughed and charged him, and they wrestled through the parking lot. Two minutes later, they were all gone.

"Go get it," Donna whispered.

"Did you see where it went?"

"Right under the stands . . ."

John slipped out of the car and found the wiener in the dirt. He wiped it on his shirt, brought it back and offered it to his sister. "It's still hot," she said. "God, it's perfect."

Her eyes were shining. John looked at her and the anger that washed over him almost snapped his spine. This was his *sister*: his fuckin' *little sister*. He wanted to kill someone, but he didn't know whom, or how. Not then. Later, when he met the Crows, he learned whom and how.

•   •   •

"Everybody's got a story," Sam said somberly. "Every fuckin' one of us. If it's not about us, it's about somebody in the family. Jesus Christ."

The phone rang.

"Shadow Love?" Sam asked.

Aaron shrugged and picked up the phone. " 'Lo?"

"The cops are coming," a man said. *"They'll be there in ten minutes."*

"What?"

"The cops are coming. Get out now."

Sam Crow was on his feet. "What?"

Aaron stood with the receiver in his hand, confused. "Somebody, I don't know. Said the cops are on their way. In ten minutes."

"Let's go. . . ."

"I gotta get . . ."

"Fuck it, let's go!" Sam yelled. He grabbed Aaron's jacket, threw it at him, picked up his own.

"The typewriter . . ." Aaron seemed dazed.

"Fuck the typewriter!" Sam had the door open.

"I got to get my letters. I don't know what's in them. Maybe something about Barbara or something . . ."

"Ah, shit . . ." Sam grabbed a brown supermarket bag and sailed it at Aaron. "Get as much as you can in there," he said. He jerked open a closet door, pulled a green army duffel bag out and started pushing in their clothing. "Don't look at that shit, just stuff it in the bag," he shouted at Aaron, who seemed to be moving in slow motion, thumbing through his personal papers.

It took them four minutes to fill the duffel and collect Aaron's papers. The rest of their possessions would be left behind.

"Whoever it was, maybe they were wrong," Aaron panted as they started down the stairs.

"They weren't wrong. You think somebody'd just call . . . ?"

"No. And it was an Indian guy. He had the accent. . . ."

Sam stopped at the first-floor landing and peered out at the street.

"Through the back," he said after a second. "There's a guy walking down the street."

"What about the truck?" Aaron asked as he trailed behind his cousin.

"If they know us, if they've got our names, they'll know about the truck. And our fingerprints are all over that room. . . ."

They went down another flight into the basement, then out past the furnace and a storage room, and up a short flight of concrete steps into an alley. The darkness was broken by lights from back windows of the apartments and of houses on the other side of the alley.

"Right through the yard," Sam said in a whisper.

"They'll think we're window peepers," Aaron said.

"Shhh."

They crossed the yard, crouching, staying close to the garage and then to a hedge.

"Watch the clothesline," Sam muttered a second too late. The wire line snapped Aaron across the bridge of the nose.

"Ah, boy, that hurt," he said, holding his nose.

"Quiet . . ."

They stopped behind a bridal-wreath bush by the corner of the house. A car was moving along the street; it slowed and stopped at the corner. A few seconds later, two men got out. One leaned against the fender of the car and lit a cigarette. The other wandered down the sidewalk toward the back of the Crows' apartment house. They looked like street people but walked with a hard confidence.

"Cops," Sam whispered.

"We got to get across the street before everything is blocked," Aaron said.

"C'mon." Sam led the way again, dragging the duffel bag. They went down the length of the block, crossing yards behind the houses. Most windows were still lit. They heard music from several, or television dialogue muffled by the closed windows.

Aaron suddenly laughed, a delighted sound that stopped Sam in his tracks.

"What?"

"Remember back in Rapid City, when we was hitting

those houses? Shit, we wasn't hardly teenagers. . . . It feels kind of good."

"Asshole," Sam grunted, but a moment later he chuckled. "I remember that broad with the yellow towel. . . ."

"Oh yeah . . ."

At the last house, they moved into a hedge and looked into the street.

"Nobody," said Sam. "Unless they're sitting in one of those cars."

"Right straight across and into the alley," Aaron said. "Go."

They crossed the street as quickly as they could, the duffel banging against Sam's legs. They hurried down the length of the alley.

"I can't carry this motherfucker much farther," Sam panted.

"There's a phone up by the SuperAmerica store. One more block," Aaron said.

They humped down another alley, Aaron helping with the duffel bag. At the end of the alley they stopped, and Aaron sat down behind between a bush and a chain-link fence. The Superamerica was straight across the street, the phone mounted on an outside wall.

"I'll call Barbara," Sam said, fumbling for change. "You wait here. Stay out of sight. I'll have her pull right into the alley."

"What about Shadow Love? If this is right, if there are cops, he'll walk right into them."

"There's nothing we can do about that," Sam said bleakly. "We gotta hope that he spots them, or calls Barb."

"Maybe it's nothing," Aaron said.

"Bullshit," said Sam. "Those were cops. They figured us out, cousin. They're on our ass."

CHAPTER
17

Two pickups and a car with a Sioux Falls television logo were angle-parked outside the all-night coffee shop. A single man in a cowboy hat sat in a window booth, hunched over a cup of coffee and a grilled-cheese sandwich. Lucas hesitated outside the window, looking in, then followed Lily through the door.

"Checking for Jennifer?" she asked with a small smile.

Lucas blushed. "Well, it'd be better if she weren't . . ."

"Sure." He followed her down the row of booths, watching her hips. She'd changed from slacks to a dress and low heels. She still carried the shoulder bag with the .45.

The waitress, a tired young woman with vagrant strands of black hair dangling in her face, took their order of cheeseburgers and coffee and slouched away.

"What do you think about this Crows business?" Lily asked while they waited for the food.

"I don't know. Larry sounded weird. And shit, I was talking to this other guy, this Shadow Love. I knew at the time there was something not right about him. He . . . vibrated, you know?"

"Fruitcake?"

"There was something wrong. I don't know." The coffee came, scalding hot, oily.

There was nothing like the Minneapolis Indian community in New York, Lily said. Indians were there, all right, but weren't as visible. "They look kind of . . . mysterious," she said. "You see them on the street, on the corners. They're not threatening, not hostile. They just seem to watch. . . ."

Lucas nodded. "Sometimes they're like the biggest up-country Scandinavian redneck shitkickers in the world. They bang around in old pickups and work in the lumber business or ranching. Then other times you'll be out fuckin' around somewhere and you'll come across a bunch of Indians doing a ceremony. It looks like a tourist thing, but it's not. It's real. . . ."

They talked for an hour. Lucas at one point decided he was babbling. On the way back to the motel, in the car, they spoke almost not at all. Lucas parked behind the motel and locked the car.

"Think they'll know anything?" she asked as they walked down the hall toward their rooms.

"Maybe. We can call."

"Come on in. We can call from my room." She pushed the door open and Lucas followed her inside. She gestured at the phone, and he sat on the bed, picked up the receiver and dialed. Daniel answered on the first ring.

"Chief: Lucas. What happened?"

"We went in, but we missed them," Daniel said. "They're the right guys, though. There were a couple of press releases balled up and tossed in a garbage bag under the sink and the typewriter's right . . ."

"They left the typewriter?"

"Yeah. Sloan's down there, with Del, and they say it's kind of odd. They left a lot of junk behind, but the personal stuff is gone. Sloan thinks they blew out of the place in a hurry—maybe when they heard that Liss wasn't dead. Figured he might talk."

"Are you talking to the neighbors?"

"Yeah. Nobody saw them much. They are two old Indians, though. And they left prints all over the place, the

FBI's running them now. And somebody said they drove a truck, and that's still parked out front. . . ."

"Jesus. Maybe you ought to shut down the scene and watch it, maybe they'll be back. . . ."

"We're doing that, but Del doesn't think it'll work. He says word'll be up and down the street in an hour, about the raid."

"That's probably right," Lucas said. "Damn."

"We'll talk to you tomorrow—we ought to have everything figured out by then. We'll meet at one o'clock, if you can make it."

"We'll be there," Lucas said. He hung up and turned to Lily, shaking his head. "Missed them."

"But they're the right guys?"

"Yeah, they left some stuff behind. They got a definite ID."

"God damn it," Lily said irritably. She dropped her head and reached back with one hand and rubbed her neck. She was less than a foot away and Lucas could smell the elusive scent she'd worn the first day he'd met her.

"How much longer are we going to fool around?" he asked quietly.

"I'm all done," she said.

"Say what? You're all done?"

"Yeah." She stood and stepped across the room. Lucas started after her, but she reached the lights, snapped them off and then stepped back into the dark, her arms crossed in front of her breasts.

"I'm really scared," she said.

"Jesus." He wrapped her tightly with his left arm, caught the back of her neck in his right hand and pulled her face to his. The kiss locked them together, swaying, for ten seconds; then she pulled her chin back, gasping, and they stumbled sideways together and fell on the bed.

"Lucas, dammit, give me a minute in the shower. . . ."

"Fuck the shower," he said. His voice was coarse, fevered. He kissed her again, his body pressing her into the bed, one hand tugging at the buttons that held the top of her dress together.

"Jesus, let me . . ."

"I got it." A button popped and his hand was on her warm skin, her stomach, then around behind, unlatching her brassiere. Lily began to moan, trying to catch his lips. They rolled across the bed, she fumbling with his belt, he with his hand now beneath her dress, pulling at her underpants.

"My God, a garter belt, what's it made out of, steel mesh? I can't . . ."

"Slow down, slow down. . . ."

"No."

He got the garter belt off one leg, though it was still twisted around her ankle, and then her underpants were off one leg, and his hands were on her. Finally he entered her and she nearly screamed with the intensity of the feeling . . . and sometime later, she thought, she did scream.

"Christ, I wish I still smoked," he said. He'd turned on a bedside lamp and was sitting up, still mostly dressed. She was gasping for air. Like a carp, she thought. She'd never seen one, but had read in good books about carp gasping for air on riverbanks. He looked down at her. "Are you okay?"

"Yeah. My God . . ."

"Can I . . . let me take some of this stuff . . ."

After the violence of the first episode, he was suddenly tender, moving her body, lifting her, stripping off her remaining clothing. She felt almost like a child, until he kissed her on the front of her thigh, just where it joined her hip, and the fire ran through her belly again and she gasped. Lucas was on her again and the bedside lamp seemed to grow dimmer. Then again, after a while, she thought, she may have screamed again.

"Did I scream?" she blurted. She stood facing the shower head, the water beating off her breasts. Lucas stood behind her. She could feel him pressing against her buttocks, his soapy hand on her stomach.

"I don't know. I thought it was me," he said.

She giggled. "What are you doing?"

"Just washing."

"I think you already washed there."

"A little more couldn't hurt."

She closed her eyes and leaned back against him, his soapy hand moving, and it started once again. . . .

CHAPTER
18

Barbara Gow's house had gray siding, once white, and a red asbestos-shingle roof. A single box elder stood in the front yard and a swayback garage hunkered hopelessly in back. A waist-high chain-link fence surrounded her holdings.

"It looks pretty bad," she said sadly. They were ten minutes off the expressway, in a neighborhood of tired yards. The postwar frame houses were crumbling from age, poor quality and neglect: roofs were missing shingles, eaves showed patches of dry rot. In the dim illumination of the streetlights, they could see kids' bikes dumped unceremoniously on the weedy lawns. The cars parked in the streets were exhausted hulks. Oil stains marked the driveways like Rorschachs of failure.

"When I bought it, I called it a cottage," she said as they rolled into the driveway. "God damn, it makes me sad. To think you can live in a place for thirty years, and in the end, not care about it."

Sam Crow closed one eye and stared at her with the other, gauging the level of her unhappiness. In the end, he grunted, got out of the car and lifted the garage door.

"I hope Shadow Love's okay," she said anxiously as she pulled into the garage.

She had picked them up ten minutes after Sam called her.

As they headed back to her house, they crossed the street that the apartment was on. There were cars in the street. Cops. The raid was under way.

"He was due back," Sam said as they got out of the car. "With all those cops in the street . . ."

"If he wasn't there when they arrived . . ."

"If they didn't get him, we should be hearing from him," said Aaron.

Barbara's house was musty. She was never a housekeeper, and she smoked: the interior, once bright, was overlaid with a yellowing patina of tobacco tar. Sam Crow dragged the duffel bag up the stairs. Aaron headed for a sitting room that had a foldout couch.

"You guys got any money?" Barbara asked when Sam came back down.

"A couple of hundred," he said, shrugging.

"I'll need help with the groceries if you stay here long."

"Shouldn't be too long. A week, maybe."

Twenty minutes later, Shadow Love called. Barbara said, "Yes, they're here. They're okay," and handed the phone to Sam.

"We were afraid they got you," Sam said.

"I almost walked right into them," Shadow Love said. He was in a bar six blocks from the Crows' apartment. "I was thinking about something else, I was almost on the block when I realized something was wrong, with all those cars. I watched for a while, I was worried I'd see them taking you out."

"You coming here?" Sam asked.

"I better. I don't know where they got their information, but if they're tracking me . . . I'll see you in a half-hour."

When Shadow Love arrived, Barbara stood on her tiptoes to kiss him on the cheek and took him straight into the kitchen for a sandwich.

"Somebody betrayed us," Shadow Love said. "That fuckin' Hart was in the street outside the apartment. He's passing out money now. The hunter cop too."

"We're not doing as well as I hoped," Sam confessed. "I'd hoped Billy would get at least one more and that John would make it out of Brookings. . . ."

"Leo's still out and I'm available," Shadow Love said. "And you can't complain about the media. Christ, they're all over the goddamned Midwest. I saw a thing on television from Arizona, people out on the reservations there, talking. . . ."

"So it's working," Aaron said, looking at his cousin.

"For now, anyway," Sam said.

Later that night, Sam watched Barbara move around the bedroom and thought, She's old.

Sixty, anyway. Two years younger than he was. He remembered her from the early fifties, the Ojibway bohemian student of French existentialists, her dark hair pulled back in a bun, her fresh heart-shaped face without makeup, her books in a green cloth sack carried over her shoulder. Her beret. She wore a crimson beret, pulled down over one eye, smoked Gauloises and Gitanes and sometimes Players, and talked about Camus.

Barbara Gow had grown up on the Iron Range, the product of an Ojibway father and a Serbian mother. Her father worked in the open-pit mines during the day and for the union at night. Her mother's Bible sat in a small bookcase in the living room. Next to it was her father's *Das Kapital*.

As a teenager, she had done clerical work for the union. After her mother died, leaving a small insurance policy, she'd moved to Minneapolis and started at the university. She liked the university and the talk, the theory. She liked it better when she heard the news from existential France.

Sam could still see all of that in her, behind the wrinkled face and slumping shoulders. She shivered nude in the cold air and pulled on a housecoat, then turned and smiled at him, the smile lighting his heart.

"I'm surprised that thing still works, much as you abuse it," she said. Sam's penis curled comfortably on his pelvis. It *felt* happy, he thought.

"It'll always work for you," Sam said. He lay on top of the blankets, on top of the handmade quilt, impervious to the cold.

She laughed and left the room, and a moment later he heard the water start in the bathroom. Sam lay on the bed, wishing he could stay for a year or two years or five, wrapped in the quilt. Scared. That's what it was, he thought. He put the thought out of his mind, rolled off the bed and walked to the bathroom. Barbara was sitting on the toilet. He stepped in front of the vanity and turned on the water to wash himself.

"Shadow Love's still watching that movie," Barbara said. The sounds of TV gunfire drifted up the stairs.

"*Zulu,*" said Sam. "Big fight in Africa, a hundred years ago. He says it was better than the Custer fight."

Barbara stood up and flushed the toilet as Sam dried himself with a towel. "Is this the end?" she asked quietly as they walked back into the bedroom.

He knew what she meant, but pretended he did not. "The end?"

"Don't give me any bullshit. Are you going to die?"

He shrugged. "Shadow Love says so."

"Then you will," Barbara said. "Unless you go away. Now."

Sam shook his head. "Can't do that."

"Why not?"

"The thing is, these other people have died. If it comes my turn and I don't fight, it'll be like I turned my back on them."

"You've got a gun?"

"Yeah."

"And this is all necessary?"

"Yes. And it's almost necessary that we . . . die. The people need this story. You know, when we were kids, I knew people who rode with Crazy Horse. Who's alive now to talk to the kids? The only legends they have are dope dealers. . . ."

"So you're ready."

"No, of course not," Sam admitted. "When I think about dying . . . I can't think about dying. I'm not ready."

"Nobody ever is," Barbara said. "I look at myself in the mirror, on the door . . ." She pushed the bedroom door shut, and the full-length mirror mounted on the back reflected the two of them, naked, looking into it. ". . . and I see this old woman, shriveled up like last year's potato. A clerk at the historical society, all gray and bent over. But I feel like

I'm eighteen. I want to go out and run in the park with the wind in my hair, and I want to roll around on the grass with you and Aaron and hear Aaron putting the bullshit on me, trying to get into my pants . . . and I can't do any of that because I'm old. And I'm going to die. I don't want to be old and I don't want to die, but I will. . . . I'm not ready, but I'm going."

"I'm glad we had this talk," Sam said wryly. "It really cheered me up."

She sighed. "Yeah. Well, the way you talk, I think when the time comes, you'll use the gun."

Shadow Love paced.

Sam lay at Barbara's right hand, asleep, his breathing deep and easy, but all during the night Barbara could hear Shadow Love pacing the length of the downstairs hallway. The television came on, was turned off, came on again. More pacing. He'd always been like that.

Almost forty years earlier, Barbara had lived a half block from Rosie Love, and had met the Crows at her house. They had been radical hard-cases even then, smoking cigarettes all night, drinking, talking about the BIA cops and the FBI and what they were doing on the reservations.

When Shadow was born, Barbara was the godmother. In her mind's eye, she could still see Shadow Love walking the city sidewalks in his cheap shorts and undersize striped polo shirt, his pale eyes calculating the world around him. Even as a child, he had had the fire. He was never the biggest kid on the block, but none of the other kids fooled with him. Shadow Love was electric. Shadow Love was crazy. Barbara loved him as she would her own child, and she lay in her bed and listened to him pace. She looked at the clock at 3:35, and then she drifted off to sleep.

In the morning, she found him sitting, asleep, in the big chair in the living room, the chair she once called her man-trap. She tiptoed past the doorway toward the kitchen, and his voice called to her as she passed: "Don't sneak."

"I thought you were asleep," she said. She stepped back to the doorway. He was on his feet. Light was coming in the window behind him and he loomed in it, a dark figure with a halo.

"I was, for a while." He yawned and stretched. "Is this house wired for cable?"

"Yeah, I got it for a while. But when there was nothing on, I had them turn it off."

"How about if I give you the money and you have them turn it back on? HBO or Cinemax or Showtime. Maybe all of them. When the heat gets heavy, we'll really be cooped up."

"I'll call them this morning," she said.

At midmorning, after breakfast, Barbara got a stool, a towel and a pair of scissors and cut Sam's and Shadow Love's hair. Aaron sat and watched in amusement as the hair fell in black wisps around their shoulders and onto the floor. He told Sam that when old men get their hair cut, they lose their potency.

"Nothin' wrong with my dick," Sam said. "Ask Barb." He tried to slap her on the butt. She dodged his hand and Shadow Love flinched. "Watch it, God damn it, you're going to stick the scissors in my ear."

When she finished, Shadow Love put on a long-sleeved cowboy shirt, sunglasses and a baseball cap.

"I still look pretty fuckin' Indian, don't I?"

"Get rid of the sunglasses," Barbara said. "Your eyes could pass for blue. You could be a tanned white man."

"I could use some ID," Shadow Love said, tossing the sunglasses on the kitchen table.

"Just a minute," Barbara said. She went upstairs and came back a few minutes later with a man's billfold, all flat and tired and shaped to another butt. "It was my brother's," she said. "He died two years ago."

The driver's license was impossible. Her brother had been four years older than she, and bald and heavy. Even with the bad picture, there was no way Shadow Love could claim to be the man in the photo.

"All this other stuff is good," he said, thumbing through it. Harold Gow had credit cards from Amoco, Visa and a local department store. He had a membership card from an

HMO, a Honeywell employee's ID without a photo, a Social Security card, a Minnesota watercraft license, a credit-union card, a Prudential claim card, two old fishing licenses, and other odd bits and pieces of paper. "If they shake me down, I'll tell them I lost my license on a DWI. When an Indian tells them that, they believe you."

"What about you guys?" Barbara asked the Crows.

Sam shrugged. "We got driver's licenses and Social Security cards under our born names. I don't know if the cops have those figured out yet, but they will."

"Then you shouldn't go out on the street. At least not during the day," Barbara said.

"I've got to talk to people, find out what's going on," Shadow Love said.

"You be careful," Barbara said.

Shadow Love was in a bar on Lake Street when an Indian man came in and ordered a beer. The man glanced sideways at Shadow Love and then ignored him.

"That Welfare guy's down at Bell's Apartments handing out money again," the Indian man told the bartender.

"Christ, half the town is drinking on him," the bartender said. "I wonder where they're getting all the loot?"

"I bet it's the CIA."

"Boy, if it's the CIA, somebody's in trouble," the bartender said wisely. "I met some of those boys in 'Nam. You don't want to fuck with them."

"Bad medicine," the Indian man said.

A man at the back of the bar yelled, "Nine-ball?" and the Indian man called, "Yeah, I'm coming," took the beer and wandered back. The bartender wiped the spot he'd been leaning on with a wet rag and shook his head.

"The CIA. Man, that's bad business," he said to Shadow Love.

"That's bullshit, is what it is," Shadow Love said.

He finished his beer, slid off the stool and walked outside. The sun was shining and he stopped, squinting against the bright light. He thought for a moment, then turned west and ambled down Lake Street toward the apartments.

Bell's Apartments were an ugly remnant of a sixties housing program. The architect had tried to disguise an underlying prison-camp barrenness by giving each apartment a different-colored door. Now, years later, the colored doors together looked like a set of teeth with a few punched out.

Behind the building, an abandoned playground squatted in a rectangle of dead weeds. The hand-push merry-go-round had broken off its hub years before and had rusted into place, like a bad minimalist sculpture. The basketball court offered pitted blacktop and bare hoops. The swing sets had lost all but two swings.

Shadow Love sat in one of the swings and watched Larry Hart working his way down to the first floor of the building. Hart would look at a piece of paper in his hand, knock on a door, talk to whoever answered, then move on. Sometimes he talked for ten seconds, sometimes for five minutes. Several times he laughed, and once he went inside and came back out a few minutes later, chewing something. Frybread.

The problem, Shadow Love thought, was that there were too many people in on the Crows' secret. Leo and John and Barbara, and a bunch of wives who might know or have guessed something.

The Crows had been proselytizing for years. Though they had stayed resolutely in the background, their names were known, as was the extreme nature of their gospel. Once those names popped up on a police computer as suspects, they'd go right to the top of the hunters' list. That normally wouldn't be too much of a problem. The cops' resources in the Indian community were minimal.

Hart was something else. Shadow Love had known him in high school, but only from a distance, in the days when the boys in one grade didn't mix with the boys in the grades above. Hart had been popular then, with both Indians and whites. He still was. He was one of the people and he had friends and he had money.

Shadow Love watched him working down through the building, heard him laughing, and before Hart reached the bottom level, Shadow Love knew that something would have to be done.

•   •   •

Hart saw Shadow Love sitting in the swing as he walked toward the steps that would take him to the bottom floor, but he didn't recognize him. He watched the man swinging, then dropped into a blind section of the stairwell. Five seconds later, when he came out of the stairwell, the man was gone.

Hart shivered. The man must have simply gotten off the swing, walked around the bush at the edge of the playground and gone down the street. But that was not the effect Hart felt. The man was there when he went into the stairwell and gone a few seconds later. He had vanished, leaving behind a swing that still rocked back and forth from his energy.

It was as though he had disappeared, as Mexican wizards were said to do, changing into crows and hawks and jumping straight up in the air.

Indian demons.

Hart shivered again.

A block away, Shadow Love was on the phone.

"Barb? Could you pick me up?"

CHAPTER
19

Lucas woke in the dark, listening, and finally identified the sound that had woken him. He reached across the bed and touched her.

"Crying?"

"I can't help it," she squeaked.

"A little guilt, maybe."

She choked, unable to answer for a moment. Then came a muffled "Maybe." She rolled over to face him, her knees pulled up in fetal position. "I've never done this before."

"You told me that," he said into the dark. He groped around for a moment, found the switch on the bedside lamp and turned it on. Her head was down, her face concealed.

"The thing is, I knew I would be. Unfaithful. That one night, in my room, I almost didn't stop you. I shouldn't have. But it was . . . too quick. I couldn't handle it," she said. "Then when Hood went down and I was freaked out and you were freaked out and I got out of town. . . . On the way to New York, on the plane. I cried. I thought I wouldn't see you again, wouldn't get to sleep with you. But I was relieved, you know. When they told me I had to come back, I was crying again. David thought I was crying because I didn't want to come back. But I was crying because I knew what would happen. I was so . . . hungry."

"Hey, look. I've been through this," Lucas said. "I feel bad about it sometimes, but I can't stay away from women. A shrink would probably find something weird is wrong with me. But I just . . . want women. It's like you said, I get hungry. I can't stop it. It's a drug, you crave it."

"Just the sex?" She rolled over a bit, her head cocked toward him, watching his eyes.

"No. The woman. The back-and-forth. Hanging around. The sex. Everything."

"You're a relationship junkie. Always need something new."

"No, that's not quite right. There's a woman in Minneapolis, I think I've gotten in bed with her once or twice a year since I was a rookie. Sixteen, eighteen years. I see her and I want her. I call her up, she calls me up, I want her. It's not newness. It's something else."

"Is she married?"

"Yeah. For fifteen years, must be. Has a couple of kids."

"That is strange." There was a moment of silence, then she said, "Part of the guilt is that I don't feel worse than I do. You know what I mean? I liked it. I haven't had sex that good since . . . I don't know. Ever, I think. It was like a blackout. With David, it's soft and gentle and the orgasms come, most of the time anyway, but nothing feels . . . driven. Everything is always under control. David is thin and doesn't have much hair. You're hard, and you've got all this body hair. It's like . . . it's so different."

"Too much analysis," Lucas said after a moment. She reached out and touched his face. "I just wanna fuck," he said in a gravelly parody of lust.

"That's ridiculous," she said. She pulled herself closer to him, snuggled on his arm. "Do you think the guilt will go away?"

"I'm pretty sure of it," he said.

"That's what I think too," she said.

They left early, Lucas grumpy in the morning sunlight, but touching her often, on the elbow, the cheek, the neck, brushing hair out of her face. "Let's go for a while. We can stop on the road for breakfast. I can't eat when I'm up this early," he grumbled.

"Your internal clock is screwed up," Lily said as they settled into the Porsche. "You need to get reoriented."

"Nothing happens in the morning, so why get up?" Lucas said. "All the bad people are out at night. And most of the good ones, as far as that goes."

"Let's just try to make it back to the Cities in one piece," she said as he spun the drive wheels and left the motel parking lot. "If you want me to drive . . ."

"No, no."

They drove straight into the morning sun. Lily was feeling chatty and craned her neck at the oddities of the prairie.

"I'm going back a different way, a little further south," Lucas said. "I like to see as many roads as I can. I don't get out here very often."

"That's fine."

"It won't add much time," he said.

The day started cold but rapidly warmed up. A few minutes after they crossed the Minnesota line, Lucas pulled into a roadside diner. They were the only customers. A fat woman worked in the kitchen behind a chest-high stainless-steel counter. They saw only her head. The counterman was a thin, big-eyed man wearing a dirty apron. He had two days of beard and rolled a Lucky Strike, half smoked and now unlit, between his thin lips. Lucas ordered two hard-fried eggs and bacon.

"I'd recommend that," he said to Lily.

"I'll have the eggs, anyway," she said. The waiter yelled back to the cook and then stumped off to a chair and picked up the local weekly.

"Have you been here before?" Lily asked quietly when the waiter's back was turned.

"No."

"So how can you recommend the bacon and eggs?"

Lucas looked around the diner. Paint was peeling off the ceiling and a black mold was attacking the seams of the aging wallpaper. "Because they've got to fry it and that ought to sterilize it," he said under his breath.

She glanced around and suddenly giggled, and Lucas thought he might be in love.

After breakfast, when they were back in the car, the talk slowed and Lily moved her seat to a reclined position. Her eyes fell shut.

"A nap?" asked Lucas.

"Relaxing," she said. Her breathing grew steady, and Lucas drove on. Lily dozed but didn't sleep, opening her eyes and sitting forward at turns and stops. After a while, she found the steady soft vibration of the car had become arousing. She opened her eyes just a crack. Lucas had put on sunglasses and was driving with a steady, relaxed watchfulness. Now and then he turned his head to look at passing attractions that she couldn't see from her low position. She reached out and put a hand on his leg.

"Uh-oh," he said. He glanced at her and grinned. "The animal is alive."

"Just thinking," she said. She stroked his thigh, her eyes closed again, letting herself feel the coarse weave of his jeans.

"Dammit," Lucas said after a few more minutes. "My dick is going to break off." He pushed himself up in the seat, reached down the front of his pants and changed things around. She laughed, and when he sat down, she put her hand back in his lap. He was erect, his penis reaching up beneath his fly to his belt.

"Ooo, too bad we're in a car," she said.

He looked over at her, grinned and said, "You've played this game before?"

"What game?" She stroked and he pushed her hand away.

"You're done," he said. "It's my turn. Take off your panty hose."

"Lucas . . ." she said. She sounded shocked, but she sat upright and looked out the car windows. They were alone on the rural highway.

"Come on, chicken. Off with the pants."

She looked at the speedometer. A steady sixty miles per hour. "You could kill us."

"Nope. I've played before."

"Mr. Experience, huh?"

"Come on, come on, you're bullshitting now. Off with the pants. Or live with the consequences."

"What consequences?"

"Deep in your heart, you'll know that I know you're chicken."

"All right, Davenport." She pushed herself off the seat, and with some difficulty pulled off her panty hose.

"Now the pants."

She pushed herself up again and took off her underpants.

"Here, I'll take them," Lucas said. Without thinking, she handed him the pants; he quickly dropped his window and threw them out.

"Davenport, for Christ's sakes . . ." She was looking back down the highway where the underpants had disappeared into a roadside ditch.

"I'll buy you new ones."

"Goddamn right," she said.

"So now you lean back and close your eyes." She looked at him and felt a blush crawling up her face. "Come on," he said.

She leaned back and his hand touched her thighs, the fingers just trailing along, from the joint of her hip to her knee, and back again. It was warm in the car and she felt the blood moving to her groin. Her mouth dropped open and the warmth continued to build.

"Oh, boy," she said after a few minutes. "Boy . . ."

"Moan for me," he said.

"What?"

"Moan for me. One good moan and Davenport stops the car."

She reached over and touched him. He felt huge under the jeans and she giggled. "I've got to stop giggling," she said lazily. She reached out again; then Lucas hit the brake and she rocked forward.

"What?" She looked wildly out the window.

"Jeffers petroglyphs," he said. "I've heard about them, but I've never seen them."

"What?" Lily was gasping, like a fish out of water. The

car rocked as Lucas pulled into a grass-covered parking area. She pulled her skirt down.

"Indian carvings on some exposed rock," Lucas said. There were two other cars in the parking area, although a sign said the petroglyph monument was closed for the season. Lucas hopped out of the car and Lily got out on her side. In the distance, across a fence, they could see a half-dozen people looking down at a slab of reddish rock.

"Must have climbed the fence," Lucas said. "Come on." Lucas vaulted the gate, then helped Lily clamber over.

"Christ, this is the last time I wear a dress on the road. And I feel so bare . . . you and your fucking games," she said. "From now on, it's tennis shoes and pants."

"You look good in a dress," he said as they walked up a graveled path. "You look terrific. And you look great without the underpants."

The petroglyphs were scratched into the flat surfaces of exposed red rock. There were outlines of hands, drawings of animals and birds, unknown symbols.

"Look how small their hands were," Lily said. She stooped and placed her own hand over one of the glyphs. Her hand was larger.

"Maybe it was a kid or a woman," Lucas said.

"Maybe." She stood straight and looked around at the rolling prairie and the adjoining cornfield. "I wonder what in the hell they would have been doing out here. There's nothing here."

"I don't know." Lucas looked around. The sky seemed huge, and he felt as though he were standing on the point of the planet. "You've got this rise, you can see forever. But I suppose it was really the rock. Further out west, there's an Indian quarry. It's old. The Indians would take out a soft red rock called pipestone. They made pipes and other stuff out of it."

The petroglyphs were carved on a gently sloping hillside and Lucas wandered with Lily down the slope, passing the other visitors. The others were on their hands and knees, tracing out the glyphs with their fingers. One woman was doing a charcoal rubbing on brown paper, transferring the designs. Two of them said hello. Lucas and Lily nodded.

"We've got to get going pretty soon if we want to make that meeting," Lucas said finally, glancing at his watch.

"Okay."

They walked slowly back to the car, the prairie wind blowing Lily's hair around her face. At the fence, she put one foot on the wire, and Lucas caught her from behind and squeezed.

"One small kiss," he said.

She turned and tipped up her face. The kiss started small and turned warmer, until they were dancing around slowly in the tall grass. She pushed him away after a moment and, breathing hard, looked down.

"These shoes . . . these heels, I'm going to twist my ankle."

"All right. Let's go." He helped her over the fence, then followed. As they walked to the car, he slipped his arm around her waist.

"I'm still turned on from fooling around in the car," he said.

"Hey. It's only three hours back to the Cities," she said playfully.

"And about two meetings after that."

"Tough luck, Davenport . . ."

He led her around the car, opened the passenger-side door, caught her by the arm, sat in the car and pulled her on top of him. "Come on."

"What?" She struggled for a moment, but he pulled her in.

"They can't see us from the road, and those other people are looking at the rocks," he said. "Face me."

"Lucas . . ." But she turned to face him.

"C'mon."

"I don't know how . . ."

"Just bend your knees up and sit, that's good, that's good."

"The car's too small, Lucas. . . ."

"That's fine, you're fine. Jeez, has anybody ever told you that you've got one of the great asses in Western history?"

"Lucas, we can't . . ."

"Ah . . ."

She sat astride him, facing him, her knees apart, just enough room to move a half-dozen inches, and he began to rock, and she felt the morning's play coalescing around her. She closed her eyes, and rocked, and rocked, and the orgasm gathered and flowed and washed over her. She came back only when she heard Lucas say, "Oh, man, man . . ."

"Lucas," she said, and she giggled again and caught herself. She never giggled and now she was giggling every fifteen minutes.

"I needed that," he said. He was sweating and his eyes looked distant and sated. The door was partway open, and Lily looked out the window, then pushed it open with a foot and eased out onto the grass and pulled her skirt down. Lucas followed awkwardly, zipped up, then leaned forward and kissed her. She wrapped her arms around him and pushed against his chest. They swayed together for a moment, then Lucas released her, looking dazed, and half staggered around the car.

"We better get going," he said.

"Right . . . okay." She got into the car, and Lucas started it and found the reverse gear. He slowly eased out onto the roadway, watching for traffic. The road was empty, but Lucas was preoccupied, so Lily saw them first.

"What are they doing?" she asked.

"What?" He looked in the same direction she was. The people who had been looking at the petroglyphs were lined up along the fence, facing them, repeatedly slapping their hands together.

Lucas stared for a moment, perplexed, then caught it and threw back his head and laughed.

"What?" asked Lily, still puzzled, looking at the line of people across the fence. "What are they doing?"

"They're applauding," Lucas laughed.

"Oh, no," Lily said, her face flaming as they accelerated away. She looked back and after a moment added, "They certainly got their money's worth. . . ."

CHAPTER
20

In the car, Barbara looked him over.

"Why am I doing this? Driving you?"

"I'm looking for a guy," Shadow Love said. "I want you to talk to him on the telephone."

"You're not going to do anything, are you?"

"No. Just want to talk," Shadow Love said. He turned away and watched the street roll by. It took an hour of cruising and a half-dozen stops, with Barbara growing increasingly anxious, but Shadow Love finally spotted Larry Hart as he went into the Nub Inn.

"Let's find a phone," Shadow Love said. "You know what to say."

"What're you going to do?" Barbara asked.

"I want to talk to him. See what he's getting. If there's any possibility that we'll be seen, I'll call it off. You can wait out of sight down the road. If anything goes wrong and they grab me, I just won't show up and you can drive away."

"All right. Be careful, Shadow."

Shadow Love glanced at her. Her knuckles were white on the steering wheel. *She knows what's coming.* The pistol he'd used to kill Yellow Hand pressed into his side. His fingers touched the cold stone knife in his pocket.

●   ●   ●

Hart took the bait. Barbara called him at the Nub Inn, explained that she'd seen him go inside, and said that she had some information. But she was scared, she said. Scared of the assassins, scared of the cops. She was an old client of his, she said, and knew him by sight. She said she'd meet him by the green dumpster outside the sheet-rock warehouse by the river.

"You've got to come alone, Larry, please. The cops scare me, they'll beat me up. I trust you, Larry, but the cops scare me."

"Okay. I'll see you in ten minutes," Hart said. "And don't be scared. There's nothing to be scared of."

She looked through the glass of the phone booth toward her car. Shadow Love was slumped in the passenger seat, and she could just see the top of his head. "Okay," she said.

It took Hart fifteen minutes to get out of the inn, into his car and down to the warehouse. "There he is," Shadow Love said as Hart pulled over to the curb near the warehouse. They watched as he got out of the car, locked it, looked around and began walking cautiously toward the dumpster at the corner of the building.

"Drive around the block, like I told you. I'll look for cops," Shadow Love said.

Nothing moving on the street, nobody sitting in parked cars. Shadow Love took a breath. "Okay," he said. "Up behind the warehouse. And then you go on down where I showed you, and wait."

When they finished circling the block, they were on the back side of the warehouse. Shadow Love got out of the car. "Take care," Barbara said. "And be quick."

As she drove away, Shadow Love walked across a vacant lot littered with construction debris to the warehouse. He slipped carefully around the corner and was then directly behind the dumpster. Through a narrow space between the warehouse wall and the dumpster, he saw, for just a second, the dark sleeve of a man's coat on the other side. Hart was wearing a black jacket. Shadow Love touched the pistol under his shirt and stepped around the dumpster.

"Larry," he said. Hart jumped and spun around.

"Jesus," he said, his face stricken. "Shadow."

"It's been a long time," Shadow Love said. "I think I saw you a time or two out on Lake Street, after you graduated."

"Yeah, long time," Hart said. He tried to smile. "Are you still living around here?"

Shadow Love ignored the question. "I heard in the bars that you've been looking for me," he said, stepping closer. Hart was bigger than he was, but Shadow Love knew that Hart would be no contest in a fight. Hart knew it too.

"Yeah, yeah. The cops have. They want to talk to you about your fathers."

"My fathers? The Crows?"

"Yeah. Some people think they might, you know . . ." Hart bobbed his head uncomfortably.

". . . have a connection with these killings?"

"Yeah."

"Well, I don't know about that," Shadow Love said. He was standing on the sides of his feet, the fingers of both his hands in his jeans pockets. "Are you a cop now, Larry?"

"No, no, I still work for the Welfare."

"You're sure talking like a cop, out on the street," Shadow Love said, pressing.

"Well, I know," Hart said. "I don't like it either. I got my clients, but the cops won't leave me alone, you know? They don't have anybody else who knows the people."

"Mmmm." Shadow Love looked down at the toes of his cowboy boots, then up at the sky. It had been slate-gray for a day and a half, but now there was a big blue hole in the clouds right over the river. "Come on, Larry. I want to talk some more. Let's go on down where we can see the river. Nice day."

"It's cold," Hart said. He shivered but walked along. Shadow Love stayed just a few inches behind him, his fingers still in his pockets.

"That's a big old hole, there," Shadow Love said, looking at the sky.

"They call it a sucker hole, pilots do," Hart said, looking up at it. "I took a couple of flying lessons once. That's what they called those things. Sucker holes."

"What do you think, that the Crows are behind all this?" Shadow Love asked.

Hart had to half turn to talk to him, and he lost his footing for a moment and stumbled. Shadow Love caught his elbow and helped him regain his balance. "Thanks," Hart said.

"The Crows?" Shadow Love prompted. They continued walking.

"Well, old man Andretti shipped a lot of money out here —that's the money the cops have been spreading around town—and those were the names that came up," Hart said. "The Crows."

"How about me?"

"Well, the cops know you're their son. They thought maybe you'd know . . ."

". . . where they are? Well, yeah. I do," Shadow Love said.

"You do?"

"Mmm." They got off the blacktopped street and walked along the grassy top of the hill that ran down to the Mississippi. Shadow Love stopped and looked down the river. The black spot floated out in front of his eyes, a funnel of darkness in the day. Fuckin' Hart, probing to find his fathers. "Love the river," he said.

"It's a hell of a river," Hart agreed. A harbor tow was pushing a single empty barge downstream toward the Ford lock and dam. The light from the sucker hole poured down on it, and from the height of the hillside, the boat and barge looked like kids' toys, every detail standing out in high relief.

"Look up there," Shadow Love said. "There's an eagle."

Hart looked up and saw the bird, but he thought maybe it was a hawk. He didn't say so but stood looking at it, aware of Shadow Love beside and slightly behind him. Shadow Love slipped his hand in his pocket and felt the knife. He'd never used it before, never thought of it as a real weapon.

"Breathe it in, Larry, the cold air. God, it feels good on your skin. Breathe it in. See the eagle circling? Look at the hillside over there, Larry. Look at the trees, you can pick them all out. . . . Breathe it in, Larry. . . ."

Hart stood with his back to Shadow Love, his eyes half closed, taking great gulping breaths of the cold air, feeling the tingle on his skin, on the back of his neck. He turned his head up again and said, "You know, I talked . . ."

He was going to tell Shadow Love that he'd called the Crows from the police station, to tell them about the coming raid. But he couldn't do that. It would sound as though he were trying to ingratiate himself, as if he were crawling. Tears started down his cheeks. The cold, he thought. Just the cold.

He was taking it all in, breathing it, feeling the eagle soar, when Shadow Love put a hand on his shoulder. Hart turned his head, but the other man had stepped behind him.

"What—" Hart began to say, and then he felt the fire in his throat, a stinging, and looked stupidly at the blood on his coat, pouring like a stream onto his hands. Hart sank to his knees in wonder, then fell on his face, rolled a few feet and stopped, the eagle gone forever.

Shadow Love watched his body for a moment, then put the knife back in his jacket and looked around. Nobody.

That's two, he thought. He turned and climbed the embankment, and as he did, the TV tape of the killing of Billy Hood unrolled before his eyes, the woman cop with her pistol, blasting young Billy in the face. Lillian Rothenburg, the TV said.

He crossed the top of the hill, walked down the street, turned the corner and got in the car with Barbara.

"You okay?" Barbara asked fearfully. She looked quickly around. "See anybody around? Where's Hart?"

"Hart's gone," Shadow Love said, slumping in the passenger seat, his eyes half closed. "Saw an eagle. Great big fuckin' bald eagle, floating out over the river."

He looked away from her fear, out the window. In the reflections on the glass, he saw Lily's face, and nodded to it.

CHAPTER
21

Daniel was in a dark mood. He prowled his office, peering at the political photographs that lined his walls.

"I thought we were doing good," Sloan ventured.

"So did I," said Lester. He had his loafers off and his feet hung over the side of his chair. He was wearing white sweatsocks with his blue suit.

"I can't complain," Daniel admitted. He was nose to nose with a black-and-white photo of Eugene McCarthy that dated back to the Children's Crusade of '68. McCarthy looked pleased with himself. Daniel scowled at him and counted the coups.

"One: We took out Bluebird and cleared the only killings on our turf. Two: We got Hood with Lily's help. Three: We broke the names out of Liss and damn near nailed the Crows at their apartment. That's all good."

"But?" Lily asked.

"Something's going to happen," Daniel said, turning back toward the group around his desk. "And it'll happen here. I feel it in my bones."

"Maybe the Crows'll call it off for a while, cool out," Lucas suggested. "Maybe they'll figure that if they lie low, the heat'll die down, give them a break."

Daniel shook his head. "No. The tempo's wrong," he

243

said. "This has been a planned progression. They kill two people to establish a philosophical basis, then Andretti to grab major headlines, then the judge and the attorney general, major federal and state law officials. The next act is going to be something big. It won't get smaller."

Anderson arrived as Daniel was talking. He took a chair and nodded to Lucas and Lily.

"Got something?" Daniel asked.

Anderson cleared his throat. "It ain't good," he said.

South Dakota authorities had located Shadow Love's driver's license. The license showed an address at Standing Rock. Standing Rock cops said he hadn't lived there for years. They had no idea where he was. The news from the National Crime Information Center was both bad and good: there was plenty of information on Shadow Love, and it was all frightening. Most of it came from California, where he'd served two years on an assault charge.

"Two years? Must have been a hell of an assault," Lily said.

"Yeah. There was a race fight outside a bar. Shadow Love took some guy down and put the boot to him. Damn near kicked him to death."

"How about here in Minnesota?" Daniel asked. "He grew up here?"

"Yeah. Went to Central. We've got Dick Danfrey over at the school board now, looking through their records. He should be getting back anytime. We're looking for addresses, friends, attorneys, anything that might make a connection."

"Is he a psycho? Shadow Love?" asked Lucas.

"The California people did a pretty thorough psychiatric evaluation on him," Anderson said, shuffling through his papers. "They're going to fax the records to us. There were indications of schizophrenia. They say he talked to invisible friends and sometimes invisible animals. And the prison shrink said the other inmates were scared of him. Even the guards. And this was in a hard-core California prison."

"Jesus," Lucas said.

"We'll have a whole file on him later this afternoon," Anderson said. "Pictures, prints, everything. Pretty recent too. Last five years, anyway."

There was nothing on the Crows. "Zilch," Anderson said. "Nothing?"

"Well, Larry's heard of them and he knows some stuff. Mostly rumors, or legend. Nothing that would track them."

"Where is Larry?" asked Daniel, looking around.

Sloan shrugged. "He's been pretty down in the mouth since that business with the Liss kid, and us putting the money on the street."

"What the fuck, he think we're playing tic-tac-toe or something?" Daniel asked angrily.

Sloan shrugged again and Lucas asked Anderson, "What about the feebs and the fingerprints? What about the truck?"

"The FBI's still running the prints, but they say if they're old . . . it could take a while. The truck has different plates front and back. When we checked, the plates were supposedly lost off trucks out in South Dakota. There was no theft report, because the owners thought they'd just bounced off. So we got more prints, but no IDs."

"What you're telling us is, we've probably got them in the system, pictures and all, but we don't have any way to figure out which ones they are?" Daniel asked.

"That's about it," said Anderson. "The feebs are giving top priority to picking out the prints. . . ."

"Maybe you could check with State Vital Records. Look for a birth certificate on Shadow Love, see who the father is, if one is listed," Lucas suggested.

"I'll do that," Anderson said. He made a note on a file cover.

"What else?" asked Daniel. The question met with silence. "Okay. Now. Something's going to happen. It's given me the creeps. We gotta get these motherfuckers. Today. Tomorrow. God damn it. And when you see Larry, tell him I want his ass in here for these meetings."

Two kids found Hart's body. They were playing on the hillside in the late-afternoon shadows when they saw him, crumpled in the weeds. For a few seconds, the older of the two thought it was a bum; but the lump was so unmoving, so awkwardly piled on itself without regard to tendon or muscle strain that even the younger one quickly realized that it must be death.

They looked at the body for a moment, then the older boy said, "We better go get your mom to call the cops."

The younger boy stuck his thumb in his mouth; it was something he hadn't done for two years. When he realized what he was doing, he pulled his thumb out and thrust his hands in his pants pockets. The older one grabbed him by the shirt and tugged him up the hillside.

The first cop on the scene was a patrolman riding single in his squad. He stepped close enough to see the blood, leaned forward to feel the cold neck and backed away. If there was evidence around the body, he didn't want to destroy it.

Two Homicide cops arrived fifteen minutes later, but nobody had yet recognized Hart.

"Throat cut," one cop said. "Could be a Crow hit. That'd be bad. Look at his clothes—decent clothes, the guy's got some bread."

The second cop, the same bespectacled investigator who'd caught the Benton murderer, eased Hart's billfold out of his hip pocket, stood up, opened it and looked at the driver's license behind the plastic window.

"Sweet bleedin' Jesus," he said aloud, his face suddenly ashen.

His partner, who was on his knees, looking at the side of Hart's head, looked up when he heard the tone of his voice. "What?"

"This is Larry Hart, the guy working with the special squad on the Indian killings."

His partner stood up and said, "Gimme the license." His voice was tight, choked. He took the license and carefully pinched a lock of Hart's hair and tugged on it, rolling the dead man's face just slightly. He compared it to the photo on the license.

"Aw, fuck," he said. "It's him."

•   •   •

Lily picked up the bedside phone and said hello. It was Daniel: "Lily, is Lucas there?"

"Lucas?" she said.

"Lily, don't dog me around, okay? We got big fuckin' trouble."

"Just a minute."

Lucas was in the shower. She pulled him out, and wet as a duck dog, he took the phone. "Daniel," Lily told him quietly.

"Yeah?" Lucas said.

"Larry Hart's been hit," Daniel said, his voice shaky. "He's dead. Throat cut."

"Sonofabitch," Lucas groaned.

"What?" Lily stood up. She was wearing a slip and nylons, and she watched Lucas while she groped for her dress.

"When did it happen?" he asked. As an aside to Lily he said, "Hart's been killed."

"We don't know shit," Daniel said. "A couple of kids found him on the hill above the river by the Franklin Avenue bridge, about an hour ago. He'd been dead for a while. The last time anybody talked to him was about noon. Sloan saw him down on Lake. Sloan's down there now, trying to backtrack him."

"All right, I'll get down there," Lucas said.

"Lucas, this isn't what I thought was coming. This is something else. I still think we're going to get hit big. Hart's personal and it makes me feel like shit, but something else is coming." Daniel had started quietly, but by the time he finished, his voice was rising and the words were tumbling out in anger.

"I hear you," Lucas said.

"Find it, God damn it. Stop it," Daniel roared.

In the car on the way down, Lily said, "Why did they call my room, looking for you?"

Lucas accelerated through a red light, then turned and looked at her in the dark. "Daniel knows. He probably knew five minutes after we got in bed. I told you he was smart; but he'll keep his mouth shut."

Sloan was standing at the edge of the hill, his hands in

his coat pockets. A half-block away, three television trucks sat at the side of the street, their engines running, their microwave dishes pointed at the sky. A reporter and photographer from the *StarTribune* were sitting on the hood of their car, talking to a TV cameraman.

"Ain't this the shits?" Sloan asked when Lucas and Lily came up.

"Yeah." Lucas nodded at the reporters. "Have we put anything out yet? To the newsies?"

"Nothing, yet," Sloan said. "Daniel's calling a press conference. He's decided to release the names, by the way—the Crows and Shadow Love. He's going to ask for help and come down hard on the idea that the Crows are killing other Indians."

"People liked Hart," Lucas said.

"That's what they say," Sloan agreed.

Down the hill, under portable lights, the assistant medical examiners were lifting Hart's body onto a stretcher. "Did anybody see anything at all?" Lucas asked.

"Yeah. A woman back up the hill," Sloan said. "She's on her way downtown now, to look at Shadow Love's pictures. She saw a couple of guys walk over the hill, and then later she saw one of them getting in a car. Younger guy, skinny, wearing a fatigue jacket."

"Shadow Love," said Lucas.

"Could be. A woman was driving the car. She was real short. She could barely see over the steering wheel. She had dark hair pulled back in a bun."

"What about the car?"

"Older. No make or model. The witness never looked at the license number. She said one of the back corner windows—you know, one of those little triangle things?—had been knocked out and there was a piece of box cardboard in it. That's about it. It was green. Pale green."

"You saw Larry earlier, right?"

"Yeah. Just before noon. He said he was heading back down Lake. He was planning to hit the bars up at the top of the street. I backtracked him as far as the Nub Inn. The bartender who was on duty earlier in the day had already gone home, but I talked to him on the phone and he said

Hart got a call there. He said he seemed surprised, like he couldn't figure out how anybody would know he was there. Anyway, he took the call and a couple of minutes later went running out of the place."

"Setup," said Lily.

"That's what I figure," Sloan said. "We've got a guy over, talking to the bartender, but I don't think he'll have much more to say."

"Christ, what a mess," Lucas said, running his fingers through his hair.

"My wife is going to be excreting bricks when she finds out one of our people got hit," Sloan said.

"I never heard of it before, not around here," Lucas said, shaking his head. He glanced at Lily. "You get this kind of stuff?"

"Every once in a while. Some dealers hit a cop a couple years ago, just to show they could do it."

"What happened?"

"The guys that did it . . . they're not with us anymore."

"Ah." Lucas nodded.

The bespectacled Homicide cop made his way up the hill, pushing his knees down with his hands as he climbed the last few feet. He was breathing heavily when he got to the top.

"How's it going, Jim?" Lucas asked.

"Not so good. Not a goddamned thing down there."

"No shell?"

"Nope. Not so far. We've worked it over pretty good. I think it was all the knife. Hell of a way to go."

"Tracks?"

"Can't find any," the Homicide cop said. "Too grassy. That long stuff is like walking on sponges. They must have come off the street, right onto it. . . . You know, Hart had his back to the guy, the cutter. No struggle. Nothing. I wonder if it was somebody he trusted?"

"Probably held him at gunpoint, like Hood did with Andretti," Lily said.

"Yeah, there's that," the cop said. He looked down the steep embankment. "But you'd think that he'd have tried to run or jump. One big jump down that hill, he'd be ten or fifteen feet from the shooter . . . but there was no sign of a jump. No place where his feet dug in. No grass stains on his pants. Nothing."

"He gave up," Lily said, looking at Lucas.

A crowd had gathered behind the reporters. Several of the onlookers were Indian, and Lily decided to mingle, hoping that someone else had seen something. While she worked the crowd, Lucas went down the block to a pay phone and called TV3. A receptionist hunted down Jennifer. "A tip," Lucas said when she came on the line.

"Is there a price?"

"Yeah. We'll get to that later."

"So what's the tip?"

"You've got some guys out by the river, working a homicide?"

"Yes. Jensen and . . ."

"It's Larry Hart. The Indian expert from Welfare that we brought in to help track these assassins."

"Holy shit," she said. Her voice was hushed. "Who else knows?"

"Nobody, at the moment. Daniel's calling a press conference, probably in a half-hour or so. . . ."

"He already did, we've got people on the way."

"If you go on the air ahead of time, you've got to cover me. Don't give it to that fuckin' Kennedy, because everybody knows you guys lay off stories on each other."

"Okay, okay," she said, a touch of intensity in her voice. "What else? Cut?"

"Yeah. Just like the others. Throat cut, bled to death."

"When?"

"We don't know. This afternoon. Early afternoon, probably. He was found by a couple of kids who were playing along the hill."

"Okay. What else? Was he breaking the case? Was he close?"

"He wasn't this morning, but maybe he ran into something. We don't know. Now: Here's the price."

"Yeah?"

"We think the guy who did it is named Shadow Love.

Thirties, Sioux, skinny, tattoos on his arms. Daniel's going to release the name. Don't use it until he does, but when he does, pound it. I want Shadow Love's name on the air every ten seconds. I want you to pound on the idea that he's killing other Indians. Push Daniel for some photos—they've got good photos of him from California, and don't let them bullshit you on that. Demand the fuckin' photos. Give them as much airtime as you can. Tell the boss that if you cooperate, I feed you more exclusive stuff."

"Hammer Shadow Love," she said.

"Hard as you can," Lucas said.

Lily got nothing from the crowd. When she was done, she asked Lucas to drop her at her room: "I need some sleep, and I need to think. Alone."

Lucas nodded. "I could use some time myself."

At her door, Lily turned to him. "What the fuck are we going to do, Davenport?" she blurted, her voice low and gravelly.

"I don't know," Lucas said. He reached out and brushed a lock of dark hair away from her cheek, back over her ear. "I just can't stop with you."

"I'm having a little trouble myself," Lily said. "But I've got too much with David to make a break. I don't think I'd want to break . . ."

"And I don't want to lose Jen," Lucas said. "But I just can't stop with you. I'd like to take you right now. . . ." He pushed her back into the room, and she had her arms around his neck, and they rocked together for a minute, the heat growing until she pushed him back.

"Get out of here, God damn it," she said. "I need some rest."

"All right. See you tomorrow?"

"Mmm. Not too early."

After dropping Lily off, Lucas drove back through town. Four trucks equipped with microwave dishes were clustered around the door to City Hall, black electronics cables snaking across the sidewalk into the building. On impulse, he pulled into a vacant cops-only parking spot and went inside.

The press conference was almost over. Lucas watched from the back as Daniel went through his routine. The television reporters were looking at their watches, ready to break away, while they listened to the the newspaper people ask a few final questions.

As he turned to leave, Jennifer stepped into the room and bumped him with an elbow.

"Thanks again. We were on the air an hour ago," she said quietly. "Look at Shelly. . . ."

Shelly Breedlove, a reporter for Channel 8, was staring spitefully at them from across the room. She'd made the connection on TV3's exclusive break on Larry Hart's murder.

Jennifer smiled pleasantly back and said, "Fuck you, bitch," under her breath. To Lucas she said, "Are you on your way home?"

"Yeah."

"I've got a baby-sitter. . . ."

Lucas slept poorly, his legs twitching, curling, uncurling. Jennifer curled against his bare back, her forehead against the nape of his neck, tears trickling down her cheeks. She could smell the perfume on him. It wasn't hers and it wasn't something he'd picked up sitting next to another woman. There'd been contact. A lot of contact. She lay awake, with the tears, and Lucas dreamed of a cold round circle of a shotgun pressed against his head, and of Larry Hart tumbling down the hillside above the Mississippi, the barges curling away, rolling down the river, their pilots unaware of the light going out on the hill above them. . . .

CHAPTER
22

Sam Crow raged through the house while Aaron sat silently in the La-Z-Boy, bathed in flickering light from the television set. Shadow Love's picture was everywhere, views from the front and both sides, close-ups of his tattooed arms.

"That fuckin' kid is ruinin' us," Sam shouted. He crowded against Barbara, who, frightened by his anger, wrapped and rewrapped her hands with a damp dish towel and pretended to do dishes between bouts of weeping. "How could you fuckin' go along?"

"I didn't want to," she cried, "I didn't know . . ."

"You knew." Sam spat. "For Christ's sakes, did you think he was delivering a fuckin' Christmas card?"

"I didn't know . . ."

"Where'd you leave him?"

"He got out by Loring Park. . . ."

"Where was he going?"

"I don't know. . . . He said you wouldn't want him here. He said he had to work alone. . . ."

"Fuck meee," Sam called out. "Fuck meee. . . ."

Aaron appeared in the doorway. "C'mere, look at this."

Sam followed him back to the living room. For the past half-hour, they'd seen report after report from Minneapolis: from the hillside where Hart's body had been found, from

253

the chief's office, from Indian Country. Man-in-the-street interviews. Lily, working the crowd, an NYPD badge pinned to her coat. People talking to her, thrusting their faces in front of the camera.

Now that had changed. A room with light blue walls. An American flag. A podium with a circular American-eagle seal under a battery of microphones, and a man in a gray double-breasted suit with a handkerchief in his breast pocket.

"It's Clay," Aaron said.

". . . terrorist group has now begun striking at its own people. That doesn't make them any less dangerous but will, I hope, make it obvious to the Indian people that these killers don't care any more about Indians than they do about whites. . . ."

And later:

". . . worked with Indian people during my entire career, and I'm asking my old friends of all Indian nations to call us at the FBI with any information about this group . . ."

And more:

". . . I will be accompanied by a task force of forty specialists, men and women from around the nation who will be brought in to break this ring. We are prepared to stay in Minnesota until we are successful in this endeavor. We will remain in full and immediate contact with the Washington center. . . ."

"Lawrence Duberville Clay," Sam said, almost reverently, as he stared at the man on the TV screen. "Hurry up, motherfucker. . . ."

"There's somebody here," Barbara called from the kitchen, fear thick in her voice. "Somebody on the porch."

The doorbell rang as Aaron hurried into the back bedroom, where he had been sleeping, and returned with an old blue .45. The bell rang again and then the front door pushed open. A dark figure, short hair, black eyes; Aaron, flattened against the hallway wall, at first thought it might be Shadow Love, but the man was too big. . . .

"Leo," Aaron called in delight. A smile lit the old man's face and he dropped the pistol to his side. "Sam, it's Leo. Leo's home."

CHAPTER
23

"You're sleeping with that New York cop. Lily." Jennifer looked at him over the breakfast bar. Lucas was holding a glass of orange juice and looked down at it, as if hoping it held an answer. The newspaper sat next to his hand. The headline read: CROWS KILL COP.

He wasn't a cop, Lucas thought. After a moment he glanced away from the table and then back at the newspaper and nodded. "Yes," he said.

"Are you going to again?" Her face was pale, tired, her voice low and whispery.

"I can't help it," he said. He wouldn't look at her. He turned the glass in his hand, swirling the juice.

"Is this . . . a long-term thing?" Jennifer asked.

"I don't know."

"Look at me," she said.

"No." He kept his eyes down.

"You can come back and see the baby, but call first. Once a week for now. I won't continue our sexual relationship and I don't want to see you. You can see the baby on Saturday nights, when I have a sitter. After Lily goes back to New York, we'll talk. We'll make some kind of arrangement so you can visit the baby on a regular basis."

Now he looked up. "I love you," he said.

Tears started in her eyes. "We've been through this before. You know what I feel like? I feel pathetic. I don't like feeling pathetic. I won't put up with it."

"You're not pathetic. When I look at you . . ."

"I don't care what you see. Or anybody else. I'm pathetic in my own mind. So fuck you, Davenport."

When Jennifer left, Lucas wandered around the house for a few moments, then drifted into the bedroom, undressed, and stood under a scalding shower. Daniel wanted every man on the street, but after Lucas had toweled off, he stood in front of an open closet, looking at the array of slacks and shirts, and then crawled back into bed and lapsed into unconsciousness. The Crows, Lily, Jennifer, the baby and game monsters from Drorg all crawled through his head. Every once in a while he felt the pull of the street scene outside Hood's apartment: he'd see the bricks, the negotiating cop, a slice of Lily's face, her .45 coming up. Each time he fought it down and stepped into a new dream fragment.

At one o'clock, Lily called. He didn't answer the phone, but listened as her voice came in through his answering machine.

"This is Lily," she said. "I was hoping we could get some lunch, but you haven't called and I don't know where you are and I'm starving so I'm going out now. If you get in, give me a call and we can go out to dinner. See you."

He thought about picking up the phone, but didn't, and went back to the bed. The phone rang again a half-hour later. This time it was Elle: "This is Elle, just calling to see how you are. You can call me at the residence."

Lucas picked up the receiver. "Elle, I'm here," he croaked.

"Hello. How are you?"

"A down day," he said.

"Still the shotgun dream?"

"It's still there. And sometimes during the day. The sensation of the steel."

"It's a classic flashback. We see it all the time with burn victims and shooting victims and people who've gone through other trauma. It'll go away, believe me. Hold on."

"I'm holding on, but it's scary. Nothing's ever gotten to me like this."

"Are you going to play Thursday night?" Elle asked.

"I don't know."

"Why don't you come a half-hour early? We can talk."

"I'll try to make it."

The bed was like a drug. He didn't want it, but he fell back on the sheets and in a minute was gone again. At two o'clock, suddenly touched with fear, he sat up, sweating, staring at the clock.

What? Nothing. Then the cold ring of the shotgun muzzle rapped him behind the ear. Lucas clapped a hand over the spot and let his head fall forward on his chest.

"Stop," he said to himself. He could feel the sweat literally pop out on his forehead. "Stop this shit."

Lily called again at five o'clock and he let it go. At seven, the phone rang a fourth time. "This is Anderson," a voice said to the answering machine. "I've got something. . . ."

Lucas picked up the phone. "I'm here," he said. "What is it?"

"Okay. Lucas. God damn." There was the sound of computer printouts rustling. Anderson was excited; Lucas could picture him going through his notes. Anderson looked, talked and sometimes acted like an aging hillbilly. A few months earlier he had incorporated his private computer business and was, Lucas suspected, on his way to becoming rich with customized police software. "I went into Larry's genealogical files for the Minnesota Sioux—you know how he had them stored in the city database?"

"Yeah, I remember."

"I looked up all the Crows. They were all too old—not many Crows in Minnesota. So I got a typist and had her put all the names from Larry's file into my machine in a sort routine. . . ."

"What?"

"Never mind. She put them in my machine in a list. Then I went over to State Vital Records and found all the women named Love who had babies between 1945 and 1965. You said this Shadow Love dude looked like he was in his thirties. . . ."

"Yeah."

"So I pulled all of those. There were a hell of a lot of them, more than four hundred. But I could eliminate all the girl babies. That got rid of all but a hundred and ninety-seven. Then I put the names of the fathers into my machine—"

"So you could run them against the genealogy—"

"Right. I got about halfway through and found a Rose E. Love. Mother of Baby Boy Love. No name for the kid, but that wasn't uncommon. Get this. I don't know how she did it, but she got them to list two names in the space for the father."

"Interesting . . ."

"Aaron Sunders and Samuel Close."

"Shit, Aaron and Sam, it's gotta be . . ."

"Their race is listed as 'other.' This was back in the fifties, so it's probably Indian. And they turn up on Larry's genealogy. They are the grandsons of a guy named Richard Crow. Richard Crow had two daughters, and when they married, the Crow name ended. We got Sunders and Close—but I'd bet my left nut those are the real names for Aaron and Sam Crow."

"God damn, Harmon, that's fuckin' terrific. Have you run—"

"They both had Minnesota driver's licenses, but only way back, before the picture IDs. The last one for Sunders was in 1964. I called South Dakota, but they were shut down for the day. I asked for a special run and the duty guy told me to go shit in my hat. So then I rousted the feebs and they got on the line to the SoDak people. They got to the duty guy and now *he's* shitting in *his* hat. Anyway, we got the special run. They're checking the records now. I figure with everything that's happened, that's the most likely place. . . ."

"How about NCIC?"

"We're running that now."

"We ought to check prison records for Minnesota and the Dakotas and the federal system. Be sure you check the feds. The federal system gets the bad-asses off the reservations. . . ."

"Yeah, I've got that going. If the Crows were inside in the last ten or fifteen years, it'll show at the NCIC. The feebs said they'll check with the Bureau of Prisons to see about their records before that."

"How about vehicles? Besides the truck?" Lucas asked.

"We're looking for registrations. I doubt they'd leave a car on the street, but who knows?"

"Any chance that Rose Love is still alive?"

"No. Since I was over there anyway, I went through the death certificates. She died in 'seventy-eight in a fire. It was listed as an accident. It was a house in Uptown."

"Shit." Lucas pulled at his lip and tried to think of other data-run possibilities.

"I went through old city directories and followed her all the way back to the fifties," Anderson continued. "She was in the 'fifty-one book, in an apartment. Then she missed a couple of years and was in 'fifty-four, in an apartment. Then in 'fifty-five she was in the Uptown house. She stayed there until she died."

"All right. This is great," Lucas said. "Have you talked to Daniel?"

"Nobody's at his house, that's why I called you. I had to tell *somebody*. It freaked me out, the way it all came out of the machines, boom-boom-boom. It was like a TV show."

"Get us some fuckin' photos, Harmon. We'll paper the streets with them."

Anderson's discoveries brought a flush of energy. Lucas paced through the house, still naked, excited. If they could put the Crows' faces on the street, they'd have them. They couldn't hide out forever. Names were almost nothing. Pictures . . .

Half an hour later Lucas was back in bed, falling into unconsciousness again. Just before he went out, he thought, *So this is what it's like to be nuts. . . .*

"Lucas?" It was Lily.

"Yup."

He looked down at the bed. He could see the outline of

where his body had been from the sweat stains. The dreams
had stayed with him until he woke, a little after seven in
the morning. He reached out, popped up the window shade,
and light cut into the gloom. A moment later, the phone
rang.

"Jesus, where were you yesterday?" Lily asked.

"In and out," he lied. "Tell you the truth, I went back
to my old net, to see if any of my regulars had heard anything. They're not Indians, but they're on the street. . . ."

"Get anything?" she asked.

"Naw."

"Daniel's pissed. You missed the afternoon meet."

"I'll talk to him," Lucas said. He yawned. "Have you had
any breakfast yet?"

"I just got up."

"Wait there. I'll get cleaned up and come get you."

"Turn on a TV before you do that. Channel Eight. But
hurry."

"What's on?"

"Go look," she said, and hung up.

Lucas punched up the TV and found an airport press conference with Lawrence Duberville Clay.

". . . in cooperation with local enforcement officials . . .
expect to have some action soon . . ."

"Bullshit, local officials," Lucas muttered at the television. The camera pulled back and Lucas noticed the screen
of bodyguards. There were a half-dozen of them around
Clay, professionals, light suits, identical lapel pins, backs to
their man, watching the crowd. "Thinks he's the fuckin'
president . . ."

Lucas' heart jumped when Lily came out of the hotel elevator. The angles of her face. Her stride. The way she brushed
at her bangs and grinned when she saw him . . .

Anderson had a stack of files for the morning meeting.
South Dakota, he said, had files on Sunders and Close.
There were photos in the driver's-license files, bad but re-
cent. And when the white names were run through the
NCIC files, a list of hits came back, along with fingerprints.

With a direct comparison available, fingerprint specialists confirmed that Sunders and Close were the men the Minneapolis cops had just missed in the apartment raid. An FBI computer specialist said later that the wide-base search of the fingerprint files would have identified them in "another four to six hours, max."

The South Dakota files had been faxed to Minneapolis, and the best possible reproductions of the driver's-license photos arrived on an early-morning plane. Copies were being made for distribution to all the local police agencies, the FBI and the media.

"Press conference at eleven o'clock," Daniel said. "I'll hand out the photographs of the Crows."

"We got some more coming from the feds," Anderson announced. "Sunders spent time in federal prison, fifteen years ago. He shot a guy out at Rosebud, wounded him. He spent a year inside."

"Old man Andretti has agreed to put up an unofficial reward for information leading to the Crows. They don't have to be arrested or anything. He'll pay just to find out where they are," Daniel said. He looked at Lucas. "I'd like to get that out to the media through the back door. . . . I'll confirm it, but I don't want to come right out and say there's a price on their heads. I want to keep some distance from it. I don't want it to sound like we're turning a bunch of vigilantes loose on the Indians. We've got to live with these people later."

Lucas nodded. "All right. I can set that up. I'll get the guy from TV3 to ask a question at the press conference."

Daniel flipped through his Xerox copies of the rap sheets. "It doesn't seem like they've done much. A couple of small-time crooks. Then this."

"But look at the pattern," Lily said. "They weren't small-time crooks like most small-time crooks. They weren't breaking into Coke machines or running a pigeon-drop. They were organizing, just like Larry said."

The files on Sunders and Close showed a sporadic history of small crime, except for the shooting that sent Sunders to prison. Most of it was trespassing on ranches, unlawful discharge of firearms, unlawful threats.

The latest charge was six years old, on Sunders, who had been arrested for trespassing. According to the complaint file, he had entered private property and allegedly damaged a bulldozer. He denied damaging the bulldozer, but he did tell police that the rancher was putting a service trail through a Dakota burial ground.

Close's file was thinner than Sunders'. Most of the charges against him were misdemeanors, for loitering or vagrancy, back when those were legal charges. There was a notation by a Rapid City officer that Close was believed to have been responsible for a series of burglaries in the homes of government officials, but he had never been caught.

On a separate slip of paper was a report from an FBI intelligence unit that both Sunders and Close had been seen at the siege of Wounded Knee, but when the siege ended, they were not among the Indians in the town.

"I'd say they've got a deep organization, going all the way back to the sixties, and maybe back to the forties," Lily said, looking at the file over Lucas' shoulder. A lock of her hair touched his ear, and tickled. He moved closer and let her scent settle over him. He had not yet told her about Jennifer. The thought of it made him uncomfortable.

"The *StarTribune* this morning called them our first experience with dedicated domestic terrorists," Lucas said.

"They picked that up from the *Times*," Lily said. "The *Times* had an editorial Friday, said the same thing."

Daniel nodded gloomily. "It'll get worse when they do whatever it is they're planning to do. Something big."

"You don't think . . . like the airport?" Anderson asked.

"What?" asked Sloan.

"You know, like the Palestinians? I mean, if you were going to do something big, shooting up the airport or blowing up a plane would do it. . . ."

"Oh, Christ," Daniel said. He gnawed on his lower lip, then got up and took a turn around his desk. "If we go out there and suggest tighter controls and the word gets out, the airlines'll take it right in the ass. And I'll be right there with them, gettin' it in the same place."

"If we don't tell them, and something happens . . ."

"How about just a light touch . . . just talk to the security, a hint to the FBI, maybe put some people out there under-cover?" suggested Sloan.

"Maybe," said Daniel, sitting down again. He looked at Anderson. "Do you really think . . . ?"

"Not really," Anderson said.

"I don't think so either. All the people they've hit so far have been symbols of something. Shooting up an airport full of innocent people wouldn't prove anything."

"How about the Bureau of Indian Affairs?" Lucas asked. "A lot of old-line Indians hate the BIA."

"Now that's something," Daniel said, his eyes narrowing. "An institution instead of an individual . . . It'd be a logical step, to go after the people they see as their oppressors. I better talk to the feebs. Maybe they could put a couple of people in the BIA office."

"Wait a minute," Lucas said. He stood up and walked around his chair, thinking. Then he looked at Daniel and said, "Jesus—it could be Clay."

They all thought about it for a moment, and Daniel shook his head. "Everything they've done has been pretty well planned. Nobody knew that Clay was coming in until the last couple of days."

"No, no, think about it," said Lucas, jabbing a finger at Daniel. "If you look at this whole . . . progression . . . in the right way, you could see it as a lure to pull Clay in. The terrorist angle, the publicity. . . . That's exactly the kind of thing Clay'd bite on."

"That's an awful big jump," Daniel argued. "They couldn't be sure he'd come. You could wind up killing a half-dozen people and getting all of your own people killed, and Clay might sit on his ass in Washington."

"And why Clay?" Sloan asked.

"Because he's a big target and he's got a bad rep among Indians," Lily said. "You remember that hassle out in Arizona with the two factions on that reservation? I can't re-member what the deal was. . . ."

"Yeah, he sent in all those agents to kick ass . . ." Ander-son said.

"If I remember right, there was an article in *Time* that

said Clay has had a bunch of run-ins with Indians over the years. Doesn't like them . . ." Lucas said.

"The Crows can't get at him," said Sloan. "He's got an unbelievable screen of bodyguards—you should have seen them this morning. If the Crows tried to shoot their way through them . . . I mean, these guys got Uzis in their armpits."

"All it takes is a guy on a rooftop with a deer rifle," said Lucas.

"Ah, shit," said Daniel. He whacked the desktop with an open palm. "We can't take a chance. We'll talk to Clay's security people. And let's put some people around his hotel. Up on the rooftops, in the parking garage. Just put some uniforms in street clothes. . . . Christ, the guy is a pain in the ass."

"We oughta take a look at the hotel too," Lucas said. He was still moving around the office, thinking about it. The idea fit: but how could the Crows get at Clay? "Look for a hole in the security. . . ."

"I still don't think it's Clay. It's gotta be something they could plan for," Daniel said. "Keep thinking about it. Let's get some more ideas going."

The meeting broke up, but ten minutes before the press conference, Daniel called them back together.

"I'm going to tell you this quick and I don't want any argument. I've been talking to Clay and his people, and the mayor. Clay will come here and will make the announcement about the identification of the Crows. He'll pass out the photos."

"God damn it," said Anderson, white-faced. "That's our work. . . ."

"Take it easy, Harmon. There's a lot going on here. . . ."

"They bought the information from us, is that right?" Anderson demanded. "What'd we get?"

"You won't believe it." Daniel smiled a self-satisfied smile, spread his arms and peered at the ceiling, as though receiving manna from heaven. "You're looking at the new Midwest on-line information-processing center. . . ."

"Holy shit," Anderson whispered. "I thought Kansas City had that wrapped."

"They just came unwrapped. We're doing the deal right now."

"Our own Cray II," Anderson said. "The fastest fucking machine ever built . . ."

"What a crock of shit," said Lily.

"Let's try to keep that opinion to ourselves," Daniel said. "After the press conference, Clay wants to talk to the *team*. I think he wants to give us a pep talk."

"What a crock of shit," Lily repeated.

"Did you suggest that he might be the target?" asked Lucas.

"Yeah," Daniel nodded. "He agreed with me that it was unlikely, but he also went along with the idea of a screen of cops on the buildings around the hotel. And his guys are looking for holes in the security."

Four advance men arrived ahead of Clay. One waited outside City Hall, where Clay's car would unload. The other three, guided by a cop, walked the hallway to the room where the press conference would be held. Lucas and Lily, lounging outside the door of the conference room, watched them coming. Two of the men stopped, a pace away.

"Police officers?" he asked.

"Yeah," said Lucas.

"Got an ID?"

Lucas shrugged. "Sure."

"I'd like to see it," the advance man said. His tone was courteous, but his eyes were not.

Lucas looked at Lily, who nodded and flashed her NYPD case. Lucas handed over his ID. "Okay," said the advance man, still courteous. "Could you point out the other plain-clothes people inside . . . ?"

It was quick and professional. In five minutes, the room was secure. When Clay arrived, he got out of his car alone, but two more advance men blocked either end of the car. The mayor came out and met Clay at the car, and they walked, chatting as casual friends, into City Hall. If any of the newsies noticed that the two men were walking through an invisible corridor of professional security, none of them said anything.

Clay and Daniel did the press conference together, the mayor beaming from the wings. Anderson and an FBI functionary passed out photos of the Crows.

"An hour from now, the Crows won't be able to go on the streets," Lucas said as the conference ended.

"We've had Shadow Love's face out there, and that hasn't gotten anywhere . . ." Lily said, when he got in the car beside her.

"We're tightening down. It'll work, with a little time."

"Maybe. I just hope they don't pull some shit first. We better get down to Daniel's office for this meeting with Clay."

Sloan, Lucas, Lily, Anderson, Del and a half-dozen other cops had been waiting ten minutes when Daniel and Clay arrived, trailed by the mayor, two of Clay's bodyguards and a half-dozen FBI agents.

"Your show, Larry," Daniel said.

Clay nodded, stepped behind Daniel's desk and gazed around the crowded office. He looked like an athlete gone to fat, Lucas thought. You wouldn't call him porky, but you could get away with "heavyset."

"I always like to talk to local police officers, especially in serious situations like this where everything depends on cooperation. I spent several years on the streets as a patrolman—got to the rank of sergeant, in fact . . ." Clay began, and he nodded at a uniform sergeant standing in the corner of the room. He was a solid speaker, picking out each local cop in turn, fixing him with his eyes, soliciting agreement and cooperation. Lily glanced up at Lucas after Clay had given them the treatment, and cracked a smile.

"Good technique," she whispered.

Lucas shrugged.

". . . wide experience with Indians, and I will tell you this. Indian rules are not our rules, are not the rules of a rational, progressive society. That statement—I'd prefer to keep it in this room—is not a matter of prejudice, although it can be twisted to sound that way. But it's a solid fact; and most

Indians themselves recognize it. But we don't have two sets of rules in America. We have law, and it applies to everybody. . . ."

"Heil Hitler," Lucas muttered.

When they finished, Clay whipped out of the building in his cloud of bodyguards.

"Let's go look at his hotel," Lucas suggested.

"All right," Lily said. "Though I'm starting to have my doubts. His guys are pretty good."

Clay's chief of security was a nondescript, pale-eyed man who looked like a desk clerk until he moved. Then he looked like a viper.

"We've got it nailed down," he said after Lucas and Lily identified themselves. "But if you think you might see something, I'd be happy to walk you through."

"Why?" asked Lucas.

"Why what?"

"Why are you happy to walk us through, if it's all nailed down?"

"I never figured myself to be the smartest guy in the world," the security man said. "I can always learn something."

Lucas looked at him for a minute, then turned to Lily. "You're right. They're good," he said.

They took the tour anyway. Clay was on the fourteenth floor. There were higher buildings around, but none closer than a half-mile.

"Couldn't take him through a window," the security man said.

"How about something set up in advance? Clay's stayed at this hotel before, right?"

"Like what?"

Lucas shrugged. "A bomb in an elevator?"

"We sniffed the place out. Routine," the security man said.

"How about a suicide run? The Crows are crazy. . . ."

"We've checked the staff, of course. No Indians at all, nobody with the kind of background that we'd worry about.

Most of them are career people, been here a while. A few
new people on the desk and kitchen staff, but we screen
them out when the boss comes and goes. . . . And when he
does come and go, we check the lobby and the street first.
He's in and out in a hurry, with no warning. So it wouldn't
be anybody on the street."

"Hmmph," said Lucas.

They were headed back down in the elevator and Lucas
asked, "Is there any way to get up on top of the elevator
from the basement or the roof, ride up that way?"

The security man allowed himself a small grin. "I'm not
going to talk about that," he said, glancing at Lucas. "But
in a word, no."

"You've got the elevators wired," said Lily.

The security man shrugged as the elevator stopped at the
third floor. An elderly woman wearing a fur wrap got on,
peered nearsightedly at the lighted buttons and finally
pushed the button for the second floor. A room-service
waiter pushed a dinner cart past the elevators just as the
doors were closing.

"How about a disguise?" Lucas asked after the old lady
had gotten off. "What if somebody came in disguised as an
old lady . . ."

"Metal detectors would pick up the gun."

". . . and had a gun stashed on the third floor. Rode up
to the third floor, picked it up and then went up to
fourteen . . ."

The security man shrugged again. "That's a fantasy. And
when they got up there, they'd have to shoot their way past
three trained agents. And the boss is armed, and he knows
how to use it."

Lucas nodded. "All right. But I got a bad feeling," he
said.

He and Lily left the security man in the lobby and headed
for the doors. Just as they were about to go out, Lucas said,
"Wait a minute," and turned back.

"Hey," he called to the security man. "How did that
room-service food get up on three?"

The security man looked at Lucas, then at Lily, then at the elevators.

"Let's go ask," he said.

"In a dumbwaiter," a cook told them. He pointed to an alcove, where they could see the opening for the chain-driven lift.

The security man looked from the dumbwaiter to the cook to Lucas. "Could a man ride up in that?" he asked the cook.

"Well . . . I guess a couple guys have. Sometimes," the cook said, his eyes shifting nervously.

"What do you mean, 'sometimes'?"

"Well, when it's busy, you know, the boss doesn't want a lot of waiters riding up in the elevators with the customers. The waiters are supposed to take the stairs. But sometimes, I mean, if it's on the tenth floor . . ."

"How often do guys ride up?" the security man asked.

"Look, I don't want to get anybody in trouble. . . ."

"Nobody'll hear a word from us," Lily promised.

The cook wiped his hands on his apron, then lowered his voice and said, "Every day."

"Shit," said the security man.

The security man laid it out: "A suicide run. Four guys. They come down the alley to the service dock. They push the bell. One of the staff opens the door to see who it is. The Crows stick a gun in his stomach. One guy stays in the kitchen while the other three ride up in the dumbwaiter, one at a time. They come out in the service area on fourteen. They've got automatic weapons or shotguns. They check the hall, somehow . . . maybe just peek, or they use a dental mirror . . . they come out and take the two agents in the hall. That leaves one guy with the chief. They knock the door out with a shotgun, and then it's three on two, maybe three machine guns or shotguns against two pistols. . . ."

"It's a possibility," said Lily.

Now it was Lucas' turn to shake his head. "You know, when you lay it out like that, it sounds pretty unlikely. . . ."

"The Crows are pretty unlikely," the security man said.

"I'll tell you what we're going to do. We'll freeze the kitchen. Stick a monitor somewhere. If they come in, we'll snap them up."

"A trap," said Lily.

"Right. Well—excuse me, I gotta go talk to the chief. And listen: Thanks."

On the sidewalk in front of the hotel, Lucas shook his head again.

"It was a hole, but that's not what the Crows are up to," he said.

"Then what?"

"I don't know."

In the car, Lily looked at her watch. "Why don't we talk about it over lunch?"

"Sure. Want to go to my place?" Lucas asked.

Lily looked at him curiously. "This is a new attitude," she said. "What happened?"

"Jennifer . . ."

". . . figured us out," she finished, sitting up straight in her seat. "Oh, shit. Did she throw you out?"

"That's about it," Lucas conceded. He cranked the car and pulled away from the curb.

"You don't think she'd call David, do you?" Lily asked anxiously.

"No. No, I don't. She's spent some time in bed with married men—I know some of them—and she'd never have thought of talking to their wives. She wouldn't break up a marriage."

"It makes me nervous," Lily said. "And that must be why you're so bummed out. You sat in Daniel's office looking like your dog had died."

"Yeah. It's Jen and it's this fuckin' case. Larry killed, executed. And I've been useless. That feels weird, you know? When something important is happening—drugs, gambling, credit-card scams, burglary rings—I've got these contacts. Daniel comes to me and says, 'Talk to your net. We got thirty-six burglaries on the southeast side last week, all small shit, stereos and TVs.' So I go out and talk to the net. A good part of the time, I'll find out what's happening. I'll squeeze a gambler and get sent to a fence and squeeze the fence and find a junkie, and squeeze the junkie and get the whole ring. But this thing . . . I got nobody. If they were regular crooks, I could find them. Dopers need dope or need to sell it, so they're out and about. Burglars and credit-card hustlers need fences. But who do these guys need? An old friend. Maybe a former university professor. Maybe an old sixties radical. Maybe some kind of right-wing lunatic. Maybe Indian, maybe white. Who the fuck knows? I spent my whole goddamn life in this town, and most of the time I lived right around where the Indians live and I never saw them. I know a few, but it's because they're in drugs or burglary, or because they're straight and I go to their stores. Other than that, I just don't have a net out there. I've got a black net. I've got a white net. I've even got an Irish net. I don't have an Indian net."

"Stop feeling sorry for yourself," Lily said. "You got the tip on the trouble out at Bear Butte and found the photograph that I picked Hood out of."

"I got tied up like a fuckin' pig by Hood and almost got my brains blown out. . . ."

"You figured out how to squeeze the Liss woman and got the names of the Crows out of her. You're doing all right, Davenport."

"It's been luck, and that ain't going to hack it from here on out," Lucas said, glancing at her. "So stop trying to cheer me up."

"I'm not," she said cheerfully. "We don't have a lot to be cheerful about. As a matter of fact, unless we get real lucky, we're completely fucked."

"Not completely," Lucas said. He downshifted, let the car wind down to a red light and touched her thigh. "But in an hour, who knows?"

Lily prowled through the house like a potential buyer, checking each of the rooms. Once, Lucas thought, he caught her sniffing the air. He grinned, said nothing and got two beers.

"Pretty good," she said finally, as she came up the stairs from the basement. "Where'd you get that old safe?"

"I use it as a gun safe," Lucas said, handing her a beer.
"I picked it up cheap when they were tearing out a railroad
ticket office here in St. Paul. It took six guys to get it in the
house and down the stairs. I was afraid the stairs were going
to break under the weight."

She took a sip of beer and said, "When you invited me
for lunch . . ."

"Yeah?"

". . . am I supposed to make it?"

"Oh, fuck no," he said. "You got your choice. Pasta salad
or chicken-breast salad with slices of avocado and light
ranch dressing."

"Really?"

"It's a zoo over on Franklin and down on Lake," Lily said
as she worked down into her salad. "With Clay in town,
the feebs are crawling all over the place."

"Assholes," Lucas grunted. "They've got no contacts, the
people hate them, they spend twenty-four hours a day stepping on their dicks. . . ."

"They're doing that now, in major numbers," Lily
agreed. She looked up from her chicken-breast salad and
said, "That was delicious. That pasta looks pretty good
too. . . ."

"Want a bite?"

"Maybe just a bite?"

After lunch, they went to the study and Lily pulled out one
of Anderson's notebooks for review. They both drank another beer, and Lucas put his feet up on a hassock and
dozed.

"Warm in here," Lily said after a while.

"Yeah. The furnace kicked in. I looked at the thermome-
ter. It's thirty-six degrees outside."

"It felt cold," she said, "but it's so pretty, you don't notice
it. With the sun and everything."

"Yeah." He yawned and dozed some more, then cracked
his eyes open as Lily peeled off her cotton sweater. She had
a marvelously soft profile, he thought. He watched her read,
nibbling at her lower lip.

"Nothing in the notebooks," he said. "I've been through them."

"There must be something, somewhere."

"Mmm."

"Why did the Crows kill Larry? They must have known that it would be counterproductive, in the political sense. And they didn't *have* to kill him—he wasn't helping us that much."

"They didn't know that. He was on TV after the raid on the Crows' apartment. . . . Maybe they thought . . ."

"Ah. I didn't think of that," she said. Then she frowned. "I was on TV the other night. After Larry was cut."

"Might be a good idea to lie low for a while," Lucas said. "These guys are fruitcakes."

"I still can't figure Larry," she said. "Or this other guy, Yellow Hand. Why kill Yellow Hand? Revenge? But revenge doesn't make any sense in this kind of situation, against one of your own people. It just muddies things up. And they never mention those shootings in their press releases. . . ."

"I got no ideas," Lucas said. After a moment he added, "Well, that's not *quite* right. I do have one idea. . . ."

"What's that?"

"Why don't we sneak back to the bedroom?"

She sighed, smiled a sad smile and said, "Lucas . . ."

When they talked about it later, Lucas and Lily agreed that there wasn't anything notable about the time they spent in bed that afternoon. The love was soft and slow, and they both laughed a lot, and between times they talked about their careers and salaries and told cop stories. It was absolutely terrific; the best of their lives.

"I've decided what I'm going to do about David," Lily said later in the day, rolling out to the edge of the bed and putting her feet on the floor.

"What are you going to do?" Lucas asked. He had been putting on his jockey shorts, and he stopped with one foot through a leg hole.

"I'm going to lie to him," she said.

"Lie to him?"

"Yeah. What we've got going, David and I, is pretty good. He's a good guy. He's attractive, he's got a nice sense of humor, he worries about me and the kids. It's just . . ."

"Keep talking."

"There's not the same kind of heat as there is with you. I can look at him sometimes and I get a lump in my throat, I can't even talk. I just feel so . . . *warm* toward him. I love him. But I don't get that kind of driving hot feeling. You know what I mean?"

"Yeah. I know."

"I was thinking about it the other night. I was thinking, Here's Davenport. He's large and he's rough and he makes himself happy first. He's not always asking me if I'm okay, have I come. So what is this, Lily? Is this some kind of safe rape fantasy?"

"What'd you decide?"

"I don't know. I didn't decide anything, really. Except to lie to David."

Lucas got fresh underwear from his chest of drawers and said, "Come on. I'll give you a shower."

She followed him into the bathroom. In the shower she said, "David wouldn't do this either. I mean, you just kind of . . . work me over. Your hands are . . . in everything, and I . . . kind of like it."

Lucas shrugged. "You're hurting yourself. Stop talking about David, for Christ's sake."

She nodded. "Yeah. I better."

When they got out of the shower, he dried her, starting the rough towel around her head and slowly working down her legs. When he finished, he was sitting on the side of the bathtub; he reached around her and pulled her pelvis against his head. She ruffled his hair.

"God, you smell good," he said.

She giggled. "We've got to stop, Davenport. I can't handle much more of this."

They dressed slowly. Lucas finished first and lay on the bed, watching her.

"The hardest part of lying to him will be the first ten or fifteen minutes," he said suddenly. "If you can get through the first few minutes, you'll be okay."

She looked up, a guilty expression on her face. "I hadn't thought of that. The first . . . encounter."

"You know when you bust a kid for something, a teenager, and you're not sure that they did it? And they get that look on their face when you tell them you're a cop? And then you *know*? If you're not careful, you'll look like that."

"Ah, Jesus," she said.

"But if you can get through the first ten minutes, just keep bullshitting along, you'll stop feeling guilty and it'll go away."

"The voice of experience," she said, with the tiniest stain of bitterness in her voice.

"I'm afraid so," he said, a little despondently. "I don't know. I love women. But I look at Sloan. You know, Sloan's *wife* calls him Sloan? And they're always laughing and talking. It makes me jealous."

Lily dropped onto the foot of the bed. "Let's not talk about this," she said. "It'll put me in an early grave. Like Larry."

"Poor old Larry," Lucas said. "I feel for the sonofabitch."

The next day was sunny. Lucas had on his best blue suit with a black wool dress coat. Lily wore a dark suit with a blue blouse and a tweed overcoat. Just before they left Lily's hotel room, TV3 had begun live coverage of Larry Hart's funeral. The coverage opened with a shot of Lawrence Duberville Clay arriving at the funeral. Clay spoke a few clichés into a microphone and went inside.

"He thinks he's the fuckin' president," Lucas said.

"He might be, in six more years," Lily said.

The Episcopalian church was crowded with welfare workers and clients, cops and Indian friends and family. Daniel spoke a few words, and Hart's oldest friend, whom he'd called brother, spoke a few more. The casket was closed.

The cortege to the cemetery shut down traffic in central Minneapolis for five minutes. The line of funeral cars ran bumper to bumper through the Loop, escorted by cops on motorcycles.

"It's better out here," Lily said as they walked into the cemetery. "Churches make me nervous."

"This is the first place I ever saw you," Lucas said. "Bluebird's buried here."

"Yup. Weird."

Gravestones were scattered over twelve acres of slightly shaggy grounds, beneath burr oaks. Lucas supposed it would be a spooky place on moonlit nights, the oaks looming like shadows cast by the Headless Horseman. Anderson, stiff in a black suit, looking more like an undertaker than the undertaker, wandered over to stand beside them.

"This is where Rose E. Love is buried," he said after a while.

"Oh, yeah? Where'd you find that out?" Lucas said.

"I found it in some notes with the old coroner's files. There weren't any relatives handy when she died, so they made a note on the death certificate about the funeral home and cemetery, in case somebody came looking for her."

"Hmph."

"Bluebird too," Lily said.

"Mmm."

After a while, Anderson wandered away, edging around the accumulation of funeralgoers. Film crews from all the local television stations and several foreign and national news services stood as close as seemed circumspect, as the cops rolled out their most martial ceremony. When it was over, they passed a folded flag to Hart's mother and fired a military salute.

When the service ended, Anderson strolled up again.

"She's right along here," he said.

"Who?"

"Rose E. Love. I had them look up the gravesite in the cemetery office."

Lucas and Lily, pulled along by Anderson's interest, followed him a hundred yards to a gravesite under the boughs of an aging oak, a dozen feet from the wrought-iron fence surrounding the cemetery.

"Nice spot," Anderson said, looking up into the spreading oak tree with its hand-size leaves still clinging to the branches.

"Yeah." The grave had been kept up spotlessly; on the oblong pink granite stone was inscribed ROSE E. LOVE, in large letters, and below that MOTHER, in smaller script. Lucas looked around. "The grave looks a lot better than the other ones around here. You don't think maybe Shadow Love stops by and works on it?"

Anderson shook his head. "Naw. The cemeteries don't allow that. They'd get all kinds of shit going on. Me and my old lady bought our plots, you know, a couple of years back. They had all these care plans you could sign up for. Give them two thousand bucks now and they'll take care of your grave in perpetuity. It's called Plan Perpetual. You can put it right in your will."

"That's a little steep, isn't it?" Lily asked. "Two thousand bucks?"

"Well, I mean, it's *forever*," Anderson said. "When the next ice age comes through, they'll have a guy out here with a heater. . . ."

"Still a little steep."

"If you can't afford it all at once, you can pay by the year. You know, like seventy-five, a hundred bucks."

"Gives me the creeps thinking about it," Lucas said.

"He doesn't plan to die," Lily confided to Anderson.

"I hate to tell you this," Anderson said as they wandered away from Rose Love's grave, "but there comes a time in every man's life . . ."

Lucas thought of a question for Anderson. As he opened his mouth to speak, the cold steel of a gun barrel touched him behind the ear. He jerked to a halt, staggered, closed his eyes, slapped his neck and let out a deep breath.

"Lucas?" asked Lily. She had stopped and was looking up at him. "What's wrong?"

"Nothing," he said after a moment. "I was just day-dreaming."

"Jesus, I thought you had a heart attack or something." Anderson was looking at him curiously, but Lucas shook his head and took Lily's arm. Anderson broke off just before they got to the fence, and headed across the slope toward the cemetery road. Lily and Lucas strolled out of the cemetery through a side exit, away from the remnants of the somber crowd.

The question was lost.

"What do you want to do?" Lily asked.

"I think I might go back out on my regular net," Lucas said. He had been thinking about his lie of the day before, and decided that talking to his regulars might be a good idea.

"Okay. You can drop me at the hotel," Lily said. "I'm going to sit around and read Anderson's notebooks for a while. Maybe go for a run before dinner."

"I told you. There's nothing in it—Anderson's stuff," Lucas said. "We won't find them on paper. If the Crows are lying low, we need somebody to talk to us."

"Yeah. But somewhere, there's something. A name. Something. Maybe somebody from their prison days . . ."

The day was chilly, but the bright sunlight felt fine on Lily's face. She walked with her head tilted back as they crossed the street, taking in the rays, and Lucas' heart thumped as he walked behind her, marveling.

Shadow Love was parked a block away, watching them.

CHAPTER
24

Shadow Love stole a Volvo station wagon from the reserved floor of an all-day parking ramp. He drove it to the cemetery and waited a half-block from the hillside where they'd bury Hart.

The wait was a short one: Hart's funeral moved like clockwork. The funeral cortege came in from the other side of the graveyard, but Davenport and the New York woman came in from his side. They all gathered on the hillside and prayed, and Shadow Love watched, slipping back to the warm moment when he slashed Hart, feeling the power of the knife. . . . The knife was in his pocket, and he touched it, tingling. No gun had ever affected him the same way, nor had the knife, before the Hart killing.

Blood made the stone holy. . . .

When the funeral ended, Davenport and the New York cop walked away from the crowd with another man, down the hill toward his mother's grave. When they stopped, Shadow Love's forehead wrinkled: They were *at* his mother's grave. What for? What did they want?

Then they split up. The other man wandered away, and Davenport and the woman continued on until they crossed through the wrought-iron fence onto the sidewalk. The woman tilted her head back, smiling, the sunlight playing

across her face. Davenport caught her arm as they got to
the car and bumped his hip against hers. *Lovers.*

He would have trouble staying with the Porsche, Shadow
Love thought, if Davenport stayed on city streets. He
couldn't get too close. But Davenport went straight to I-
35W and headed north. Shadow stayed several cars back
as Davenport drove into the Loop, made one left and
dropped the woman in front of her hotel.

As Shadow Love waited at the curb, Davenport pulled
out of the hotel's circular driveway, crossed two lanes of
traffic and headed straight back toward him. Shadow Love
turned in his seat and looked out the passenger window until
Davenport was past. Following him would be impossible.
Davenport would see the U-turn close behind him, and the
tomato-red Volvo was not inconspicuous. The woman, on
the other hand . . .

Lily.

Shadow Love touched the stone knife, felt it yearning for
drink. . . .

Shadow Love had worked intermittently as a cab driver, and
he knew the Minneapolis hotels. This was a tough one: it
was small, mostly suites, and played to a wealthy clientele.
Security would be good.

Shadow Love left the car at the curb, walked to the hotel
entrance, and carefully stepped into the lobby and looked
around. No sign of the woman. She had already gone up.
Three bellhops were leaning on the registration desk, talking
to the woman behind it. If he went farther inside, he'd be
noticed. . . .

A flower shop caught his eye. It had an exterior entrance,
but it also had a doorway that led directly into the hotel
lobby. He thought for a moment, then checked his billfold.
Forty-eight dollars and change. He went back outside and
walked to the flower shop.

"One red rose? How romantic," the woman said, her eyebrows arching, a skeptical note in her voice. The hotel was
expensive. Shadow Love was not the kind of man who
would have a lover inside.

"Not my romance," Shadow grunted, picking up her skepticism. "I just dropped her off in the cab. Her old man give me ten extra bucks for the rose."

"Ah." The woman's face broke into a smile. Everything was right in the world. "For ten dollars you could buy two roses. . . ."

"He said one and keep the change," Shadow Love said grumpily. He had forty-eight dollars between himself and the street, and this flower shop was selling roses at five dollars a pop. "Her name is Rothenburg. I don't know how you spell it. Her old man said you could get the room."

"Sure." The woman wrapped a single red rose in green tissue paper and said, "Is the card to be signed?"

"Yeah. 'Love, Lucas.'"

"That's nice." The woman picked up the phone, rapped in four numbers and said, "This is Helen. You got a Rothenburg? Don't know the spelling. Yeah . . . Four-oh-eight? Thanks."

"We'll send it right up," the woman said as she gave Shadow Love his change.

Room 408. "Thanks," he said.

He left the shop and went outside. It was late afternoon, getting cooler. He looked both ways, then walked away from the car toward Loring Park and took a long turn around the pond, thinking. The woman was good with a gun. He couldn't fuck up. If he waited awhile, then went straight in to the elevators, as though he belonged there, he might get up. Then again, maybe not—but if they stopped him, they wouldn't do more than throw him out. He dug in a pocket, took out a Slim Jim sausage and chewed on it.

If he got up, what then? If he knocked on her door and she opened it, bang. But what if the chain was on? He had no faith in the idea of shooting through the door. The pistol was a .380, good enough for close work, but it wouldn't punch through a steel fire-liner. Not for sure. She'd recognize him. And she was a killer. If he missed, she'd be all over him. It'd be hell just getting out of the hotel. . . .

Have to think.

He was still working it out when he got back to the car. A Federal Express truck stopped across the street and the driver hopped out. Shadow Love, his mind far away, automatically tracked him as he went into the lobby of an office building and began emptying the local package box. A moment later, when the driver came out with his load of packages, Shadow Love skipped out of the car and walked into the lobby.

The Federal Express box had an open rack of packaging envelopes and address slips, with ballpoint pens on chains. *Lily Rothenburg, Police Officer,* he wrote. *Room 408 . . .*

He still didn't know how he'd get in her door. Sometimes you had to pray for luck. When he got back on the sidewalk, it was dark. . . .

The rose was totally unexpected: the last thing she would have expected, but it thrilled her. David sent flowers; Davenport did not. That he should . . .

Lily put it in a water glass and set it on top of the television set, looked at it, adjusted it and sat down with Anderson's computer printouts. In two minutes, she knew she couldn't read.

Davenport, God damn it. What's this rose shit? She took a turn around the room, caught her image in a mirror. *That's the silliest smile I've seen on you since you were a teenager.*

She couldn't work. She glanced at a copy of *People,* put it aside and walked around the room again, stopping to sniff at the rose.

She was in a *feeling* mood, she decided. *A hot bath . . .*

Shadow Love went straight through the lobby with the Federal Express package in his hand, slightly in front of his body, so the bellhops could see the colors. He stopped at the elevators, poked 4 and resolutely *did not* look at the desk and the bellhops. The elevator chimed, the doors opened . . . he was in, and alone.

He gripped the knife, feeling its holy weight, then touched his belly, feeling the gun there. But the knife was the thing.

The doors opened on the fourth floor and he stepped out, still holding the package in front of him. Room 408. He

turned right and heard a vacuum cleaner behind him. He
stopped. Luck.

He turned back, went around the corner and found a
maid with a vacuum cleaner. There was nobody else in the
hallway.

"Got a package," he grunted. "Where's four-oh-eight?"

"Down there," the maid said, flipping a thumb down the
hall behind her. She was a short woman, slender, early twenties; already worn out.

"Okay," Shadow said. He slipped a hand under his
jacket, looked around once to make sure they were alone,
pulled the gun and pointed it at the woman's head.

"Oh, no . . ." she said, backing away, her hands out toward him.

"Down to the room. And get your keys out. . . ." The
woman continued backing away, Shadow matching her
pace for pace, the muzzle of the gun never leaving her face.
"The keys," he said.

She groped in her apron pocket and produced a ring with
a dozen keys.

"Open four-oh-eight . . . but let me knock first." He thrust
the package at her, his voice rising, an edge of madness to
it. "If she answers, tell her you've got a package. Let her
see it. If you try to warn her, if you do anything to spook
her, bitch cunt, I'll blow your motherfuckin' brains out. . . ."

The thought that the maid might betray him gripped
Shadow Love's stomach, and the black spot popped into his
line of vision, obscuring her face. He forced it down, down,
concentrating: *Not this one; not yet.*

The maid was terrified. She clutched at the package, holding it to her chest.

"Here," she squeaked.

The black spot was still there, smaller, floating like a mote
in God's eye, but he could read the number on the door:
408. Shadow reached out and knocked, quietly. No answer.
The killing rush was coming now, like cocaine, even
better. . . . He knocked again. No answer.

"Open it," he said. He pressed the gun against the
woman's forehead. "If there's a noise, I'll fuckin' kill you,
bitch. I'll blow your fuckin' brains all over the hall."

The woman slipped the key into the lock. There was a tiny metallic click and she flinched, and Shadow Love tapped her with the barrel. "No more," he whispered. "Open it."

She turned the key. There was another click and the door eased open.

Lily got out of the bathtub, steam rolling off her body; she felt languid and soft from the bath oils. She heard the knock and stopped toweling. It wasn't a maid's knock. It was too soft, too . . . furtive. She frowned, took a step toward the bathroom door, looked through the bedroom to the outer sitting room; it was dark. A lamp was on in the bedroom, as were the lights in the bathroom. There was another knock, a pause, then a click. Somebody coming in.

Lily looked around for her purse, with the gun in the concealed holster: outer room. *Shit.* She reached back, hit the bathroom light switch and started for the lamp.

Shadow Love pushed the maid forward. The door opened and the woman went through. There was little light, apparently coming from a bathroom. . . . *No. There's another room. Fuckin' rich bitch has a suite. . . .* The light suddenly went out, and they were in darkness, Shadow Love and the maid silhouetted against the light from the hallway.

Lily killed the lamp as the door opened. She felt a tiny surge of relief when she saw the small woman and the familiar colors on the package. She reached again for the wall switch, then saw the man behind the woman and what looked like a gun.

"Freeze, motherfucker," she screamed at the dark figures, dropping automatically into her Weaver stance, her hands empty. But the movement, in the dark, might be convincing. . . .

The scream startled him. Shadow Love sensed the cop woman dropping into a shooter's stance, and swept the maid's feet from under her and went down on top of her. He could feel the woman moving sideways in the minimal

light in the room, and he pivoted and kicked the outer door
shut. The dark was complete.

"Got a woman, here, a maid," Shadow Love called. He
pointed the gun toward where he thought the other door
was, although he was disoriented and felt he might be off.
But if she fired at him, he'd get her in the muzzle blast.
"Come out and talk; I just want to talk about the Indians,
about the Crows. I've worked with the police."

Bullshit. Shadow Love. Must be.
"Bullshit. You move, motherfucker, and I'll spread you
around like spaghetti sauce."

Lily, nude, crawled across the bedroom floor in the dark,
her hands sweeping from side to side, looking for a weapon.
Anything. *Nothing. Nothing.* Back toward the bathroom,
creeping in silence, waiting for the killing light . . . Into the
bathroom. Groping. Up the walls. A towel rack. She tugged
on it. It held. She put her full weight on it, bouncing frantically, and suddenly, explosively, it came free. She went flat
again, frozen, waiting for the light, but nothing came. She
went back to the floor and, with the towel bar in her hand,
crawled out the bathroom door toward the front room.

There was a sudden, terrific clatter. Shadow Love started,
put his face next to the maid's and whispered, "Move, bitch,
and I'll slit your fuckin' throat." He could feel the woman
trembling in her thin maid's uniform. "And I got the gun;
if you go for the door, I'll shoot you."

He left her then, and crawled toward the spot where he
thought the inner door was, feeling his way across the carpet
in the dark.

*What was the noise? What was she doing? Why hadn't she
risked a light? She wouldn't be any worse off. . . .*

The problem was, the first one to turn on a light would
be most exposed. . . .

"I'm not here to hurt anybody," he called.

His voice was a shock: he was so close. Two feet away, three.
And now she could smell him: his breath. He'd been eating
something spicy, sausage maybe, and his warm breath trick-

led toward her over the carpet. Could he smell the bath oils
on her? She thought she might be a yard from the door, and
he was coming through. She rolled to one side, a slow, inch-
ing, agonizing movement, holding the towel bar between her
breasts.

Where was she? Why wasn't she answering? She could be
standing over him, pointing a .45 at his skull, tightening on
the trigger. The injustice of his death gripped him, and for
a full beat, two beats, he waited for the crashing blow that
would kill him. There was nothing. He reached ahead in the
dark, feeling the baseboard on the wall ahead, sliding his
hand to the right, finding the corner and the doorway. *The
bathroom . . . that noise she made, that sounded like it came
out of a bathroom, the hollow-sharp sound you get from tile
walls . . . What was she doing in there?* Moving a few inches
at a time, he crossed through the doorway, low-crawling toward the bathroom. *Nothing from her. Nothing. Maybe she's
not armed. . . .*

"Don't got no gun, bitch. That's it. Well, I'm putting my
gun away, you know? You know why? 'Cause I'm getting
my knife out. Cut open Larry Hart with it, you know? You
know what I did then? After I cut him? You know?"

Where is she? Where is the bitch? He strained into the
darkness. Got to scare her, got to make her move.

"I sucked the blood, that's what I did," Shadow Love
called. "All hot. Better'n deer's blood. Sweeter . . . Bet
yours'll be sweeter yet . . ."

Where the fuck is she?

There was a change in the darkness next to her, a movement
through it. Shadow Love, on the floor next to her, not more
than two feet away, low-crawling toward the bathroom. She
couldn't see him, but she could sense him there, moving in
the dark. Moving as slowly as he was, she pulled her feet
under her and quietly stood up, her hand sliding up the
woodwork along the edge of the door. She could no longer
sense him—standing, she was quite literally too far away—
but she figured he had to be through the door.

• • •

"You don't have a gun, do you, bitch?" Shadow Love screamed. The cry was as hard and sharp as a sliver of glass and Lily gasped involuntarily. He heard the gasp and froze. She was close by. He could feel it. *Very close. Where?* He swung an arm out to the right, then his gun hand to the left. And he touched her, raked the back of her calf with his gun hand as she went through the door, into the outer room, and he pivoted and fired the pistol once through the door. . . .

No, she thought. *He must have heard . . .*

She took a fast step through the door, high, over him, in case his legs were still in the doorway, and was pushing off with her back leg when his hand struck her calf. Shit. She dodged sideways; there was a flash and a deafening crack, and she twisted sideways toward the television set, crawling. . . .

"Noooo . . ." The scream clutched at Lily as she hit a body in the dark. *Soft . . . woman . . .* She had just registered the thought as the other woman, sobbing frantically, clubbed at her and she went down, twisting, back on her hands and knees, crawling toward the television, reaching out, sweeping the carpet for the purse. . . .

The muzzle blast blinded him for a second, but now he knew for sure: She had no gun and was heading for the door. The maid's scream froze him, then Shadow Love struggled to his feet, groping for the wall and a light switch. He found the wall and ran his hand toward the switch, watching the doorway in case the cop tried for the door.

And then, in the instant before he would turn on the light . . .

He heard the slide.

There was no other sound like it. A .45, at full cock.

And then Lily, her voice like a gravedigger's: "I'm out here, motherfucker. Go ahead—turn on the light."

Shadow Love, poised in the doorway, felt the voice coming from his left. One chance: he took it. With the gun in his hand he launched himself straight through the dark toward the other door, where he could hear the maid sobbing.

Two steps, three, and then he hit her. She was standing and she screamed, and he held her for an instant as he found the door, gripped the knob and then thrust the woman toward the place Lily's voice had come from. He felt the maid go, stumbling, and he wrenched open the door. As he went through, he fired once, toward the two women, and then ran toward the stairs, waiting for the bite from the .45. . . .

Light from the hallway flooded the room, and Lily saw movement toward her and realized it was too small to be Shadow Love: *maid.*

She pivoted to a shooting line past the falling woman and saw Shadow Love in the doorway, his gun arm out toward her. She was still turning past the woman, and then he was gone, his arm trailing behind, like a bat in a drag bunt. Lily was still following with the .45 when Shadow Love pulled the trigger.

The bullet hit her in the chest.

Lillian Rothenburg went down like a tenpin.

CHAPTER
25

Lucas was chatting with a gambler outside a riverfront bar when his handset beeped. He stepped off the curb, reached through the open window of the Porsche and thumbed the transmit switch.

"Yeah. Davenport." The sun had set and a chill wind was blowing off the river. He stuck his free hand in his pants pocket and hunched his back against the cold.

"Lucas, Sloan says to meet him at Hennepin Medical Center just as fast as you can get there," the dispatcher said. "He says it's heavy-duty. Front entrance."

"Okay. Did he say what it's about?"

After a second's hesitation, the dispatcher said, "No. But he said lights and sirens and get your ass over there."

"Five minutes," Lucas said.

Lucas left the gambler standing on the sidewalk and pushed the Porsche across the bridge, south through the warehouse district to the medical center, wondering all the time. A break? Somebody nailed a Crow? There were three squad cars and a remote television truck at emergency receiving. Lucas wheeled around front, dumped the car in a no-parking space, flipped down the sunshade with the police ID and walked up the steps. Sloan stood waiting behind the glass doors, and Lucas saw a patrol captain and a woman sergeant standing in the lobby. They seemed to be staring at him. Sloan pushed the glass door open, and when Lucas stepped inside he linked his arm through Lucas'.

"Got your shit together?" Sloan asked. His face was white, drawn, deadly serious.

"What the fuck you talking about?" Lucas said, trying to pull away. Sloan hung on.

"Lily's been shot," Sloan said.

For just a second, the world stopped, like a freeze frame in a movie. A guy being wheeled across the lobby in a wheelchair: frozen. A woman behind an information desk: caught with her mouth half open, staring carplike at Lucas and Sloan. All stopped. Then the world jerked forward again and Lucas heard himself saying, "My fuckin' Christ." Then bleakly, "How bad?"

"She's on the table," Sloan said. "They don't know what they got. She's breathing."

"What happened?" Lucas said.

"You okay?" asked Sloan.

"Ah, man . . ."

"A guy—Shadow Love—forced a maid to open her hotel room. Lily was taking a bath, but she got to her gun, and there was some kind of fight and he shot her. He got away."

"Motherfucker," Lucas said bitterly. "We were over looking at Clay's hotel security, we never thought about hers."

"The maid's all shook up, but she's looked at a picture and she thinks it was Shadow. . . ."

"I don't give a fuck about that, what about Lily? What are the docs saying? Is she bad? Come on, man."

Sloan turned away, shrugged, then turned back and gestured helplessly. "You know the fuckin' docs, they ain't gonna say shit because of the malpractice insurance. They don't want to say she's gonna make it, then have her croak. But one of the hotel guys was in combat in Vietnam. He says she was hit hard. He said if she'd of been in Vietnam, it would of depended on how fast they got her back to a hospital whether she made it. . . . He thinks the slug took a piece of lung, and he rolled her up on her side to keep her from drowning in blood. . . . The paramedics were there in two or three minutes, so . . . I don't know, Lucas. I think she'll make it, but I don't know."

Sloan led the way through the hospital to the surgical suite. Daniel was already there with a Homicide cop.

"You okay?" Daniel asked.

"What about Lily?"

"We haven't heard anything yet," Daniel said, shaking his head. "I just ran over from the office."

"It's Shadow Love, you know. Doing security work for the Crows."

"But why?" Daniel's forehead wrinkled. "We're not that close to them. And there's no percentage in killing Lily, not for political reasons. I'm a politician and they're politicians, and I can see what they're doing. It makes sense, in a bizarre way. They were so careful to explain the others—Andretti, the judge in Oklahoma, the guy in South Dakota. This doesn't fit. Neither did Larry. Or your snitch."

"We don't know exactly what's going on," Lucas said, his voice on the edge of desperation. "If I could just find something . . . some little hangnail of information, just a fuckin' scrap . . . anything."

They thought about it in silence for a moment, then Daniel, in a lower voice, said, "I called her husband."

Two hours later, long done with conversation, they were staring bleakly at the opposite wall of the corridor when the doors from the operating suite banged open. A redheaded surgeon came through, still wrapped in a blue surgical gown dappled with blood. She snapped the mask off her face and tossed it into a bin already half full of discarded masks and gowns, and began peeling off the gown. Daniel and Lucas pushed off the wall and stepped toward her.

"I'm good," she said. She tossed the used gown in the discard bin and wiggled her fingers in front of her face. "Seriously gifted."

"She's okay?" Lucas asked.

"You the family?" the surgeon asked, looking from one of them to the other.

"The family's not here," Lucas said. "They're on their way from New York. I'm her partner and this is the chief."

"I've seen you on TV," she said to Daniel, then looked back at Lucas. "She'll be okay unless something weird happens. We took the slug out—it looks like a light thirty-eight, if you're interested. It entered through her breast, broke a rib, pulped up a piece of her lung and stuck in the muscle wall along the rib cage in back. Cracked the rib in back too. She's gonna hurt like hell."

"But she'll make it?" Daniel said.

"Unless something weird happens," the surgeon nodded. "We'll keep her in intensive care overnight. If there aren't any problems, we'll have her sitting up and maybe walking around her bed in a couple of days. It'll take longer before she's feeling right, though. She's messed up."

"Aw, Jesus, that's good," said Lucas, turning to Daniel. "That's decent."

"Bad scars?" asked Daniel.

"There'll be some. With that kind of wound, we can't fool around. We had to get in to see what was going on. We'll have the entry wound from the slug, and then the surgical scars where I went in. In a couple or three years, the entry wound will be a white mark about the size and shape of a cashew on the lower curve of her breast. In five years, the surgical scars will be white lines maybe an eighth-inch across. She's olive-complected, so they'll show more than they would on a blonde, but she can live with them. They won't be disfiguring."

"When can we see her?"

The surgeon shook her head. "Not tonight. She won't be doing anything but sleeping. Tomorrow, maybe, if it's necessary."

"No sooner?"

"She's been *shot*," the surgeon said with asperity. "She doesn't need to talk. She needs to heal."

David Rothenburg came in at two o'clock in the morning on a cattle-car flight out of Newark, the only one he could get. Lucas met him at the airport. Daniel wanted to send Sloan, or go himself, but Lucas insisted. Rothenburg was wearing a rumpled blue seersucker suit and a wine-colored bow tie with a white shirt; his hair was messed up and he wore half-moon reading glasses down on his nose. Lucas had talked to the airline about the shooting, and Rothenburg was the first person out of the tunnel into the gate area. He had a black nylon carry-on bag in his left hand.

"David Rothenburg?" Lucas asked, stepping toward him.

"Yes. Are you . . ." They moved in a circle around each other.

"Lucas Davenport, Minneapolis Police."

"How is she?"

"Hurt, but she'll make it, if there aren't any complications."

"My God, I thought she was dying," Rothenburg said, sagging in relief. "They were so vague on the phone. . . ."

"Nobody knew for a while. She's had an operation. They didn't know until they got inside how bad it was."

"But she'll be okay?"

"That's what they say. I've got a car. . . ."

Rothenburg was two inches taller than Lucas but slender as a rope. He looked strong, like an ironman runner, long muscles without bulk. They walked stride for stride across the terminal and out to the parking ramp to the Porsche.

"You're the guy she bailed out of trouble. The hostage, when she shot that man," Rothenburg said.

"Yeah. We did some work together."

"Where were you tonight?" There was an edge to the question, and Lucas glanced at him.

"We split up. She went back to her hotel to read some stuff while I was out working my regular informant net. This guy we're looking for, Shadow Love, tracked her there."

"You know who did it?"

"Yes, we think so."

"Jesus Christ, in New York the guy'd be in jail."

Lucas looked directly across at Rothenburg and held the stare for a moment, then grunted, "Bullshit."

"What?" Rothenburg's anger was beginning to show.

"I said 'bullshit.' He fired one shot and got lost. He's got a safe house somewhere and he knows what he's doing. The

New York cops wouldn't do any better than we're doing. Wouldn't do as good. We're better than they are."

"I don't see how you can say that, people are being shot down here."

"We have about one killing a week in Minneapolis and we catch all the killers. You have between five and eleven a night in New York and your cops hardly catch any of them. So don't give me any shit about New York. I'm too tired and too pissed to listen to it."

"It's my wife who's shot . . ." Rothenburg barked.

"And she was working with me and I liked her a lot, and I feel guilty about it, so stay off my fuckin' back," Lucas snarled.

There was a moment of silence; then Rothenburg sighed and settled further into his seat. "Sorry," he said after a moment. "I'm scared."

"No sweat," said Lucas. "I'll tell you something, if it makes you feel better. As of tonight, Shadow Love is a dead motherfucker."

Lucas left Rothenburg at the hospital and went back on the street. There were few places open; he found a bar in a yuppie shopping center, drank a scotch, then another, and left. The night was cold and he wondered where Shadow Love was. He had no way to find out, not without a break.

CHAPTER
26

Leo came in at three in the morning. "No sign of Clay, but his man's at home."

"Drake? You saw him?"

"Yeah. And he's got a girl with him."

"Blonde?" asked Sam.

"Yeah. Real small."

"Far out . . . real young?"

"Probably eight or ten years old. Took Drake's hand when they walked up to the door."

"Clay'll be coming," Aaron said with certainty. "When you got his kind of twist, you don't get away from it." When he said 'twist,' he made a twisting motion with his fist.

Sam nodded. "Another night," he said. "Tomorrow night."

"Did you hear about the cop?" asked Aaron.

Leo took off his jacket and tossed it at the couch. "The woman? Yeah. It's Shadow."

"God damn, the fool will ruin us," Aaron said bitterly.

"One more night," said Leo. "One or two."

"Killing cops is bad medicine," Aaron said. He looked at his cousin. "If it's gonna happen with Clay, it's gotta be soon. We might start thinking about taking him at the hotel or on the street."

Sam shook his head. "The plan is right. Don't fuck with the plan. Clay's got a platoon of bodyguards with machine guns. They'd flat kill us on the street and Clay'd be a hero. If we can get him at Drake's, he'll be alone. And he won't be no hero."

"Tomorrow night," said Leo. "I'd bet on it."

Shadow Love hid in a condemned building six blocks out from the Loop. The building, once a small hotel, became a flophouse and finally was condemned for its lack of maintenance and the size of its rats. Norway rats: the fuckin' Scandinavians ran everything in the state, Shadow Love thought.

There were a few other men living in the building, but Shadow Love never really saw them. Just shambling figures darting between rooms, or moving furtively up and down the stairs. When you took a room, you closed the door and blocked it with a four-by-four from a pile of lumber on the first floor. You braced one end of the timber against the door, one end against the opposite wall. It wasn't foolproof, but it was pretty good.

The three-story structure had been built around a central atrium with a skylight at the top. When the men had to move their bowels—a rare event, most of them were winos—they simply hung over the atrium railing and let go. That kept the upper rooms reasonably tidy. Nobody stayed long on the bottom floors.

When Shadow Love moved in, he brought a heavy coat, a plastic air mattress, a cheap radio with earphones, and his gun. Groceries were slim: boxes of crackers, cookies, a can of Cheez Whiz, and a twelve-pack of Pepsi.

After the shooting, Shadow Love had run down the stairs, tried to *stroll* through the lobby, then hurried on to the Volvo. He drove it until he was sure he couldn't have been followed, and dumped it. He stopped once at a convenience store to buy food and then settled into the hideout.

There was nothing on the radio for almost two hours. Then a report that Detective Lillian Rothenburg had been shot. Not killed but shot. More than he'd hoped for. Maybe he got her. . . .

Then, a half-hour later, word that she was on the operating table. And two hours after that, a prognosis: The doctors said she'd live.

Shadow Love cursed and pulled the coat around him. The nights were getting very cold. Despite the coat, he shivered.

The bitch was still alive.

CHAPTER
27

Lucas spent the next day working his net, staying in touch with the hospital by telephone. In the early afternoon, Lily woke up and spoke to David, who was sitting at her bedside, and later to Sloan. She could add little to what they knew.

Shadow Love, she said. She had never seen his face, but it felt right. He was middle-height, wiry. Dark. Ate sausage.

That said, she went back to sleep.

At nine, Lucas called a friend at the intensive care unit: he had been calling her hourly.

"He just left, said he was going to get some sleep," the friend told Lucas.

"Is she awake?"

"She comes and goes. . . ."

"I'll be right there," he said.

Lily was wrapped in sheets and blankets, propped half upright on the bed. Her face was pale, the color of notebook paper. A breathing tube went to her nose. Two saline bags hung beside her bed, and a drip tube was patched into her arm below the elbow.

Lucas' friend, a nurse, said, "She woke up a while ago, and I told her you were coming, so she knows. Don't stay long, and be as quiet as you can."

Lucas nodded and tiptoed to Lily's bedside.

"Lily?"

After a moment, she turned her head, as if the sound of his voice had taken a few seconds to penetrate. Her eyes, when she opened them, were clear and calm.

"Water?" she croaked. There was a bottle of water on the bedstand with a plastic straw. He held it to her mouth and she sucked once. "Damn breathing tube dries out my throat."

"You feel pretty bad?"

"Doesn't . . . hurt much. I feel like I'm . . . really sick. Like I had a terrible flu."

"You look okay," Lucas lied. Except for her eyes, she looked terrible.

"Don't bullshit me, Davenport," she said with a small grin. "I know what I look like. Good for the diet, though."

"Jesus, it freaked me out." He couldn't think of anything else to say.

"Thanks for the rose."

"What?"

"The rose . . ." She turned her head away, then back and forth, as though trying to loosen up her neck muscle. "Very . . . romantic."

Lucas had no idea what she was talking about, and then she said, "I got through the first fifteen minutes . . . with David. I hurt so bad I wasn't thinking of you or anything, I was just happy to be here. And we were talking and when I thought of you, the first fifteen minutes were gone . . . and it was okay."

"Jesus, Lily, I feel so bad."

"Nothing you could do: but you be careful," she said in her rusty voice. Her eyelids drooped. "Are you getting any-where?"

Lucas shook his head. "We've got a screen of people around Clay—I still think it's him. I just haven't figured out how. We're watching the dumbwaiter, but that's not it."

"I don't know," she said. Her eyes closed and she took two deep breaths. "I'm so damn sleepy all the time. . . . Can't think . . ."

And she was gone, sleeping, her face going slack. Lucas

sat by her bed for five minutes, watching her face and the slow rise and fall of her chest. He was lucky, he thought, that he wasn't walking beside her coffin across another cemetery, just as with Larry. . . .

Larry.

It came back in a flash, as real as the shotgun behind his ear. He'd been walking across the cemetery grass with Lily and Anderson, after leaving Rose Love's well-tended grave. Anderson was talking about the cost of grave maintenance and the perpetual-care contract he and his wife had bought. . . .

And the question popped into his head: Who paid to take care of Rose Love's grave? Neither Shadow Love nor the Crows had enough money to endow a perpetual-care fund, so they must pay it annually or semiannually. But if they were on the road all the time, where would the bill be sent? Lucas stood, looked down at Lily's sleeping face, paced out of the ICU, past a patient who looked as though he were dying, and then back in, until he was standing by her bed again.

The Crows or Shadow Love, whoever paid for maintenance, might simply remember to write a check once or twice a year and mail it, without ever getting a bill. But that didn't feel right; there must be a bill. Maybe they had a postal box; but if they had their mail sent to a box, and didn't get back into town for a while, important messages might sit there for weeks. Lucas didn't know what the Crows had done, but he knew what he would do in their circumstances. He'd have a mail drop. He'd have the cemetery bill and other important stuff sent to an old, trustworthy friend. Somebody he could rely on to send the mail on to him. He half ran from the ICU to the nurses' station.

"I gotta have a phone," Lucas snapped at his friend. She stepped back and pointed at a desk phone. He picked it up and called Homicide. Anderson was just getting ready to leave.

"Harmon? I'm heading out to Riverwood Cemetery in a hurry. You get on the line, find out where Riverwood does its paperwork and call me. I've got a handset. If the office

is closed, run down somebody who can open it up, somebody who does the bills. I'll be there in ten minutes."

"What have you got?" Anderson asked.

"Probably nothing," Lucas said. "But I've got just the
smallest fuckin' hangnail of an idea. . . ."

Clay and a security man stood in the parking garage and
argued.

"It's a fuckin' terrible idea," the security man said intently.

"No, it's not. When you get a little higher in management, you'll recognize that," Lawrence Duberville Clay re-
plied. An undertone in his voice hinted that it was unlikely
the security man would ever rise higher in management.

"Look: one car. Just one. You wouldn't even see it."

"Absolutely not. You put a car on me and you better
warn the people inside that I'll fire their asses. And you with
them. No. The only way for me to do this is to go out on
my own. And I'll probably be safer than if I was here. Nobody'll expect me to be out on the street."

"Jesus, boss . . ."

"Look, we've been through this before," Clay said. "The
fact is, when you're surrounded by a screen of security, you
don't have any *feel* for anything. I *need* to get away, to be
effective."

They had a car for him, a nondescript rental that one of
the agents had picked up at the airport. Clay took the wheel,
slammed the door and looked out at the unhappy security
man.

"Don't worry, Dan. I'll be back in a couple, three hours,
no worse for the wear."

Lucas had to wait ten minutes at the cemetery office, watching the moon ghost across the sky behind dead oak leaves.
He shivered and paced impatiently, and finally a Buick
rolled up and a woman got out.

"Are you Davenport?" she asked in a sour voice, jingling
her keys.

"Yes."

"I was at a dinner," she said. She was a hard woman in her early thirties, with a beehive hairdo from the late fifties. "Sorry."

"We really should have some kind of papers," she said frostily as she unlocked the door.

"No time," Lucas said.

"It's not right. I should call our chairman."

"Look, I'm trying to be fuckin' nice," Lucas said, his voice rising as he spoke. "I'm trying as hard as I can to be a nice guy because you seem like an okay woman. But if you drag your feet on this, I'll call downtown for a warrant. It'll be here in five minutes and we'll seize your whole goddamn billing system. If you get lucky, you'll get it back sometime next year. You can explain that to your chairman."

The woman stepped away from him and a spark of fear touched her eyes. "Please wait," she said. She went into a back room, and soon Lucas could hear her typing on a computer keyboard.

It was all bullshit, Lucas told himself. Not a chance in a fucking million. A moment later a printer started, and then the woman came out of the back room.

"The bills have always been sent to the same place, every six months, forty-five dollars and sixty-five cents. Sometimes they're slow-pay, but they always pay."

"Who?" asked Lucas. "Where'd you send the bill?"

The woman handed Lucas a sheet of computer paper, with one short line pinched between her thumb and forefinger. "It's right here," she said. "A Miss Barbara Gow. That's her address under her name. Does that help?"

Corky Drake had been born with a silver spoon in his mouth, only to have it rudely snatched away in his teens. His father had for some years neglected to report his full income to the Internal Revenue Service. When the heathens had learned of Corky Senior's oversight . . . well, the capital barely covered what was owed, much less the fines.

His father had removed himself from the scene with a garden hose that led from the tailpipe of a friend's Mercedes into the sealed car. The friend had refused to forgive him, even in death, for what he had done to the upholstery.

Corky, who was seventeen, was already a person of refined taste. A life of poverty and struggle simply was not on the menu. He did the only thing he was qualified to do: he became a pimp.

Certain friends of his father's had exceptional interests in women. Corky could satisfy those, for a price. Not only were the women very beautiful, they were very young. They were, in fact, girls. The youngest in his current stable was six. The oldest was eleven, although, Corky assured the wits among his clientele, she still had the body of an eight-year-old. . . .

Corky Drake met Lawrence Duberville Clay at a club in Washington. If they hadn't become friends, they had at least become friendly. Clay appreciated the services offered by Drake.

"My little perversion," Clay called it, with a charming grin.

"No. It's not a perversion, it's perfectly natural," Drake said, swirling two ounces of Courvoisier in a crystal snifter. "You're a connoisseur, is what you are. In many countries of the world . . ."

Drake would serve his clients in Washington or New York, if they required it, but his home base was in Minneapolis, and his resources were strongest there. Clay, in town on business, visited Corky's home. After that, the visits became a regular part of his life. . . .

Drake was talking to the current queen of his stable when he heard the car in the driveway.

"Here he is now," he said to the girl. "Remember, this could be the most important night of your life, so I want you to be good."

Leo Clark sat in a clump of brush thirty yards from Drake's elaborate Kenwood townhouse. He was worried about the cops. Barbara Gow's car was parked up the street. It didn't fit in the neighborhood. If they checked it and had it towed, he'd be fucked.

He sat in the leaves and waited, looking at his watch every

few minutes and studying the face of the Old Man in the Moon. It was a clear night for the Cities, and you could see him staring back at you, but it was nothing like the nights on the prairie, when the Old Man was so close you could almost touch his face. . . .

At ten minutes after nine, a gray Dodge entered Corky's circular driveway. Leo put up a pair of cheap binoculars and hoped there'd be more light when Corky opened the door. There was, and just enough: the elegant gray hair of Lawrence Duberville Clay was unmistakable. Leo waited until Clay was inside the house, then picked his way through the wood to Barbara's car, quickly started it and headed back to her house. He stopped only once, at a pay phone.

The message was simple: "Clay's at the house."

Anderson was waiting in his office when Lucas hurried in.

"What you got?"

"A name," Lucas said. "Let's run it through the machine."

They put Barbara Gow's name into the computer and got back three quick hits.

"She's Indian, and she's a rad, or used to be," Anderson said, scanning down the monitor. "Look at this. Organizing for the union, busted in a march . . . Christ, this was way back in the fifties, she was ahead of her time. . . . Civil rights and then antiwar stuff there in the sixties . . ."

"She'd of known the Crows," Lucas said. "There weren't that many activist Indians back in the fifties, not in Minneapolis. . . ."

Anderson was scanning through one of his notebooks; he found a page and held it up to the screen. "Look at this," he said. He tapped an address in the notebook and touched an address on the screen. "She lived just a couple blocks from Rose E. Love, and at the same time."

"All right, I'm going down there," Lucas said. "Get onto Del and some of his narcs, tell them I might need surveillance help. I'll look the place over now. It's too much to hope that they'll be there."

"You want me to start some squads that way, just in case?"

"Yeah, you could start a couple, but keep them off the block unless I holler."

Leo pulled into Barbara Gow's driveway and Aaron lifted the garage door. Leo rolled the car inside but left the engine running. Sam stepped out of the house carrying a chopped-down shotgun. Leo had cut the gun down himself. What had been a conventional Winchester Super-X, a four-shot semiauto, wound up as an ugly illegal killing machine that looked as much like a war club as a shotgun. Sam opened the car door and slipped the shotgun under the passenger seat, and then helped Aaron load a six-foot chunk of rail-road tie into the cargo space. They'd sharpened one end with an ax and screwed handles to the top. When it was in, Aaron slammed the tailgate and he and Sam got in.

"You want to leave the garage door up?" Leo asked.

"Yeah. If we gotta get off the street in a hurry when we come back, it'll get us an extra minute."

Lucas cruised by the side of the Gow house, moving as slowly as he could without being conspicuous. There were lights on in both front and back, probably the living room and the kitchen or a bedroom. The upper floor was dark. He turned the corner to pass in front of the house and saw that the garage door was up, the garage empty. As he passed, a shadow crossed the living room blind. Someone inside. Since the car was gone, that meant more than one person was living in the house. . . .

He picked up the handset and put in a call to Anderson.

"Get me the description of the woman who was seen with Shadow Love," he said.

"Just a second," Anderson said. "I've got the notebook right here. Can't get Del, he's on the street, but one of his guys has gone after him. There are a couple of squads waiting out on Chicago."

"Okay."

There was a moment of silence. Lucas took another corner and went around the block. "Uh, there's not much. Very small, barely see over the steering wheel. Indian. Maybe an older woman. She didn't seem young. Green car, older, a wagon, with white sidewall tires."

"Thanks. I'll get back to you."

He took another corner, then another, and came back up along the side of Gow's house. As he did, a man walked out of the house across the street from Gow's, leading a dog. Lucas stopped at the curb as the man strolled out to the sidewalk, looked both ways, then headed around the side of his house, the dog straining at the leash. Lucas thought about it, let the man get a full lot down the opposite block, then called Anderson.

"I need Del or a couple of narcs in plain cars."

"I got a guy looking for Del; we should have him in a minute."

"Soon as you can. I want them up the block from Gow's place, watching the front."

"I'll pass the word."

"And keep those squads on Chicago."

The dog was peeing on a telephone pole when Lucas pulled up next to the night walker. He got out of the car, his badge case in hand.

"Excuse me. I'm Lucas Davenport, a lieutenant with the Minneapolis Police Department. I need a little help."

"What d'you want?" the man asked curiously.

"Your neighbor across the street. Mrs. Gow. Does she live alone?"

"What'd she do?" the man asked.

"Maybe nothing at all . . ."

The man shrugged. "She usually does, but the last few days, there's been other people around. I never seen them, really. But people are coming and going."

"What kind of car does she drive?"

"Old Dodge wagon. Must be fifteen years old."

"What color?"

"Apple green. Ugly color. Never seen anything like it, except in those Dodges."

"Huh." Lucas could feel his heart pounding harder. "White sidewalls?"

"Yep. You don't see them like that anymore. Bet she

don't drive a couple thousand miles a year. The tires are probably originals. What's she done?"

"Maybe nothing," Lucas said. "Thanks for your help. I'd appreciate it if you'd keep this to yourself."

As Lucas started back to the car, the man said, "Those other people . . . they left about five minutes ago. Somebody drove up in her car and somebody else opened the garage door, and one minute later, they left."

Lucas called Anderson: "I got something," he said. "I'm not sure what, but the Crows may be on the street."

"Sonofabitch. You think they're hitting somebody?"

"I don't know. Don't let those squads get away, though. I don't care what happens. And get me Del's man."

"I got Del. He was maybe a mile away, he oughta be there anytime."

"All right. Tell him I'll wait at Twenty-fourth and Bloomington, right by Deaconess Hospital."

Del was waiting when Lucas arrived. The street was empty, and Lucas crossed into the left lane until their cars were door to door. Both men rolled their windows down.

"Got something?"

"Could be heavy," Lucas said. "I think I got the Crows' hideout, but they're on the street."

"What do you want from me?"

"I was gonna ask for some surveillance help, but if the Crows are on the street . . . I'm going in. I need some backup."

Del nodded. "Let's do it."

"Let me introduce you to Lucy," Drake said. He turned toward the back and called, "Lucy? Darling?"

They were standing in front of the fireplace, glasses in their hands. A moment after he called, Lucy appeared from the back. She was tiny, blonde, shy, and wore a pink kimono.

"Come over here, darling, and meet a friend of mine," Drake said.

•   •   •

"Cop," Leo said.

"Shit. He's going in," Sam said.

Drake's house was on a long loop road, to the left. The cop had just turned into the loop, then stayed to the right. If he continued along the loop, he'd pass Drake's house on the way back out.

"We gotta wait," Sam said. He pointed at a supermarket parking lot. "Pull in there. We can watch for him to come out."

"What if Clay leaves?"

Aaron looked at his watch. "He's only been there a half-hour. He usually stays two or three. This is not something you do quick. Not if you can help it."

Lucas and Del left their cars just down the block, and Lucas led the way to the porch. Del took a short black automatic out of a hip holster and stood to one side of the door as Lucas knocked.

He knocked once, then again.

A woman's voice: "Who is it?"

Before Lucas could answer, Del piped up, in a childish falsetto, *"StarTribune."*

There was a moment's hesitation and then the door started to open. As it opened, Lucas realized that it was on a chain. A woman's eye appeared in the crack. Lucas said, "Police," and the woman screamed, "No," and tried to push the door shut. She was small and dark and not young, and Lucas knew for sure. As she tried to push the door shut he rocked back and kicked it; the chain ripped off and they were inside, the woman running awkwardly toward the back. Lucas was on her, punching her between the shoulder blades, and she went down on her face in the hallway. Del was braced in the entrance to the living room, his gun in front of him, scanning.

"You don't fuckin' move," Lucas snarled at the woman. "You don't fuckin' move, you hear?"

Lucas and Del went through the house in thirty seconds, rotating down the hallway, clearing out the two bedrooms, then taking the stairs, cautiously, ready . . . Nothing.

At the top, Lucas heard the woman on her feet, and as

Del held the stairs, Lucas shouted, "Wait here," and ran back down. Gow was headed for the front door when Lucas hit her again. She yelped and went down, and he dragged her to a radiator and cuffed her to it. Del was still waiting at the top of the stairs; Lucas came and they cleaned out the second floor. Nobody.

Downstairs they checked the bedrooms again, this time for any sign of the Crows. It was all there: a stack of un-mailed press releases, letters, two different sets of men's clothing.

"I'm gonna talk to this woman," Lucas told Del. "You shut the front door and call Anderson, tell him what we've got. Get a warrant down here, maybe we can finesse things later. And tell him we may want an ERU team for when the Crows come back."

While Del went to call, Lucas walked back to Barbara Gow, who was lying on her side with her knees up to her face, weeping. Lucas uncuffed her and prodded her back with his foot.

"Sit up," he said.

"Don't hurt me," she wailed.

"Sit the fuck up," Lucas said. "You're under arrest. Seven counts of first-degree murder. You have the right to remain silent . . ."

"I didn't do anything."

"You're an accomplice . . ." Lucas said, squatting next to her, his face two inches from hers. He was not quite shouting, and he deliberately let spittle rain on her face.

"I didn't do anything."

"Where are the Crows . . . ?"

"I don't know any Crows. . . ."

"Bullshit. All their stuff is in back." He grabbed her by the blouse and shook her.

"I don't know," she said. "I don't know where they went. They took my car."

"She's lying," Del said. Lucas looked up and found Del standing over them. His eyes were dilated and he hadn't shaved for several days. "Stay with her for just a second. I wanna run down to the bathroom."

Lucas waited, watching the woman's face. A few seconds later, they heard the bath water running.

"What're you going to do?" Lucas asked when Del returned. He tried to sound interested—curious—but not worried.

"She's got nice hot water," Del said. "So I thought maybe I'd give the bitch a bath."

"Shit, I wish I'd thought of that," Lucas said happily.

Gow tried to roll away from him but Del caught the old woman by the hair. "You know how many old women drown in the bathtub? Suck in that scalding hot water and can't get out?"

"It's a tragedy," Lucas said.

"Let me go," Gow screamed, struggling now. Del dragged her toward the hallway by the hair. She flailed at him, but he ignored it.

"There's some coffee in the kitchen," Del called. "Why don't you go heat up some water, we can have a cup. This'll only take a minute. She don't look too strong."

"They went to kill Clay," Gow blurted.

"Jesus Christ." Del let her go and the two men crouched over her.

"They can't get to him. He's got round-the-clock bodyguards," Lucas argued.

"He sneaks out," Gow said. "He has sex with little girls, so he sneaks out."

Lucas looked at Del: "Motherfucker. They don't crack the security. They get Clay to come out. Call Anderson and have him get onto the feebs. Find out where Clay is. And get Daniel."

Del dashed down the hall toward the telephone and Lucas gripped the old woman's hair.

"Tell me the rest. I'll testify in court for you. I'll tell them you helped; it might get you off. Where'd they go?"

Tears ran down her face and she sobbed, unable to talk.

"Talk to me," Lucas screamed, shaking the old woman's head.

"There's a man named Christopher Drake. Corky Drake. He lives up in Kenwood somewhere," Barbara Gow sobbed. "Clay goes to his house for the girls."

Lucas let her go and ran into the kitchen, where Del was on the phone. "I gotta go," he shouted. "Stay with her. Tell Anderson I'll call in ten seconds, tell him I'll need those squads."

Lucas sprinted to the Porsche, cranked it, picked up the handset and called Dispatch.

"A Christopher Drake," he told the dispatcher. "In Kenwood. I need the address now."

Twenty seconds later, as he turned onto Franklin Avenue, he had it.

"I need everything you've got. No sirens, but make it fast," he told Dispatch.

Anderson came on: "I'm talking to Del, we're going out to the FBI now. How long before you make this Drake's place?"

Lucas ran a red light and calculated. "If I don't hit anything, about two minutes," he said. He crossed the center line into the left lane and blew past two cars, the speedometer nudging sixty.

The squad car came out of the loop road, turned away from them and kept going. Aaron grunted, checked his watch again and said, "Let's go."

Drake's house was a quarter-mile down the lane. They did a U-turn in front of the house, so the car would be pointed out, and left it on the street. The yards were wooded, and the brush would screen them as they approached the house.

"Let's get the tie," Sam said as they climbed out of the car.

Aaron looked up at the sky as Sam popped the tailgate. "Good moon for a killing," Aaron said.

In the soundproofed privacy of the bedroom, the girl dropped the kimono around her feet and slipped onto the bed. Lawrence Duberville Clay peeled off his underwear and slipped in beside her, and she put her arm over her chest.

"Smell so good," she said. He looked over her shoulder

at the video camera and the monitor screen. The light was just right. It would be an evening to remember.

Leo held the cut-down shotgun by his side as they pulled the railroad tie out of the car and held it by the handles. A battering ram. Nearly a hundred pounds, swung hard, focused on a point no bigger than a hammerhead. Better than any sledgehammer made.

Swinging the tie, they moved swiftly through the dark into Drake's yard.

"Go through it one more time," Leo said.

Sam recited in a monotone. "Aaron and I swing it. When the door goes down, we drop it and you run right over it, freeze anyone inside. Aaron takes the ground floor, blocking anyone out, and you and I go up the stairs. There are four bedrooms up the stairs, and they'll be in one of them."

"Drop the tie, go in, freeze anyone, then Aaron takes over and we go up the stairs."

"Clay carries a gun; you've seen the pictures," Aaron said. He looked up at the moon. "So be careful."

They stayed in a screen of trees as they came up the drive, then broke across an open space to a lilac bush, paused to adjust their holds on the railroad tie.

"You got it?" Aaron asked.

"Let's go," said Sam.

Running awkwardly, they rushed at the door, then stopped at the last second and swung the tie as hard as they could. It hit the door two inches from the knob and blew it open as effectively as a stick of dynamite. They let go as the door flew open; the tie fell half inside, and Leo was in the living room. Drake was there, coming off the couch, a pearl-gray suit and pink open-necked shirt, his mouth open. Leo, his face twisted into a mask of hate, shoved the shotgun at him and said in a coarse whisper:

"Where is he?"

Integrity had never been one of Drake's burdens. "Up the stairs," he blurted. "First door on the left."

"If he's not there, motherfucker, you gonna be sucking on this shotgun," Leo snarled.

"He's there. . . ."

Aaron held Drake as Leo and Sam took the stairs, struggling with the railroad tie as they went, their footfalls muffled by the thick carpet. At the top, they looked at each other, and Leo held the shotgun over his head. They went at the bedroom door with the tie. The bedroom door was no more match for the ram than the front door had been. It blew open and Leo went through.

Music was playing from a stereo; the lights were low enough for comfort, bright enough for spectating. A video camera was mounted on a steel tripod, with a television flickering beside it. Clay was there, his flesh obscenely white, sluglike, on the red satin sheet. The girl was beside him, nearly as pale as he was, except for a streak of scarlet lipstick.

"Get away," Leo said to the girl, gesturing with the shotgun.

"Wait," said Clay. The girl rolled away from him and off the bed.

"Wait, for Christ's sakes," Clay said.

"On your feet," Leo said. "This is a citizen's arrest."

"What?"

"On your feet and turn around, Mr. Clay," Leo said. "If you don't, I swear to God I'll blow you to pieces."

Clay, frightened, crawled off the bed and turned. Sam slipped his pistol into his pocket, took out his obsidian knife and stepped behind him.

"We're going to handcuff you, Mr. Clay," Sam said. "Put your hands behind your back. . . ."

"You're the Crows. . . ."

"Yeah. We're the Crows."

"Do I know you? I've seen you? Your faces . . ."

Clay was facing curtains that covered windows overlooking the driveway. A set of headlights swept into the drive, then a set of red flashers.

"Cops," said Leo.

"We met a long time ago," Sam said. "In Phoenix."

Clay started to turn his head, recognition lighting his eyes, and Sam reached up from the other side, grabbed his hair and dragged the knife across his throat. Clay twisted away screaming, and the girl broke for the door. Blood pumped through Clay's hands and he fell faceup on the bed, trying to hold himself together. Sam shouted, "Let's go."

Leo shouted, "Run," and as Sam went, he stepped close to the supine Clay and fired the shotgun into his chest.

Lucas turned into the loop road fifty yards in front of the first cruiser. He had to slow to find the address, then saw Barbara Gow's wagon in the street and the open door of the white Colonial house. He slid into the circular drive, stood on the brake and piled out, the P7 in his hand. The cruiser was just behind him, and then there were more lights on the lane, more cops coming in. He waited just a second for the first cruiser and heard the shotgun roar. . . .

"Cops," Sam screamed from the top of the stairs, his scream punctuated by the shotgun blast. Both he and Aaron favored old-model .45s, and had them in their hands. The girl, nude, ran down the stairs, saw Aaron waiting and stopped. Sam pushed past her, with Leo just behind.

Drake had his hands on his head and began to back away. "Fucker," Aaron said, and shot him in the chest. Drake flipped back over a sofa and disappeared.

"Try the back?" Leo shouted.

"Fuck it," said Aaron. "Clean the driveway out with the shotgun, then get out of the way."

Leo ran to the door. The car's headlights were focused on it but he could see figures behind the lights. He fired three quick shots, emptying the gun, and ducked back inside as a hail of bullets tore through the doorway into the living room.

"Go out the back," Aaron said to him. He kissed Leo on the cheek, looked at his cousin.

"Time to die, you flatheaded motherfucker," Sam shouted.

The return fire from outside had stopped. There were shouts, and Sam lifted his head, smelling the perfume of the house. Then Aaron was out the door at a dead run, Sam a step behind, the .45s jumping in their hands.

•　　　•　　　•

Lucas looked at the cop and said, "Get somebody around back. They're in there, I just heard . . ."

He never finished the sentence. There was a shot inside the house, a pause, and then a shotgun opened from the doorway. The muzzle blast flickered like lightning in the dark and the cop who'd started for the back went down. More squads were roaring into the driveway, one sliding sideways as another cop went down.

Lucas fired a quick three shots at the doorway and started toward it as the gunner ducked inside. Then the Crows were there, coming out the door at a run, their pistols firing wildly. Lucas fired twice at the first one as the other cops opened up. The Crows were down a half-second later, bullets kicking up dirt around them, plucking at their shirts, their jeans, enough lead to kill a half-dozen men.

And then there was silence.

Then a few words, like morning birds outside a bedroom window. "*Jesus God,*" somebody was saying. "*Jesus God.*"

Sirens. Static from the radios. More sirens. Lots of them. Lucas crouched behind the car.

"Where's the shotgun?" he screamed. "Anybody see the shotgun?"

A cop was crying for help, the pain on him. Another was a lump in the dirt.

"Who's around back?" somebody called.

"Nobody. Get somebody around back."

A uniform dashed into the headlights, stopped next to the cop who was lying still in the dirt, and began tugging him out of the light. Lucas stood, aiming his pistol through the doorway, and squeezed off two suppression shots.

"He's gone," the uniform screamed, holding the dead cop in his arms. "Jesus, where are the paramedics?"

More lights in the lane, then Sloan coming up the driveway.

"Heard you on the radio," he grunted. "What have we got?"

"Maybe a shotgun inside."

There was a figure at the door, and two or three separate voices screamed warnings.

"Hold it, hold it," somebody shouted.

The girl appeared in the doorway, her eyes as wide as a deer's, shambling out of the wreckage.

"Who's in there?" Lucas called as she came across the driveway.

"Nobody," she wailed. She half turned to the house as though she couldn't believe it. "Everybody's dead."

CHAPTER
28

"I don't know what else we could have done," Lucas said. In his own ears, the words sounded like excuses, quick and chattery as if tumbling out of a teletype, harsh with guilt. "If we hadn't gone straight in, we'd have lost Clay for sure. We knew they weren't far in front of us."

"You did okay," Daniel said grimly. "It was that fuckin' Clay, sneaking out like that. The Crows must have known. They set him up, slicker'n shit. Fuckin' Wilson is dead, Belloo's maybe crippled, it's that fuckin' Clay's fault."

"It must have been Shadow Love with the shotgun," Lucas said. He was leaning against the wall, his hands in his pockets and his head down. His shirt was covered with blood. He thought it might be Belloo's. He was missing the heel of one shoe. Shot off? He wasn't sure. That foot hurt, but there were no wounds. Not a scratch. A uniformed captain, his face pale as the moon, stood down the hall and watched them talk. "He did Clay and Wilson and Belloo, all three. One of the Crows must have shot Drake. But that motherfucker Shadow Love, he caught us with that shotgun. . . ."

"The whole thing lasted no more than eight seconds," Daniel said. "That's what they're getting from the tapes. . . ."

"Christ . . ."

"The main thing is Shadow Love," Daniel said. "He must have gone out the back. We've got the neighborhood blocked off. We'll get him in the morning; I just hope he didn't get out before we set up the line."

"What if he's in somebody's house? What if he went in somewhere and he's got somebody's family on the wall?"

"We'll be going door to door."

"Motherfucker's a fruitcake and he's carrying a shotgun and we just killed his fathers. . . ."

They were standing in the antiseptic hallways of Hennepin Medical Center, outside the surgical suite, one set of doors closer to the operating rooms than was usually permitted. Two dozen family members, friends and cops were corralled one set of doors farther out, waiting for news.

And beyond the next set, a hundred newsmen, maybe more. Doctors and nurses shuttled in and out of the operating suite, half of them with no business there, but officiously correct in demeanor. They wanted to see what was going on.

Clay had been taken in, but he was gone; so was Drake, shot in the heart. The first cop shot was brain dead, but they had him on a respirator; the hospital was talking to his family about organ donations. The second cop was still on the table. A nurse had pointed out the doc working on Belloo, the same redheaded surgeon who'd done Lily. Two more surgeons joined her, and an hour after Belloo went on the table, she came through the doors into the waiting area.

"You guys are giving me more business than I need," she said grimly.

"What's the story?"

"It'll be a while before we know. We've got a neurosurgeon looking at some crap around his spinal cord. There's some bone splinters in there but he's still got function. . . ."

"He can walk?"

The surgeon shrugged. "He's going to lose something but not all of it. And we had to get a urologist down. A couple pellets went through a testicle."

Lucas and Daniel both winced. "Is he going to lose . . . ?"

"We're evaluating that. I don't know. He'd still be functional, even with one, but there's some plumbing in there. . . . Do you know if he has kids?"

"Yeah, three or four," said Daniel.

"Good," said the surgeon. She looked tired as she dumped her mask and gloves in the discard bin. "I better go talk to the family."

She was headed toward the family waiting area when the automatic doors swung open. The mayor and one of his aides came through, followed by the FBI's agent in charge.

"We gotta do something for the TV," the mayor snapped.

"I think we need more investigation . . ." the AIC said urgently.

"Bullshit, we got Davenport and a half-dozen cops saw the girl and we've got her statement and his body. There's no question. . . ."

"There's always a question," said the AIC.

"There's a videotape," said Daniel.

"Aw, Jesus," said the AIC. He turned to a hospital wall and leaned his head against it.

"We could deal," the mayor said to Daniel. "He was one of the administration's point men on crime. I don't know what we could get, but it'd be a lot. More urban renewal; new sewage treatment; our own air force; you name it."

Daniel shook his head. "No."

"Why not?" the AIC asked heatedly. "Why the fuck not? We stood down in that surveillance post after the fuckup with Bill Hood and we cut a deal. Remember what you said? You said, 'You always deal. Always.' "

"There's a corollary to that rule," Daniel said.

"What's that?"

"You always deal, except sometimes," Daniel said. He looked at the mayor. "This is one of those times."

The mayor nodded. "First, it just wouldn't be right."

"And second, we'd get caught," said Daniel. "You want to tell the TV, or you want me to?"

"You do it; I'm going to call somebody in the White House," the mayor said. "It's going to be bad, but there are levels of badness. Maybe I can cut a deal to make it less bad. . . ."

The AIC argued that the mayor should talk to the president before any announcement; the aide suggested that they had nothing to lose. Daniel pointed out that the discussion they were having could already bring big political trouble: they were talking about a conspiracy to cover up a crime. The politicians began backing away. The AIC still wanted to talk. As tempers got hotter, the night seemed to close in on Lucas, until he felt he might suffocate.

"I'm going," he told Daniel. "You don't need me and I need to sit down somewhere."

"All right," Daniel nodded. "But if you can't help thinking about it, think about Shadow Love."

Sloan was coming in as Lucas left.

"You okay?" Sloan asked.

"Yeah," Lucas said wearily. "Considering."

"How's Wilson?"

"Dead. They're selling off his heart and lungs and liver and kidneys and probably his dick. . . ."

"Jesus fuckin' Christ," Sloan blurted, appalled.

"Belloo's gonna make it. Might lose one of his balls."

"Jesus . . ." Sloan ran a hand through his hair. "You stop to see Lily?"

"No . . ."

"Look, man . . ." Sloan started.

He hesitated, and Lucas said, "What?"

"Do you feel bad about her now? With her husband here and all?"

Lucas thought about it for a second before he shook his head. "No," he said.

"Good," said Sloan. "'Cause you shouldn't."

"Got my goddamn car shot up," Lucas said. "My fuckin' insurance agent is gonna jump out a window when he hears about it."

"I got no sympathy for you," Sloan said. "You're the luckiest motherfucker on the face of the earth. Cothron said you walked right into the Crows' guns, like Jesus walking across the water, and never anything happened."

"I can't remember too well," Lucas said. "It's just all fucked up in my head."

"Yeah. Well, take it easy."

"Sure." Lucas nodded and limped away down the hall.

The Porsche had three bullet holes in it, each in a separate piece of sheet metal. Lucas shook his head and climbed in.

The night was not quite cold. He ran down through the Loop, in sync with traffic lights, and made it out to the interstate without stopping. He was flying on automatic: east across the river, off at the Cretin Avenue exit, south down Cretin, right to Mississippi River Boulevard, south to home.

Jennifer was waiting.

Her car was in the driveway, a light was on in a window of the house. He pulled into the drive and jabbed the transmitter for the garage door opener. As he waited for the door to open, she came to the window and looked out. She had the baby on her arm.

"I freaked out," she said simply.

"I'm all right," he said. He was limping from the lost heel.

"How about the other guys?"

"One dead. One pretty busted up. The Crows are dead."

"So it's over."

"Not quite. Shadow Love got away."

They were staring at each other across the narrow space of the kitchen, Jennifer unconsciously bouncing the baby on her arm.

"We've got to talk. I can't just walk away from you. I thought I could, but I can't," she said.

"Man, Jen, I'm fuckin' crazy right now. I don't know what's going on. . . ." He looked around wildly, the peaceful neighborhood hovering around them like a joke. "Come on," he said. "Come on and talk. . . ."

Shadow Love had heard about the shootout on his radio, and now he waited in a thicket just over the lip of the slope that went down to the river. He'd planned to take Davenport when he got out of the car, but he hadn't counted on the automatic garage door opener. The door rolled up with

Davenport still in the car, waiting. Shadow Love crouched, considered a dash across the street, but Davenport's house was set too far back from the road. He'd never make it.

When the door went down, Shadow Love walked fifty feet down the street, into the shadow of a spreading oak, and hurried across the street, through a corner of another yard and into the dark space beside Davenport's garage. Front doors were usually stout. Back doors, on garages, usually were not, since they didn't lead directly into the house. Shadow Love slipped around the garage to the back door and tested the knob. Locked.

The door had two panes of inset glass. Shadow Love peeled off his jacket, wrapped a sleeve around the middle joints of his fingers and pressed on the glass, hard, harder, until it cracked. There was almost no noise, but he paused, counted to three, then put more pressure along the crack. Another crack radiated out from the pressure point, then another. Two small pieces of glass fell almost noiselessly into the garage. Shadow Love stopped and checked the night around him: nothing moving, no *sense* of anything. Still using the jacket as padding, he pushed his little finger through the hole and carefully pulled two of the larger shards of glass from the door. In another minute, he had a hole large enough to reach through. He turned the lock knob and eased the door open.

The garage was not quite pitch dark: some light filtered in from the neighbor's house in back, enough that he could see large shapes, such as the car. With his left hand on the Porsche's warm hood, he moved carefully toward the door that led into the house. His right hand was wrapped around the pistol grip of the M-15. Once he was lined up on it, he would blow the knob off the door, and he'd be inside in a matter of a second or two. . . .

He never saw the shovel hanging from a nail on the garage wall. His sleeve hooked the blade and the shovel came down like a thunderclap, hammering into a garbage can, rattling off the car and onto the floor.

"What?" said Jennifer, starting at the noise.

Lucas knew. "Shadow Love," he whispered.

CHAPTER
29

"The basement," Lucas snapped.

He grabbed Jennifer by the shoulder and threw her toward the stairs as he drew his gun. She wrapped her arms around Sarah and went down, taking three steps at a time and leaping the last four, staggering as she hit the bottom.

In the garage, Shadow Love, stunned by the thunderclap of the falling shovel, brought the M-15 to his hip and fired three shots at the door's knob plate. One shot missed and blew through the door, into the kitchen cabinets and stove. The other two hit the knob plate, battering the door open. Half blinded by the flash from the weapon, his brain unconsciously registering the stink of the gunpowder, Shadow Love took two steps toward the door, then dropped to his face as three answering shots punched through the opening into the garage.

Lucas took the stairs a half-second behind Jennifer, but stopped three steps from the bottom. Jennifer was flattened against the wall, her arms wrapped around the baby, holding its head to her shoulder. Her face was distorted, as though she wanted to cry out but couldn't: it was a face from a macabre fun-house mirror. Lucas would remember it for the rest of his life, a split-second tableau of total terror. As the first of Shadow Love's shots smashed through the door, Sarah began to scream and Jennifer clutched her tighter, shrinking against the wall.

"Workroom," Lucas shouted, flattening himself against the stairwell wall, his gun hand extended up the stairs. "Get under the workbench."

Shadow Love's next two shots blew open the door from the garage, the slugs ricocheting through the kitchen. The door was at an angle to the stairway. Lucas fired three shots through the opening, hoping to catch Shadow Love coming in. There was a clatter in the garage, then a whip-quick series of flashes with the crack of the rifle. Lucas slid to the bottom of the stairs as the vinyl flooring came apart at the top of the stairs, the slugs slamming into the slanting head-wall over the steps. Shooting from the garage, with the rifle, Shadow Love had the advantage: he could fire down with a good idea of where his shots were going, but Lucas couldn't see to shoot up. Shadow Love knew that. The garbage can rattled and Lucas risked a quick step up and put two more shots through the wall where the can was. Shadow Love opened up again. This time, the shots were angled down into the stairwell. Though they were still overhead, Lucas was forced out of the stairwell and into the work-room, with the door left open.

Shadow Love controlled the stairs.

The garage stank of burnt gunpowder, auto exhaust and gasoline from the lawn mower. Shadow Love, panting, squatted by the step into the house and tried to figure the shots he'd taken. Eight or nine, total: better count it as nine. The gun was loaded with a thirty-shot banana clip, and he had one more clip in his jacket. He might need everything he had—they might not be enough—if Davenport barricaded himself in the basement.

The black spot was there, and he could feel the anger cooking in his heart. There was a very good chance that Davenport would kill him. The cop was on his home ground; he was well trained; and Shadow Love felt his luck had broken when he'd failed with the New York woman.

Still he had to try. The black spot grew, calling him in, and the anger rode into his veins like fire.

Jennifer was huddled under the workbench, wrapped protectively around Sarah, who was screaming beyond comfort.

"What are we doing?" she cried. "What are we doing?"

"The St. Paul cops should be coming in. We've only got to hold out a few minutes," Lucas said. "He'll have to make a move or get out. You stay put."

Lucas scrambled crabwise across the basement to his gun safe and spun the combination dial. He missed the second number, cursed and started over.

Upstairs, Shadow Love was torn between attack and retreat. He wouldn't stay free on the streets for long. He had no place to hide, his picture was everywhere. If he was careful, very careful, he might grab a car somewhere and make it out into the countryside. But with Clay's killing, the hunt would be remorseless. He would never have another chance at Davenport. Never have another chance to avenge his fathers. On the other hand, the hunter cop was armed and waiting in a house he knew intimately. An attack straight down the stairs would be suicide.

He held his breath, listening. No sirens. With the cool nights of October, windows were closed and furnaces were running; the firefight would not be particularly audible. On the other hand, Mississippi River Boulevard was a favorite jogging route. He'd be lucky if a passerby hadn't already heard the gunfire. Somehow, he had to pry Davenport out of the basement, and quickly. . . .

Squatting just outside the garage door, the M-15 pointed diagonally through the door at the stairwell, he noticed a telephone on the wall.

Shit. An extension in the basement?

Shadow Love crouched in a sprinter's position, listened for a second, then sprang through the open door into the kitchen, rolling when he hit the floor, coming up with the gun pointed at the stairwell. Nothing. He was inside.

With the gun leveled at the stairway door, he took a step

backward, picked up the phone with his free hand. Just a
dial tone. *Okay.* He let the phone dangle off the hook and
eased back to the doorway, silent in his sneakers.

He needed a way to blow them out. Chancing a look
down the stairwell, he stepped forward, feeling the vinyl
kitchen floor creak below his weight. The floor. The floor
would never stop a slug from an M-15. . . .

Moving in a gunman's crouch, he crossed quickly in front
of the open stairway door into the living room, listened
again, then took a half-dozen strides farther into the house.
A picture window looked out toward the street. Nobody.
Shadow Love pointed the rifle at the floor and pulled the
trigger a half-dozen times.

Lucas pulled open the safe door as Shadow Love opened
fire. The barrage came as a shock. Splinters exploded
through the basement and shrapnel from the .223 slugs
filled the air like hundreds of tiny bees. Jennifer screamed
once and rolled, one arm wrapped over her head, her body
covering the crying baby.

"The baby," she screamed. "The baby," and she plucked
at the baby's back.

"Over here," Lucas shouted as the firing stopped. Changing magazines? "Jen, Jen, over here . . ."

Jennifer was partially sheltered by the workbench and sat
sobbing, plucking at the baby. Lucas crawled across the
floor and pulled her out and she flailed at him, resisting, not
understanding.

"Into the safe, into the safe . . ."

Lucas dragged her and the screaming Sarah to the turn-
of-the-century safe, threw the guns out on the floor and unceremoniously shoved them both inside.

"The baby," Jennifer screamed at him. She turned Sarah,
and Lucas saw the splinters protruding from the baby's
back.

"Don't touch them," he shouted. He and Jennifer were
inches from each other, shouting, and Sarah was beyond
tears: she'd reached the stage where she could barely
breathe, her eyes wide with terror.

"Hold the door open an inch. An inch. An inch. You understand? You'll be okay," Lucas shouted. "Do you understand me?"

"Yes, yes . . ." Jennifer nodded, still wrapped around Sarah.

Lucas left them.

He owned twelve guns; he carried four away from the safe, along with three boxes of ammunition. He crawled into the space under the workbench where Jennifer had been. It would give him some protection from direct hits coming through the floor, and he could see the stairs. He first loaded the Browning Citori over and under; he used the twenty-gauge shotgun for hunting. His only shells were number-six shot, but that was fine. At a short distance, they would punch a convincing hole through a man's head.

Next he loaded the two Gold Cup .45s that he'd used in competition, seven rounds per magazine, one round in each chamber, both weapons cocked and locked. Then the P7, loaded with nine-millimeter rounds, waiting. As he finished loading the P7, he began to wonder if Shadow Love had fled: the firing had been stopped for nearly a minute. . . .

Shadow Love could hear the woman screaming, could hear Davenport's voice, but not what he said. Damn walls, it was hard to tell where they were, but he thought to the right, and they sounded somehow distant, toward the far end of the basement. He watched the stairs for a few seconds, then took a fast dozen strides through the house, almost to the end, and once again began to pour gunfire through the floor. This time, though, he fired as he ran back to the basement door, blowing a trail of bullet holes through the carpet. . . .

In the basement, the metal fragments and splinters filled the air, plucking at Lucas' back and sleeve. He was hit and it hurt, but it felt superficial. He rubbed at his back and left a trail of pain where the slivers stuck through his shirt. If he stayed in the basement, he could be blinded. Shadow Love's last run had gone the whole length of the basement. Lucas got the Gold Cups ready. If he tried it again . . .

•   •   •

Shadow Love had been counting on the bullets to ricochet rather than fragment. He imagined the basement as a blizzard of wildly careening slugs. Pleased with the idea of making a trail the length of the house, he waited near the top of the stairs for a rush, waited, waited . . . Nothing. He refigured his ammunition supply. He'd fired at least twenty shots, he decided. He pulled the clip, slapped in the new one and checked the first. Six rounds left. Still plenty for a fight.

He waited another few seconds, then hurried again through the house, picked out a new pattern and raced back toward the stairwell, firing as he went. He was almost at the stairs when the rug suddenly popped up once, then again, not six feet away, and he realized that Davenport was shooting back through the floor, something big, something coming up through the carpet and into the ceiling, close, and Shadow Love dove into the garage. . . .

Lucas watched the firing pattern develop, tried to anticipate where Shadow Love would move and fired back with one of the .45s. He had little hope of hitting him, but he thought it might force Shadow Love to stop firing through the floor.

As the firing run ended at the back of the house, Lucas stood and walked quickly across the width of the basement to the safe.

"Jen, Jen?"

"What?"

"The next time he fires through the floor, I'm going to pull the circuit breaker and try the stairs. The lights will be out. Stay cool."

"Okay." The baby was gasping. Jennifer now sounded remote and cold; she had it under control.

One of the .45s was almost empty. Lucas laid it on the floor, stuck the other in his pants pocket with the butt sticking out, and crossed the basement floor and waited, the shotgun pointing at the base of the stairs, the switch box open.

Shooting through the floor wasn't good enough: Shadow Love wouldn't know when or if Davenport was hit, and his time must be running out. The black spot, larger, pressed against his consciousness. Attack now. He had to attack.

The door to the garage was still open, and in the shaft of light coming from the kitchen, he saw the gas can for the lawn mower.

"Motherfucker," he whispered. He glanced at the stairwell, groped for a minute, found the switch for the garage light and turned it on.

There was a rack of shelves next to the door, with a variety of bottles, mostly plastic. One, containing a tree-borer insecticide, was made of brown glass. Keeping the M-15 pointed at the stairwell, Shadow Love unscrewed the top of the insecticide bottle, turned it upside down and drained it. When it was empty, he stepped over to the gas can, picked it up, then stepped back to a position that would keep the stairwell covered. Moving as quickly as he could, he filled the quart bottle with gasoline, then looked around for a plug. Newspaper. There were bundles of newspapers along the garage wall. He ripped off a sheet of paper, soaked it in gasoline and plugged the neck of the bottle.

When he was ready, he vaulted through the door, past the open stairwell and into the living room. From there he could lob the bottle down the stairs to the tiled floor at the bottom.

"Hey, Davenport," he yelled.

No answer. He lit the newspaper with a cigarette lighter, and it flamed up.

"Hey, Davenport, suck on this," he yelled, and threw the bomb down the stairs. It hit and smashed, the gasoline igniting in a fireball. Shadow Love braced himself against the living room wall, waiting.

". . . suck on this," Shadow Love yelled, and a bottle came down the stairs. There was a *crack* and a *whoosh* and the gasoline went up in a fireball.

"Sonofabitch," Lucas said. He looked around wildly and spotted a gallon paint can. He pulled the main circuit breaker, throwing the house into darkness, except for the light from the fire. Dashing across the basement floor, he grabbed the paint can, vaulted the fire at the base of the stairs, fired one barrel of the shotgun up the stairs and went up them two at a time. Three steps from the top, he hurled the paint can through the door.

The sudden and virtually complete darkness disoriented Shadow Love for a moment, and then Davenport was on the stairs, coming, and Shadow Love, not waiting, fired a shot through the wall from the living room, then tracked the dimly seen movement out of the stairwell and fired once, the muzzle blast blinding him, firing again, seeing the can and thinking, *No. . . .*

The first shot nearly took Lucas' head; it sprayed his face with plaster and blinded him in one eye. The second shattered the paint can. The third gave him a muzzle blast to follow. Lucas fired once with the shotgun, panning behind the blast; he dropped the long gun and pulled the .45.

Thinking, *No,* Shadow Love saw Davenport and dragged the muzzle of the M-15 around, the movement taking an eternity, then Davenport's face froze as though caught by a strobe light, but it was no strobe, it was the flash from a shotgun muzzle reaching out, and Shadow Love soaked up the impact as if he had been hit in the side with a baseball bat. He flattened back against the wall and rebounded, still desperately struggling to bring the muzzle around, still trying, his finger closing spasmodically on the trigger. . . .

Lucas saw Shadow Love in the flash of the shotgun, just the pale eyes, saw the M-15 coming around, the muzzle flash, the bullet going somewhere, and then he was firing the .45, and Shadow Love went over, falling, tumbling. The M-15 stuttered again, three shots that went through the ceiling, and Lucas fired again and again and again, and then the pain and the smell hit him, and he turned, seeing the fire on his leg, and he rolled into the kitchen, rolling it out. . . .

Shadow Love couldn't move. He didn't hurt, but he couldn't move. He couldn't sit up. He couldn't move the gun. *I'm dying; why's my mind so clear? Why's it all so clear?*

•   •   •

Lucas crawled across the kitchen floor in the dark and groped under the sink for the fire extinguisher, thinking that it was old and might not work. He pulled the seals and squeezed the trigger, and it worked, spraying a stinging foam on his leg, wiping out the small tongues of flame that crawled over the surface of his trousers. He took his hand off the trigger and dragged himself back to the stairs. The gasoline was still burning and the carpet had caught fire, but nothing else. He hosed the fire down, wiped it out, then crossed in the dark to the switch box and turned the lights on.

Jennifer: "Lucas?"

"We're all right," Lucas said, his voice creaking. The stench of gasoline, burnt carpet, gunpowder and fire-extinguisher fluid was almost overpowering. He had to hold on to the doorjamb to keep himself upright. "But I'm hurt."

He staggered back across the basement and pulled himself up the stairs and looked carefully around the corner. Shadow Love was lying on the rug like a pile of dirty clothing. Lucas stepped over to him, keeping the .45 centered on the man's chest, and kicked the M-15 across the room.

He felt Jennifer behind him.

"You're a mean sonofabitch," Shadow Love groaned. Nothing moved but his lips.

"Die, motherfucker," Lucas croaked.

"Is he dead?" Jennifer asked.

"In a few minutes," Lucas said.

"Lucas, we gotta call . . ."

Lucas grabbed Jennifer's coat and sank to the floor, pulling her down with him. She had the baby, who now looked almost sleepy.

"Lucas . . ."

"Give him a few minutes," Lucas said. He looked at Shadow Love. "Die, motherfucker," he said again.

"Lucas," Jennifer screamed, trying to pull away, "we got to call an ambulance."

Lucas looked at her and shook his head. "Not yet."

Jennifer tore at her coat, but Lucas wrapped her up and

pinned her on the floor. "Lucas . . ." She beat at him with her free hand and the baby started to whimper again.

"Who told? Who gave us away?" Shadow Love coughed. Still no pain, only a growing cold. Davenport was a *mean* sonofabitch, Shadow Love thought.

"You did," Lucas snapped.

"I did?"

"Yeah. Your mom's grave. You had them send the bills to Barbara Gow."

"I?" Shadow Love asked again. As he exhaled, a blood bubble formed on his lips and then burst. The salty taste of the blood was his last sensation.

"Die, motherfucker," Lucas said.

He was talking to a dead man. After another moment, with no further movement from Shadow Love, Lucas released Jennifer. She was looking at him in horror.

"Call the cops," he said.

CHAPTER
30

"You got him?" Daniel asked.

"He's dead," Lucas said. "I'm looking at him," he explained, and told him that Jennifer and the baby had been injured, but the injuries didn't appear serious.

"How bad are you?"

"My leg's burned. I'm full of splinters. My house is fucked up," Lucas said.

"So take the day off," Daniel said. His voice was flat, not funny.

"Pretty fuckin' funny," Lucas said coldly.

"What do you want me to say? You're so fucked up I don't know why you're talking to me on the telephone."

"I needed to tell somebody," Lucas said. He looked out of the kitchen to the open front door. After Jennifer had called 911, she'd stalked past him, out the door and into the yard to wait. When he'd called after her, she'd refused to look at him.

"Get your ass to the hospital," Daniel said. "I'll see you there in ten minutes."

Jennifer had a sliver taken from her arm. The anchor from TV3 called her at the hospital and Jennifer told him to go fuck himself.

The baby had a half-dozen splinters in her back. The docs said that by the time she was old enough to be told about the fight, the scars would be virtually invisible.

Lucas spent the night, the next day and part of the following day at Ramsey Medical Center, first receiving treatment for the burns on his leg and the plaster particles in his right eye. He wouldn't need skin grafts, but it was a near thing. The plaster was washed out: the eye would heal. When the docs had finished with the eye, a physician's assistant went to work on the splinters. They weren't in deep, but there were dozens of them, from his thigh across his butt and up his back and his left arm.

He got out early the second afternoon, still wearing a massive gauze bandage that covered his eye, and went to look at his house. The insurance man, he decided, would jump out of his window twice when he saw it.

Late that night, after a number of calls to clear the way, he drove to Hennepin Medical Center and took a back elevator to the surgical floor. At ten minutes past midnight, he got out of the elevator and walked down a tiled corridor to a nursing station, where he found his friend.

"Lucas," she said, "I told her you were coming. She's still awake."

"Is she alone?"

"Do you mean, 'Has her husband gone?' Yeah, he's gone," the nurse said, grinning wryly.

A younger nurse, barely out of her teens, leaned on the station counter and said, "The guy is really something else. He reads to her, gets videos for her, gets snacks. He's here all the time. I've never seen anybody so . . ." She groped for the word. ". . . *faithful.*"

"Just like my cocker spaniel," said the older nurse.

Lily was propped up in bed, watching the Letterman show.

"Hey," she said. She touched the remote and Letterman winked out. Her face was pale, but she talked easily. "You got him. And he got you. You look like shit."

"Thanks," Lucas said. He kissed her on the lips and eased himself into the bedside chair. "I got him more."

"Mmm," she said. "The legend of Lucas Davenport grows another couple of inches."

"So how do you feel?" Lucas asked.

"Not too bad, as long as I don't laugh or sneeze," Lily said. She looked tired, but not sick. "My ribs are messed up. They had me walking around today. It hurt a lot."

"How much longer will you be here?"

Lily hesitated, then said, "I get out tomorrow. They're going to brace me up. I'm taking Andretti's plane to New York tomorrow afternoon."

Lucas frowned and sat back in the chair. "That's pretty quick."

"Yes." There was another silence, then Lily said, "I can't help it."

Lucas looked down at her. "I think we have some unfinished business. Somehow." He shrugged. There was another space of silence.

"I don't know," she said finally.

"David?" Lucas asked. "Do you love him?"

"I must," she said.

A while later she said, "Will you get back with Jennifer?"

Lucas shook his head. "I don't know. She's . . . kind of freaked out after what happened in the house. I'll see her tomorrow. Maybe."

"Don't come see me off," Lily said. "I don't know if I could handle things, if you and David were there at the same time."

"Okay," Lucas said.

"And could you . . ."

"What?"

"Could you leave?" she said, in a tiny, distant voice that squeaked toward despair. "If you stay any longer I'll cry, and crying hurts. . . ."

Lucas stood awkwardly, shuffled his feet, then leaned over and kissed her again. She caught his shirt in her hand, pulling him, and the kiss went on, fiercer, with heat, until suddenly she let go and instead of pulling him, pushed against his chest.

"Get the fuck out of here, Davenport," she said. "We can't start this again, God damn it, get the fuck out of here."

"Lily . . ."

"Lucas, please . . ."

He nodded and took a breath, let it go. "See you." He couldn't think of anything else to say. He backed out of the hospital room, looking into her eyes until the swinging door flapped shut.

At the nurses' desk, he asked his friend what time Lily would check out. Ten o'clock, he was told, with an ambulance scheduled to drive to the St. Paul municipal airport, where she would be loaded into a private jet.

Lucas drove out to the airport the next morning in his Ford four-by-four, and sat and watched as Lily was lifted from the ambulance and wheeled in a chair through the gate to the waiting jet. David bent over her, still wearing the blue seersucker suit, his hair rumpled in the wind. He looked like an academic. David.

They had to carry Lily up the steps to the jet. As they picked her up, Lucas felt her eyes on him, but she never raised a hand. She looked at him for three seconds, five, and then was gone.

The jet left and Lucas rolled out of the airport toward the Robert Street bridge.

He talked to Jennifer that afternoon. She wanted to set up a visitation schedule, she said, so Lucas could see Sarah. Lucas said he wanted to talk. She asked if Lily was gone and Lucas said yes. She wasn't sure if she wanted to talk, Jennifer said, but she would meet him. Not today, not tomorrow. Sometime soon. Next week, next month. She couldn't forget about those last minutes at the house, when Shadow Love was dying, the baby was hurt, and Lucas wouldn't let her call. . . . She was trying to forget, but she couldn't. . . .

That was Thursday. He went to the games group that night, and played. Elle asked him about the shotgun. It was gone, he said. He hadn't felt its touch since the shootout. He felt fine, he said, but he thought he might be lying.

Everything should have been fine, but it didn't feel quite

right. He felt as though he were in the last hours of a prolonged journey on speed, in the mental territory where everything has more contrast than it does in real life, where buildings overhang in a threatening way, where cars move too fast, where people talk too loud, where sideways looks in bars can mean trouble. That lasted through the weekend, and began to fade early in the next week.

A little more than three weeks after the shootout, on a Saturday afternoon, Lucas sat in an easy chair and watched an Iowa–Notre Dame football game. Notre Dame was losing and no amount of prayer would help. It was a relief when the phone rang. He picked it up and heard the hiss of the long-distance satellite relay.

"Lucas?" Lily, her voice soft and husky.

"Lily? Where are you?"

"I'm at home. I'm looking out the window."

"What? Out the window?" He flashed on the first time he'd seen her in the hallway at the police station: her dark eyes, her hair slightly askew, strands of it falling across her graceful neck. . . .

"David and the boys are down in the street, loading the van. They're leaving for Fort Lauderdale, on a father-son big-game fishing trip. First time for the boys . . ."

"Lily . . ."

"Lucas, Jesus, I'm starting to cry. . . ."

"Lily . . ."

"They'll be gone for a week, Lucas—my husband and the boys," she groaned. "Ah, fuck, Davenport, this is so fuckin' miserable. . . ."

"What? What?"

"Can you come to New York?" Her voice had gone rough, sensual, dark. "Can you come in tomorrow?"

In the End . . .

Leo climbed the dark side of Bear Butte, through the loose rubble, through the fine black sand, slipping at times, using his hands, moving steadily toward the peak.

The night still gripped the world when he reached the top. He eased himself down on a convenient hump, took the blanket-roll off his shoulders and wrapped the rough army wool around himself.

To the south, he could see the lights of Sturgis and I-90, and beyond that, the Stygian darkness of the Black Hills. In every other direction, the only break in the night came from yard lights on the scattered ranches.

The sunrise was spectacular when it came.

In the west, the stars were as bright and as profuse as ever; in the east, there was a growing pale light at the knife-edged horizon. Suddenly, with the unexpectedness of a shooting star, there was a flame at the horizon, a flowing golden presence as the world turned into the sun.

The sunlight touched the top of the butte long before it flooded the flatlands, so from the top he could watch the dawn racing toward him, rippling over the empty countryside below. Leo sat with the blanket around his shoulders, his eyes half closed. When the light crossed through the base of the

341

butte, he sighed, turned and looked west, watching the day chase the night into Wyoming.

There was a lot to do.

A lot of talk about the Crows and about Shadow Love.

Legends to build.

Leo said a quick prayer and started down. The last of the stars were going and he looked up at them as he dropped over the crest.

"See you guys," he said. "Flatheaded motherfuckers."

•　　•　　•

Carlo Druze was a stone killer.

He sauntered down the old gritty sidewalk with its cracked, uneven paving blocks, under the bare-branched oaks. He was acutely aware of his surroundings. Back around the corner, near his car, the odor of cigar smoke hung in the cold night air; a hundred feet farther along, he'd touched a pool of fragrance, deodorant or cheap perfume. A Mötley Crüe song beat down from a second-story bedroom: plainly audible on the sidewalk, it must have been deafening inside.

Two blocks ahead, to the right, a translucent cream-colored shade came down in a lighted window. He watched the window, but nothing else moved. A vagrant snowflake drifted past, then another.

Druze could kill without feeling, but he wasn't stupid. He took care: he would not spend his life in prison. So he strolled, hands in his pockets, a man at his leisure. Watching. Feeling. The collar of his ski jacket rose to his ears on the sides, to his nose in the front. A watch cap rode low on his forehead. If he met anyone—a dog-walker, a night jogger—they'd get nothing but eyes.

From the mouth of the alley, he could see the target house and the garage behind it. Nobody in the alley, nothing moving. A few garbage cans, like battered plastic toadstools, waited to be taken inside. Four windows were lit on the ground floor of the target house, two more up above. The garage was dark.

Druze didn't look around; he was too good an actor. It wasn't likely that a neighbor was watching, but who could know? An old man, lonely, standing at his window, a linen shawl around his narrow shoulders . . . Druze could see him in his mind's eye, and was wary: the people here had money, and Druze was a stranger in the dark. An out-of-place furtiveness, like a bad line on the stage, would be noticed. The cops were only a minute away.

With a casual step, then, rather than a sudden move, Druze turned into the darker milieu of the alley and walked down to the garage. It was connected to the house by a glassed-in breezeway. The door at the end of the breezeway would not be locked; it led straight into the kitchen.

"If she's not in the kitchen, she'll be in the recreation room, watching television," Bekker had said. Bekker had been aglow, his alluring face pulsing with the heat of uncontrolled pleasure. He'd drawn the floor plan on a sheet of notebook paper and traced the hallways with the point of his pencil. The pencil had trembled on the paper, leaving a shaky worm trail in graphite. "Christ, I wish I could be there to see it."

Druze took the key out of his pocket, pulled it out by its string. He'd tied the string to a belt loop so there'd be no chance he'd lose the key in the house. He reached out to the doorknob with his gloved left hand, tried it. Locked. The key opened it easily. He shut the door behind him and stood in the dark, listening. A scurrying? A mouse in the loft? The sound of the wind brushing over the shingles. He waited, listening.

Druze was a troll. He had been burned as a child. Some nights, bad nights, the memories ran uncontrollably through his head, and he'd doze, wretchedly, twisting in the blankets, knowing what was coming, afraid. He'd wake in his childhood bed, the fire on him. On his hands, his face, running like liquid, in his nose, his hair; his mother screaming, throwing water and milk; his father flapping his arms, shouting, ineffectual . . .

They hadn't taken him to the hospital until the next day: his mother had put lard on him, hoping not to pay, as Druze howled through the night. But in the morning light, when they'd seen the nose, they took him.

He was four weeks in the county hospital, shrieking with pain as the nurses put him through the baths and the peels, as the doctors did the skin transplants. They'd harvested the skin from his thighs—he remembered the word, all these years later, *harvested:* it stuck in his mind like a tick—and used it to patch his face.

When they finished he looked better, but not good. The features of his face seemed fused together, as though an invisible nylon stocking were pulled over his head. His skin was no better, a patchwork of leather, off-color, pebbled, emotionless, like a quilted football. His nose had been fixed, as best the doctors could, but it was too short, his nostrils flaring straight out, like black headlights. His lips were stiff and thin, and dried easily. He licked them, unconsciously, his tongue flicking out every few seconds with a lizard's touch.

The doctors had given him the new face, but his eyes were his own.

His eyes were flat black and opaque, like weathered paint on the eyes of a cigar-store Indian. New acquaintances sometimes thought he was blind, but he was not. His eyes were the mirror of his soul: Druze hadn't had one since the night of the burning. . . .

The garage was silent. Nobody called out, no telephone rang. Druze tucked the key into his pants pocket and took a black four-inch milled-aluminum penlight out of his jacket. With the light's narrow beam, he skirted the car and picked his way through the litter of the garage. Bekker had warned him of this: the woman was a gardener. The unused half of the garage was a littered with shovels, rakes, hoes, garden trowels, red clay pots, both broken and whole, sacks of fertilizer and partial bales of peat moss. A power cultivator sat next to a lawn mower and a snowblower. The place

smelled of earth and half of gasoline, a pungent, yeasty mix-
ture that pulled him back to his childhood. Druze had
grown up on a farm, poor, living in a trailer with a propane
tank, closer to the chicken coop than the main house. He
knew about kitchen gardens, old, oil-leaking machinery and
the stink of manure.

The door between the garage and the breezeway was
closed but not locked. The breezeway itself was six feet wide
and as cluttered as the garage. "She uses it as a spring green-
house—watch the tomato flats on the south side, they'll be
all over the place," Bekker had said. "You'll need the light,
but she won't be able to see it from either the kitchen or
the recreation room. Check the windows on the left. That's
the study, and she could see you from there—but she won't
be in the study. She never is. You'll be okay."

Bekker was a meticulous planner, delighted with his own
precise work. As he'd led Druze through the floor plan with
his pencil, he'd stopped once to laugh. His laugh was his
worst feature, Druze decided, with his actor's ear. Harsh,
scratching, it sounded like the squawk of a crow pursued
by owls. . . .

Druze walked easily through the breezeway, stepping
precisely toward the lighted window in the door at the end
of the passage. He was bulky but not fat. He was, in fact,
an athlete: he could juggle, he could dance, he could balance
on a rope. He could jump in the air and click his heels and
land lightly enough that the audience could hear the *click,*
alone, like a spoken word. Midway through, he heard a
voice and paused.

A voice, singing. Sweet, naive, like a high school choral-
ist's. A woman, the words muffled. He recognized the tune
but didn't know its name. Something from the sixties. A
Joan Baez song, maybe. The focus was getting tighter. He
didn't doubt that he could do her. Killing Stephanie Bekker
would be no more difficult than chopping off a chicken's
head or slitting the throat of a baby pig. Just a shoat, he
said to himself. It's all meat. . . .

·   ·   ·

He'd done another murder, years earlier. He'd told Bekker about it, over a beer. It wasn't a confession, simply a story. And now, so many years later, the killing seemed more like an accident than a murder. Even less than that: like a scene from a half-forgotten drive-in movie, a movie where you couldn't remember the end. A girl in a New York flophouse. A hooker maybe, a druggie for sure. She gave him some shit. Nobody cared, so he killed her. Almost as an experiment, to see if it would rouse some feeling in him. It hadn't.

He never knew the hooker's name, doubted that he could even find the flaphouse, if it still existed. At this date, he probably couldn't figure out what week of the year it had been: the summer, sometime, everything hot and stinking, the smell of spoiled milk and rotting lettuce in sidewalk dumpsters . . .

"Didn't bother me," he told Bekker, who pressed him. "It wasn't like . . . Shit, it wasn't like anything. Shut the bitch up, that's for sure."

"Did you hit her? In the face?" Bekker was intent, the eyes of science. It was, Druze thought, the moment they became friends. He remembered the moment with perfect clarity: the bar, the scent of cigarette smoke, four college kids on the other side of the aisle, sitting around a pizza, laughing at inanities . . . Bekker wore an apricot-colored mohair sweater, a favorite, a sweater from the sixties, a sweater that framed his face.

"Bounced her off a wall, swinging her," Druze had said, wanting to impress. Another new feeling. "When she went down, I got on her back, got an arm around her neck, and *jerk* . . . that was it. Neck just went pop. Sounded like when you bite into a piece of gristle. I put my pants on, walked out the door. . . ."

"Scared?"

"No. Not after I was out of the place. Something that simple . . . what're the cops going to do? You walk away. By the time you're down the block, they got no chance. And in that fuckin' place, they probably didn't even find her for two days, and only then 'cause of the heat. I wasn't *scared*, I was more like . . . hurried."

"That's something." Bekker's approval was like the rush Druze got from applause, only better, tighter, more concentrated. Only for him. Druze got the impression that Bekker had a confession of his own but held it back. Instead the other man asked, "You never did it again?"

"No. It's not like . . . I enjoy it."

Bekker sat staring at him for a moment, then smiled. "Hell of a story, Carlo."

He hadn't felt much when he'd killed the girl. He didn't feel much now, ghosting through the darkened breezeway, closing in. Tension, stage fright, but no distaste for the job.

Another door waited at the end of the passage, wooden, with an inset window at eye level. If the woman was at the table, Bekker said, she would most likely be facing away from him. If she was at the sink, the stove or the refrigerator, she wouldn't be able to see him at all. The door would open quietly enough, but she would feel the cold air if he hesitated.

What was that song? The woman's voice floated around him, an intriguing whisper in the night air. Moving slowly, Druze peeked through the window. She wasn't at the table: nothing there but two wooden chairs. He gripped the doorknob solidly, picked up a foot, wiped the sole of his shoe on the opposite pant leg, then repeated the move with the other foot. If the gym shoe treads had picked up any small stones, they would give him away, rattling on the tile floor. Bekker had suggested that he wipe, and Druze was a man who valued rehearsal.

His hand still on the knob, he twisted. The knob turned easily and silently under his glove, as slowly as the second hand on a clock. The door was on a spring and would ease itself shut. . . . And she sang: Something, Angelina, *ta-dum, Angelina.* Good-bye, Angelina? She was a true soprano, her voice like bells. . . .

The door was as quiet as Bekker had promised. Warm air pushed into his face like a feather cushion, the sound of a dishwasher, and Druze was inside and moving, the door closed behind him, his shoes silent on the quarry tile. Straight ahead was the breakfast bar, white-speckled Formica with a single short-stemmed rose in a bud vase at the far end, a cup and saucer in the center and, on the near end, a green glass bottle. A souvenir from a trip to Mexico, Bekker had said. Hand-blown, and heavy as stone, with a sturdy neck.

Druze was moving fast now, to the end of the bar, an avalanche in black, the woman suddenly there to his left, standing at the sink, singing, her back to him. Her black hair was brushed out on her shoulders, a sheer silken blue negligee falling gently over her hips. At the last instant she sensed him coming, maybe felt a rush in the air, a coldness, and she turned.

Something's wrong: Druze was moving on Bekker's wife, too late to change course, and he knew that something was wrong. . . .

Man in the house. In the shower. On his way.

Stephanie Bekker felt warm, comfortable, still a little damp from her own shower, a bead of water tickling as it sat on her spine between her shoulder blades. . . . Her nipples were sore, but not unpleasantly. He'd shaven, but not recently enough. . . . She smiled. Silly man, must not have nursed enough as a baby . . .

Stephanie Bekker felt the cool air on her back and turned to smile at her lover. Her lover wasn't there; Death was. She said, "Who?" and it was all there in her mind, like a fistful of crystals: the plans for the business, the good days at the lakes, the cocker spaniel she had had as a girl, her father's face lined with pain after his heart attack, her inability to have children . . .

And her home: the kitchen tile, the antique flour bins, the wrought-iron pot stands, the single rose in the bud vase, red as a drop of blood . . .

Gone like a beggar's wink.

Something wrong . . .

"Who?" she said, not loud, half turning, her eyes widening, a smile caught on her face. The bottle whipped 'round, a Louisville Slugger in green glass. Her hand started up. Too late. Too small. Too delicate.

The heavy bottle smashed into her temple with a wet crack, like a rain-soaked newspaper hitting a porch. Her head snapped back and she fell, straight down, as though her bones had vaporized. The back of her head slammed the edge of the counter, pitching her forward, turning her.

Druze was on her, smashing her flat with his weight, his hand on her chest, feeling her nipple in his palm.

Hitting her face and her face and her face . . .

The heavy bottle broke, and he paused, sucking air, his head turned up, his jaws wide; he changed his grip and smashed the broken edges down through her eyes. . . .

"Do it too much," Bekker had urged. He'd been like a jock, talking about a three-four defense or a halfback option, his arm pumping as though he was about to holler *Awright*. . . . "Do it like a junkie would do it. Christ, I wish I could be there. And get the eyes. Be sure you get the eyes."

"I know how to do it," Druze had said.

"But you must get the eyes. . . ." Bekker had had a little white dot of drying spittle at the corner of his mouth. That happened when he got excited. "Get the eyes for me. . . ."

Something wrong.

There'd been another sound here, and it had stopped. Even as he beat her, even as he pounded the razor-edged bottle down through her eyes, Druze registered the negligee. She wouldn't be wearing this on a cold, windy night in April, alone in the house. Women were natural actors, with an instinct for the appropriate that went past simple comfort. She wouldn't be wearing this if she were alone. . . .

He hit her face and her face and her face, and heard the thumping on the stairs, and half turned, half stood, startled, hunched like a golem, the bottle in his gloved hand. The man came 'round the corner at the bottom of the stairs, wrapped in a towel. Taller than average, too heavy but not actually fat. Balding, fair wet hair at his temples, uncombed. Pale skin, rarely touched by sunlight, chest hair gone gray, pink spots on his shoulders from the shower.

There was a frozen instant, then the man blurted "Jesus" and bolted. Druze took a step after him, quickly, off balance. The blood on the kitchen tile was almost invisible, red on red, and he slipped, his feet flying from beneath him. He landed back-down on the woman's head, her pulped features imprinting themselves on his black jacket. The man, Stephanie Bekker's lover, was up the stairs. It was an old house and the doors were oak. If he locked himself in a bedroom, Druze would not get through the door in a hurry. The man might already be dialing 911. . . .

Druze dropped the bottle, as planned, and turned and trotted out the door. He was halfway down the length of the breezeway when it slammed behind him, a report like a gunshot, startling him. *Door,* his mind said, but he was running now, scattering the tomato plants. His hand found the penlight as he cleared the breezeway. With the light, he was through the garage in two more seconds, into the alley, slowing himself. *Walk. WALK.*

In another ten seconds he was on the sidewalk, a troll, thick, hunched, his coat collar up. He got to his car without seeing another soul. A minute after he left Stephanie Bekker, the car was moving. . . .

Keep your head out of it.

Druze did not allow himself to think. Everything was rehearsed, it was all very clean. Follow the script. Stay on schedule. Around the lake, out to France Avenue to Highway 12, back toward the loop to I-94, down 94 to St. Paul.

Then he thought:

He saw my face. And who the fuck was he? So round, so pink, so startled. Druze smacked the steering wheel once in frustration. *How could this happen? Bekker so smart . . .*

There was no way for Druze to know who the lover was, but Bekker might know. He should at least have some ideas. Druze glanced at the car clock: 10:40. Ten minutes before the first scheduled call.

He took the next exit, stopped at a SuperAmerica store and picked up the plastic baggie of quarters he'd left on the floor of the car: he hadn't wanted them to clink when he went into Bekker's house. A public phone hung on an exterior wall, and Druze, his index finger in one ear to block the street noise, dialed another public phone, in San Francisco. A recording asked for quarters and Druze dropped them in. A second later, the phone rang on the West Coast. Bekker was there.

"Yes?"

Druze was supposed to say one of two words, "Yes" or "No," and hang up. Instead he said, "There was a guy there."

"What?" He'd never heard Bekker surprised; not before this night.

"She was fuckin' some guy," Druze said. "I came in and did her and the guy came right down the stairs on top of me. He was wearing a towel."

"What?" More than surprised. He was stunned.

"Wake up, for Christ's fuckin' sake. Stop saying 'What?' We got a problem."

"What about . . . the woman?" Recovering now. Mentioning no names.

"She's a big fuckin' Yes. But the guy saw me. Just for a second. I was wearing the ski jacket and the hat, but with my face . . . I don't know how much was showing. . . ."

There was a long moment of silence, and then Bekker said, "We can't talk about it. I'll call you tonight or tomorrow, depending on what happens. Are you sure about . . . the woman?"

"Yeah, yeah, she's a Yes."

"Then we've done that much," Bekker said, with satisfaction. "Let me go think about the other."

And he was gone.

Driving away from the store, Druze hummed, harshly, the few bars of the song: Ta-dum, Angelina, good-bye, Angelina . . . That wasn't right, and the goddamned song would be going through his head forever until he got it. Ta-dum, Angelina. Maybe he could call a radio station and they'd play it or something. The melody was driving him nuts.

He put the car on I-94, took it to Highway 280, to I-35W, to I-694, and began driving west, fast, too fast, enjoying the speed, running the loop around the cities. He did it, now and then, to cool out. He liked the wind whistling through a crack in the window, the oldie-goldies on the radio. Ta-dum . . .

The blood-mask on the back of his jacket had dried, invisible now. He never knew it was there.

• • •

Stephanie Bekker's lover had heard the strange thumping
as he toweled himself after the shower. The sound had been
unnatural, violent, arrhythmic, but it had never crossed his
mind that Stephanie had been attacked, was dying there on
the kitchen floor. She might be moving something, one of
her heavy antique chairs, maybe, or perhaps she couldn't
get a jar open and was rapping the lid on a kitchen
counter—he really didn't know what he thought.

He wrapped a towel around his waist and went to look.
He walked straight into the nightmare: A man with a beast's
face, hovering over Stephanie, the broken bottle in his hand
like a dagger, rimed with blood. Stephanie's face . . . What
had he told her, there in bed, an hour before? You're a beautiful woman, he'd said, awkward at this, touching her lips
with his fingertips, so beautiful. . . .

He'd seen her on the floor and he'd turned and run. *What
else could he do?* one part of his mind asked. The lower part,
the lizard part that went back to the caves, said: *Coward.*

He'd run up the stairs, flying with fear, reaching to slam
the bedroom door behind him, to lock himself away from
the horror, when he heard the troll slam out through the
breezeway door. He snatched up the phone, punched numbers, a *9*, a *1*. But even as he punched the *1*, his quick mind
was turning. He stopped. Listened. No neighbors, no calls
in the night. No sirens. Nothing. Looked at the phone, then
finally set it back down. Maybe . . .

He pulled on his pants.

He cracked the door, tense, waiting for attack. Nothing.
Down the stairs, moving quietly in his bare feet. Nothing.
Wary, moving slowly, into the kitchen. Stephanie sprawled
there, on her back, beyond help: her face pulped, her whole
head misshapen from the beating. Blood pooled on the tile
around her; the killer had stepped in it, and he'd left tracks,
one edge of a gym shoe and a heel, back toward the door.

Stephanie Bekker's lover reached down to touch her
neck, to feel for a pulse, but at the last minute, repelled, he
pulled his hand back. She was dead. He stood for a moment,
swept by a premonition that the cops were on the sidewalk,
were coming up the sidewalk, were reaching toward the

front door. . . . They would find him there, standing over the body like the innocent man in a Perry Mason television show, point a finger at him, accuse him of murder.

He turned his head toward the front door. Nothing. Not a sound.

He went back up the stairs, his mind working furiously. Stephanie had sworn she'd told nobody about their affair. Her close friends were with the university, in the art world or in the neighborhood: confiding details of an affair in any of those places would set off a tidal wave of gossip. They both knew that and knew it would be ruinous.

He would lose his position in a scandal. Stephanie, for her part, was deathly afraid of her husband: what he would do, she couldn't begin to predict. The affair had been stupid, but neither had been able to resist it. His marriage was dying, hers was long dead. To find love again . . .

He choked, controlled it, choked again. He hadn't wept since childhood, couldn't weep now, but spasms of grief, anger and fear squeezed his chest. Control. He started dressing, was buttoning his shirt when his stomach rebelled, and he dashed to the bathroom and vomited. He knelt in front of the toilet for several minutes, through dry heaves, then finally stood up and finished dressing, except for his shoes. He must be quiet, he thought.

He did a careful inventory: billfold, keys, handkerchief, coins. Necktie, jacket. Coat and gloves. He forced himself to sit on the bed and mentally retrace his steps through the house. What had he touched? The front doorknob. The table in the kitchen, the spoon and bowl he'd used to eat her cherry cobbler. The knobs on the bedroom door and bathroom door, the water faucets, the toilet seat . . .

He got a pair of Stephanie's cotton underpants from her bureau, went down the stairs again, started with the front door, and worked methodically through the house. In the kitchen, he didn't look at the body. He couldn't look at it, but he was always aware of it at the edge of his vision, a leg, an arm . . . enough to step carefully around the blood.

In the bedroom again, and the bathroom. As he was wiping the shower, he thought about the drain. Body hair. He listened again. Silence. *Take the time.* The drain was fastened down by a single brass screw. He removed it with a dime, wiped the drain as far as he could reach with toilet paper, then rinsed it with a direct flow of water. The paper he threw into the toilet, and flushed once, twice. Body hair: the bed. He went into the bedroom, another surge of despair shaking his body. He would forget something. . . . He pulled the sheets from the bed, threw them on the floor, found another set—a blue set, one of Bekker's—and spent five minutes putting them on the bed and rearranging the blankets and the coverlet. He wiped the nightstand and the headboard, stopped, looked around.

Enough.

He rolled the underpants in the dirty sheets, put on his shoes and went downstairs, carrying the bundle of linen. He scanned the living room, the parlor and the kitchen one last time. His eyes skipped over Stephanie. . . .

There was nothing more to do. He put on his coat and stuffed the bundle of sheets in the belly. He was already heavy, but the sheets made him gross: good. If anybody saw him . . .

He walked out the front door, down the four concrete steps to the street and around the long block to his car. They'd been discreet, and their discretion might now save him. The night was cold, spitting snow, and he met nobody.

He drove down off the hill, around the lake, out to Hennepin Avenue, and spotted a pay telephone. He stopped, pinched a quarter in the underpants, dialed 911. Feeling both furtive and foolish, he put the pants over the mouthpiece of the telephone before he spoke:

"A woman's been murdered . . ." he told the operator.

He gave Stephanie's name and address. With the operator pleading with him to stay on the line, he hung up, then carefully wiped the receiver and walked back to his car. No. Sneaked back to his car, he thought. Like a rat. They would never believe, he thought. Never. He put his head on the steering wheel. Closed his eyes. Despite himself, his mind was calculating.

The killer had seen him. And the killer hadn't looked like a junkie or a small-time rip-off artist killing on impulse.

He'd looked strong, well fed, purposeful. The killer could be coming after him. . . .

He would have to give more information to the investigators, he decided, or they'd focus on him, her lover. He'd have to point them at the killer. They'd know that Stephanie had had intercourse, the county's pathologists would be able to tell that. . . .

God, had she washed? Of course she had, but how well? Would there be enough semen for a DNA-type?

No help for that. But he could give the police information they'd need to track the killer. Type a statement, xerox it through several generations, with different darkness settings, to obscure any peculiarities of the typewriter. . . .

Stephanie's face came out of nowhere.

At one moment, he was planning. The next, she was there, her eyes closed, her head turned away, asleep. He was seized with the thought that he could go back, find her standing in the doorway, find that it had all been a nightmare. . . .

He began to choke again, his chest heaving.

And Stephanie's lover thought, as he sat in the car: Bekker? Had he done this? He started the car.

Bekker.

It wasn't quite human, the thing that pulled itself across the kitchen floor. Not quite human—eyes gone, brain damaged, bleeding—but it was alive and it had a purpose: the telephone. There was no attacker, there was no lover, there was no time. There was only pain, the tile and, somewhere, the telephone.

The thing on the floor pulled itself to the wall where the telephone was, reached, reached . . . and failed. The thing was dying when the paramedics came, when the glass in the window broke and the firemen came through the door.

The thing called Stephanie Bekker heard the words "Jesus Christ," and then it was gone forever, leaving a single bloody handprint six inches below the Princess phone.

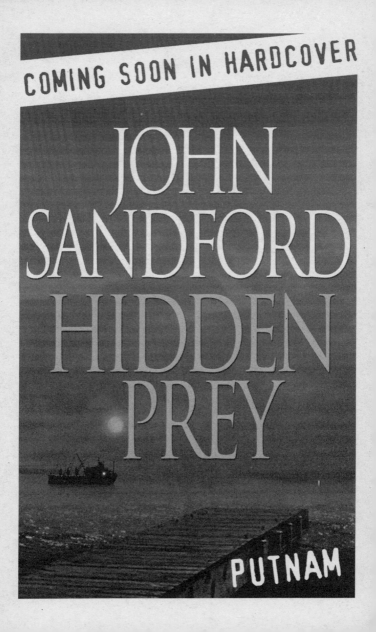

COMING SOON IN HARDCOVER

JOHN
SANDFORD
HIDDEN
PREY

PUTNAM